DEBBIE MACOMBER

Twenty-One Wishes

mira

Recycling programs for this product may not exist in your area.

ISBN-13: 978-0-7783-0963-5

Twenty-One Wishes

Copyright © 2020 by Harlequin Books S.A.

Twenty Wishes
First published in 2008. This edition published in 2020.
Copyright © 2008 by Debbie Macomber

The Twenty-First Wish
First published in 2011. This edition published in 2020.
Copyright © 2011 by Debbie Macomber

This edition published by arrangement with Harlequin Books S.A.

For questions and comments about the quality of this book, please contact us at CustomerService@Harlequin.com.

Mira
22 Adelaide St. West, 40th Floor
Toronto, Ontario M5H 4E3, Canada
www.Harlequin.com

Printed in U.S.A.

Also available from Debbie Macomber and MIRA

Midnight Sons

Alaska Skies
(*Brides for Brothers* and
The Marriage Risk)
Alaska Nights
(*Daddy's Little Helper* and
Because of the Baby)
Alaska Home
(*Falling for Him,*
Ending in Marriage and
Midnight Sons and Daughters)

This Matter of Marriage
Montana
Thursdays at Eight
Between Friends
Changing Habits
Married in Seattle
(*First Comes Marriage* and
Wanted: Perfect Partner)
Right Next Door
(*Father's Day* and
The Courtship of Carol Sommars)
Wyoming Brides
(*Denim and Diamonds* and
The Wyoming Kid)
Fairy Tale Weddings
(*Cindy and the Prince* and
Some Kind of Wonderful)
The Man You'll Marry
(*The First Man You Meet* and
The Man You'll Marry)
Orchard Valley Grooms
(*Valerie* and *Stephanie*)
Orchard Valley Brides
(*Norah* and *Lone Star Lovin'*)
The Sooner the Better
An Engagement in Seattle
(*Groom Wanted* and
Bride Wanted)
Out of the Rain
(*Marriage Wanted* and
Laughter in the Rain)
Learning to Love
(*Sugar and Spice* and
Love by Degree)

You…Again
(*Baby Blessed* and
Yesterday Once More)
The Unexpected Husband
(*Jury of His Peers* and
Any Sunday)
Three Brides, No Groom
Love in Plain Sight
(*Love 'n' Marriage* and
Almost an Angel)
I Left My Heart
(*A Friend or Two* and
No Competition)
Marriage Between Friends
(*White Lace and Promises* and
Friends—And Then Some)
A Man's Heart
(*The Way to a Man's Heart* and
Hasty Wedding)
North to Alaska
(*That Wintry Feeling* and
Borrowed Dreams)
On a Clear Day
(*Starlight* and
Promise Me Forever)
To Love and Protect
(*Shadow Chasing* and
For All My Tomorrows)
Home in Seattle
(*The Playboy and the Widow*
and *Fallen Angel*)
Together Again
(*The Trouble with Caasi* and
Reflections of Yesterday)
The Reluctant Groom
(*All Things Considered* and
Almost Paradise)
A Real Prince
(*The Bachelor Prince* and
Yesterday's Hero)
Private Paradise
(in *That Summer Place*)

Debbie Macomber's
Cedar Cove Cookbook
Debbie Macomber's
Christmas Cookbook

CONTENTS

TWENTY WISHES

To June Scobee Rodgers
My dear friend
An inspiration
and a joy

One

It was six o'clock on Valentine's Day, an hour that should have marked the beginning of a celebration—the way it had when she and Robert were married. When Robert was alive. But tonight, on the most romantic day of the year, thirty-eight-year-old Anne Marie Roche was alone. Turning over the closed sign on the door of Blossom Street Books, she glanced at the Valentine's display with its cutout hearts and pink balloons and the collection of romance novels she didn't read anymore. Then she looked outside. Streetlights flickered on as evening settled over the Seattle neighborhood.

The truth was, Anne Marie hated her life. Well, okay, *hate* was putting it too strongly. After all, she was healthy, reasonably young and reasonably attractive, financially solvent, *and* she owned the most popular bookstore in the area. But she didn't have anyone to love, anyone who loved her. She was no longer part of something larger than herself. Every morning when she woke, she found the other side of the bed empty and she didn't think she'd ever get accustomed to that desolate feeling.

Her husband had died nine months ago. So, technically, she was a widow, although she and Robert had been separated. But they saw each other regularly and were working on a reconciliation.

Then, suddenly, it was all over, all hope gone. Just when they were on the verge of reuniting, her husband had a massive heart attack. He'd collapsed at the office and died even before the paramedics could arrive.

Anne Marie's mother had warned her about the risks of marrying an older man, but fifteen years wasn't *that* much older. Robert, charismatic and handsome, had been in his midforties when they met. They'd been happy together, well matched in every way but one.

Anne Marie wanted a baby.

Robert hadn't.

He'd had a family—two children—with his first wife, Pamela, and wasn't interested in starting a second one. When she'd married him, Anne Marie had agreed to his stipulation. At the time it hadn't seemed important. She was madly in love with Robert—and then two years ago it hit her. This longing, this need for a baby, grew more and more intense, and Robert's refusal became more adamant. His solution had been to buy her a dog she'd named Baxter. Much as she loved her Yorkie, her feelings hadn't changed. She'd still wanted a baby.

The situation wasn't helped by Melissa, Robert's twenty-four-year-old daughter, who disliked Anne Marie and always had. Over the years Anne Marie had made many attempts to ease the tension between them, all of which failed. Fortunately she had a good relationship with Brandon, Robert's son, who was five years older than his sister.

When problems arose in Anne Marie and Robert's marriage, Melissa hadn't been able to disguise her glee. Her stepdaughter seemed absolutely delighted when Robert moved out the autumn before last, seven months before his death.

Anne Marie didn't know what she'd done to warrant such passionate loathing, other than to fall in love with Melissa's father. She supposed the girl's ardent hope that her parents would one day remarry was responsible for her bitterness. Every child wanted his or her family intact. And Melissa was a young teen when Anne Marie married Robert—a hard age made harder by the family's circumstances. Anne Marie didn't blame Robert's daughter, but his marriage to Pamela had been dead long before she entered the picture. Still, try as she might, Anne Marie had never been able to find common ground with Melissa. In fact, she hadn't heard from her since the funeral.

Anne Marie opened the shop door as Elise Beaumont approached. Elise's husband, Maverick, had recently passed away after a lengthy battle with cancer. In her midsixties, she was a retired librarian who'd reconnected with her husband after nearly thirty years apart, only to lose him again after less than three. She was a slight, gray-haired woman who'd become almost gaunt, but the sternness of her features was softened by the sadness in her eyes. A frequent patron of the bookstore, she and Anne Marie had become friends during the months of Maverick's decline. In many ways his death was a release, yet Anne Marie understood how difficult it was to let go of someone you loved.

"I was hoping you'd come," Anne Marie told her with a quick hug. She'd closed the store two hours early, giving Steve Handley, her usual Thursday-night assistant, a free evening for his own Valentine celebration.

Elise slipped off her coat and draped it over the back of an overstuffed chair. "I didn't think I would and then I decided that being with the other widows was exactly what I needed tonight."

The widows.

They'd met in a book group Anne Marie had organized at the store. After Robert died, she'd suggested reading Lolly Winston's *Good Grief*, a novel about a young woman adjusting to widowhood. It was through the group that Anne Marie had met Lillie Higgins and Barbie Foster. Colette Blake had joined, too. She'd been a widow who'd rented the apartment above A Good Yarn, Lydia Goetz's yarn store. Colette had married again the previous year.

Although the larger group had read and discussed other books, the widows had gravitated together and begun to meet on their own. Their sessions were often informal gatherings over coffee at the nearby French Café or a glass of wine upstairs at Anne Marie's.

Lillie and Barbie were a unique pair of widows, mother and daughter. They'd lost their husbands in a private plane crash three years earlier. Anne Marie remembered reading about the Learjet incident in the paper; both pilots and their two passengers had been killed in a freak accident on landing in Seattle. Lillie's husband and son-in-law were executives at a perfume company and often took business trips together.

Lillie Higgins was close to Elise's age, but that was all they shared. Actually, it was difficult to tell exactly how old Lillie was. She looked barely fifty, but with a forty-year-old daughter, she had to be in her mid-sixties. Petite and delicate, she was one of those rare women who never seemed to age. Her wardrobe consisted of ultra-expensive knits and gold jewelry. Anne Marie had the impression that if Lillie wanted, she could purchase this bookstore ten times over.

Her daughter, Barbie Foster, was a lot like her mother and aptly named, at least as far as appearances went. She had long blond hair that never seemed to get mussed, gorgeous crystal-blue eyes, a flawless figure. It was hard to believe she had eighteen-year-old twin sons who were college freshmen; Anne Marie would bet that most people assumed she was their sister rather than their mother. If Anne Marie didn't like Barbie so much, it would be easy to resent her for being so…perfect.

"Thanks for closing early tonight. I'd much rather be here than spend another evening alone," Elise said, breaking into Anne Marie's thoughts.

There was that word again.

Alone.

Despite her own misgivings about Valentine's Day, Anne Marie tried to smile. She gestured toward the rear of the store. "I've got the bubble wrap and everything set up in the back room."

The previous month, as they discussed an Elizabeth Buchan novel, the subject of Valentine's Day had come up. Anne Marie learned from her friends that this was perhaps the most painful holiday for widows. That was when their small group decided to plan their own celebration. Only instead of romantic love and marriage, they'd celebrate friendship. They'd defy the world's pitying glances and toast each other's past loves and future hopes.

Elise managed a quivering smile as she peered into the back of the store. "Bubble wrap?"

"I have tons," Anne Marie informed her. "You can't imagine how many shippers use it."

"But why is it on the floor?"

"Well…" It seemed silly now that Anne Marie was trying to explain. "I always have this insatiable urge to pop it, so I thought we could do it together—by walking on it."

"You want us to step on bubble wrap?" Elise asked, sounding confused.

"Think of it as our own Valentine's dance and fireworks in one."

"But fireworks are for Independence Day or maybe New Year's."

"That's the point," Anne Marie said bracingly. "New beginnings."

"And we'll drink champagne, too?"

"You bet. I've got a couple bottles of the real stuff, Veuve Clicquot."

"*Veuve* means widow, you know. The widow Clicquot's bubbly—what else could we possibly drink?"

The door opened, and Lillie and Barbie entered in a cloud of some elegant scent. As soon as they were inside, Anne Marie locked the shop.

"Party time," Lillie said, handing Anne Marie a white box filled with pastries.

"I brought chocolate," Barbie announced, holding up a box of dark Belgian chocolates. She wore a red pantsuit with a wide black belt that emphasized her petite waist. Was there no justice in this world? The woman had the figure of a goddess and she ate *chocolate?*

"I read that dark chocolate and red wine have all kinds of natural benefits," Elise said.

Anne Marie had read that, too.

Lillie shook her head in mock astonishment. "First wine and now chocolate. Life is good."

Leading the way to the back room, Anne Marie dimmed the lights in the front of the shop. Beside the champagne and flutes, she'd arranged a crystal vase of red roses; they'd been a gift from Susannah's Garden, the flower shop next door. All the retailers on Blossom Street were friends. Hearing about the small party, Alix Turner from the French Café had dropped off a tray of cheese, crackers and seedless green grapes, which Anne Marie had placed on her worktable, now covered with a lacy cloth. Lydia had insisted they use it for their celebration. It was so beautiful it reawakened Anne Marie's desire to learn to knit.

She wished she could see her friends' gifts as more than expressions of sympathy, but her state of mind made that impossible. Still, because of the other widows, for their sake as well as her own, she was determined to try.

"This is going to be fun," Elise said, telling them why Anne Marie had spread out the bubble wrap.

"What a wonderful idea!" Barbie exclaimed.

"Shall I pour?" Anne Marie asked, ignoring the sense of oppression she couldn't seem to escape. It had been present for months and she'd thought life would be better by now. Perhaps she needed counseling. One thing was certain; she needed *something*.

"By all means," Lillie said, motioning toward the champagne.

Anne Marie opened the bottle and filled the four glasses and then they toasted one another, clicking the rims of the flutes.

"To love," Elise said. "To Maverick." Her voice broke.

"To chocolate!" Barbie made a silly face, perhaps to draw attention away from Elise's tears.

"And the Widow's champagne," Lillie threw in.

Anne Marie remained silent.

Although it'd been nine months, her grief didn't seem to diminish or become any easier to bear. She worked too much, ate too little and grieved for all the might-have-beens. It was more than the fact that the man she'd loved was dead. With his death, she was forced to give up the dream of all she'd hoped her marriage would be. A true companionship—and the foundation of a family. Even if she were to fall in love again, which seemed unlikely, a pregnancy past the age of forty was risky. The dream of having her own child had died with Robert.

The four sipped their champagne in silence, each caught up in her own memories. Anne Marie saw the sorrow on Elise's face, the contemplative look on Lillie's, Barbie's half smile.

"Will we be removing our shoes in order to pop the bubble wrap?" Lillie asked a moment later.

"Mom has this thing about walking around in stocking feet," Barbie said, glancing at her mother. "She doesn't approve."

"It just wasn't done in our household," Lillie murmured.

"There's no reason to take our shoes off," Anne Marie said. "The whole idea is to have fun. Make a bit of noise, celebrate our friendship and our memories."

"Then I say, let 'er rip," Elise said. She raised her sensibly shod foot and stomped on a bubble. A popping sound exploded in the room.

Barbie went next, her step firm. Her high heels effectively demolished a series of bubbles.

Pop. Pop. Pop.

Pop.

Lillie followed. Her movements were tentative, almost apologetic.

Pop.

Anne Marie went last. It felt…good. Really good, and the noise only added to the unexpected sense of fun and exhilaration. For the first time since the party had begun, she smiled.

By then they were all flushed with excitement and champagne. The others were laughing giddily; Anne Marie couldn't quite manage that but she could *almost* laugh. The ability to express joy had left her when Robert died. That wasn't all she'd lost. She used to sing, freely and without self-consciousness. But after Robert's funeral Anne Marie discovered she couldn't sing anymore. She just couldn't. Her throat closed up whenever she tried. What came out were strangled sounds that barely resembled music, and after a while she gave up. It'd been months since she'd even attempted a song.

The popping continued as they paraded around on the bubble wrap, pausing now and then to sip champagne. They marched with all the pomp and ceremony of soldiers in procession, saluting one another with their champagne flutes.

Thanks to her friends, Anne Marie found that her mood had begun to lift.

Soon all the bubbles were popped. Bringing their champagne, they sat in the chairs where the reader groups met and toasted each other again in the dimly lit store.

Leaning back, Anne Marie tried to relax. Despite her earlier laughter, despite spending this evening with friends, her eyes filled with tears. She blinked them away, but new tears came, and it wasn't long before Barbie noticed. Her friend placed a reassuring hand on Anne Marie's knee.

"Does it ever hurt any less?" Anne Marie asked. Searching for a tissue in her hip pocket, she blotted her eyes. She hated breaking down like this. She wanted to explain that she'd never been a weepy or sentimental woman. All her emotions had become more intense since Robert's death.

Lillie and Barbie exchanged knowing looks. They'd been widows the longest.

"It does," Lillie promised her, growing serious, too. "But it takes time."

"I feel so alone."

"That's to be expected," Barbie said, passing her the box of chocolates. "Here, have another one. You'll feel better."

"That's what my grandmother used to say," Elise added. "Eat, and everything will seem better."

"Mine always said I'd be good as new if I did something for someone else," Lillie said. "Grams swore that showing kindness to others was the cure for any kind of unhappiness."

"Exercise helps, too," Barbie put in. "I spent many, many hours at the gym."

"Can't I just buy something?" Anne Marie asked plaintively, and hiccuped a laugh as she made the suggestion.

The others smiled.

"I wish it was that easy," Elise said in a solemn voice.

Anne Marie's appetite had been nonexistent for months and she didn't really enjoy going to a gym—walking nowhere on a treadmill seemed rather pointless to her. She didn't feel like doing volunteer work, either, at least not right now—although helping another person might get her past this slump, this interval of self-absorption.

"We're all looking for a quick fix, aren't we?" Barbie said quietly.

"Maybe." Lillie settled back in her chair. "Of these different options, the one I could really sink my teeth into is buying something."

"So could I," Barbie said with a laugh.

"I realize you're joking—well, partly—but material things won't help," Elise cautioned, bringing them all back to reality. "Any relief a spending spree offers is bound to be temporary."

As tempting as the idea of buying herself a gift might be, Anne Marie supposed she was right.

"We all need to take care of ourselves physically. Eat right. Exercise," Elise said thoughtfully. "It's important we get our finances in order, too."

"I couldn't agree with you more on *that*," Lillie said.

"Let's make a list of our suggestions," Elise went on. Reaching for her purse, she took out a small spiral notebook.

"If I'm going to make a list," Lillie piped up, "it won't be about eating cauliflower and going jogging. Instead, I'd plan to do some of the things I've put off for years."

"Such as?" Anne Marie asked.

"Oh, something fun," Lillie said, "like traveling to Paris."

Anne Marie felt as if a bolt of lightning had struck her. When they were first married, Robert had promised her that one day he'd take her to Paris. They talked about it frequently, discussing every aspect of their trip to the City of Light. The museums they'd visit, the places they'd walk, the meals they'd eat...

"I want to go to Paris with someone I love," she whispered.

"I want to fall in love again," Barbie said decisively. "Head over heels in love like I was before. A love that'll change my life."

They all grew quiet for a long moment, considering her words.

Anne Marie couldn't believe Barbie would lack for male companionship. They'd never discussed the subject, but she was surprised that a woman as attractive as Barbie didn't have her choice of men. Maybe she did. Maybe she simply had high standards. If so, Anne Marie couldn't blame her.

"We all want to be loved," Lillie said. "It's a basic human need."

"I had love," Elise told them, her voice hoarse with pain. "I don't expect to find that kind of love again."

"I had it, too," Barbie said.

Another hush fell over them.

"Making a list is a good idea," Elise stated emphatically. "A list of things to do."

Anne Marie nodded, fingering one of the suspended Valentine's decorations as she did. The idea had caught her interest. She needed to revive her enthusiasm. She needed to find inspiration and motivation—and a list might just do that. She was a list-maker anyway, but this would be different. It wouldn't be the usual catalog of appointments and everyday obligations.

"Personally I don't need another to-do list," Lillie murmured, echoing Anne Marie's thought. "I have enough of those already."

"This wouldn't be like that," Anne Marie responded, glancing at Elise for verification. "This would be a…an inventory of wishes," she said, thinking out loud. She recognized that there were plenty of *shoulds* involved in widowhood; her friends were right about that. She did need to get her financial affairs in order and pay attention to her health.

"Twenty wishes," she said suddenly.

"Why twenty?" Elise asked, leaning forward, her interest obvious.

"I'm not sure. It sounds right." Anne Marie shrugged lightly. The number had leaped into her head, and she didn't know quite why. *Twenty.* Twenty wishes that would help her recapture her excitement about life. Twenty dreams written down. Twenty possibilities that would give her a reason to look toward the future instead of staying mired in her grief. She couldn't continue to drag from one day to the next, lost in pain and heartache because Robert was dead. She needed a new sense of purpose. She owed that to herself—and to him.

"Twenty wishes," Barbie repeated slowly. "I think that works. Twenty's a manageable number. Not like a hundred, say."

"And it's not too few—like two or three," her mother said.

Anne Marie could tell that her friends were taking the idea seriously, which only strengthened her own certainty about it. "Wishes and hopes for the future."

"Let's do it!" Lillie proclaimed.

Barbie sat up straighter in her chair. "You should learn French," she said, smiling at Anne Marie.

"French?"

"For when you're in Paris."

"I had two years of French in high school." However, about all she remembered was how to conjugate the verbs *être* and *avoir*.

"Take a refresher course." Barbie slid onto the edge of her cushion.

"Maybe I will."

"I might learn how to belly dance," Barbie said next.

The others looked at her with expressions of surprise; Anne Marie grinned in approval.

"Lillie mentioned this earlier, but I think it would do us all a world of good to be volunteers," Elise said. "I've become a Lunch Buddy at my grandson's school and I really look forward to my time with Malcolm."

"Lunch Buddy? What's that?"

"A program for children at risk," Elise explained. "Once a week I visit the school and have lunch with a little boy in third grade. Malcolm is a sweet-natured child, and he's flourished under my attention. The minute I walk into the school, he races toward me as if he's been waiting for my visit all week."

"So the two of you have lunch?"

"Well, yes, but he also likes to show me his schoolwork. He's struggling with reading. However, he's trying hard, and every once in a while he'll read to me or I'll read to him. I've introduced him to the Lemony Snicket books and he's loving those."

"You tutor him, then?"

"No, no, he has a reading tutor. It's not that kind of program. I'm his *friend*. Or more like an extra grandmother."

The idea appealed to Anne Marie, but she didn't know if this was the right program for her. She'd consider it. Her day off was Wednesday and every other Saturday when Theresa came into the store. She had to admit that volunteering at an elementary school would give her something to do other than feel sorry for herself.

It wasn't a *wish*, exactly. Still, Elise claimed she felt better because of it. Helping someone else—perhaps that was the key.

The party broke up around nine-thirty, and after she'd waved everyone off, Anne Marie locked the front door. Then she climbed the stairs to her tiny apartment above the bookstore. Her ever-faithful Baxter was waiting for her, running circles around her legs until she bent down and lifted him up and lavished him with the attention he craved. After taking him out for a brief walk, she returned to the apartment, still thinking about the widows' new project.

She made a cup of tea and grabbed a notepad, sitting on the couch with Baxter curled up beside her. At the top of the page she wrote:

Twenty Wishes

It took her a long time to write down the first item.

1. Find one good thing about life

She felt almost embarrassed that all she could come up with was such a plaintive, pathetic desire, one that betrayed the sorry state of her mental health. Sitting back, she closed her eyes and tried to remember what she used to dream about, the half-expressed wishes of her younger years.

She added a second item, silly though it was.

2. Buy myself a pair of red cowboy boots

In her twenties, long before she married Robert, Anne Marie had seen a pair in a display window and they'd stopped her cold. She absolutely *had* to have those boots. When she'd gone into the store and tried them on, they were a perfect fit. Perfect. Unfortunately the price tag wasn't. No way could she afford $1500 for a pair of cowboy boots! With reluctance she'd walked out of the store, abandoning that small dream.

She couldn't have afforded such an extravagance working part-time at the university bookstore. But she still thought about those boots. She still wanted them, and the price no longer daunted her as it had all those years ago. Somehow, she'd find herself a pair of decadent cowboy boots. Red ones.

Chewing on the end of her pen, she contemplated other wishes. Really, this shouldn't be so difficult...

It occurred to her that if she was going to buy red cowboy boots, she should think of something to do in them.

3. Learn how to line dance

She suspected line dancing might be a bit passé in Seattle—as opposed to, say, Dallas—but the good thing was that it didn't require a partner. She could show up and just have fun without worrying about being part of a couple. She wasn't ready for another relationship; perhaps in time, but definitely not yet. After a few minutes she crossed out the line-dancing wish. She didn't have the energy to be sociable. She read over her first wish and scratched that out, too. She didn't know how to gauge whether she'd actually found something good about life. It wasn't specific enough.

A host of possibilities bounced around in her head but she didn't bother to write any of them on her list.

Lillie was right; she needed to get her finances in order. She wrote that down on a second sheet of paper, along with getting her annual physical and—maybe—signing up for the gym. The only thing on the first sheet, her wish list, was those boots.

So now she had two separate lists—one for wishes and the second for the more practical aspects of life. Not that each wish wouldn't ultimately require its own to-do list, but that was a concern for another day. She closed her eyes and tried to figure out what she wanted most, what wish she hoped to fulfill. The next few ideas were all sensible ones, like scheduling appointments she'd postponed for months. It was a sad commentary that her one wish, the lone desire of her heart, was an outrageously priced pair of boots.

That was the problem; she no longer *knew* what she wanted. Shrouded in grief and lost dreams, her joy had vanished, the same way laughter and singing had.

So far, her second list outnumbered the wish list. It included booking appointments with an accountant, an attorney, the vet and a couple of doctors. Sad, sad, sad. She could well imagine what Lillie and Barbie's lists looked like. They'd have wonderful ideas. Places to go, experiences to savor, people to meet.

Anne Marie stared at her wish list with its one ridiculous statement, tempted to crumple it up.

She didn't. For reasons she couldn't explain, she left it sitting on her kitchen counter. Lists were important; she knew that. Over the years she'd read enough about goal-setting to realize the value of writing things down. In fact, the store carried a number of bestselling titles on that very topic.

Okay, this was a start. She wasn't going to abandon the idea. And at least she'd taken control of some immediate needs. She'd identified what she *had* to do.

Sometime later, she'd list what she *wanted* to do.

She ran her finger over the word *boots*. Foolish, impractical, ridiculous—but she didn't care. She was determined to have the things.

Already the thought of listing her wishes was making a difference; already she felt a tiny bit of hope, a whisper of excitement. The thawing had begun.

Eventually other desires, other wishes, would come to her. She had nineteen left. She felt as if the genie had finally escaped the lamp and was waiting to hear her greatest desires. All she had to do was listen to her own heart and as soon as she did, her wildest dreams would come true.

If only life could be that simple.

It wasn't, of course, but Anne Marie decided she was willing to pretend.

Two

All that next week Anne Marie continued to look at her list. The sheet of paper with TWENTY WISHES written across the top became a patchwork of scribbles and scratched-out lines. She wrote *I want to sing again,* then changed her mind, deciding it was unnecessary to waste a wish on something she was convinced would return in its own time.

Eventually she transferred her list, such as it was, to a yellow legal pad, which somehow made her wishes seem more official. Then on Wednesday, her day off, she walked past a craft store on her way back from the accountant's and noticed the scrapbooking supplies in the window. She stared at the beautifully embellished pages displayed in the showcase. She used to possess a certain decorative flair. She wasn't sure she did anymore, but the idea of creating pages like that for her meager list of wishes appealed to her. A scrapbook to compile her wishes, make her plans and document her efforts. Those wishes would encourage her to look forward, to focus on the future with an optimism that had been lacking since her separation from Robert.

With that in mind, Anne Marie bought the necessary supplies, then lugged them home. As she passed A Good

Yarn, the shop just two doors down from the bookstore, she impulsively stepped inside. First, she wanted to thank Lydia for the table covering and second…she'd ask about classes.

She'd add knitting to her wish list. Anne Marie wondered why she hadn't thought of that earlier. Elise was a consummate knitter and often encouraged the others to learn. She described the satisfactions of knitting in such a compelling way, Anne Marie had flirted more than once with the idea of taking a class. Lydia Goetz, who owned A Good Yarn, was a much-loved and admired member of the Blossom Street neighborhood. Anne Marie was friendly with her and had often gone inside the yarn store, but never with the serious intent of learning to knit. Now, the prospect of knitting filled her with unfamiliar enthusiasm.

Lydia was sitting at the table in the back of the shop with her sister, Margaret. Although Lydia was petite and graceful, her sister was rather big-boned, a little ungainly. At first glance it was hard to believe they were even related. Once the surprise of learning they were sisters wore off, the resemblance revealed itself in the shape of their eyes and the thrust of their chins.

When Anne Marie entered the store, the sisters were obviously involved in their conversation; as they spoke, Lydia was knitting, Margaret crocheting. The bell above the door jingled, startling them both.

A smile instantly broke out on Lydia's face. "Anne Marie, how nice to see you! I'm glad you stopped by."

Lydia had a natural warmth that made customers feel welcome.

"Good morning," Anne Marie said, smiling at the two women. "Lydia, I came to thank you again for the gorgeous tablecloth."

"Oh, you're welcome. You know, it's really a lace shawl I knit years ago. I hope you'll have occasion to use it again."

"Oh, I will."

"I've been meaning to visit the bookstore," Lydia told her. "I want to pick up a couple of new mysteries. By the way, how did the Valentine's party go?"

"It was wonderful," Anne Marie said, gazing around. Whenever she went into the yarn shop, she was astonished by the range of beautiful colors and inviting textures. She walked over to the blue, green and teal yarns that lined one area of the shelves. Putting down her packages, she reached out a hand to touch a skein of irresistibly soft wool.

"Can I help you find something?" Lydia asked.

Anne Marie nodded and, strangely, felt a bit hesitant. "I'd like to learn to knit." This was the first positive step she'd taken toward acting on her wish list. She'd been searching for somewhere to start, and knitting would do very well. "I...saw the notice in the window for a beginners' class last week, but there isn't a sign now. Do you have one scheduled anytime soon?"

"As it happens, Margaret and I were just discussing a beginners' class for Thursday afternoons."

Anne Marie shook her head. "I work all day on Thursdays."

"I'm also thinking about starting a new class for people who work. How about lunchtime on Tuesdays?" Lydia suggested next. "Would you like to sign up for that?"

Before Anne Marie could respond, Margaret was on her feet. "That's too many classes," she muttered. "Lydia's teaching far too many classes and it exhausts her."

"Margaret!" Lydia protested and cast a despairing look at her sister.

"Well, it's true. You need to get someone else in here

who can teach. I do as much as I can," she said, "but there are times I've got more customers than I can handle and you're involved with all those classes."

Lydia ignored her sister. "Anne Marie, if you want to learn how to knit, I'll teach you myself."

It occurred to Anne Marie that what she really wanted was a class. She'd rejected line dancing because that had seemed like an overwhelming social occasion; a small knitting group was far less threatening. Other than the Valentine's event with the widows, she hadn't gone anywhere or done much of anything since Robert's funeral. Until now, the mere thought of making cheerful conversation with anyone outside the bookstore was beyond her. She decided she could ease into socializing with a knitting class. A few like-minded women, all focused on the same task...

"I appreciate the offer," Anne Marie told Lydia. "However, I think Margaret's probably right. You've got a lot on your plate. Let me know if that noontime beginner class pans out."

"Of course."

After they'd exchanged farewells, Anne Marie picked up her shopping bags and left the yarn store. As she strolled past the shop window she noticed Whiskers, Lydia's cat, curled up in a basket of red wool. When Anne Marie walked Baxter, he often stood on his hind legs, front paws against the window, fixated on Lydia's cat—who wanted nothing to do with him.

Hauling the scrapbooking supplies upstairs to her apartment, Anne Marie set her bags on the kitchen table, then scooped up her dog, stroking his silky fur. "Hey, Mr. Baxter. I just saw your friend Whiskers."

He wriggled excitedly and she put him down, collecting a biscuit from a box on the counter. "Here you go." She smiled as he loudly crunched his cookie, licking up each and every crumb. "Maybe I'll knit you a little coat sometime...and maybe I won't."

Now that a knitting class apparently wasn't a sure thing, Anne Marie was shocked at how discouraged she felt. One roadblock, and she was ready to pack it in. Less than a year ago, hardly anything seemed to defeat her, but these days even the most mundane problems were disheartening.

At least Baxter's needs were straightforward and easily met, and he viewed her with unwavering devotion. There was comfort in that.

Eager to start her scrapbook project, she got to work. The three-ring binder was black with a clear plastic cover. For the next thirty minutes she cut out letters, decorated them with glitter glue and pasted them on a bright pink sheet. Then she slipped it behind the cover so the front of the binder read TWENTY WISHES. In addition to the binder, Anne Marie had purchased twenty plastic folders, one for each wish.

She became so involved in her work that it was well past one before she realized she hadn't eaten lunch. She emptied a can of soup into a bowl, and it was heating in the microwave when her phone rang.

Startled, she picked up the receiver on the first ring. The beeper went off at the same time, indicating that her meal was ready.

"Hello," she said, cradling the phone against her shoulder as she opened the microwave. She rarely got calls at home anymore. In the weeks after Robert's funeral, she'd heard from a number of couples they'd been friends with, but those people had gradually drifted away. Anne Marie hadn't made the effort to keep in touch, either. It was easier to lose herself in her grief than to reach out to others.

"Anne Marie, it's Lillie. Guess what?" her friend said breathlessly.

"What?" Hearing the excitement in Lillie's voice lifted her own spirits.

"Remember what you said Valentine's night?"

Anne Marie frowned. "Not exactly. I said various things. Which one do you mean?"

"Oh, you know. Elise was talking about eating something to feel better and then someone else—me, I think—brought up volunteering and you said…" She giggled. "You asked why we couldn't just buy ourselves something."

Anne Marie smiled. She'd been joking at the time, but it appeared that Lillie had taken her seriously. "Are you about to tell me you bought yourself something?"

"I sure did," Lillie said gleefully.

"Well, don't leave me in suspense. What did you get?"

Lillie giggled again. "A brand-new shiny red convertible."

"No!" Anne Marie feigned shock.

"Yes. Can you imagine me at sixty-three buying myself a sports car?"

"What kind is it?" Anne Marie knew next to nothing about cars, which was why she belonged to Triple A. In truth, Robert had been pretty helpless, too.

"A BMW."

It must've been expensive; Anne Marie knew that much. Well, Lillie could afford it. The perfume company had been more than generous to her and Barbie after the plane crash, and they were both financially secure.

"Want to go for a ride?"

Anne Marie's first inclination was to decline. Almost immediately she changed her mind. Why not go? Lillie's excitement was so contagious, she couldn't resist joining in.

"I'd love to," she said warmly.

"Great. I'll meet you in front of the bookstore in twenty minutes."

"Uh, what about Jacqueline?" She knew Lillie had plenty of other friends and that she and Jacqueline Donovan were especially close. They'd raised their children together, belonged to the same country club and were active members of several charitable organizations. Jacqueline, too, was a frequent customer at Blossom Street Books, not to mention all the other neighborhood stores.

"Rest assured, she'll get her turn," Lillie told her. "So, do you want to go for a ride or not?"

"I do. I just thought…never mind. I'd love to ride in your shiny new red convertible."

Gulping down her soup and then grabbing her coat, Anne Marie waited outside by the curb. Lillie pulled up right on time. The car, a convertible, was certainly bright red, and it shone from fender to fender. Despite the overcast skies, her friend had the top down.

Anne Marie stepped forward, gawking at the vehicle. "Lillie, it's fabulous!"

The older woman grinned. "I think so, too."

"What did Barbie have to say?"

Lillie shook her head. "She doesn't know yet. No one does. I'd just driven it off the showroom floor when I called you."

"Why me?"

"You're the one who inspired the idea. So it's only fitting that you be the first one to ride in it."

Anne Marie remembered the "eat something," "do something" conversation, but she never would've guessed she'd end up riding in a brand-new BMW because of it.

"It's the first time in my life that I've purchased my own car. I negotiated the deal myself," Lillie announced proudly. "And I had all my facts straight before I even walked inside. Those salesmen take one look at me and see dollar signs. I needed to prove to them—and to myself—that I'm no pushover."

"I'm sure you did—and then some."

Lillie nodded. "I got on the internet and found a website that showed the invoice price, and then broke out the dealer's typical overheads and advertising costs."

Anne Marie was more impressed by the minute. "You really did your research."

"My dear, you can find out just about anything on the internet." She raised her eyebrows. "I also discovered that the dealer cost includes a holdback for profit." Lillie smiled roguishly as she continued her story. "The salesman was a charming fellow, I will say that. He expected to walk away with a substantial commission check, but I quickly disavowed him of *that* notion."

Anne Marie stared at her, astonished. "How did you do it?"

"We started negotiating and I had him at the point of accepting my offer when I remembered that dealers sometimes get incentives and rebates on cars sold."

"You mentioned that, too?"

"Darn right I did and he agreed to my terms."

"Lillie, congratulations." Anne Marie had no idea the older woman had such a head for business. As far as she was aware, Lillie hadn't worked a day in her life, or at least not outside the home. In many ways Barbie was a younger version of her mother. Both women had married young, and each had chosen a husband ten or so years her senior. That was something Anne Marie had in common with them; the fact that they were both mothers was not. They'd promptly delivered the requisite child, in Barbie's case, twin sons. If Anne Marie recalled correctly, the Foster boys, Eric and

Kurt, were enrolled in separate East Coast schools—very elite ones, naturally.

"It feels so good to drive a vehicle I negotiated for myself," Lillie said. "And this came about because of you."

"Really, I just made an offhand comment."

"It's more than purchasing my own car," she said, as though Anne Marie hadn't spoken, "it was managing everything myself instead of handing the task over to someone else. I've always felt I could be a good businesswoman if I'd been given the opportunity." She rubbed her hand over the arc of the steering wheel. "No one seemed to consider me capable of running my own affairs. Ironically, the person I needed to convince most was me. Thanks to you, I did."

Anne Marie felt a bit uncomfortable; Lillie was giving her far more credit than she deserved.

"Come on," Lillie said. "Get in."

Swinging open the passenger door, Anne Marie climbed into the convertible and fastened her seat belt.

Lillie gripped the steering wheel tightly, throwing back her head. "I have to tell you, I'm really getting into this Twenty Wishes thing."

"I am, too," Anne Marie said. "When you phoned I was in the middle of making a scrapbook, a page for each wish. I'm going to cut out magazine pictures to visualize them and to document the various steps."

Lillie turned to smile at her. "What a great idea."

The praise encouraged her and Anne Marie quickly went on to describe the craft-store supplies she'd purchased. "I don't have much of a list as yet, but I'm working on it. How about you?"

Lillie was silent for a moment. "I've decided I want to fall in love." She spoke with a determination Anne Marie had never heard from her.

"Barbie said the same thing at our Valentine's party," Anne Marie pointed out.

"I know."

Anne Marie waited.

"I've had plenty of men ask me out," Lillie told her. "I don't mean to sound egotistical, but I'm not interested in most of them."

Anne Marie nodded, not surprised that "plenty of men" would find Lillie attractive.

"I've learned a thing or two in the last sixty-odd years," Lillie was saying, "and I'm not as impressed with riches or connections as I once was. When I fall in love, I want it to be with a man of integrity. Someone who's decent and kind and—" She paused as though searching for the right word. "Honorable. I want to fall in love with an honorable man." She seemed embarrassed at having spoken her wish aloud, and leaned forward to start the engine. "As you might've guessed, my marriage—unlike my daughter's—wasn't a particularly good one. I don't want to repeat the mistakes I made when I was younger." The car roared to life, then purred with the sound of a flawlessly tuned engine.

Checking behind her, Lillie backed out of the parking space on Blossom Street. From there they headed toward the freeway on-ramp. Lillie proposed a drive through the Kent Valley and along the Green River, and Anne Marie agreed.

Closing her eyes, Anne Marie let the cold February wind sweep past her. Lillie turned on the radio just as the DJ announced a hit from the late 1960s. Soon she was crooning along to The Lovin' Spoonful's "Did You Ever Have To Make Up Your Mind." Anne Marie remembered her mother singing that song as a girl. Perhaps it was unusual to find herself good friends with a woman who was her mother's contemporary. Sadly, although Anne Marie was an only child, she and her mother weren't close. Her parents had divorced when she was in sixth grade, and the bitterness, especially on her mother's part, had lingered through the years. It didn't help that Anne Marie resembled her father. She'd had little contact with him after the divorce, and he died in a boating accident on Lake Washington when she was twenty-five. Her mother had never remarried.

Because they had such an uneasy relationship, Anne Marie avoided frequent visits home. She made a point of calling her mother at least once a month. Even then, it seemed they didn't have much to discuss. Sad as it was to admit, Anne Marie had more in common with Lillie than she did with her own mother.

As Lillie's voice grew louder, Anne Marie stayed quiet, afraid that if she attempted to sing she'd embarrass herself. After about twenty minutes, Lillie exited the freeway and drove toward the road that ran beside the banks of the Green River.

This was about as perfect a moment as Anne Marie could remember since Robert's death. They had the road to themselves. The sun was on her face and the wind tossed her hair in every direction and she couldn't have cared less.

Lillie, however, had wrapped a silk scarf over her elegantly arranged hair, which held it neatly in place.

Darting around the twisting country roads, Lillie revealed her skill as a driver. Then, in the middle of a sharp turn, she let out a small cry of alarm.

"What's wrong?" Anne Marie was instantly on edge. She grasped the passenger door as Lillie struggled to control the vehicle.

"The steering wheel," she gasped. She pulled the car over to the side of the road and cut the engine. She looked wide-eyed at Anne Marie. "There's something wrong with the steering."

"This is a brand-new car!"

"You don't need to remind me," Lillie said through clenched teeth. She opened the car door and got out, then reached behind the seat for her purse. Taking out her cell phone, she exhaled slowly. "Fortunately I have the dealership's number in my Calls Received." She wrapped one arm around her waist while she waited for someone to answer.

"Hello," she said, speaking without even a hint of irritation in her voice. "This is Lillie Higgins. I was in the dealership earlier this afternoon. Could I speak with Darryl Pierpont, please? He's the salesman who sold me this vehicle." She waited, and it seemed the salesman was unavailable because Lillie asked to speak with the manager, who was apparently out of the office, as well. Lillie then said, "All right, answer me this. Has the dealership deposited the check I wrote?" She turned to Anne Marie, eyes fierce. "I suggest you don't, as I'm about to put a stop payment order on it."

That quickly got her the attention she sought. After explaining what had happened and listening for a moment, then describing her location, Lillie closed the cell.

"The dealership's sending a tow truck for the car. The service manager is bringing me a replacement vehicle until they can determine what's wrong with mine."

"As they should."

"Until then we have to sit here and wait."

They climbed back into the car and chatted for half an hour or so until another BMW arrived, followed by a tow truck. A Hispanic man stepped out of the car. "Ms. Higgins?" he asked with a slight Mexican accent, looking at Lillie.

"Yes."

"I'm Hector Silva, manager of the service department. I would like to personally apologize for this inconvenience."

"I've owned this car for less than two hours!"

Hector shook his head. "I give you my word that we will find out what caused the problem and repair it properly. Until then, the dealership would like you to use this loaner car."

Anne Marie liked the man immediately. He was around Lillie's age, she guessed, with lovely tanned skin and salt-and-pepper hair. He handed Lillie some papers to sign and then the keys to the other car.

"Would you like a ride back to the dealership, Mr. Silva?" Lillie offered, surprising Anne Marie.

"No, thank you, I'll escort your convertible with the tow truck driver. I'll have your car back to you as soon as possible."

"Thank you."

He bowed his head. "It is my pleasure, Ms. Higgins."

While Hector Silva and the driver of the tow truck conferred, Lillie and Anne Marie slipped into the second car, a luxury sedan.

"He was so nice," Anne Marie commented. The service manager couldn't have been more accommodating or polite.

"I was looking forward to giving the dealership a piece of my mind," Lillie said with a sigh. "But how can I when everyone's being so wonderful? Well," she said, grinning, "after I threatened them."

"That had nothing to do with Mr. Silva, though."

"I agree," Lillie said. "He struck me as genuine."

They resumed their drive, except that this time Lillie headed straight back to the city, stopping in front of Blossom Street Books.

"Thank you, Lillie," Anne Marie said as she climbed out. "I've never enjoyed a car ride more."

"Bye." And with a smile that shone from her eyes and her heart, Lillie drove off.

Three

Standing in front of Woodrow Wilson Elementary School, Anne Marie took a deep breath. Elise Beaumont had repeatedly encouraged her to become a volunteer and had recommended the Lunch Buddy program. Elise herself was a Lunch Buddy at a different school—her grandson's—but Woodrow Wilson was closer to Blossom Street. She'd sounded so positive about the experience that Anne Marie had felt inspired to make the initial call. Volunteering was now number three on her list of Twenty Wishes, after the red boots and learning to knit.

Lillie had bought her red BMW convertible and despite the problems that first day, she was thrilled with her purchase. Buoyed by that sense of exhilaration, Lillie had decided to look more closely into the financial matters she'd left in the hands of others. She, too, was working on her list, as were Barbie and Elise.

Last week Elise had said she was applying for a part-time job. For the last three years of her husband's illness, she'd been Maverick's primary caregiver. Now that her husband was gone, Elise needed some kind of activity to fill her time. Maverick wouldn't have wanted her to mope uselessly around the house, she insisted.

Although Anne Marie had only met Maverick Beaumont—a professional poker player—once or twice, she felt Elise was right. Maverick was obviously a man of action and he would've urged his wife to do something constructive and meaningful with her remaining years. The Lunch Buddy program was a worthwhile start, but Elise had extra time, lots of it, and energy to spare.

Anne Marie wasn't sure how Robert would react if he were to find out she'd volunteered as a Lunch Buddy—let alone that she'd begun a list of Twenty Wishes. Would he consider it frivolous? Self-involved? Or would he think it was a good idea, a good way of recapturing her enthusiasm for life? They'd been married almost eleven years and there were days Anne Marie felt she'd never really known her husband.

Robert was a private person who kept his feelings hidden from the world and sometimes even from her. When she first told him she wanted a child, Robert had simply left the room. Not until three days later was he willing to discuss the matter. He'd told her that a second family was out of the question; as far as he was concerned, they'd made that decision before their marriage. He was right. She'd agreed there'd be no children. What he didn't understand or seem capable of acknowledging was that she'd been at a very different point in her life when she'd married him. She'd been too young to realize how intense the desire for a baby would become as the years went on.

Robert said he already had his family, that it was time to think about grandchildren, not more children. She'd agreed to his terms and, according to him, that agreement was binding.

Anne Marie had tried to ignore her yearning for a child. With Robert's encouragement and support, she'd purchased Blossom Street Books with a small inheritance from her grandparents' estate, which she'd invested years before. That hadn't solved the problem, nor had Baxter, the Yorkie he'd surprised her with one evening. Much as she loved Robert, her bookstore and her dog, her need for a baby was still there, growing until she could no longer ignore it.

She wanted a baby. Robert's baby. The promise she'd made him had been more than eleven years ago. She'd changed her mind, but he refused to change his. She'd pleaded and cajoled, all to no avail.

To complicate everything, Robert had discussed this personal and private matter with his daughter, who'd naturally sided with her father. That made Anne Marie's relationship with Melissa—and with Robert—even more difficult.

Melissa had hated Anne Marie from the day she married Robert. Granted, the girl had only been thirteen at the time, but she'd rejected Anne Marie's overtures in no uncertain terms, and her attitude had become more adamant, more intolerant, with age. His daughter had always been Daddy's little girl and her resentment toward Anne Marie was unyielding. Melissa had done everything possible to make her feel like an outsider. Anne Marie hadn't been invited to graduations, birthdays or other family events. Brandon, her stepson, had accepted her from the beginning, and they'd held their own little celebrations. During the first few years, Robert had tried to build a bridge between her and his daughter, but that effort had fallen by the wayside. After a while both she and Robert had given up. His relationship with Melissa had become something completely separate from his marriage.

Still, Anne Marie felt deeply betrayed when her husband took a private matter between the two of them to his daughter. He'd been disloyal to her. Even worse was learning about it from Melissa, who'd taunted Anne Marie with what she knew. That had added humiliation to the pain.

Robert listened stoically as she wept and cried out her fury. Nothing she said seemed to affect him. He listened, his face impassive, and then a few days later, packed a bag and moved out. Just like that.

The shock of it had left Anne Marie reeling for weeks. After a month in which she refused to give him the satisfaction of calling, Robert had briefly returned to the house to suggest a legal separation.

Remaining as unemotional as possible, Anne Marie had agreed. Perhaps living apart would be best while they both considered their options. By then, Anne Marie had been angry. Okay, furious. She'd wondered if Robert had ever really loved her. How selfish, how unfair, how…male of him.

Anne Marie felt it was imperative that Robert know she was serious about a baby. He'd moved out of the house and, following his lead, she'd moved out, too, leaving the place to sit vacant. Fortunately she had the apartment above the bookstore, which had recently become available. She hoped such a drastic action would give Robert notice that she was more than able to support herself—more than capable of living her life without him. In his own fit of defiance, Robert had listed the house, which was in his name. Everyone was surprised when it sold the first week. Anne Marie's things, whatever she hadn't moved to the apartment, had been taken to a storage unit. It had all been so petty, so juvenile.

Their separation had become a battle of wills, each of them intent on showing how unnecessary and superfluous the other was. They were clearly destined for the divorce court, until Anne Marie decided enough was enough. After all, this was the man she loved. Despite everything—her disappointment, her anger toward Melissa—her feelings for her husband hadn't changed. The day she called Robert at the office had been a turning point. She admitted she missed him and was sorry the situation had deteriorated so far. He seemed surprised to hear from her and at the same time delighted. He said he was sorry, too, and they'd agreed to meet for dinner.

The one stipulation was that there be no talk about Anne Marie having a baby. Although she didn't like it, she'd promised. Dinner was wonderful and Robert had gone out of his way to make the evening as romantic as possible.

Robert Roche could certainly be charming when he put his mind to it, and that night he'd charmed himself right into her bed. Their lovemaking had always been powerful and it felt so wonderful to be with him again. Then, in the morning when she awoke, Anne Marie discovered he'd left during the night. That was like a slap in the face. It would serve him right if she ended up pregnant, she'd thought angrily.

Only she hadn't.

They'd continued to meet and to talk regularly but that was the last time they'd made love.

Shaking her head, trying to free herself from the memories, Anne Marie realized she'd been standing in front of the elementary school for ten minutes without moving. Making a determined effort, she walked into the building.

She had an appointment with the school counselor, Ms. Helen Mayer, at ten-thirty and she was already five minutes late.

As soon as Anne Marie entered the school, the hallway immediately filled with noisy youngsters, all of them trying to get past her and outside. But for the first time that day, the sun peeked out through dark clouds, and she took that as a favorable sign.

Eventually Anne Marie located the school office, which had a small waiting area, a large counter that stretched across the room and a number of offices behind it.

"May I help you?" the woman at the counter asked.

"I'm Anne Marie Roche. I have an appointment with Ms. Mayer."

"You're here for the Lunch Buddy program?"

"That's right." Anne Marie nervously brushed her hair away from her face. She wore it straight, shoulder-length, and had dressed in wool slacks and a white turtleneck sweater. Now that she was actually at the office, her uncertainty returned. She wasn't convinced this was the best project for her, wish list or not. She didn't know anything about children of elementary-school age, or any age for that matter. Her experience with Melissa hadn't exactly inspired confidence in her ability to relate to kids.

"Ms. Mayer is meeting with the other volunteers in Room 121," the woman told her. "There's an orientation first."

"Okay," Anne Marie said with a nod, figuring the orientation would help her decide. "How do I find Room 121?"

"It's easy. Just go out the way you came in, take a left and follow the hallway to the end."

"Thank you."

"You're welcome," the secretary mumbled as she turned back to her computer screen.

Mentally repeating the directions, Anne Marie stepped out of the office. For a moment she hesitated, thinking she could just leave now, simply walk out. She didn't know any young children and couldn't imagine what they'd want to talk about. But her hesitation was brief. The prospect of confessing to Elise that she hadn't even tried compelled Anne Marie to go to Room 121.

Two other women and one man were already seated on metal folding chairs at a long conference table. There was a chalkboard behind them. Helen Mayer welcomed her with a gesture toward an empty seat.

"You must be Anne Marie," she said. "Meet Maggie, Lois and John."

Anne Marie nodded in the direction of the other volunteers and pulled out a chair. She still felt the urge to make an excuse and walk out. She couldn't, though. Not without at least going through the orientation.

"I believe that's everyone," Helen said, reaching for a piece of chalk. She walked over to the board and wrote each person's name.

During the next thirty minutes, Anne Marie learned that this was a four-month commitment. She must agree to meet faithfully with her Lunch Buddy once a week for that period of time.

"Every week?" one of the other women asked.

"Yes, the same day if possible but it's understandable if you occasionally need to change days. It's best for the children to have a sense of routine and trust that you'll be here for them."

The others all nodded. A little belatedly, Anne Marie did, too.

"Next, we ask that you eat the food from the cafeteria. Lunch Buddy kids get their lunch free, thanks to a government subsidy, but you can buy yours at a minimal charge. If you must bring in food from outside, please check to be sure the child you're paired with doesn't have any food allergies."

That was reasonable, Anne Marie thought.

"After lunch you can let the child take you to his or her classroom. Or you can go outside for recess if you prefer. The idea is to spend the entire lunch period with your assigned child."

"Do they still jump rope?" Lois asked.

Ms. Mayer nodded. "With the same rhymes we used when I was a girl."

The women exchanged smiles.

"The important thing is to interact with the child," the school counselor continued. "Get to know him or her and forge a friendship."

"What about seeing the child outside school?" This question came from Maggie, who appeared to be in her early fifties.

"That'll have to be approved by the child's parent or guardian."

Anne Marie couldn't imagine seeing the child other than inside the protected walls of the school. She didn't want to get emotionally attached. Besides, that wasn't part of the deal. All that was required was to come in and have lunch with her young charge. If he or she wanted to show off school assignments, fine. But that was the limit of what Anne Marie could handle. She had enough to cope with; she didn't need to add anything else to the mix. Any relationship with an at-risk child would have to remain casual. Nothing beyond the most basic obligations.

The orientation meeting took the full half hour. Several additional questions were asked, but Anne Marie only half listened. While the others chatted, she struggled, asking herself over and over if this was the right volunteer program. She couldn't imagine why Elise seemed to think she'd be a perfect Lunch Buddy. Anne Marie didn't feel perfect. What she felt was…nothing. Nothing at all. Zoned out. Emotionally dead. Disinterested.

Ms. Mayer handed out the assignments, leaving Anne Marie for last. She must have sensed her doubts because she asked, "Do you have any further questions?"

Anne Marie shook her head. "Not really. I'm just wondering if I'm really a good candidate for this."

"Why not give it a try? I suspect you'll enjoy it. Almost everyone does."

The other woman's reassurance warmed her. "Okay, I will."

"The child I have in mind for you is named Ellen Falk," she went on to say. "Ellen is eight years old and in second grade. Because of the Right to Privacy Laws, I'm not allowed to reveal any details about her home background. However, I can tell you that Ellen is currently living with her maternal grandmother."

"Has she been in this school long?"

"Ellen's been a student here for the past two years."

"Okay."

Before Anne Marie could ask why the school counselor had decided to pair her with this particular child, Helen Mayer continued. "Ellen is an intense child. Very quiet. Shy. She doesn't have a lot to say, but don't let that discourage you."

"Okay," Anne Marie said again.

"Talk to her and be patient. She'll speak to you when she's ready."

Oh, great. She'd have to carry the entire conversation for heaven only knew how many weeks. "Is there a reason you decided to match me up with this child?" she asked. Surely there was another one, another little girl who was more personable. Anne Marie wasn't much of a talker herself these days, and she wasn't sure that pairing her with an intense, reticent child would work.

"That's an excellent question," Helen Mayer said approvingly. "Ellen loves to read, and since you own Blossom Street Books…well, it seemed to be a good fit."

"Oh."

"Ellen is one of our top second-grade readers."

Rather than suggest being paired with a different child, Anne Marie decided to go ahead with this arrangement. "I look forward to meeting her," she said, wincing inwardly at the lie.

"Ellen has first lunch, which starts in a few minutes, so if you'll come with me, I'll introduce you."

Anne Marie still wasn't convinced she was ready for this. However, it was now or never. Once she walked out of Room 121, Anne Marie knew that unless she met the child immediately, she wouldn't be back.

Ms. Mayer led her down the hallway to a row of classrooms, each door marked with the grade and the teacher's name. Ellen was in Ms. Peterski's class. Helen Mayer waited until a young woman—obviously Ms. Peterski—and twenty or so children had filed out, then walked inside, Anne Marie a few steps behind her.

The first thing Anne Marie noticed was how impossibly small the desks were. The second was the child sitting in the far corner all alone. Her head was lowered, and her stick-straight hair fell forward, hiding her eyes.

"Ellen," the school counselor said, her voice full of enthusiasm. "I want you to meet your Lunch Buddy."

The little girl, dressed in dirty tennis shoes, jeans and a red T-shirt, slid out of her chair and moved toward them, her gaze on the floor.

"Anne Marie, meet Ellen."

"Hello, Ellen," Anne Marie said dutifully. She kept her voice soft and modulated.

Ellen didn't acknowledge the greeting.

After an awkward silence, Ms. Mayer spoke again. "Ellen, would you please escort your guest to the lunch-room?"

In response Ellen nodded and walked quickly out of the room. She stood outside the door until Anne Marie caught up.

"That's a nice T-shirt you're wearing," Anne Marie said, testing the waters. "Red is one of my favorite colors."

No response.

The noise from the cafeteria grew louder as they made their way down the hall. Ellen joined the other students in the lunch line and Anne Marie stood behind her.

"What's for lunch today?" Anne Marie asked.

Ellen pointed to one of the students at a nearby table, spooning macaroni and cheese into her mouth. "That."

At last! The eight-year-old actually had a voice.

The line started to move. "Macaroni and cheese used to be one of my favorite lunches," Anne Marie said. "Do you like it, too?"

Ellen shrugged.

"What's your favorite?"

She expected the universal response of pizza. Instead Ellen said, "Chili and corn bread."

"I like that, too." Well, she didn't hate it, but it wasn't one of Anne Marie's favorites. Thus far they didn't seem to have a lot in common.

Their lunch consisted of macaroni and cheese, a gelatin salad, carrot sticks, milk and an oatmeal cookie. Carrying her tray, Anne Marie followed the girl to a table near the back of the room. Ellen chose to sit at the far end, away from the other children.

Anne Marie set her tray across from Ellen, then pulled out her chair and sat down. Ellen bowed her head and folded her hands on her lap for a silent moment before she reached for her silverware. Apparently she was saying grace before eating her lunch.

Anne Marie took a sip of milk once Ellen had taken her first bite. "I understand you like to read," she said conversationally.

Ellen nodded.

"I own a bookstore. Have you read any of the Harry Potter books?"

Ellen shook her head. "My grandma said they're too advanced for me. She said I could read them in fourth grade."

"Your grandmother's probably right."

Ellen crunched down on a carrot stick.

"Who's your favorite author?" Anne Marie asked, encouraged by the girl's response.

Ellen swallowed. "I like lots of authors."

Again, this was progress. Of a sort. *And* the girl didn't talk with her mouth full, which meant she'd been taught some manners.

"When I was your age, books were my best friends." Anne Marie could recall reading in her bedroom with the door closed to drown out the sound of her parents arguing.

That comment didn't warrant a response. Anne Marie took another bite of her lunch as she mentally sorted through potential topics of conversation. It was hard to remember what she'd liked when she was eight. She didn't think Ellen would be interested in hearing about her widowed friends or her list of Twenty Wishes.

They continued to eat in silence until an idea struck Anne Marie. "Do you like dogs?"

Ellen nodded vigorously.

"I have a dog."

For the first time since they'd sat at the table, Ellen looked up. "A boy dog or a girl dog?"

"A boy. His name is Baxter."

"Baxter." A hint of a smile flashed in her eyes.

Anne Marie felt a surge of relief. She'd hit pay dirt. Ellen liked dogs. "He's a Yorkshire terrier. Do you know what kind of dog that is?"

Ellen shook her head.

"Baxter is small but he has the heart of a tiger. He's not afraid of anything."

Ellen's eyes brightened.

"Would you like to meet him one day?"

Ellen nodded again. "What color is he?"

"Mostly he's black but his face is sort of a tan, and he has funny-looking ears that stick straight up."

"My ears stick out, too," Ellen said in a solemn voice.

Anne Marie studied the child. She could see the faint outline of Ellen's ears beneath her straight hair, which hung just below her chin. "I had ears like that when I was your age," Anne Marie told her. "Then I grew up and my ears stayed the same size and everything else got bigger."

Ellen took another bite of her macaroni and cheese.

Anne Marie did, too. She finished the lunch period by telling the girl stories about Baxter. Ellen asked dozens of questions and even giggled once.

The other children gradually left the lunchroom, drifting out to the schoolyard. The muted sound of their play could be heard through the windows. Anne Marie looked out several times; when she asked if Ellen wanted to go outside, the youngster declined.

The bell finally rang, signaling the end of lunch. Ellen stood.

So did Anne Marie.

Ellen carried her dirty tray to the kitchen and showed Anne Marie where to place it.

"I guess you have to go back to class now," Anne Marie said.

Ellen nodded. Anne Marie walked her to the classroom door and just as she was about to leave, Ellen whispered something she couldn't quite hear.

"What did you say?" Anne Marie asked.

Ellen glanced up. "Thank you," she said more loudly.

"You're welcome, Ellen. I'll see you next Wednesday."

Ellen smiled, then quietly entered the room and walked to her desk.

As Anne Marie watched, her chest constricted with a sensation that felt alien to her. It was a good feeling, though—one that came from reaching out to someone else.

Elise was right; Anne Marie did feel better for volunteering. Little Ellen Falk needed a friend.

The ironic thing was that Anne Marie needed one even more.

Four

After leaving Woodrow Wilson Elementary, Anne Marie ran a few errands in the neighborhood. She bought groceries, went to the post office and picked up some dry cleaning. Her Wednesdays were generally crowded with appointments and chores.

When she brought the groceries up to her apartment, she noticed that the light on her answering machine was flashing. After greeting a sleepy Baxter and putting the perishables in the refrigerator, she grabbed a pen and pad and pushed the message button.

The first one was from the school counselor. "Anne Marie, this is Helen Mayer. I wanted to see how everything went with Ellen. If you have any questions, please feel free to contact me at the school." She then repeated the phone number. "See you next Wednesday."

The second message began. "Anne Marie—" Melissa Roche's voice stopped Anne Marie cold.

"Could you call me at your earliest convenience?" Her question was followed by a slight hesitation. "It's important."

The recording ended with Melissa reciting her phone

number. "This is a new number. If I don't hear from you by the end of the day, I'll call the bookstore."

That sounded almost like a threat.

Anne Marie wondered about Melissa's request as she finished putting the groceries away. When she was done, she tentatively reached for the phone. If Melissa was seeking her out, it had to be something serious, although she couldn't imagine what. The call connected and the phone rang twice. Anne Marie was hoping for a reprieve. She didn't get one.

"Hello," Melissa answered. Her voice seemed clipped, defensive.

"This is Anne Marie," she said, trying to keep her own voice as unemotional as possible.

"I know who it is," Melissa said. "I have caller ID."

"You left a message for me," Anne Marie reminded her. The enmity between them remained, despite the fact that Robert was gone.

"I need to talk to you," Melissa told her.

"I'm free now." Anne Marie would rather get this over with.

"I mean, I need to talk to you face-to-face."

That was exactly what Anne Marie had hoped to avoid. Naturally, she was suspicious of Melissa's sudden need for a meeting. "Why?"

"Anne Marie, please, I wouldn't ask if it wasn't necessary."

She exhaled slowly. "All right. When?"

"What about tomorrow night? We could meet for dinner…"

"I close the store on Thursday nights. It would have to be after eight."

"What about Friday night then?" Melissa suggested.

"Okay." Anne Marie knew her reluctance must be evident. She could think of a dozen ways she'd rather spend Friday evening than sitting across a table from her stepdaughter.

Melissa chose a restaurant and they set the time. The conversation ended shortly thereafter, and when she put the phone back, Anne Marie felt queasy. Everything about their short conversation had unnerved her. She hated going into this meeting with Melissa so unprepared, but then it occurred to her that perhaps Brandon knew what was going on. She hadn't spoken to her stepson in a few weeks, and this was a good excuse to catch up with him. She hoped he could clear up the mystery; if he had any idea why Melissa had contacted her after all these months, he'd certainly tell her.

Anne Marie opened a drawer in the kitchen and removed the telephone directory, then flipped through the pages until she found her stepson's work number.

Brandon answered immediately, obviously pleased to hear from her.

"Anne Marie! How are you doing?" he asked. Although Robert had been especially close to Melissa, the relationship between father and son was often strained.

"I'm fine. How about you?"

"Good. Good. What can I do for you?"

Brandon was a claims adjuster for an insurance company and she was well aware that he didn't have time to waste on idle chitchat.

"I heard from Melissa this afternoon."

"Melissa called you?" That was strange enough to instantly get his attention. "What did she want?" he asked curiously.

"To talk to me, or so she says. We're meeting for dinner. Can you tell me what that's about?"

"Melissa called you?" Brandon repeated. He seemed completely at a loss. "I couldn't begin to tell you what she wants."

Anne Marie sighed. "I can't figure it out, either. She insists we talk face-to-face."

"Would you like me to give her a call?" he asked.

"No, that's okay. I'll find out soon enough." Whatever it was didn't appear to involve Brandon.

"Let me know what's up, will you?"

"You haven't heard from her?" Brandon and Melissa had always been fairly close, even though he openly disapproved of his sister's attitude toward Anne Marie.

"Not in a couple of weeks, which isn't like her. After Dad died, I heard from her practically every day. Lately, though, she's been keeping to herself."

"You haven't called her?"

"I've left her a couple of messages. Apparently she's been spending all her time with that guy she's seeing. If I'm reading the situation right, it sounds like she and Michael are serious."

"Is that good news or bad?" Anne Marie asked.

"I think it's good. I like Michael and as far as I can tell, he really cares about Melissa."

"So you've met him?"

"Yeah, a couple of times. He came to Dad's funeral."

Anne Marie had been too grief-stricken to remember who'd been there; not only that, Michael would've been a stranger to her, one among many.

Was Melissa planning to confide in her about this young man? Hard to believe, but Anne Marie's curiosity was even more pronounced now.

She replaced the phone, staring out the kitchen window onto the alley behind Blossom Street. She'd just have to wait until Friday to learn the reason for Melissa's phone call.

On Friday, Anne Marie got to the restaurant shortly before the predetermined time of seven. Based on past experience, she expected Melissa to be late; that was usually the case, especially if the event happened to include Anne Marie—like dinner at her and Robert's house or a holiday get-together. It was yet another way she displayed her complete lack of regard for her stepmother. But when Anne Marie arrived Melissa was already there, pacing outside the restaurant. Anne Marie was shocked, to say the least.

Melissa had suggested a well-known seafood place on the waterfront close to Pike Place Market. Walking fast, it was about twenty minutes from the bookstore, and Anne Marie had worn an extra sweater against the cold wind coming off Elliot Bay.

Her stepdaughter abruptly stopped her pacing the moment she saw her. Because of their long, unfortunate history, Anne Marie didn't—couldn't—lower her guard. She'd been sucker punched too many times by some slyly cruel comment or unmistakable slight.

"Hello, Melissa," she said, maintaining a cool facade. "You're looking well." Her stepdaughter was an attractive woman, tall and willowy in stature. Her hair was dark and fell in soft natural curls about her face. She was wearing black jeans and an expensive three-quarter-length khaki raincoat. Even as a girl, she'd been almost obsessed with fashion and appearances, an obsession her father had indulged.

"You look good, too," Melissa said carelessly. "Are you dating anyone?"

Anne Marie bit her tongue. "No. If that's what you want to talk about, I think I should leave now."

"Calm down, would you?" Melissa snapped. "This doesn't have anything to do with you dating."

The derisive, scornful attitude was there in full display, and Anne Marie wondered why she still tried. Her stepdaughter seemed unreachable—by her, anyway—and had been from the day they met.

"I… I shouldn't have asked," Melissa murmured in what might have passed for an apology if her voice hadn't held the same level of hostility. "It isn't really any of my business."

"Shall we go inside?" Anne Marie said. The wind was growing stronger, and the rain seemed about to start any minute.

"Yes," Melissa agreed, moving quickly to the door.

Melissa had made a reservation, and they were soon seated at a table by the window. The water was as dark as the sky but Anne Marie gazed out at the lights, dimly visible in the fog. Then she turned to her menu. She and Melissa both seemed determined to make a thorough study of it. With her nerves on edge, Anne Marie didn't have much of an appetite. She decided on clam chowder in a bread bowl and when the server came, she was surprised to hear Melissa order the same thing.

"I'd like some coffee, too," Melissa told him.

"I would, as well."

Once the waiter had left, Melissa nervously reached for her linen napkin, which she spread carefully across her lap. Then she rearranged her silverware.

"Are you ready to tell me what this is about?" Anne Marie asked. Any exchange of pleasantries was pointless.

There was a pause. "It's probably unfair to come to you

about this," Melissa finally said, "but I didn't know what else to do."

Anne Marie closed her eyes briefly. "Rather than hint at what you want to say, why don't you just say it?"

Melissa placed her hands in her lap and lowered her head. "I... I haven't been doing well since Dad died."

Anne Marie nodded. "I haven't, either."

Melissa looked up and bit her lip. "I miss him so much."

Anne Marie tried to swallow the sudden lump in her throat. "Me, too."

"I thought if I went into his office and talked to his friends I'd feel better."

The waiter brought their coffee, and Anne Marie welcomed the distraction. She could feel tears welling up and she didn't want the embarrassment of crying in front of Melissa.

When they were alone again, Melissa dumped sugar in her coffee. "Like I said, I decided to stop by the office," she muttered, scooping up three tiny half-and-half cups and peeling away the tops. "Dad was always so proud of his role in the business."

Robert had every right to be proud. He'd worked for the data storage business almost from its inception and much of the company's success could be attributed to his efforts. He enjoyed his job, although the demands on his time had increased constantly. For three consecutive years, Robert had planned to take Anne Marie to Paris for their wedding anniversary. Each year he'd been forced to cancel their vacation plans because of business.

"Everyone must've been happy to see you," Anne Marie commented politely.

Melissa shrugged. "Even in this short amount of time, there've been a lot of changes."

That was understandable. Robert had died almost ten months ago, and life had a way of creeping forward, no matter what the circumstances.

"Do you remember Rebecca Gilroy?" Melissa asked.

"Of course." The young woman had been Robert's personal assistant. As Anne Marie recalled, Rebecca had started working for the company a year or so before Robert's heart attack.

"She had a baby."

"I didn't know she was pregnant." Had she learned of it, Anne Marie would've sent her a gift. She'd only met Rebecca on a few occasions, but she'd liked her.

"She isn't married." Melissa's gaze held hers.

Anne Marie didn't consider that significant. "It's hardly a prerequisite these days."

Melissa picked up her coffee and Anne Marie noticed that her hands were trembling.

"Do you remember exactly when you and my dad separated?"

Anne Marie expelled her breath. "It's not something I'm likely to forget, Melissa. Of course I remember. He... left on September 18th the year before last." She lifted her shoulders as she took in a deep breath, feeling raw and vulnerable. "I was miserable without your father. I still am." She wasn't sure where this conversation was leading and strained to hold on to her patience. Exhaling, she added, "Despite the fact that you dislike me, we've always had something very important in common. We both loved your father."

Melissa didn't acknowledge the comment; instead she stared down at the table. "One night a couple of months after you and Dad separated, I decided to treat him to dinner. He was working too hard and he often stayed late at the office."

That was a fairly typical occurrence throughout their marriage. As a company executive, Robert put in long hours.

"I picked up a couple of sandwiches and some of his favorite soup and went over there to surprise him."

Anne Marie nodded patiently, wondering when her stepdaughter would get to the point.

"The security guard let me in and when I walked into the office…"

The waiter approached the table with their order; Melissa stopped talking and even seemed grateful for the intrusion.

Anne Marie took her first taste, delicious despite her lack of appetite. Realizing Melissa hadn't continued, she gestured with her spoon. "Go on. You walked into the office and?"

Melissa nodded and reluctantly picked up her own spoon. "Rebecca was there, too."

"Mandatory overtime was one of the job requirements."

"She wasn't exactly…working."

Anne Marie frowned. "What do you mean?"

Melissa glared at her then. "Do I have to spell it out for you?" she demanded. "If you're going to make me say it, then fine. Rebecca and my father were…they were having sex."

Anne Marie's spoon clattered to the floor as the shock overwhelmed her. Her body felt mercifully numb, and her mind refused to accept what she'd heard. It was like the day the company president had come to the bookstore to personally tell her Robert had died. The same kind of dazed unbelief.

"I'm sorry, Anne Marie," Melissa whispered. "I… I

shouldn't have been so straightforward, but I didn't know how else to say it."

Melissa's words had begun to fall together in her mind. Robert and Rebecca sexually involved. Rebecca pregnant and unmarried. *Rebecca had a child.*

Anne Marie could no longer breathe.

"Rebecca's baby…"

Melissa's eyes held hers. "I'm not positive…but I think so. You know her better than I do. I only saw her the one time…with Dad, and then when I stopped by the office recently. I… I had the impression that she isn't the type to sleep around. Oh, and she was at the funeral."

Anne Marie closed her eyes and shook her head. All of a sudden, the few spoonfuls of soup she'd managed to swallow came back up her throat. Grabbing her napkin, she held it over her mouth and leaped from her chair. She weaved unsteadily around the tables, then bolted for the ladies' room and made it inside just in time. Stumbling into a vacant stall, Anne Marie was violently ill. When she finished, she was so weak she couldn't immediately get up.

Melissa was waiting for her as she came out of the stall and handed her a dampened paper towel. Tears had forged wet trails down the younger woman's cheeks. "I'm so sorry… I shouldn't have told you. I… I had no idea what else to do."

Anne Marie held the cold, wet towel to her face with both hands. Shock, betrayal, outrage—all these emotions bombarded her with such force she didn't know which one to react to first.

"I should've talked to Brandon," Melissa whispered, leaning against the wall. She slid down until she was in a crouching position. "I shouldn't have told you… I shouldn't have told you."

A waitress came into the ladies' room. "Is everything all right?" she asked, looking concerned. "The manager asked me to make sure there wasn't anything wrong with your dinner."

As Melissa straightened, Anne Marie tried to reassure the woman that this had nothing to do with the food. "We're fine. It wasn't the soup…it's nothing to worry about."

"There'll be no charge for your dinners."

"No, please. I'll pay." The anger had begun to fortify her now, and she washed her hands with a grim determination that was sure to kill any potential germs.

Melissa waited for her by the washroom door, following her back to the table. Anne Marie scooped up her purse and slapped two twenty-dollar bills down on the table. That should more than cover their soup and coffee. Like a stray puppy, her stepdaughter trailed her outside, a foot or two behind.

The rain had begun in earnest by then and was falling so hard large drops bounced on the sidewalk. Anne Marie flattened herself against the side of the building while she struggled to comprehend what she'd heard. It seemed impossible. Unbelievable.

It *couldn't* be right. Robert would never risk getting Rebecca pregnant. Even the one night they'd spent together— She froze. They hadn't used protection. She'd told him she was off her birth control pills and it was as if it no longer mattered to him. His lack of concern had thrilled Anne Marie. She saw it as the first crack in his stubborn unwillingness to accept her need for a baby.

"Anne Marie…" Melissa choked out her name. The tears ran down her stepdaughter's face, mingling with the rain. Her hair hung in wet clumps but she didn't seem to notice. "Someone needs to talk to Rebecca—to ask her…"

"Not me."

"I can't," Melissa wailed.

"Why not?" she asked. "What difference does it make now?"

"If the baby's Dad's, then…then it's related to me. And if that baby really *is* Dad's, then… I have to know. I've got a right to know."

Anne Marie wondered if Robert's daughter would have been as tolerant toward a child she might have had. "Did Rebecca—did she have a boy or a girl?"

"A boy."

The pain was as searing as a hot poker against her skin. It took her a moment to find her voice. "If the child is Robert's, why hasn't Rebecca said anything?"

"I… I don't know," Melissa whispered. "I shouldn't have told you…"

"You wanted to hurt me," Anne Marie said coldly.

"No!" Melissa's denial was instantaneous.

"There's no love lost between us." Anne Marie had no illusions about her stepdaughter's motives. "You don't like me. You never have. All these years you've been trying to get back at me, to *punish* me, and now you have."

Not bothering to deny the accusation, Melissa buried her face in her hands and started to weep uncontrollably. "I'm sorry, so sorry."

Anne Marie wanted to turn her back on Robert's daughter and walk away. But she couldn't bear to hear Melissa weep. Even though *she* was the one Robert had betrayed, Anne Marie reached for his daughter and folded her arms around Melissa.

The two women clung together, hardly aware of the people scurrying by.

Anne Marie's reserve broke apart and the pain of Robert's betrayal came over her in an explosive, unstoppable rush. She wept as she never had before, even at Robert's funeral. Her shoulders heaved and the noisy, racking sobs consumed her.

Then it was Melissa who was holding her, comforting her. After all the years of looking for common ground with her stepdaughter, Anne Marie had finally found it.

In her husband's betrayal.

Five

Barbie Foster stood in line at the movie theater multiplex, waiting to purchase a ticket, preferably for a comedy. She needed a reason to laugh. Her day had started early when she opened Barbie's, her dress shop, two blocks off Blossom Street. The shop was high-end, exclusive and *very* expensive. Her clientele were women who could easily afford to drop four figures on a dress. Barbie made sure they got their money's worth, providing advice, accessories and free alterations. She had a number of regular customers who counted on her for their entire wardrobes. Her own sense of style had served her well.

She didn't want to sound conceited, but Barbie was aware that she was an attractive woman. Since Gary's death, she'd received no shortage of attention from the opposite sex. Men wanted a woman like her on their arm—and, she suspected, they wanted her money. Barbie, however, wasn't easily swayed by flattery. She'd been happy in her marriage and had loved her husband. At this point in her life she wasn't willing to settle for mere companionship or, heaven forbid, no-strings sex. She wanted *love*. She longed for a man who'd treat her like a princess the way Gary had. Her friends told her that was a dated attitude; Barbie didn't care. Unfortunately there weren't many princes around these days.

She'd married young. In retrospect she recognized how fortunate she'd been in finding Gary. She'd had no real life experience, so the fact that she'd met a really wonderful man and fallen in love with him was pure luck. He was ten years her senior; at thirty, he'd had a wisdom beyond his years and a great capacity for love, for loyalty. He'd been working for her father at the time and came to the house often. She'd had a crush on him that developed into genuine love, although it took her a few years to recognize just how genuine it was. At nineteen, she always made sure she happened to be around whenever he stopped by, and enjoyed parading through the house to the pool—in her bikini, of course. She still smiled at the way Gary had looked in every direction except hers.

They'd married when she was twenty-one, with her father's blessing and, surprisingly perhaps, her mother's. She got pregnant the first week of their honeymoon. When she'd delivered identical twin sons, Gary had been over the moon. The pregnancy had been difficult, however, and he'd insisted the two boys were family enough.

The twins, Eric and Kurt, filled their lives and they were idyllically happy. Not that she and Gary didn't have their share of differences and arguments, but they forgave each other quickly and never confused disagreement with anger. Their household had been calm, orderly, contented. The plane crash ended all that. Barbie had always been close to her sons, but following the tragic deaths, of Gary and her father, the three of them were closer than ever. They helped one another through their grief, and even now they talked almost every day.

Encouraged by her mother and sons, a year after Gary's death Barbie started her own business. The dress shop helped take her mind off her loneliness and gave her purpose. Her sons were eighteen and growing increasingly independent. They'd be on their own soon. As it happened, they were attending colleges on the opposite side of the country. Swallowing her natural instinct to hold on to her children, she flew out to Boston and New York with her sons, got them settled in their respective schools and then flew home. She'd wept like a baby throughout the entire five-hour flight back to the West Coast.

Her house seemed so empty without the boys—her house and her life. She'd never felt more alone than she had since last September when she'd accompanied Kurt and Eric to their East Coast schools. Thankfully, though, they'd both come home for Thanksgiving and Christmas.

She'd kept herself occupied with the shop, but the Valentine's get-together with the other widows had revealed a different kind of opportunity. Barbie had begun to compose her list of Twenty Wishes, hoping to discover a new objective, some new goal to pursue. Her mother had leaped at this idea with an enthusiasm she hadn't shown in years, and if for no other reason, Barbie had followed suit. They often did things together and, in fact, her mother was Barbie's best friend.

The line moved. Barbie approached the teenage cashier and handed her a ten-dollar bill.

"Which movie?"

Barbie smiled at her. "You decide. Preferably a comedy."

The girl searched her face. "There are three or four showing. You don't care which one?"

"Not really." All Barbie wanted to do was escape reality for the next two hours.

The teenager took her money and a single ticket shot up, which she gave Barbie, along with her change. "Theater number twelve," she instructed. "The movie starts at four twenty-five."

Although she wasn't hungry, the instant Barbie stepped into the lobby, the scent of popcorn made her mouth water. She purchased a small bag and a soft drink, then headed for theater number twelve.

The previews were underway, and Barbie quickly located a seat in a middle row. She settled down with her popcorn and drink, dropping her purse in the empty seat beside her.

Glancing about, Barbie saw nothing but couples, most of them older and presumably retired. She nibbled on her popcorn and all at once her throat went dry. The entire world seemed to be made up of people in love. She envied the other women in the audience their long-lasting relationships, their forever loves, which was what she and Gary should have had. She wanted another chance. She was attractive, well-off, a nice person—and alone. Falling in love again was first on her list of wishes. But she didn't want another relationship unless she could find a man like Gary and there didn't seem to be many of those.

Until the other widows had started talking about those stupid wishes, Barbie's life had seemed to be trudging along satisfactorily enough. Her mother's list was nearly complete. Not Barbie's. She'd written down a few things besides falling in love. She wanted to learn how to belly dance. She and Gary had seen a belly dance performance during a brief stopover in Cairo years before and she'd been intrigued by the sensuous, feminine movements. She'd listed something else, too. She wanted to go snorkeling in Hawaii and shopping in Paris and sightseeing in London—all of which she'd done with Gary and enjoyed. But she didn't want to do them alone.

At the moment, her desire to fall in love again seemed an illusion beyond her grasp. But she wasn't exactly *looking* for a relationship. If she truly wanted to love and be loved, she had to be receptive to love, open to it, willing to risk the pain of loss.

She shook her head, telling herself there was no point in believing that a man might one day love her the way Gary had. Love *her*. Not her money, not her beauty. Her.

All of a sudden tears welled in her eyes and she dashed them angrily away. She didn't have a thing to cry about. Not a single, solitary thing. Dozens of women, hundreds of them, would envy her life. She had no money problems, her children were responsible adults, and at forty she didn't look a day over thirty. The tears made no sense whatsoever, and yet there was no denying them.

Reaching for her purse, Barbie pulled out a pack of tissues, grabbed one and loudly blew her nose.

The previews for upcoming features were still flashing across the screen. They were apparently comedies because the audience found the clips amusing. Sporadic laughter broke out around her.

Sniffling and dabbing her eyes, she noticed a man in a wheelchair approaching the row. He was staring at her, which wasn't uncommon. Men liked to look at her. Only it wasn't appreciation or approval she saw in his gaze. Instead, he seemed to be regarding her with irritation.

Maneuvering his chair into the empty space beside Barbie, he turned to glare at her. "In case you weren't aware of it, you're sitting in the row reserved for people with wheelchairs and their companions."

"Oh." Barbie hadn't realized that, although now he'd mentioned it, she saw the row was clearly marked.

"You'll need to leave." His words lacked any hint of friendliness.

He must have someone with him and wanted the seat for that person. No wonder he frowned at her as if she'd trespassed on his personal property.

Retrieving her large purse, she draped it over her shoulder, grabbed her popcorn and soft drink and stood. Instead of walking all the way through the empty row, she tried to get past him.

In an effort to give her the necessary room, he started to roll back his wheelchair and somehow caught the hem of her pants. Barbie stumbled and in the process of righting herself, dumped the entire contents of her soft drink in his lap.

The man gasped at the shock as the soda drenched his pants and ice cubes slid to the floor.

"Oh, I am so sorry." Barbie plunged her hand in her purse for the tissue packet and managed to spill her popcorn on him as well.

"I... I couldn't be sorrier," she muttered, more embarrassed than she'd ever felt before.

"Would you kindly just *leave*."

"I—"

He pointed in the direction he wanted her to go, then shook his head in disgust.

Barbie couldn't get out of the row fast enough. Feeling like a clumsy fool, she rushed into the empty lobby. She yanked a handful of napkins from the dispenser and hurriedly returned to the theater.

The man was still brushing popcorn off his lap when she offered him the napkins.

"Can I get you anything else?" she asked in a loud whisper.

His intense blue eyes glared back at her. "I think you've already done enough. The best thing you could do is *leave me alone.*"

"Oh."

He didn't need to be so rude. "I said I was sorry," she told him.

"Fine. Apology accepted. Now if it's possible, I'd like to enjoy the movie."

Barbie gritted her teeth. She felt like dumping another soft drink on his head. It wasn't as if she'd purposely spilled the soda. It'd been an accident and she'd apologized repeatedly. She felt her regret turn into annoyance at his ungracious reaction.

Because he'd made it abundantly clear that he wanted her far away, Barbie took an empty seat on the aisle five rows back from the wheelchair section. She made a determined effort to focus her attention on the movie, which had started about ten minutes earlier.

It was a comedy, just as she'd requested, only now she wasn't in any mood to laugh. Instead, she tapped her foot compulsively, scowling at the unfriendly man seated below her. When she saw that her tapping was irritating others, she crossed her legs and allowed her foot to swing. In all her life she'd never met anyone so incredibly rude. He *deserved* to have that soda dumped in his lap!

The rest of the audience laughed at the antics on the screen. Barbie might have, too, if she'd been able to concentrate. Almost against her will, her eyes kept traveling to the man in the wheelchair. The little girl in her wanted to stick her tongue out at him.

He'd asked her to move and yet no one sat next to him. In fact, the entire row was empty. He hadn't come with anyone; he just didn't want *her* sitting next to him.

What exactly was wrong with her? Lots of men would have welcomed her company. And they would've been more polite about that little accident, too. She was tempted to give that…that Neanderthal a piece of her mind. He had a lot of nerve asking her to leave. It was a free country and she could sit anywhere she darn well pleased.

Barbie left halfway through the movie, pacing the lobby in her exasperation. Where did he get off acting like such a jerk—and worse, making *her* feel like one? The teenager who'd sold her the ticket watched her for several minutes.

"Is everything okay?" she called out.

Barbie whirled around, her agitation mounting. "I was just insulted," she said, although there wasn't anything the girl could do about it. "Without realizing it, I sat in the wheelchair seating and this man told me to move."

The girl looked down, but not before Barbie caught her smiling.

"Do you think that's funny?" she asked.

"No, no, I'm sorry. You didn't have to move if you didn't want to."

"I didn't know that at the time. I assumed there was someone with him and I'd taken his or her spot."

"He was alone."

"So it seems. Furthermore, I didn't mean to spill my drink on him. It was an accident."

The girl's eyes widened. "You spilled your drink? On him?"

"In his lap."

The teenager giggled and covered her mouth with her hand. "Did he get mad?"

"Well, yes, but it was an accident. The popcorn, too."

Another giggle escaped. "Oh, my gosh."

Barbie raised her eyebrows at this girl's amusement. "I

have never met a more unreasonable or ruder man in my entire life," she said pointedly.

"That's my uncle Mark," the girl explained, grinning openly now.

"He's your...uncle." Barbie seemed to leap from one fire into another. Every word she'd said was likely to be repeated to "Uncle Mark." Well, good. Someone should give that arrogant, supercilious hothead a real talking-to. Who did he think he was, anyway?

"Unfortunately, he can be a bit unreasonable," the girl said.

"Tell me about it."

"You shouldn't let him bother you."

Barbie opened her mouth to argue and then decided the girl was right. She'd paid for her ticket, the same as he had, and could sit wherever she pleased. If she chose to sit in the wheelchair area, that was her business, as long as no one legitimately needed the seat. And no one did.

"Why don't you go back in?" the girl suggested. "It's a very funny movie, you know."

"Thanks—I will." Barbie marched into the theater, determined to sit where *she* wanted.

And lost her nerve.

It just wasn't in her to create a scene. Instead she walked over to her previous seat. She slipped into it, balancing her purse on her lap, and stared at the screen. Whatever was happening in the movie bypassed her completely.

Giving up on the film, she studied the back of the man's head. He must've sensed her watching him because he shifted his position, as though he felt uncomfortable. Fine with her.

In another thirty minutes, the movie ended and the lights came on. The theater emptied, but Barbie remained in her seat. Mark whatever-his-name stayed where he was, too.

When the last person had walked out, he wheeled his chair toward the exit.

"Are you always so rude?" she asked, striding after him.

He wheeled around and for an instant seemed surprised to see her.

"I'm rude when the situation calls for it," Mark informed her.

In the darkened theater Barbie hadn't gotten a good look at him. She did now and almost did a double take. The man was gorgeous. Mean as a snake, though. Gary would never have talked to a woman the way this man did. He'd always been respectful. Polite.

"I wish I hadn't apologized," she muttered. "You didn't deserve it."

"Listen, you do whatever you want. All I ask is that you stay out of my way."

"Gladly." She marched ahead with all the righteousness she could muster. But before she left the building, Barbie decided to stop at the ladies' room.

She'd just emerged when she saw Mark wheel himself into the theater lobby.

"He was pretty annoyed," his niece said in a low voice, joining Barbie.

"I told him exactly what I thought of him."

The girl smiled gleefully. "Did you really?"

Barbie nodded. "And then some." Although she was beginning to suspect she'd overreacted.

"People tiptoe around him."

"Not me." She and Gary had believed in treating people equally. Anything else was a form of discrimination, of seeing the disability and not the person.

"It's because everyone in the family feels sorry for him and he hates that."

"Oh." Well, she certainly hadn't shown him any pity—but maybe she'd been somewhat rude herself.

"I don't, though," the girl went on, "which is one reason he stops in here on the evenings I'm working."

"Does he come to the movies often?" Barbie wasn't sure what had prompted the question.

"Uncle Mark comes to the movies every Monday night." The girl held Barbie's look for an extra-long moment. "I'm Tessa, by the way, and Mark Bassett is my uncle's name." She thrust out her hand.

Barbie shook it. "And I'm Barbie."

"You'll come again, won't you?" Tessa asked.

"I live in the neighborhood." Well, sort of. It was a twenty-minute drive, but this theater was the closest multiplex in her vicinity.

"I wish you would," Tessa said, walking her to the glass doors that led to the parking lot. She held one open. "I'll see you soon, okay?"

"You will," Barbie said, removing the car keys from her purse. Sitting inside her vehicle, she let the conversation with Tessa run through her mind. Tessa was basically asking her to return the following Monday—and she'd more or less agreed. She'd need to give that some thought. She felt an undeniable attraction to this man, not to mention a sense of challenge and the exhilaration that came with it. In fact, she hadn't reacted that strongly to anyone in…years. She didn't understand the intensity of her own response.

As she always did when she was upset or confused, Barbie phoned her mother. Lillie answered right away.

"Sweetheart, where were you?"

"I decided to go to the movies. I'm on my cell."

"I left you a message," her mother said. "I was hoping you'd come by the house and have dinner with me."

Suddenly ravenous, Barbie remembered that she hadn't eaten anything more than some toast and a few handfuls of popcorn all day.

"Thanks," she said. "Do you want me to pick anything up?"

"No, I got groceries earlier today."

"Do you have your car yet?" Barbie asked. The red-hot convertible had gone back to the dealership for the same problem as before. The shop had worked on the steering mechanism twice now.

"No, but I'm not worried."

"You're so calm about all this." Barbie marveled at her mother's patience. She hadn't complained even once.

"Is everything all right, dear?" her mother asked. "You sound agitated."

"I am, a little." Barbie went on to explain what had happened—without, for some reason, mentioning that the man was in a wheelchair. To her dismay, her mother laughed.

"Mother!" she protested. "This isn't funny."

"I know… It's just that I can't imagine you being so clumsy."

"It was his fault," Barbie insisted. "He's just fortunate I didn't land in his lap."

Instantly a picture appeared in her mind, and to her shock, it wasn't an unpleasant one. Barbie saw herself sitting on Mark's lap, her arms around his neck, their eyes meeting, their lips… She shook her head. She didn't know where that vision had come from because the man was so…unpleasant.

"You can tell me all about it once you're here," Lillie said.

"See you in a few minutes, then." Barbie was about to snap her cell phone shut when her mother's voice stopped her. "Barbie, listen, I almost forgot. Jacqueline Donovan invited us to a small gathering next Monday. You'll be able to attend, won't you?"

"Monday?" she repeated. "What time?"

"Around six."

"Sorry, Mom," she said, making her decision. "I'm afraid I've already got plans."

Mark Bassett wasn't going to get rid of her as easily as he no doubt hoped.

Six

Anne Marie had been in emotional free fall ever since her Friday-night dinner with Melissa. She'd tried to push the conversation from her mind but hadn't succeeded. Robert's unfaithfulness hung over her every minute of every day—the betrayal, the pain, the anger. It wouldn't hurt as much if she hadn't so desperately wanted her husband's child. For him to adamantly refuse her and then fall into bed with another woman, a woman who now had a child that might be his, bordered on cruelty.

Another complication was her stepdaughter. Anne Marie didn't want to believe that Melissa had purposely set out to hurt and humiliate her, and yet she was suspicious. Still, she felt that Robert's daughter was distressed by her father's actions and had told the truth when she said she wasn't sure where else to turn. Anne Marie didn't understand, though, why Melissa hadn't confided in her brother. Surely Brandon would've been a more natural choice. Had she come to Anne Marie because she wanted to talk to another woman? Because she knew that no one else had loved Robert as much? One thing was certain; the instant Melissa had seen how badly she'd hurt Anne Marie, she was genuinely regretful. In the end, Melissa had been the one comforting *her*.

On Sunday Anne Marie hid inside her small apartment with only Baxter for company. She didn't answer the phone, didn't check her messages. How she managed to work even half of Saturday was a mystery. At about noon, she pleaded a migraine and left the shop in Theresa's hands. Thankfully, the store was closed on Sundays.

Anne Marie didn't leave her apartment other than to take Baxter for brief walks. She wandered from room to room with a box of tissues while she vented her pain and her grief.

How could Robert have let this happen? How could he betray her in such a fundamental way? The phone rang a number of times but she didn't answer. Her display screen showed that most of the calls were from Melissa, the last person she wanted to hear from. The messages accumulated until her voice-mail box was full. Anne Marie didn't care. As far as she was concerned, the less contact with the outside world the better.

Monday she had to work again. Intuitively, her staff—Theresa Newman and a college student named Cathy O'Donnell—seemed to understand she needed space. As much as possible, she stayed in the office at the back and shuffled through mounds of paperwork. She didn't feel capable of dealing with the public.

At twelve-thirty, Theresa entered the office. "Someone out front would like to see you," she said.

"A customer?"

"Umm…" Theresa acted uncertain. "I think it might be your stepdaughter."

Anne Marie tensed. If Melissa had come to the store, it likely wasn't a social visit. After Friday, Anne Marie was wary; she felt too fragile to deal with anything else her stepdaughter might have to tell her.

"Anne Marie?" Melissa pushed her way past Theresa and stepped into the office.

Theresa cast Anne Marie an apologetic look and excused herself.

Melissa stood awkwardly in the doorway. "Why didn't you answer the phone?" she demanded. "I called and called. It was like you dropped off the face of the earth."

She would've thought the answer was fairly obvious. "I... I wasn't up to talking to anyone."

"I've been worried about you. Brandon has, too."

"You told him?"

Melissa nodded. "He was furious with me. He said... he said I should never have told you."

Harsh words trembled on the tip of her tongue. How she wished Melissa had gone to her brother first. But she supposed that eventually she would've uncovered the truth on her own. Now or later, did it really matter?

Melissa seemed close to tears. "Brandon's right." Her voice was shaky. "I'm sorry, Anne Marie. At the time I... I felt I should tell you. I knew it would shock you like it did me, but I didn't realize how hurt you'd be. I was stupid and thoughtless. I'm so sorry."

It would've been easy to dissolve into tears all over again. Anne Marie made an effort to maintain the tight control she held on her emotions. "In a way you did the right thing," she said, trying to speak calmly. "I would've needed to learn about this baby at some point."

Melissa advanced one step into the room. "I still feel terrible."

"Let's put it behind us," Anne Marie said. The girl would never know what it cost her to make that offer. Instinctively she wanted to blame her for this pain, but Anne Marie discovered she couldn't do it. After years of trying to find some kind of connection with her stepdaughter, she didn't want to destroy the tenuous one they now shared.

"Can I do something to make it up to you?" Melissa pleaded.

Anne Marie shook her head.

"Can I get you anything?" she implored next.

She drew in a deep breath. "Do you have a new heart for me?" she asked, in a tone she hoped was offhand and witty. From the sad look in her stepdaughter's eyes, Anne Marie knew it hadn't been.

"Maybe I should just go." Melissa's shoulders slumped as she half-turned to leave.

"Why don't we have tea one day soon," Anne Marie suggested.

"You'd do that?" Melissa asked in disbelief.

"You're Robert's daughter and no matter what you think of me, I loved your father," Anne Marie said, unwilling to be dishonest.

"Even now?" Melissa asked. "Knowing he betrayed you?"

Love was difficult to explain. Robert's actions had devastated her, and while she wanted to confront him, force him to own up to his betrayal, that possibility had been taken away from her. And yet…she loved him.

"Dad hurt you badly, didn't he?"

"Yes, he did. I could hate him for that but—"

"I would," Melissa cut in, eyes narrowed.

"And what good would that do?" Anne Marie asked her. "Believe me, I've been over this time and again. I could let the news bury me—and for a while it did."

"I know… I blame myself for that."

"Don't worry. I meant what I said about putting this behind us. Anyway, I'm dealing with everything as best I can. At first I wanted to lash out, but I couldn't see how that would help. My pain and anger aren't going to change a thing, are they?"

Melissa stared at her for a long moment. "You're a better person than I am."

"I doubt that—just a bit more experienced, a bit more broken and bruised." She'd never expected Melissa to compliment her on anything. "You're still young. Life kicks us all in the teeth sooner or later." She didn't mean to sound so negative, but at this point it was difficult not to. "I appreciate that you wanted to check up on me."

"I felt so awful about what my father did. And the news about Rebecca's baby hit me hard. So I turned to you and I shouldn't have."

Anne Marie waved one hand airily. "Like I said, I'm beyond all that." It wasn't completely true; she didn't think she'd ever recover from Robert's betrayal—and the way she'd found out.

Melissa stayed a few more minutes and then left for her afternoon class. The invitation for tea was intentionally open-ended. Anne Marie would call her when she felt more...prepared.

An hour later, she felt composed enough to meet the public again. Cathy had gone for the day, and while Theresa took her lunch break, Anne Marie handled the cash register. Mondays were generally slow and she had only two customers, neither of whom needed help. She was emotionally off balance, although she had to admit she felt better after talking to her stepdaughter. Melissa's concern, and Brandon's, had comforted her, at least a little.

The shop door opened and Elise Beaumont came inside. Her expression was speculative, but if she noticed that Anne Marie looked pale and drawn, she didn't mention it.

"Hello, Elise," Anne Marie said, trying to act cheerful. "I've put aside a couple of new titles you might like."

"Thanks." Elise walked up to the counter. "I came to see how it went with the Lunch Buddy program last week."

She'd almost forgotten about her volunteer project. "Oh, yes. It was fine."

"Did the school pair you up with a child?"

Anne Marie nodded. "Her name's Ellen Falk and she's in second grade." It took her a moment to conjure up Ellen's face, recalling how shy and awkward the young girl had been.

Elise picked up one of the books Anne Marie placed in front of her and flipped it open. "You don't seem too enthusiastic."

"I'm not sure Ellen and I are the best match." She went on to explain how the eight-year-old had barely said a word the entire lunch period. Over the weekend she'd lost whatever optimism she'd felt at the end of their previous session.

"It's early yet. Give it time," Elise urged.

"I will." However, Anne Marie still had her doubts about the project. She'd finish out the school year but then she'd look for a different volunteer organization. "I need to call the school counselor," she said. "The only real enthusiasm Ellen showed was when I talked about Baxter."

"The child's interested in dogs?"

"I think so. I thought if I got permission to bring him to the school, Ellen would enjoy meeting him." Baxter was a good-natured dog who seemed to do well with children, and Anne Marie had no worries about his behavior.

"That's an excellent idea."

Elise decided to buy one of the books Anne Marie had

recommended, a debut novel by a former journalist, and then wandered the store for a few minutes. With her own background as a librarian, she was an avid reader and a good customer. In fact, she often knew more about books and authors than Anne Marie did. With a second purchase in hand, Elise returned to the counter.

"Something's bothering you," she announced, studying Anne Marie.

"I—I'm fine," Anne Marie insisted.

"Actually, you aren't and that brave front is crumbling fast. You need someone to talk to. I'm available."

Elise liked to get to the point. She wasn't one to ease into a subject or look for a circumspect approach. Anne Marie usually appreciated her friend's directness. Now, however, she didn't feel ready to unburden herself.

"Well?" Elise pressed.

"I… I received some shocking news last Friday," she began. "But I'm dealing with it."

Elise waited patiently for her to continue.

Anne Marie glanced over her shoulder at another customer who'd just walked in and was scanning the shelves. "I don't want to talk about it here."

Elise patted her hand. "That's understandable. We'll just wait until—"

The shop door opened, as if on cue, and Theresa came back from lunch. "The French Café has a fabulous squash soup today," she said breezily. "You should try it."

"I might do that." Anne Marie hadn't eaten much of anything since Friday night. She was too thin as it was but she wasn't hungry, and this latest incident had contributed to her lack of appetite.

"I was thinking of having a bite to eat myself. Join me," Elise said.

It was more of a decree than a request; still, Anne Marie agreed. Elise was probably right—it would help to talk about this *and* to eat. With the glimmer of a smile she recalled Elise's advice at the Valentine's get-together. Theresa took over for her, and Anne Marie collected her purse and walked out with Elise.

"You should be wearing more than a sweater," the older woman told her.

Anne Marie shrugged halfheartedly. "You're beginning to sound like my mother," she murmured.

"From the look in your eyes, I'd say you need one."

That comment brought immediate tears, which Anne Marie struggled to hide as she returned to the office for her jacket. She grabbed a tissue to wipe her nose, then tossed it in the wastebasket. She certainly couldn't talk to her mother about what she'd learned. Laura Bostwick would use it as an opportunity to harangue Anne Marie about the huge mistake she'd made in marrying Robert. Laura had disapproved from the start. Trapped in her own unhappiness, she seemed to take a malevolent pleasure in destroying other people's joy.

Elise linked arms with her as they crossed the street. "You're so thin now I'm afraid a strong wind will blow you away."

"Oh, come on, Elise. Don't exaggerate."

"It's a problem I wish I had," Elise muttered. "When Maverick died, I'm afraid I buried my sorrows in food. Isn't that ridiculous, considering how closely I watched his diet?" Unexpectedly she smiled. "He said he ate like a bird—flax seed, blueberries, wheat germ… Maverick had such a delightful sense of humor. I sometimes wonder if I'll ever stop missing him." She shook her head and brought her attention back to Anne Marie.

The French Café was the most popular restaurant on Blossom Street; even now, at almost two, it was crowded with lunchtime customers.

Alix Turner, who baked all the pastries, belonged to one of Anne Marie's reader groups and often recommended the bookstore to others.

When it was their turn to order, both Anne Marie and Elise chose the squash soup. While they waited for the server to deliver their order, they sipped their coffee.

"Tell me what's wrong," Elise said.

"Why don't we wait until after we eat?" Anne Marie murmured, not eager to discuss Robert's infidelity.

Elise looked at her sternly. "Don't put it off. Whatever happened is tearing you up inside. You'll feel better if you share it—if not with me, then someone else. Frankly, I'm your best option."

Anne Marie had to laugh; some of the things Elise said verged on egotistical. Fortunately she knew the other woman well enough not to take offense.

"Let's talk about our Twenty Wishes instead," Anne Marie said. "Are you working on your list?"

"I am." Elise smiled. "I'm determined to go on a hot air balloon ride. That one's at the top of my list." She hesitated. "I have another wish…"

"Which is?"

"You promise not to laugh or try to talk me out of it?"

"Of course." There was the matter of those red cowboy boots, for one thing.

"I'm going to get a tattoo."

What? Elise? Anne Marie nearly swallowed her tongue. "Have you decided where?"

"There's a tattoo parlor near the waterfront and—"

"No, I meant where on you. Your shoulder or—"

"Oh, I'm not sure yet. Maverick had one. On his right arm." The older woman looked flustered. "But that's enough about me. Tell me what's troubling you."

Anne Marie would rather avoid the subject altogether; at the same time she was grateful for the chance to talk about it with someone she knew and trusted. She sighed. "I had dinner with my stepdaughter Friday night."

"I take it the evening wasn't pleasant."

"No... Melissa had recently gone to Robert's office and discovered that his personal assistant had a baby."

Elise straightened her shoulders. "A baby..." she repeated. "Is it Robert's?"

Anne Marie shrugged. "I'd say it's highly probable."

Elise's eyes narrowed. "But you're not sure?"

"No."

"You're going to find out, aren't you?"

"I... I don't feel it's my place to say or do anything."

"Yes, it is!" Elise said adamantly. "Who better than you? Robert was your husband."

"But..."

"And so far the identity of the father is pure conjecture."

"Well, yes, to a certain extent. Apparently while Robert and I were separated, Melissa discovered her father and Rebecca in a, uh, compromising position. Nine months later, Rebecca turns up with a baby. What else am I to think?"

Elise pursed her lips. "It does seem suspicious. The only way to know for sure is to ask her."

Anne Marie saw the wisdom of confronting Rebecca, but she couldn't do it. She wasn't convinced she'd ever have the courage to speak to her. "Brandon and Melissa are the ones who need to know."

"You, my dear, were Robert's wife. Yes, I'm aware that you'd separated. He behaved badly, and I'm positive that if he was here, he'd tell you how much he regrets everything that happened."

"He didn't want another family... Perhaps he just didn't want children with *me*."

"Don't say that," Elise said sharply. "Don't think it, either. If Robert was alive he'd be aghast at this news."

"You never knew him."

"But I know *you*," she came right back. "From what you've told me, Robert loved you."

"I thought he did." All of a sudden Anne Marie couldn't help wondering. She'd lost Robert to a heart attack and now the vision of the man she'd so desperately loved had been destroyed. Along with it, all her dreams of the future, the hopes and promises she'd hung on to during their separation, had fizzled out to nothing.

"Don't leap to any conclusions until you talk to Rebecca yourself," Elise warned her. "No one has more of a right to the truth than you."

Elise made it sound so simple, so straightforward and uncomplicated.

The server brought the steaming soup, and Anne Marie inhaled the gingery scent. For the first time in days she felt like eating. Elise reached across the table and clasped her forearm.

"Promise me you'll contact Rebecca and ask her. Do it for yourself," Elise said.

"I can't..."

"You can and you will," the other woman insisted. "Don't you remember what Scripture says? 'The truth shall set you free,' and until you know the truth you'll be held captive by your fears and doubts."

Anne Marie merely nodded as she tasted her soup. Delicious. They'd used coconut milk, she guessed, allowing herself to be momentarily distracted.

"Find out," Elise urged again as she picked up her spoon. "Don't accept all this conjecture and half-baked information. Melissa might have misjudged the situation entirely."

"I...don't think so." Naturally Anne Marie *wanted* to believe that Robert would never cheat on her. And yet she had to be realistic, too.

"But you don't know and you won't until you speak to this woman."

Anne Marie was forced to agree.

"You'll do it, then?"

Reluctantly she nodded. Not now, though, not when the pain was still so fresh and her heart was aching.

"You won't disappoint me, will you?" Elise held her gaze for a long moment.

"No," Anne Marie promised. "I'll get in touch with Rebecca and I'll ask her."

Then and only then did Elise smile. "Remember—the truth shall set you free."

Seven

The minute Anne Marie entered the school grounds at Woodrow Wilson with Baxter on his leash, she was surrounded by children, apparently out for a late recess or an early lunch. Baxter looked up at her expectantly and, fearing the small dog might be overwhelmed, she lifted him into her arms.

"I brought Baxter to visit Ellen Falk," she explained as the children gathered around.

By the time Anne Marie had walked inside, Ellen's second-grade class had been dismissed for lunch. She found the little girl waiting in the hallway by the lunchroom. She stood with her back against the wall, staring down at the floor.

"Hello, Ellen." Anne Marie spoke softly so as not to alarm her.

Ellen glanced up and when she saw Baxter, a tentative smile slid into place. "You brought him!"

"I called and Ms. Mayer said it would be all right to bring Baxter so the two of you can meet." Bending down to her constant friend and companion, Anne Marie said, "Baxter, this is Ellen."

Ellen stared at the dog. "Hi," she said and offered him her hand to sniff. "Would it be okay if I petted him?" she asked, her eyes filled with longing.

"I'm sure he'd like that."

Even with Anne Marie's permission, Ellen hesitated as she raised her hand and gently touched the top of Baxter's head. As if he understood how badly this little girl needed a friend, Baxter licked her hand.

"He likes you," Anne Marie told her. "Would you like to hold him?"

The girl's eyes grew large. "I'm allowed to do that?"

"Of course. Let me show you how to carry him." She gave Ellen a demonstration of the way she tucked Baxter between her arm and her side, then handed her the dog.

Baxter wagged his tail, and Ellen couldn't stop smiling.

"Shall we get some lunch?" Anne Marie asked. "Ms. Mayer said we'll need to take our lunches back to the classroom. Is that okay?"

"Yes." Ellen looked at her anxiously. "Baxter can come, too, can't he?"

"Of course," Anne Marie assured her.

The Yorkshire terrier attracted lots of curious attention as Ellen waited outside the busy cafeteria. "I'll get our lunch while you watch Baxter," Anne Marie said.

The menu for the day was chili with corn bread, which Anne Marie remembered was Ellen's favorite. She chose a fresh salad and canned peaches for herself. Her appetite was improving. Since her lunch with Elise the day before, she'd actually felt the faint stirrings of hunger. Talking to her friend had made her feel calmer and more rational, although Anne Marie wasn't ready to confront Rebecca yet. She would in time, as soon as she was emotionally prepared to deal with the other woman's answer.

When she'd assembled their lunch, several of the children had gathered around Ellen, asking questions about Baxter.

"I have to go now," the child told the others, and Anne Marie grinned at the importance in her voice. Ellen dutifully followed her down the hall toward the classroom, carrying Baxter as though he was the most precious burden imaginable.

The door was open and Ellen led the way to her desk. Anne Marie set the tray down and pulled up a chair next to Ellen's.

"What about Baxter?" Ellen asked, carefully putting him down. "We can't eat in front of him, can we? That would be impolite."

"Yes, it would," Anne Marie agreed. She'd brought along a small can of gourmet dog food, which was a rare treat for him. As she retrieved it from her purse, Baxter practically did flips of joy.

Ellen giggled, covered her mouth with her hand, then giggled again. "He's so funny."

"Yes, he is," Anne Marie said, smiling, too.

Ellen seemed far more interested in Baxter than in eating her own lunch. She watched Baxter wolf down his food before she turned to her own plate. "One time my mama said she'd buy me a dog."

Knowing the girl lived with her grandmother, Anne Marie wasn't sure how to comment.

"What kind of dog do you want?"

Ellen looked up from her chili. "Any kind. But Mama made lots of promises she never kept. I live with my Grandma Dolores now."

"Does she have a dog?"

Ellen shook her head. "She said she's too old to take care of a dog."

"How old is she?" Anne Marie asked.

Ellen contemplated the question. "Really, really old. I think she's over fifty."

Anne Marie managed to suppress a smile. *"That old,"* she said, exaggerating the two words. Her guess was that the woman was actually quite a bit older.

"She sleeps a lot."

"Oh."

"I don't mind. She lets me watch TV as long as I do my homework."

"She loves you very much, doesn't she?"

Ellen swallowed a bite of her corn bread. "And I love her," she mumbled.

"I'm sure you do."

"Only…only Grandma's too old to get me a dog."

"I'll be happy to share Baxter if you'd like," Anne Marie offered.

Ellen's eyes lit with pure joy. "You promise?"

"We're Lunch Buddies, aren't we?"

Ellen nodded enthusiastically. She took another spoonful of her chili and paused long enough to pet Baxter.

"We should probably take him for a walk once you finish your lunch." Anne Marie had brought a plastic bag in case nature called while Baxter was outside.

"I'm full," Ellen said decisively, planting both hands on her stomach.

"Positive?"

"Yup. Can we go now?"

They brought their trays back to the cafeteria and Anne Marie carried them inside, remembering how Ellen had instructed her the week before. When she'd put them away, the two of them walked outside.

Typical for early March in the Pacific Northwest, a fine

mist was falling. Most of the children ignored the rain, as did Ellen and Anne Marie. They strolled through the yard, making for a small grassy area nearby, and Anne Marie let Ellen take the leash. A dozen kids trailed behind as if she were the Pied Piper. They would've followed Ellen and Baxter out of the yard if the recess monitor hadn't intervened.

As usual, Baxter sniffed every inch of territory as he trotted toward the gate. "How's school?" Anne Marie asked, walking side-by-side with the eight-year-old. She hoped to become better acquainted with Ellen, although it seemed she had to drag every morsel of information from the child. Thus far, all she knew was that Ellen liked dogs and lived with her grandmother, who was over fifty and therefore "really old."

"Good."

That wasn't a lot of help. "Do you have any problems with math?"

"Nope. Grandma Dolores says I'm smart."

"I'll bet you are."

Ellen seemed to have nothing else to say. She concentrated on the dog, praising him and periodically bending down to stroke his silky ears.

Anne Marie had hoped for more progress today. She'd seen some, thanks solely to Baxter, but now that she'd made a commitment to the program and to Ellen, she was eager for the next breakthrough.

"Does he know any tricks?" Ellen asked.

"Baxter? He can sit on command."

Ellen seemed pleased. She stopped walking. "Sit," she said sternly.

Her Yorkie immediately complied, and Ellen beamed. "He's smart, too."

"Yes, he is. He doesn't know how to roll over, though.

I've tried, but I can't make him understand what I want him to do."

"I'll get a book from the library and teach him," Ellen instantly volunteered. "Can you bring him next Wednesday?"

Anne Marie had discussed the situation with Ms. Mayer. The point of the Lunch Buddy program was for Ellen and Anne Marie to become friends. Helen Mayer's concern was that Ellen would bond with Baxter and not Anne Marie. She'd suggested the dog only visit once a month.

"I'm afraid Baxter won't be able to come next week," Anne Marie explained. "But I'll bring him again soon."

The light seemed to go out of Ellen's eyes and she docilely accepted the news. "I like Baxter," she said a few minutes later.

"I can tell, and he certainly likes you."

Her returning smile was fragile, as if she'd long ago learned to accept disappointments.

What little conversation they exchanged after that was focused on Baxter. When the lunch bell rang, Ellen lingered on the playground.

"I'll see you next week," Anne Marie promised.

Ellen lowered her eyes and nodded.

Ellen was obviously accustomed to adults making promises they didn't or couldn't keep. Anne Marie wanted to reassure the youngster that if she said she'd be at the school, she would be, but actions spoke much louder than words. She hoped that over time Ellen would come to trust her.

"Can I hug Baxter goodbye?" she asked.

"Of course."

Crouching, Ellen petted the dog, then picked him up and gently gave him a hug. "Thank you for bringing him."

"You're welcome, Ellen."

With that, the girl raced toward the school building.

She was the last one to enter and Anne Marie hoped she wouldn't be late for class.

"Well, Baxter," she murmured to her pet, "you were a real hit." As she hurried toward the parking lot, Helen Mayer stepped out of the school, walking purposefully in Anne Marie's direction.

"How'd it go with Ellen this week?" she asked, quickly catching up. She wore only a sweater and shivered as she wrapped her arms around her waist.

"Okay, I think," Anne Marie said. "Thanks mostly to Baxter."

"I thought that might be the case."

"She wanted me to bring him next week, but I told her he couldn't come and it would only be me."

"That little girl's been through a great deal," Ms. Mayer said, lowering her voice. "As I explained earlier, the privacy laws prohibit me from saying any more, but rest assured that Ellen badly needs a friend."

Anne Marie immediately felt guilty for wishing she'd found another volunteer effort. But she'd made a four-month commitment and she planned to see it through. She had no intention of being another adult in Ellen's life who broke her promises.

The school counselor walked her to the parking lot. "Next Tuesday afternoon, the school's putting on a play."

Anne Marie nodded.

"Ellen has a small role in it."

"Ellen?"

"She's in the chorus."

"How nice. She didn't mention it."

Ms. Mayer didn't seem surprised. "She wouldn't. She's such a shy child. She's gifted vocally, you know."

"It'll help her self-esteem if she excels in singing." Anne

Marie didn't say that she used to sing, too. Or that she hadn't sung in months…

"Oh, I agree, this opportunity is wonderful for Ellen," Ms. Mayer said. "She's the only second-grader in the chorus."

"That's terrific." There was no personal reason for Anne Marie to feel proud of Ellen, but she did.

"Her grandmother won't be able to attend."

Despite herself, Anne Marie grinned. "Her Grandma Dolores is really old, you know. She's at least fifty."

The school counselor smiled, too. "It would mean the world to Ellen if you could come for the program."

"Me?" She thought about her Tuesday schedule. She had meetings with a publisher's rep, plus an appointment with her bookkeeper. As much as possible, Anne Marie tried to handle all her paperwork on Tuesdays.

"Ellen won't have anyone there if you don't come," the counselor continued. "If there's any chance at all…"

Anne Marie swallowed a sigh. "What time is the program?" she asked.

"Tuesday afternoon at two."

She'd been afraid of that. "I have an important meeting then. I'm sorry, but I can't make it."

Ms. Mayer didn't hide her disappointment. "Are you *sure* you can't? It would mean so much to Ellen."

Anne Marie hesitated as she tried to work out how to rearrange her schedule. Perhaps she could ask Theresa to meet with the sales rep, who was coming in at two.

"I know you're busy…"

"Everyone's busy," Anne Marie said. Her life was no different from anyone else's. She wondered if Ms. Mayer championed the other children as diligently as she did Ellen. "I'll see if I can get one of my employees to cover for me. Exactly how long will this take?"

Ms. Mayer smiled broadly. "An hour at the most. And after the program, the children will be serving cookies and juice."

"I'll see what I can do," Anne Marie promised.

"That would be wonderful." She clasped her hands together. "Thank you so much." Glancing over her shoulder, she said, "I have to get back to the school now, but thank you again."

Anne Marie opened her car door and placed Baxter inside. This volunteering was demanding more time and commitment than she'd originally assumed. The problem was, she couldn't say no.

When she returned to Blossom Street, she brought Baxter up to the apartment, then hurried into the bookstore to see Theresa. The part-time position suited Theresa well, since she had three children, one in high school and the youngest two attending junior high.

"How's it going?" Anne Marie asked.

"Fine." Theresa smiled. "I wasn't expecting to see you."

Anne Marie tried to stay as far away from the business as she could on Wednesdays. The moment she made herself available, she invariably ended up spending half her day in the store. "I'm only here for a few minutes," she said, vowing that would be the truth.

"Ms. Higgins was looking for you," Theresa told her. "She forgot this was your day off."

"Were you able to help her?"

"Oh, she wasn't interested in buying anything. She wanted to talk to you."

Anne Marie would give Lillie a call later on. She hoped the situation with her car had been settled.

"There was a phone call for you, too. A man at one of

the distributors. He asked if you'd call him back at your convenience. I wrote down all the information."

"I'll take care of that in the morning," Anne Marie said. She lingered, procrastinating because she hated to ask her employees to fill in for her. "Theresa, I was wondering if you could work next Tuesday afternoon."

"Next Tuesday?" Looking pensive, Theresa bit her bottom lip. "I think so. Can I get back to you to confirm?"

"Of course. The thing is, I'm a Lunch Buddy for this little girl named Ellen and…well, she's going to be in a school production and the counselor seemed to think it would help if I could be there." She didn't know why she was rattling on about this when it really wasn't Theresa's problem.

"I'm sure it'll be fine but I'll need to check with Jeff first."

"Thanks, and if it doesn't work out, don't worry. I'll try Cathy or Steve."

Anne Marie went upstairs to her apartment. Baxter, who was asleep in his small bed, didn't so much as stir. Apparently the excursion to the school had tired him out. "Some watchdog you are, Mr. Baxter," she muttered.

Her plan for the afternoon was to work on her list of wishes. Since her dinner with Melissa, Anne Marie hadn't really given it much thought.

1. Buy red cowboy boots

2. Learn to knit

3. Volunteer—become a Lunch Buddy

4. Take French lessons

Then, because it seemed so unlikely and yet necessary, she added the first wish, the one she'd crossed out earlier.

5. Find one good thing about life

She took out the binder she'd purchased and assembled the scrapbooking supplies and the few pictures she'd already cut out. Red cowboy boots from a catalog. A hand-knit sweater from a magazine. A photo of the Eiffel Tower. She'd need to get a picture of Ellen and... Suddenly it seemed pointless to go on, in light of what she'd discovered about Robert and her own pitiful life.

Rather than allow herself to sink into further depression, she reached for her phone and called Lillie. They arranged to meet for dinner at a Thai place they both liked.

That evening Lillie arrived at the restaurant before Anne Marie did and had already secured a table. "I'm so glad you phoned," Lillie said, kissing her cheek. "I've got lots to tell you."

"I can't wait to hear."

"It's that list."

"The Twenty Wishes?" Earlier, just reading her list had depressed her. She'd been convinced she'd never feel like dreaming again, not when she'd obviously been so wrong about her entire life.

"That list's given me a whole new burst of energy," Lillie said. "I've told my friends about it and now they're all writing their own lists."

"Really?"

"Lists are big these days. Who would've believed it?" Lillie's eyes twinkled with merriment. "I've been adding to mine nearly every day, thinking about all the things I want to do. Things I haven't considered in years. It all started when I bought that red convertible."

"Speaking of which…"

Lillie waved the question aside even before Anne Marie could ask it. "Just a minor glitch and that nice man from the service department is taking care of everything."

"You mean to say you're still driving a loaner?"

"Yes, but it doesn't matter. Everything's under control and I haven't been inconvenienced in the least."

"You shouldn't be inconvenienced. You bought their car!"

Lillie studied her menu. "I'm starved. How about you?"

Anne Marie needed to think about it, then realized she actually was hungry. "I am, too."

"Great. The way I feel right now, I'm tempted to order everything on the menu. Let's begin with the assorted appetizers, and then a green mango salad…

"And pad thai. I love their pad thai," Anne Marie said, entering into the spirit of the evening.

Between the perfectly spiced food and Lillie's invigorating company, dinner was a welcome reprieve from the low-grade depression that had been hanging over Anne Marie. Back in her apartment a few hours later, she came across the binder and the scrapbooking supplies spread out on the kitchen table.

She sat down again and read over her list. Maybe her wishes weren't so impossible, after all.

Eight

Lillie Higgins paid extra-close attention to her makeup Friday morning, chastising herself as she did. Anyone who even suspected that she was preening and primping for the service department manager at a car dealership would be aghast.

Lillie had nothing to say in her defense. She just found Hector Silva appealing; he was kind and generous and unfailingly polite. He seemed so natural, while the men who usually set out to charm her came across as self-conscious, trying too hard to impress. Not Hector Silva. His work ethic, his dignity and decency... She couldn't praise him enough.

They'd exchanged two brief conversations, and after each one Lillie had walked away feeling good. More than good, elated. She *liked* him—it was that simple—and she enjoyed talking to him. Both times she'd wished the conversations could've been longer.

Now that her car was repaired to Hector's satisfaction, she didn't have an excuse to chat with him anymore. So she'd decided to make the most of today's encounter, which would likely be their last.

Lillie arrived at the dealership with the loaner at the precise time Hector had indicated. She wore a pink linen pantsuit with a silk floral scarf tied around her head. She'd struggled with that, not wanting to look like a babushka or some latter-day hippie, and she'd finally managed to arrange it in an attractive style. Desiree, the temperamental French hairdresser she and Jacqueline Donovan shared, had insisted that if Lillie was determined to drive a convertible, she take measures to protect her hair.

When Lillie pulled into the parking space outside the service area, Hector immediately stepped outside as if he'd been standing by the door, waiting for her.

"Good morning, Ms. Higgins," he said with the slightest bow.

"Good morning, Mr. Silva."

"Please call me Hector."

"Only if you'll call me Lillie. After everything we've been through with this car, I believe we've become friends, don't you? And friends call each other by their first names." Referring to him as a friend might be presumptuous, but she couldn't seem to stop herself.

He grinned, and his dark eyes glinted with pleasure. "I feel the same way." After the briefest of hesitations, he added, "Lillie." She loved how he said her name, placing equal emphasis on each syllable. She'd never heard anyone draw it out like that. He made it sound…sensuous. Completely unlike the blunt "Lil" her husband used to call her.

"Your vehicle is ready." He gestured toward the red convertible parked near the service area.

"Did you ever find out what the problem was?" she asked, although in truth she didn't really care.

"As far as I can tell, the hydraulic hose had an air bubble in it. I worked on it myself and I had my best mechanic check it, too. He assures me the problem has been fixed. You shouldn't have any steering troubles from now on."

"Then I'm sure I won't." Instinctively, she felt certain that Hector's pledge was the only guarantee she needed.

"I've taken it out for a test drive and in my estimation it runs beautifully. However, if you'd like, the two of us could go for a short ride."

Lillie knew this was above and beyond anything that was necessary. Nevertheless she nearly squeaked with joyful anticipation. Oh, she was behaving badly, wasn't she? And she intended to go on doing it.

"I'd appreciate that very much," she told him earnestly. "But only if it won't keep you from your duties."

"You are our customer, Lillie, and it is the goal of the dealership to exceed your expectations."

"Oh." His dedication to duty dispelled the notion that he was doing this for her and her alone. In fact, he seemed to be quoting from a policy manual. That gave her pause. Perhaps what she felt toward him was imaginary, something she'd dreamed up—but she knew it wasn't. The real question was whether Hector reciprocated her feelings.

Hector held open the driver's door for her.

Lillie slipped behind the wheel as he walked around the vehicle and joined her in the passenger seat. "You're sure you have time for this?" she asked again.

"Yes, Lillie, I'm very sure." He encouraged her with a smile.

She turned the key and the engine instantly surged to life. "Is there any specific place you'd like me to drive?" she asked, hoping he'd suggest a route.

"Green River in the Kent Valley should be a good test."

That was where the vehicle had broken down the first time. It was also twenty minutes away. This was more than a short test drive, she thought excitedly. More than business.

Still, they didn't exchange a single word as she drove

down the freeway. It wasn't until they neared the river that Hector spoke.

"The car is in perfect running condition," he told her in a solemn tone.

"You can tell just by the sound?"

"Oh, yes. My wife, when she was alive, used to tease me. She said I could read cars better than I could people, and she was right."

"You're a widower?" Lillie had noticed that Hector wasn't wearing a wedding band, but she'd assumed it was because of his work.

"Yes, almost ten years now."

"I'm sorry." Lillie knew the pain of losing a life partner, even when the marriage wasn't ideal.

"Angelina was a good woman and a good wife," Hector said. "And a devoted mother. We have three beautiful children."

"My husband died in a plane crash three years ago."

"I'm sorry for your loss."

Lillie focused her attention on the road, although their conversation was of far greater interest. She might be seeing more here than was warranted but she sensed that Hector wanted her to know he was a widower. She wanted him to realize she was unattached, too.

"How old are your children?" she asked, not reacting to his sympathy, which made her a little uncomfortable. David had been an excellent provider and an adequate husband, but he'd had his weakness. Unfortunately that weakness involved other women.

For years Lillie had turned a blind eye to David's wanderings. It was easier to pretend than to confront the ugly truth of her husband's infidelities. During the last ten years of their marriage, there had been no real intimacy between them. Lillie had swallowed her pride and pretended not to know about her husband's affairs—as long as he remained discreet.

"My children are all grown now," Hector said. "They have graduated from college and taken advanced training in the fields of their choice. Manuel is an attorney. Luis is a physician and my daughter, Rita, is a teacher." His pride in his family was evident.

"My goodness, all three of your children are accomplished professionals."

"Their mother and I believed in higher education." Hector looked at her as she slowed the car's speed to take a sharp curve. "You have children?"

"A daughter. Her husband was with mine in the plane crash."

"He died, as well?"

"Unfortunately, yes."

Hector's eyes grew dark with compassion. "In one day your daughter lost both her husband and her father."

"Yes." It had been a horrific day and not one Lillie wanted to think about. David and Gary had been flying home from a business trip. The pilot and copilot had died, too.

The FAA had investigated, and after a thorough exploration of the facts had determined the cause of the accident— sudden, catastrophic engine failure. But that knowledge didn't take away the shock and the grief.

"Your daughter has a family?"

"Two sons."

"You are a grandmother, then?"

The boys were the very joy of her life. "I have twin grandsons, Eric and Kurt. They're in their first year of college."

"No." Hector wore an astounded expression. "It isn't possible you have grandchildren of that age."

"Both my daughter and I married young." Although she wasn't in the habit of divulging her age, she felt she could with Hector. "I'm sixty-three."

Again his eyes widened. "I would have said you were closer to your midforties."

With another man, Lillie might have expected such flattery. But Hector was what David would've called a straight shooter. He didn't give compliments for any reason other than that he meant them.

"I'm sixty-four," Hector admitted. "I will be retiring in a few months."

"How long have you been with the dealership?"

"Thirty-four years."

"With the same dealership?" That was practically unheard of these days.

"I started as a maintenance man and attended night school to become a mechanic. When I had my certificate, the service manager at the time offered me a job. I worked hard and within ten years I was the chief mechanic."

"When did you take over as manager?"

Hector didn't need to think about the answer. "Almost twelve years ago. I would have retired sooner, only the expenses of college made that impossible." He grimaced comically. "Private colleges."

"All of your children were in college at the same time?"

"Yes. Thankfully, each one received financial assistance through scholarships and grants. But I have to tell you the costs were staggering."

Lillie knew that from what Barbie had told her about Eric and Kurt's tuition costs and the other expenses associated with getting them started in school. Even now, Lillie could hardly believe it. She was impressed that Hector had managed to put three children through school on what he earned as a service manager. He no doubt made good money, but still...

"Your daughter attended college?" he asked.

Lillie shook her head. "Barbie married young, just as I did. Both David and I were disappointed but ultimately we approved of the marriage. She knew her own mind, and I will say she and Gary were very happy."

"That's how it is with love sometimes, isn't it?" he said, glancing in her direction. "Sometimes the heart really does know what's best."

Her own heart was speaking loud and clear at that very moment.

They'd been gone for more than an hour, and it was time to return to the dealership. Both grew quiet. Minutes earlier, their conversation had been animated; now, reality set in and there didn't seem to be anything else to say.

When Lillie pulled into the dealership's parking lot, she experienced a pang of regret. This was it; the ride—and her relationship with Hector—was over. There was no further reason to see him. It wasn't as though they'd ever encounter each other in the normal course of their lives.

He told her where to park, pointing at an empty slot.

"Thank you, Hector, for everything you've done," she said, forcing a smile.

"My pleasure."

They sat in the car, and he seemed as reluctant to move as she was.

"I should get back to work," Hector finally said.

"Yes, of course."

His hand was on the door handle. "It isn't every day I get to ride with such a beautiful woman," he said with quiet gallantry. He climbed out and gently closed the door. His eyes avoided hers. "Goodbye, Lillie."

"Goodbye, Hector."

He was a service manager for a car dealership and she was a wealthy widow. She accepted that their paths would likely never cross again. Despite that, she could do him one good turn. When she got home, Lillie phoned the dealership, leaving a message for the owner, Steve Sullivan. She praised Hector's efforts on her behalf and stressed to Steve that he had an outstanding employee.

That way, at least, she could play a small, if benevolent, role in Hector's life.

It wasn't enough but it would have to do.

Nine

Monday evening, Barbie showed up at the theater a little later than she had the previous week. Tessa Bassett was selling tickets again, and when she saw Barbie, her face lit up.

"Should I recommend another movie?" the girl asked cheerfully.

"Please do." The ill-tempered Mark Bassett was the sole reason Barbie had come back. In the last week she'd spent a lot of time thinking about him. She felt strangely invigorated by the challenge he offered, but it was more than that. She was attracted to him, not only because of his looks but because she saw in him the same loneliness she'd experienced since her husband's death. Once she made it past the barrier he'd erected against the world, perhaps they could be friends. Perhaps even more. The fact that he was physically disabled didn't bother her, nor did she find it especially daunting. She knew it didn't define or describe the person inside, any more than *her* appearance did.

Tessa mentioned a movie Barbie had never heard of and handed her the ticket, as well as her change.

"You're sure this is a good movie?" Barbie asked.

Tessa's eyes held hers. "It's the perfect movie."

Barbie was willing to take the girl's word for it. In the theater lobby, she once again purchased a small bag of popcorn and a cold soda, then walked into the dimly lit theater.

She saw that Mark was already in one of the wheelchair spaces. Tessa had been right; this was the perfect movie.

Without hesitation, Barbie moved around the back and entered the row from the opposite direction. She sat down, leaving one empty seat between her and Mark.

The instant she did, he turned to glare at her. "This space is reserved for wheelchair seating."

"Yes, I know," she said as she crossed her legs. She started to eat her popcorn as if she didn't have a care in the world. Feeling both silly and daring, she tossed a kernel in the air and caught it in her mouth. Proud of herself, she grinned triumphantly at Mark.

Clearly he wasn't impressed with her dexterity. "Would you kindly move?"

His voice was even less friendly than it had been the last time.

"I have every right to sit here should I choose to do so," she returned formally. She held out her bag of popcorn. "Here," she said.

He frowned. "I beg your pardon?"

"I'm offering you some of my popcorn."

"What makes you think I want your popcorn?"

"You're cranky. My boys get cranky when they're hungry, so I figured that might be your problem."

He looked pointedly away.

"If you're not interested, the proper response is *no, thank you.*"

He ignored that, and Barbie munched her popcorn, swaying her leg back and forth.

"Stop that."

"What?"

"Swinging your leg like a pendulum."

She crossed the opposite leg and swung it, instead.

Mark groaned.

The theater darkened, and the previews appeared on the screen. Barbie finished the small bag of popcorn. Her hands were greasy, but in her rush to get into the theater she'd forgotten to pick up a napkin. She'd also forgotten to replace the tissues she kept in her purse. She stood up to go back to the lobby. Rather than march all the way down the row, she leaned over to nudge Mark.

"Excuse me."

"You're leaving?" He actually seemed pleased.

"No, I need a napkin. Can I get you anything while I'm up?"

"No," he muttered.

She sighed audibly. "Are you always this rude or is it just me you don't like?"

"It's you."

She refused to feel insulted; instead she interpreted his response as an admission that he was aware of her. Aware and interested.

"You act as if that pleases you," he said, sounding surprised.

"Well, it doesn't hurt my feelings if that was your intent. Now, can I get by? Please?"

With exaggerated effort, he rolled back his wheelchair, allowing her to exit the row.

Barbie pushed the sleeve of her soft cashmere sweater up her arm and hung her purse over her shoulder. "Don't get too comfortable," she told him. "I'll be back in a few minutes."

"Don't hurry on my account."

"I won't."

When she entered the lobby again, she saw that Tessa was working behind the concession stand. The girl looked curiously in her direction and Barbie nodded. She grabbed some napkins to wipe her hands, then walked over to wait her turn. She made an impulsive purchase, smiling as she did.

"How's it going?" Tessa asked, handing her the change.

"He wants me to leave."

Tessa seemed worried. "You're not going to, are you?"

Barbie shook her head. "Not on your life."

Tessa nearly rubbed her hands together with glee. "This is so cool."

"What is?"

The teenager shrugged. "Well, you know. You and my uncle Mark. He needs someone in his life. He doesn't think so, but…well, it'd just be so cool if that someone was you."

"Don't get your hopes up, Tessa." Barbie felt obliged to warn her. "I'd better get back. The movie's about to start."

"Don't let him give you any crap," the girl advised. "Oops, I mean attitude."

Barbie grinned and gave her a thumbs-up.

Attitude was the right word, she mused as she made her way into the theater. It wasn't hard to figure out that his surliness was an attempt to protect himself from pain and rejection. If there was one thing she knew about, it was dealing with the insecurities of the adolescent male. And if she had her guess, he'd reverted to that kind of negative behavior after his accident. Beneath all the hostility, he was as lonely and lost as she was.

The film was just beginning as she reached their row. She stood in the aisle, waiting for him to roll his chair back.

"Excuse me," she said when he pretended not to notice. "I'd like to sit down."

"Must you?" he asked sarcastically.

"Yes, I must." Taking the initiative, she raised her leg and attempted to climb over his lap. He got the message fast enough when she presented him with an excellent view of her rear. He shot back with enough force to bolt into the empty space two rows back.

Barbie reclaimed her seat, then tossed him a chocolate bar. "Oh, here," she said. "I thought this might sweeten your disposition."

He tossed it back. "My disposition is as good as it gets. Chocolate isn't going to change it."

"Fine. I'll eat it then."

From that point on, she ignored him and he ignored her.

The movie, another romantic comedy, was delightful and Barbie quickly got involved in the plot. She and Mark didn't exchange a word until the credits were rolling and the lights came back on.

"That was really good," she said to no one in particular.

"It was sappy," Mark muttered.

"Naturally you'd say that," she protested. "Don't you believe in the power of love?"

"No."

So why had he chosen this movie? "Well, I happen to believe in it," she told him.

"Good for you." He wheeled back and started out of the theater, with Barbie keeping pace five steps behind him. Tessa, still at the concession stand, glanced at her eagerly. She gave the teenager another thumbs-up, and the girl returned a huge grin.

Just outside the complex, he unexpectedly wheeled around and confronted her. "Are you going to make a habit of this?" he demanded. The corners of his mouth curled scornfully.

"Of what?" she asked, playing dumb.

"Monday night at the movies. The only reason you're here is to irritate me."

"I didn't realize I had to pay money to do that. Couldn't I just sit out here and do it for free?"

He pinched his lips tightly closed.

"I enjoy the movies and Monday's a good night for me."

"Come another night," he said.

"I don't want to."

Frustration showed in his face. "Why are you doing this?"

"Doing what?" she asked, again feigning innocence. "You mean coming to the movies two weeks in a row on a Monday night?"

"Yes."

"Well, like I said, Monday evenings are good for me and movies are my favorite form of entertainment."

One look told her he didn't believe a word of it. "Then how come you picked the same movies I did?"

She tried to pretend she was bored with the subject. "If memory serves me, I was seated first last week. You're the one who invaded my space."

He frowned as if he'd forgotten that. "Maybe so, but this week was no accident."

"You seem to have an inflated opinion of your charms." His mouth opened and he seemed about to launch a come-back, but she didn't give him a chance. "Now, if you'll ex-cuse me, I'm going home. Good night, Mark."

He frowned. "How do you know my name?"

"I asked. I'm Barbie, by the way. Barbie Foster."

"Barbie," he repeated and snickered. Then he laughed out-right. "Barbie. It figures. You're about as plastic as they come."

"And you're about as rude as any man I've ever had the misfortune to meet."

"Then stay away from me and we'll both be happy."

"Maybe," she said flippantly as she reached for her car keys, buried deep inside her giant purse. "And maybe not. I haven't decided yet." She left him then, with a decided sway to her hips. It was an image she hoped would stay with him for a long time.

Ten

Tuesday was a good sales day at the bookstore, which wasn't typical. Anne Marie had worked out a careful method of maintaining inventory, balancing the number of mainstay and classic books she kept on the shelf with the new ones. It was crucial to have a wide range of titles. Relatively new to the business, she was learning as she went. Past experience had come from a part-time job at the University of Washington campus bookstore. Her previous career, as a customer service rep at a national insurance company, had taught her some valuable skills, too—but she hadn't loved it and was glad enough to give it up, at Robert's suggestion, to work in the bookstore, with an eye to eventually buying it.

The store was independent and needed an edge to compete with the large chains. Each bookstore, whether a chain store or an independent, was important in its own way. Blossom Street Books served the community. Over the past four years, since the renovations to the entire neighborhood, the store had developed a following and earned the loyalty of local residents. Anne Marie hadn't wanted to specialize, like some independents did, in mystery fiction

or cookbooks or children's books; she preferred to meet
all her customers' book-buying needs. She ordered books
for them, ran several reading groups, offered competitive
discounts on bestsellers and provided a cozy, intimate atmosphere. She'd made the store as inviting as possible,
with comfortable chairs, a gas fireplace and warm lighting.

Her clientele depended on Anne Marie for recommenda-
tions and updates on authors and publishing houses. She'd
managed the store before she bought it, to make sure she
really wanted to take on her own business, and in the process familiarized herself with the industry.

Even as a child, Anne Marie had been an inveterate
reader. She'd found her adventures in the pages of a book.
Never outgoing, or one to stand out in a crowd, she'd been
her husband's opposite in personality. Robert had been gre-
garious and sociable, and they'd complemented each other
well. He was fun to be around, and that had attracted her
from the beginning. Their age difference had never concerned her because he didn't seem older. Except when it
came to having another child…

Rather than sink into depression again, Anne Marie focused on creating a fresh display for the front table. Book-
stores were a low-margin business, and the real profits came
from notecards, stationery, games and other accessories.
She was working on a St. Patrick's Day exhibit, featuring
books like *How the Irish Saved Civilization* and fiction
by Maeve Binchy, Marian Keyes, Edna O'Brien and other
popular Irish novelists. Around the books she arranged
packages of greeting cards with shamrocks on them, green
candles and St. Patrick's themed paper napkins. She stepped
back, pleased with the result.

The previous owner, Adele Morris, had a bookstore in
the Fremont neighborhood, and when there was an oppor-

tunity for a second store on Blossom Street, Adele took it. Because of the renovation, she'd been offered a favorable rent and for the first couple of years she'd divided her time between the two stores. That proved to be too difficult, and Anne Marie had joined as manager soon afterward; later she purchased the business with Robert's encouragement. In her husband's eyes, the bookstore, like Baxter, was a solution to their dilemma. If Anne Marie was preoccupied with the store, she might forget about having a baby.

At one-thirty Theresa came in and for an instant Anne Marie couldn't remember why she'd shown up for work on a Tuesday.

"Ellen!" She said the child's name aloud as the memory rushed in. She was supposed to be at the school for Ellen's performance.

Theresa nodded. "You told me your Lunch Buddy was in some function at the school that you wanted to attend."

"Right." Rushing into the office, she grabbed her purse and threw on her jacket. She gave Theresa some last-minute instructions for her meeting with the children's book sales rep. Then she hurriedly left the shop via the back entrance, where she'd parked her car.

Thankfully the school was relatively close, and it only took her ten minutes to drive there. But when she arrived she discovered that the parking lot and nearby streets were jammed with vehicles and she wondered if every parent in a three-state area had decided to come for the performance. After another ten minutes she located a parking space three blocks from the school. She locked the car and ran toward Woodrow Wilson Elementary.

The music had already started by the time she entered the large gymnasium, sweaty and out of breath. The place was packed with parents and students, and if there was an available seat she couldn't find it.

Every adult in the room seemed to be in possession of a camera. Anne Marie hadn't even thought to bring one and wanted to kick herself. Ellen's grandmother would've appreciated a photograph of her granddaughter on stage.

Muttering her excuses, Anne Marie slipped past several people until she squeezed herself into a tight space where she had a good view. Sure enough, she could see Ellen standing on a riser with the other members of the chorus. She wore her Sunday best—a dress one size too small and white patent leather shoes. The stage set consisted of two large painted trees and a castle. The artwork had apparently been done by the students, as well. If she'd been told the name of the production, Anne Marie didn't remember. Clearly, though, it was the retelling of some classic fairy tale.

Anne Marie watched Ellen, who looked awkward and uncomfortable standing front row center, with two rows of children behind her.

As if she felt Anne Marie's eyes on her, Ellen glanced in her direction. When she saw Anne Marie, the girl's entire face was transformed by the beauty of her smile. Seeing how happy her presence had made Ellen, Anne Marie was glad she'd taken the trouble to show up. She sent the girl a small wave. Ellen waved back.

The music died down as the singing director stepped in front of the choir and raised both hands. The children on the risers instantly came to attention.

The performance, which turned out to be a rather inventive version of "Snow White," lasted forty minutes. No one was going to mistake it for professional theater. But the dwarves were hilarious and the singing was lively. Anne Marie nodded her head to the beat.

When the performance was finished, the principal came forward and announced that juice and cookies would be served in the children's rooms. Anne Marie checked her watch. She really should be getting back to the store. Then again, a few more minutes wouldn't hurt.

As she started toward Ellen's classroom, she nearly bumped into Helen Mayer, the school counselor.

"Anne Marie!" she exclaimed. "I'm so glad you could make it."

"Yes, the play was very well done," she said warmly. "Thank you for telling me about it."

"No, thank *you*, thank you so much."

With a quick smile, she hurried off in the opposite direction.

Anne Marie was standing by Ellen's desk when the child walked into the room, her eyes bright with happiness. "Did you hear me?" she asked. "Did you hear me sing?"

Anne Marie hadn't been able to discern Ellen's small voice among so many others. But in this case she figured a white lie was appropriate. "I did, and you were terrific."

Ellen blushed at the praise.

"You didn't tell me you like to sing."

Ellen nodded. "Mrs. Maxwell said I have a good voice. She's the music teacher."

"How many other second-grade students were part of the choir?" Anne Marie asked, although she already knew the answer.

"I was the only one."

"Just you?" Anne Marie feigned surprise.

"Yup, just me. Mrs. Maxwell said maybe by the time I'm in fourth or fifth grade I might get to sing a solo."

"Ellen, that's wonderful. Congratulations." Anne Marie had never seen the girl this excited.

The classroom had begun to fill up with other children and parents.

"Would you like some juice?" Ellen asked politely. The juice and cookies were set up on a table in the front.

Anne Marie noticed that the other students were delivering refreshments to their parents.

"That would be very nice. Thank you, Ellen."

The child waited for her turn and poured Anne Marie a small paper cup full of juice, which appeared to be some watered-down fruit punch. She also brought her two small cookies, definitely a store-bought variety.

"You didn't get anything for yourself," Anne Marie said.

"That's because you're supposed to serve your guests first," Ellen informed her solemnly.

"Of course," Anne Marie murmured. "I must've forgotten my manners."

Silently Ellen stood next to her.

Anne Marie bent down and whispered, "What's going to happen next?"

"Nothing," Ellen said. "You're supposed to drink your juice and eat your cookies."

"Okay." Anne Marie sampled a cookie, which crumbled in her mouth at the first bite. She washed it down with a gulp of juice that was far too sweet. Ellen waited until Anne Marie had finished before she returned to the refreshment table and poured a second cup of juice and took two small cookies for herself.

"Baxter wanted me to tell you hello," Anne Marie said when she came back.

Ellen swallowed the cookie she was chewing and nodded. "He's a good dog."

"A little spoiled, though."

"I'll teach him how to roll over the next time you bring him to school," Ellen promised. "I got a book from the library and I read about teaching dogs tricks. Baxter's smart and I know how to get him to roll over."

"I hope you can show me how to teach him, too."

"I will," Ellen said.

"I've tried to teach Baxter new tricks, but he doesn't seem to understand the concept." Anne Marie felt it only fair to warn Ellen; she didn't want to discourage the girl, nor did she want her to think it would be an easy task.

One of the other mothers glanced speculatively at Anne Marie and Ellen and moved toward them. "Are you Ellen's mom?" she asked Anne Marie.

"Actually, no, I'm her friend."

"Anne Marie is my Lunch Buddy," Ellen explained proudly. "She brought her dog for me to meet."

"Oh." The other woman drew a tiny long-haired girl close to her side. "I'm Shelly Lombard and this is my daughter, Cassie. She's friends with Ellen."

"Hi, Shelly, Cassie," Anne Marie said, smiling. "It's nice to meet you."

"I wanted to ask if Ellen could come over for a play date one afternoon. Would that be possible?"

This wasn't something Anne Marie could answer. "You'll have to ask her grandmother."

"Ellen lives with her grandmother, then?"

Anne Marie nodded.

"Oh...well, I don't know if that would work. I was actually hoping we could exchange play dates once in a while."

"I see."

"It's just that occasionally I have an appointment after

school and it's difficult to find someone to look after Cassie for just an hour or two."

"You could always ask her grandmother," Anne Marie said a second time.

"Yes, of course, but if she couldn't arrange to come for Ellen's performance, it's unlikely she'd be up to looking after an extra child."

Shelly had a point. Anne Marie remembered Ellen's saying that her grandmother slept a lot, which made her wonder if the woman was ill.

Shelly drifted away to chat with another parent. Anne Marie wanted to leave but she could tell that Ellen was desperate for her to stay. She searched for a topic of conversation.

"Would you like to show me your schoolwork?" Anne Marie asked. She remembered that during her brief orientation, this was an option suggested for Lunch Buddies.

"Okay." Ellen sat in her small chair and opened her desk to retrieve a notebook. Everything inside was impeccably organized.

Ellen set the notebook on top and flipped it open for Anne Marie to examine. On nearly every page the teacher had written a comment praising Ellen's work.

"You're an excellent student," Anne Marie said.

"Grandma Dolores makes me study every night." Ellen didn't seem happy about this.

"That's good, isn't it?"

"I guess." Ellen shrugged.

"Then you get to watch TV, right? That's what you told me before."

She bobbed her head. "We watch shows on the religion channel."

"What about cartoons?"

"Grandma Dolores doesn't think cartoons are good for kids. She saw *South Park* once and got upset. She hid my face in her apron and started praying to Jesus."

Anne Marie bit her lip, trying not to smile.

A buzzer rang, announcing the end of the school day. In short order, children and parents began to vacate the classroom. Ellen looked up at Anne Marie. "I need to catch my bus."

"Would you like me to walk outside with you?"

"Yes, please."

While Ellen put on her coat and gathered her things, Anne Marie went to introduce herself to the teacher. Ms. Peterski smiled at Anne Marie. "I'm so pleased you could come."

"I am, too," she said and she meant it.

She and Ellen walked out to the schoolyard, negotiating their way through the laughing, shouting throngs.

"I'll see you tomorrow at lunchtime," Anne Marie said as they neared the area where the children lined up for their buses.

"You're coming tomorrow, too?"

"It's our lunch date, remember?"

Ellen blinked hard, apparently overwhelmed that Anne Marie would come to see her two days in a row.

"I can't bring Baxter, though," Anne Marie reminded her.

"That's okay." They approached the bus stop, and suddenly Ellen slipped her hand into Anne Marie's.

It felt as if the warmth of that small hand reached all the way to her heart.

Eleven

Wednesday evening as Anne Marie prepared for bed, her phone rang. At the time she was brushing her teeth. Frowning, she turned off the tap and spit into the sink, then wiped her mouth before she went into the kitchen.

She couldn't even guess who'd be phoning after eleven o'clock. Caller ID told her nothing. It said Private Caller, which meant it was probably one of the widows. If Elise, Lillie or Barbie was calling her this late, that meant trouble of some kind, although she couldn't imagine what.

"Hello," Anne Marie answered cautiously. Nighttime phone calls usually brought bad news, and she'd had enough of that.

"This is Anne Marie?" The voice, that of an older woman, was barely audible.

"Yes."

"Anne Marie Roche?"

"Yes."

"I need...help." The woman, this stranger on the other end of the line, was close to panicking.

"Who is this, please?"

"Dolores. Dolores Falk."

"Who?"

"Ellen's grandmother."

Anne Marie sucked in her breath as a dozen disturbing possibilities ran through her mind. "Is Ellen all right?" she asked, fighting down a sense of panic.

"Yes…no. It's me who needs help… I wouldn't call you if there was anyone else." Each word seemed labored.

Anne Marie didn't know what she could possibly do. "Do you want me to call someone?" she asked, wondering how she might assist the older woman. Surely she had a neighbor or a friend she could contact. Anne Marie was a stranger.

"No, the aid car is on its way." The woman's breathing became harsh and irregular. "Just come…please. Hurry."

Anne Marie didn't understand. "Are you saying you want me to come to your house?"

"Please. Just…hurry."

"But…" How did Ellen's grandmother get her phone number? And what did she want? She was clearly in distress, but how could Anne Marie help?

"I don't have anyone else to take Ellen," Dolores gasped.

"*Me?* You want me to take Ellen? But I can't—" It was out of the question. Anne Marie didn't have room for a child.

"They're going to bring me to the hospital. Please. I'll refuse to let them unless you come."

Talk about emotional blackmail! In just the few minutes Anne Marie had been on the phone with Ellen's grandmother, she'd realized the older woman was badly in need of medical attention. As much as she resented this, Anne Marie didn't have a choice. She'd have to go and then try to sort out the situation later.

"What's the address?"

Dolores gave it to her with the added pressure of, "Hurry, please hurry."

"I'll be there as soon as I can." Exasperated, she replaced the phone and exhaled sharply. How had she ended up in this predicament? She'd volunteered to be a Lunch Buddy, not a…she didn't know what.

Pulling on jeans and a shirt, Anne Marie complained to Baxter, then promised to return as quickly as possible. With the address scribbled on a grocery-store receipt, she headed for her car. All she needed right now was to get attacked in the alley.

The alley was actually well lit, not that it would help her any if someone decided to leap out of the dark and mug her. Unlocking her car with shaking fingers, she climbed inside and started the engine.

Anne Marie considered herself the least capable person to deal with someone else's problems. If she'd had the school counselor's home number, she would've called Ms. Mayer and handed the whole mess over to her. Rescuing her Lunch Buddy in the middle of the night was *not* what she'd signed up for.

Dolores Falk's house was only about four miles away, but the neighborhood, an older working-class area, was unfamiliar. By the time Anne Marie arrived, the aid car was parked out front. A fire truck was there, too, plus paramedics. Several neighbors stood on their porches watching all the activity.

Anne Marie parked across the street, well away from the emergency vehicles. Purposefully she trudged over to the house.

The instant Ellen saw her, she bolted down the porch steps, then raced across the yard and threw her arms around Anne Marie's waist.

"What's going on?" Anne Marie asked, placing her hands on the child's shoulders.

"These men are taking Grandma to the hospital," Ellen sobbed, clinging to Anne Marie.

"But they're going to help her. Isn't that what we want?" she asked softly.

"N-o-o! She-e-e mi-gh-t *d-i-e*," the girl wailed.

"Let me talk to them," she said and gently loosened the child's arms. She walked Ellen back to the porch and left her sitting on the bottom step, still sobbing.

"Are you Anne Marie Roche?" an emergency medical technician asked as he stepped out of the house.

"Yes."

"Good. The grandmother refused medical treatment until you got here."

"Why me?"

"You'll have to ask her that yourself."

"Then let me talk to her."

He shook his head. "I'd prefer if you did that at the hospital."

"I only need a minute," she insisted stubbornly.

"The grandmother told us you'd be taking the child," the paramedic said as he started into the house.

"I'm her Lunch Buddy." She wanted to explain that her entire role in this child's life was to have lunch with her once a week. She'd met her exactly four times, if you included the brief orientation the previous month.

Lunch. That was supposed to be the full extent of her commitment.

No one had said anything about taking Ellen home with her. That was probably against the rules, anyway, and there seemed to be a lot of those.

"Isn't there someone else?" she asked, following the EMT into the house.

"Apparently not." He hurried to a bedroom in the back, Anne Marie directly behind him.

She discovered Dolores Falk on a stretcher. The woman's complexion was sickly and gray, and every rasping breath seemed to cause her pain. Her hand rested on her heart, her eyes tightly shut. Ellen had said her grandmother was over fifty; in Anne Marie's observation, she had to be in her midsixties but looked older.

"Wheel her out," the EMT instructed the other two.

The woman's eyes flew open. "Wait."

"I'm here," Anne Marie rushed to tell her.

Dolores reached out and grabbed Anne Marie's hand in a grip that was shockingly strong. "Don't let them put Ellen in a foster home. I'll lose her if they do."

"But, Mrs. Falk… Where do you want me to take her?"

The woman's eyes closed again. "Home. Take her home with you."

"With me? I can't—"

"You have to…"

The EMT came in then and they rolled the stretcher down the hallway and out of the house. Anne Marie trailed behind, watching helplessly as the emergency crew loaded Ellen's grandmother into the aid car and drove off, sirens screaming.

With her hands covering her face, Ellen sobbed as she huddled on the steps, her shoulders trembling. Her pitiful cries were drowned out by the screeching aid car.

Anne Marie crouched so they were at eye level. "Your grandmother's going to see the doctors and they're going to make her well again." She prayed with all her heart that this was true.

Ellen nodded tearfully. "When will Grandma be back?"

"I don't know, sweetheart." She was so far out of her element here that she was breaking into a cold sweat.

"Where will I go?" Ellen asked.

"For tonight," Anne Marie said, mustering as much enthusiasm as she could, "you get to come home with me."

Ellen dropped her hands long enough to look up at Anne Marie. "With you?"

"Yes, that's why your grandmother called me."

"Is Baxter there?"

Anne Marie nodded. She should've thought of that sooner. Ellen loved Baxter and he'd help take the child's mind off what was happening to her grandmother.

"Baxter's waiting for us to get back to my apartment so he can see you. Didn't you say you wanted to teach him to roll over?"

"Yes-s-s." For the first time since Anne Marie had arrived, the eight-year-old stopped weeping. She bit her lip and managed to control her sobs.

"We should pack a few things for you."

"I have my backpack," Ellen said, looking small and lost and terrified.

"Good idea. We'll put what you need in there." Taking the child by the hand, Anne Marie went into the house. It was an older single-story home, probably built soon after the Second World War. The floors were linoleum and the furniture shabby and dated. The hallway led to three bedrooms.

Ellen's room was the farthest down the hall on the right-hand side.

It was furnished with a single bed, a dresser and a child-size desk and chair. The closet was narrow but more than big enough for Ellen's few clothes.

"Just get what you'll need for school tomorrow," Anne

Marie said. In the morning she'd drive Ellen to Woodrow Wilson Elementary, then she'd talk to Ms. Mayer and find out what could be done for the child.

"I brushed my teeth already," Ellen said. Kneeling down on the braided rug next to her bed, she stuffed a pair of neatly ironed jeans and a pink sweater into her backpack.

"Don't forget your shoes and socks," Anne Marie told her. Ellen was wearing bedroom slippers and well-worn pajamas over which she'd pulled a sweatshirt. "Did you have any homework?"

Ellen nodded and hurried to the kitchen, returning with a small binder. "It's math," she explained as she added that to the pouch, along with her tennis shoes and a pair of socks.

"This is way past your bedtime," Anne Marie said.

"Grandma said she wasn't feeling well when I got home from school," Ellen told her. "She said I could have corn-flakes for dinner."

"Did you?"

Ellen shook her head. "I wasn't hungry."

Most likely Ellen was too worried about her grand-mother to have an appetite. "Who called for the aid car?"

"I did."

"You?"

"Grandma didn't look good and she didn't answer me when I talked to her and I got scared."

"That was a smart thing to do." Anne Marie had to credit the child with fast thinking. "Do you know how your grand-mother got my phone number?"

"No." Ellen lowered her eyes. "But I'm glad she did."

Now that she'd seen the situation for herself, Anne Marie was glad, too, and grateful she'd come when she had. She could only imagine how much greater the trauma of this evening would've been for Ellen if she'd been handed over to Child Protective Services and placed in temporary foster care.

"Are you ready?"

Ellen nodded solemnly and reached for Anne Marie's hand. The child turned off all the lights on the way out. She stopped on the porch and took out the house key, hidden beneath a ceramic flowerpot, then locked the front door. When she'd finished, she replaced the key.

"Will I be able to visit Grandma in the hospital?" she asked, staring up at Anne Marie with huge eyes.

"I'll find out for you in the morning, okay?"

"Please," she whispered, and the plaintive little voice broke Anne Marie's heart.

As they drove back to Blossom Street, Anne Marie suspected the girl would fall asleep on the silent ride there, but Ellen appeared wide-awake. When they got to the bookstore, Anne Marie pulled into the alley behind it.

"This is your house?" Ellen asked.

"I have a small apartment above the bookstore."

"You live over a bookstore?" she whispered, as if Anne Marie resided in some enchanted castle.

"I do. I'll bet Baxter's standing by the door, too." The Yorkshire terrier seemed to recognize the sound of her car and waited eagerly by the back entrance.

Sure enough, the minute Anne Marie unlocked the door Baxter rushed forward, leaping up and down with excitement.

"Baxter!" Despite the anguish of the evening, Ellen couldn't hide her delight at seeing the dog again. She fell to her knees and the terrier welcomed her, licking her hands and face.

"Ellen's spending the night," Anne Marie told him. Turning to the girl, she said, "Let me show you your bedroom."

"Okay." Reluctantly leaving the dog, Ellen followed Anne Marie through the apartment.

The second bedroom, which served as Anne Marie's home office, wasn't set up as guest quarters. But thankfully she had a sofa that folded out into a bed. Taking a set of sheets from the hall closet, she quickly made it up and added a couple of blankets and a pillow.

"Would you like some warm milk?" she asked when the bed was ready. "It might help you sleep."

Ellen made a face and shook her head.

"Sounds dreadful, doesn't it?" The only reason she'd offered was that her own mother used to give it to her. She hadn't liked it, either.

"Would it be okay…" Ellen hesitated.

"What is it, Ellen?"

"Could Baxter sleep with me?"

Anne Marie smiled. She should've suggested it herself. "That would be just fine."

"Thank you."

Anne Marie yawned. She was exhausted and knew Ellen must be, too. "Let me tuck you into bed," she said, "and I'll put Baxter up there with you."

"Thank you," Ellen whispered. She slipped off her sweatshirt and slippers and climbed into the newly made bed.

Once she was under the covers, Anne Marie folded them around her shoulders. She set her Yorkie on the bed. As if understanding that the child needed a friend, Baxter immediately curled up next to her.

"Good night, Ellen," Anne Marie said, about to leave the room.

"Would you say a prayer with me?" the child asked.

"A prayer?" Anne Marie couldn't remember the last time she'd prayed.

"Grandma always does."

"All right, but you say the words."

"Okay." Ellen dutifully closed her eyes and although her lips moved, she didn't speak out loud. After a moment, she said, "Amen."

"Amen," Anne Marie repeated.

"I prayed for my grandma," Ellen told her.

"I'm sure God listens to little girls' prayers," Anne Marie said, choosing to believe that He did. She turned off the light, then realized she didn't know when Ellen was supposed to be at school. "Ellen," she whispered. "What time does school start?"

"Eight-twenty."

"I'll set the alarm for seven. That'll give us plenty of time."

"Okay."

Anne Marie left the room and eased the door partially closed so she'd hear if Ellen needed her during the night. She found a night-light for the bathroom and plugged it in.

Sitting at her small kitchen table, Anne Marie inhaled a deep, calming breath. Elise Beaumont had a lot to answer for—and she planned to let her know it. This Lunch Buddy business had become a far more complicated proposition than Anne Marie had been led to expect.

She liked Ellen and she was happy to help—well, *happy* might be an exaggeration. She felt *obliged* to help, especially since the child's grandmother claimed she didn't have anyone else to ask. But in the morning, Anne Marie was driving Ellen to school and getting the name of the contact person listed for emergencies.

This was standard practice. The school would have the name of a responsible adult who'd take Ellen while her grandmother was in the hospital. Someone far more qualified than Anne Marie. Someone better equipped to look after a frightened child.

Anne Marie had her own problems. And as much as she wanted to help, she wasn't prepared to be the child's guardian for more than one night.

Twelve

Anne Marie woke before the alarm buzzed at seven and discovered Ellen sitting up in bed petting Baxter and talking to him in a voice that quavered slightly.

"Good morning," Anne Marie said as cheerfully as she could. She stretched her arms high above her head.

Ellen didn't respond.

"Would you like some orange juice?"

The girl shook her head.

"Are you sure?"

Ellen nodded.

"I'm going to take Baxter for a short walk. Do you want to come?"

"Okay." Ellen climbed out of bed and sat on the floor, where she'd left her backpack. While the child got dressed, Anne Marie prepared a pot of coffee and put on a pair of sweatpants and a fleece top.

Her usual morning routine was to take Baxter out while the coffee brewed, getting a few minutes of exercise at the same time. Their route never varied: down Blossom Street for two blocks, crossing over to a small park, going around the park twice and then back. The entire walk took twenty minutes. Once she was home again, Anne Marie always showered, changed clothes and did her hair and makeup. On a good day, everything could be accomplished in under an hour.

Ellen was ready by the time Anne Marie finished her first cup of coffee and pulled on her jacket.

"Would you like to hold the leash?" she asked.

"Yes, please."

As they headed outside, she asked Ellen a few more questions but the girl remained glum and uncommunicative. She wanted to ask Ellen what was wrong but figured it was obvious. The poor kid was worried about her grandmother, of course, and her own future. Anne Marie couldn't blame her for that, so she decided to tread carefully. If Ellen didn't want to talk, she shouldn't have to.

"When I take you to school this morning, I'm going to see the school counselor," Anne Marie said as they returned to the apartment.

"Okay."

"Do you have any relatives close by?"

"My aunt Clarisse."

That was a big relief, although Anne Marie had to wonder why Ellen's grandmother hadn't called her instead. Of course, there could be any number of reasons. Clarisse might've been out of town or at work or not answering her phone or...she ran out of excuses.

Anne Marie was confident that as soon as Clarisse learned that Dolores had been hospitalized, she'd be eager to have Ellen. Some of the tension left her now that she had the name of a responsible adult who'd step in and take care of the child.

When they entered the apartment, Anne Marie checked

her watch. Twenty-four minutes so far. That was good, especially with an eight-year-old in tow.

"What would you like for breakfast?" Anne Marie asked as they stepped into the kitchen.

Ellen shrugged.

"I don't have any kid cereals, but I do have shredded wheat. Would you like that?" Ellen had to be hungry, since she'd gone without dinner the night before.

"Okay. Thank you."

While Anne Marie got two bowls, the cereal and milk, Ellen made her bed and brushed her hair. It was straight and dark, parted in the middle with bangs that needed to be trimmed. If she'd had any little-girl hair clips, Anne Marie would've used them.

Ellen ate only a small portion of her breakfast and then placed her bowl in the sink. It was a bit early to drop her off at school, but Anne Marie wanted to be sure she had plenty of time to talk to the counselor.

"Are you ready to go?" she asked.

"Yes," Ellen replied. "Will you find out about Grandma Dolores?"

"I'll phone the hospital this morning," Anne Marie promised. She'd do it before ten, when the bookstore opened.

When Anne Marie and Ellen arrived at the school, the playground was already crowded with youngsters. The yellow buses had started to pull up, and students in bright jackets leaped down the few steps, like water cascading over a ledge. They all wore gigantic backpacks that threatened to topple them.

"Would you show me where the office is?" Anne Marie asked Ellen. She wanted the little girl to feel needed.

"Okay." Ellen silently led the way down the school's wide corridor.

"Would you like to play with your friends now?"

Ellen hesitated as if uncertain.

"Everything's going to be fine," Anne Marie assured her. "I'll call about your grandmother and let you know later."

Ellen's eyes brightened and she nodded, then ran off.

Watching Ellen join her friends, Anne Marie walked into the office; she asked to speak to Helen Mayer and within five minutes was escorted into the other woman's office.

"Is everything okay?" Helen asked immediately, a small frown between her eyes.

"Not really..." Anne Marie described the events of the night before.

Incredulous, the counselor stared at her. "Oh, my goodness."

"As you can imagine, this has all been a shock." Anne Marie pinned her gaze on the other woman. "I wonder how she got my phone number."

"Actually I gave it to her," Helen admitted a bit sheepishly. "She phoned last week and asked for it and I couldn't see any reason not to tell her. She said she wanted to talk to you about Ellen."

To be fair, the school counselor couldn't have known that Dolores would call in the middle of the night and place Anne Marie in such an awkward position. "I'm going to need the emergency contact number in Ellen's file," Anne Marie told her.

"Yes, of course." Helen turned to her computer and began to type. After a couple of minutes, she said, "The name is Clarisse McDonald." She reached for a pen and quickly wrote down the number.

Anne Marie took the piece of paper. As soon as she learned about Dolores's condition, she'd be in touch with Ellen's aunt.

"Do you know what hospital the paramedics took Dolores to?" the counselor asked.

At the time Anne Marie hadn't been thinking clearly enough to inquire, but she'd heard one of the EMTs mention Virginia Mason Hospital, which wasn't far from Blossom Street.

She was telling Helen Mayer this when a bell rang in the distance, indicating the start of classes. The sound caught Anne Marie off guard and she jerked in surprise.

"You get used to the bell," Helen said. "After a while you don't even hear it." She smiled. "You were telling me Dolores is at Virginia Mason?"

"Yes, I think so." Anne Marie would visit the hospital first. If she hurried, she should be able to make it there and get back to the store before ten.

She stood. "I'll call you as soon as I know anything."

"Thanks," Helen said as she walked Anne Marie to the office door.

Before Anne Marie left the building, she decided to check on Ellen. She stood by the classroom door and peeked in to see Ellen chatting with her friends as if nothing was awry. Relieved, she went out to the parking lot.

When Anne Marie reached Virginia Mason Hospital it was already nine-fifteen. She explained her situation to the woman at the information counter, who gave her Dolores Falk's room number.

She took the elevator to the correct floor and found Dolores alone in her room, hooked up to IV tubes. Her color seemed improved, Anne Marie thought. When she walked in, Dolores opened her eyes.

"How are you feeling, Mrs. Falk?" she asked as she approached the side of the bed.

"I'm doing better. How's Ellen?"

"She's fine. Don't worry about her."

Tears welled in the older woman's eyes. "I can't thank you enough for taking my granddaughter. I don't know what I would've done if you hadn't come."

"I'm glad to help out." Never mind that it wasn't entirely true.

Dolores's chest rose with a sigh. "The doctor says I'm going to need heart surgery."

Anne Marie squeezed the woman's hand. "They have excellent doctors here and—"

"I'm not worried for me," Dolores said, cutting her off. "My only concern is Ellen."

"You just concentrate on getting well. I have the number for Ellen's aunt Clarisse and—"

"No!" Dolores cut her off again. Her fingers tightened on Anne Marie's.

"She's the emergency contact you gave the school. So I—"

"Clarisse is in prison."

"Prison?" Anne Marie swallowed her gasp of shock.

"Fraud." Dolores closed her eyes again, as if admitting this to Anne Marie embarrassed her. Anne Marie was sure it did.

"What about Ellen's mother?"

Tears rolled from the corners of the woman's eyes and fell onto the pillow that supported her head. "Her mother is a drug addict. The state of California took Ellen away from her when she was three years old. I'd lost contact with my daughter—I didn't even know about Ellen. By the time I learned I had a granddaughter, Ellen had gone through a series of foster homes. It took me a year to get that child to sleep through the night. I won't put her back in the system. I won't do that to her."

"Oh, dear..." Anne Marie said weakly. There didn't seem to be an adequate response.

"Whatever happens to me, don't let them put her in foster care."

Her agitation grew and Anne Marie began to worry. "Promise me," she pleaded. "Promise me."

"Of course." What else could she say?

Dolores relaxed a little after that.

"What about her father?"

Dolores shook her head grimly. "My daughter probably doesn't even know who fathered this child."

"Oh."

"There's no one else."

"Perhaps her mother's clean and sober now." Anne Marie hated to sound desperate, but the options were dwindling fast.

"She's not. Last year she rescinded all rights as Ellen's mother."

"Oh." Anne Marie could feel what was coming. Dolores would ask her to watch Ellen while she was in the hospital. A rush of excuses, a dozen valid reasons she couldn't do it, were on the tip of her tongue. She couldn't make herself say them.

"That child is the only good thing I have in my life," Dolores whispered brokenly. "My daughters have both chosen paths that led to spiritual and emotional ruin. I pray for them every day."

"I'm sure you do, but—"

"I don't understand where I went wrong. Their father left us twenty years ago, and I raised them alone. I tried to show them the right way..."

Anne Marie murmured a few comforting words, although she knew there was no comfort to be had.

"I've been a proud woman all my life," Dolores continued. "I've never asked the government for help, even when I was entitled to."

With her free hand Anne Marie gripped the steel bar along the side of the bed.

"I'm asking for your help now."

Anne Marie swallowed. "But… I'm a stranger."

"Ellen talks about you constantly. You and Baxter." The faint hint of a smile came to her then.

Anne Marie was surprised she got a mention. She'd assumed the real attraction had been the dog. "But… I'm just her Lunch Buddy," she murmured.

"You're much more than that," Dolores told her. "Please take my precious Ellen and look after her for me."

"I…" Anne Marie didn't know what to say. Her place wasn't set up to take care of a child. She didn't even have a real bed for Ellen. After living alone all these months— more than a year now—she wasn't sure how she'd adjust to living with someone else. With a child.

At her obvious reluctance, Dolores said, "The doctor said once I have the surgery I should be good as new."

"You'll need recuperation time." Mentally Anne Marie tried to calculate how long that might be. A week? Two? Maybe a month. She couldn't possibly deal with this awkward situation for a whole month.

"Yes, I'll need time to heal," Dolores agreed, "but it'll go much faster if I know Ellen is well taken care of." She gazed up at Anne Marie with wide, imploring eyes. When Anne Marie didn't immediately respond, Dolores added, "Please. I'm asking you from my heart. I'm begging you not to let them take my granddaughter away from me."

Anne Marie couldn't refuse. "All right," she said, hoping she didn't sound begrudging—or afraid.

Dolores released a huge sigh. "Thank you, Lord." She

pointed to the side table next to her bed. "I've written out a statement that gives you permission to see to any medical needs Ellen might have. I also wrote a statement authorizing you to keep Ellen while I'm in the hospital."

An orderly stepped into the room. "Ready, Mrs. Falk?" he asked far too cheerfully.

"Where are you taking her?" Anne Marie asked.

The young man raised his eyebrows. "Surgery."

"So soon?"

"I'll be fine," Dolores said. "Absolutely fine."

Anne Marie felt dreadful; she should've been the one consoling the other woman.

"I'll take care of Ellen," she promised with a sense of desperation. "Just get well."

The young man directed Anne Marie to the nurses' station, where she was given a phone number to check on Dolores's progress after the surgery. Anne Marie held on to that piece of paper as if it were a winning lottery ticket. "She'll be okay, won't she?" she asked the male nurse.

The burly man sent her a stoic look. "We're going to do everything we can to make sure she's home again as soon as possible."

That was supposed to reassure her? "Thank you," she said lamely. "I'll phone later this afternoon."

"I'll have an update for you then. Ask for Dana."

"I will. Thank you." She put the phone number, plus the signed papers Dolores had mentioned, in her purse and left the hospital.

By the time she got to her car, Anne Marie's stomach was so tense she actually felt nauseous. Yesterday afternoon she'd been working out at Go Figure, the women's gym on Blossom Street, with Barbie Foster. Less than a day later, she was responsible for the care and well-being of an eight-year-old child.

At the bookstore, Anne Marie turned over the Open sign and counted out cash for the register. She had a constant flow of customers until about one o'clock, when she called the school and spoke to Helen Mayer.

"What did you find out?"

"Ellen's grandmother had heart surgery this morning."

"How's she doing?"

"I don't know. I haven't spoken to anyone at the hospital yet. I wanted to update you, though—Ellen will be staying with me while her grandmother recuperates."

"With you? What about her aunt Clarisse?"

"Apparently she…she's moved and can't be reached." That was reasonably close to the truth and should spare Dolores some humiliation.

"I'm sorry to hear that."

Not nearly as sorry as Anne Marie.

"It's good of you to look after the child. I'm surprised you agreed to it."

As much as she'd like to see Ellen with someone else, Anne Marie couldn't tell a sick woman that she preferred not to take care of her only granddaughter.

"I'll be picking Ellen up from school this afternoon and making arrangements for her to catch the bus on Blossom Street."

"I can do that for you," Helen Mayer told her. "If you need me to do anything else, just let me know. I think it's wonderful that you're willing to help out like this."

Anne Marie ended the conversation and then called the hospital. Dolores had made it through surgery without a problem, Dana informed her. She was currently in recovery, and if there were any changes, he'd call. Anne Marie gave him her phone numbers.

Fortunately Steve Handley, who worked on Thursday afternoons, was able to come in an hour early despite the short notice, which freed Anne Marie to drive to the elementary school and get Ellen. The child's face brightened when she saw her.

"How's my grandma?" she asked.

"She's in the hospital, and the doctors and nurses are taking good care of her."

"When will she be home?"

"Soon." Anne Marie bent down to look into the little girl's eyes. "Until your grandmother's home again, would you like to stay with me?"

Ellen didn't answer right away. "I guess that would be okay."

It wasn't exactly an overwhelming affirmation, but it was good enough. "We'll need to stop by your house this evening and pack a bigger suitcase."

"Can Baxter come with us?"

"I think he'd like that."

"I brought the book from the school library," Ellen announced.

It took Anne Marie a moment to realize the book she meant was the one about dog tricks.

They drove back to Blossom Street in silence, Ellen staring straight ahead. After dinner, they'd return to the house and collect her things.

Dinner.

Anne Marie hadn't given it a moment's thought. No more skipping meals. No more pity parties, either. She had to be strong for Ellen's sake. She had to hold her life together for a couple of weeks. Anne Marie figured she could manage that.

Two weeks. Maybe three.

Four at the most.

The time would pass quickly. She hoped.

Thirteen

Thanks to her list of Twenty Wishes, Barbie Foster was thinking harder, doing more and experiencing life with greater excitement. Her list was nearly complete, and she loved the way it helped her analyze what she really wanted. For years, her focus had been on Gary and the twins. But with her sons away at school, she'd been at loose ends, never quite adjusting to the change in her routine. She missed her husband so much, even now. He'd always be a part of her— and yet she was only forty, with a lot of life yet to be lived.

Instead of working at the dress shop this Saturday, Barbie decided to take a day off and go to the St. Patrick's Day concert in Freeway Park. Anne Marie Roche had arranged for the afternoon off, as well, and the two of them planned to make an occasion of it. They'd met a couple of times at Go Figure, and she'd enjoyed getting to know her better.

Her friendship with Anne Marie had deepened since their Valentine's gathering. Until that night, Barbie had viewed Anne Marie as reserved, a bit standoffish. All of that had changed when they started talking about their Twenty Wishes.

She'd begun to see Anne Marie as a kindred spirit and

discovered a wry sense of humor. Her liking had turned to respect when she learned that Anne Marie was looking after eight-year-old Ellen Falk while her grandmother recuperated from heart surgery.

Barbie had met Ellen at the bookstore the day before, when she'd come in to buy a couple of romances. The child was sweet and unpretentious; she obviously idolized Anne Marie and was completely in love with her dog, Baxter. Barbie had watched with some amusement as Ellen struggled to teach the Yorkie to roll over, with no success.

Ellen was joining them for the St. Patrick's Day concert that afternoon. When Barbie met her and Anne Marie at the bookstore shortly after twelve, they were ready and waiting.

"Where are we going?" the little girl asked, fastening the buttons on her light green coat, which looked brand-new. Thankfully it wasn't raining; that was good news, since March was notorious for drizzle in the Pacific Northwest.

"We're attending a concert with Irish music," Anne Marie explained to the youngster. "Then afterward we're visiting my mother in Ballard."

"Will we visit Grandma Dolores, too?"

"Sure thing." Anne Marie buttoned up her own jacket. "Right after we see my mother."

The child nodded thoughtfully. "What's Irish music sound like?"

Anne Marie hesitated. "Well, it's usually pretty fast and…" She shrugged, and Barbie laughed as she gave up trying to describe it. "Just wait. You'll hear it soon enough."

"Will I like it?" Ellen asked, tilting her head curiously.

"I do," Anne Marie told her. "I like it a lot."

Ellen nodded firmly. "Then I will, too."

Because Freeway Park was relatively close to Blossom Street, they decided to walk. The air was crisp, the sky clear and bright. They moved at a slow pace to accommodate Ellen's shorter steps. Barbie noticed that the child took in everything around her with huge inquisitive eyes.

When they reached Freeway Park, above Interstate 5, it was already crowded. Finding a spot to sit was difficult, although they eventually did when a couple of teenagers were kind enough to share their space. Anne Marie had remembered to bring a blanket, which she smoothed out on the grass. A platform had been built for the performance, and they had a good view of the stage.

Ellen sat cross-legged on the blanket. Barbie and Anne Marie arranged themselves close to her. Barbie hadn't done anything like this since before she'd lost Gary. It reminded her of family expeditions when the kids were little, and she felt a quiet joy, an awareness that she could be happy again.

After the accident, her primary concern had been for her children. Now that they were away at school, she was no longer insulated from the pain and the loss. It was this same loss she sensed in Mark Bassett, and one reason she was so drawn to him.

For her mother, widowhood had been a different story. They'd never really discussed it, but Barbie knew about her father's indiscretions. Lillie had chosen to ignore them. And because her mother said nothing, Barbie didn't, either. She knew that Lillie grieved for David. She'd loved him, but in some ways Barbie thought his death might have been a release for her mother—although she'd never so much as hint at such a thing.

"When will it start?" Ellen asked after sitting quietly for several minutes.

"Soon."

"Are you hungry?" Barbie asked.

The girl shook her head and tucked her hands beneath her thighs.

There was festive chatter all around them; everyone seemed to be in a cheerful mood, exchanging greetings, laughing, talking.

"Ellen likes to sing," Anne Marie told her.

"Do you?" Barbie asked, turning to the child.

At the question, Ellen's face grew red. "Anne Marie says I'm a good singer. She heard me sing in the school play." The child obviously put great stock in the compliment.

"Maybe Anne Marie can teach you a few Irish songs," Barbie suggested.

A look of such profound sadness flashed into her friend's eyes that Barbie instantly placed her hand on Anne Marie's forearm.

"I used to sing, but I don't anymore. I...can't," Anne Marie mumbled, staring down at the blanket. "I lost my voice after Robert died... I thought it would return, but it hasn't yet."

"I'm sorry." Barbie felt she had to apologize because it so clearly upset her friend.

"No, no. I mean, for heaven's sake, it's not your fault." Recovering quickly, Anne Marie dismissed her concern with a quick shake of her head.

Ellen gazed up at her, frowning. "I didn't know you can't sing."

"Don't worry, Ellen," Anne Marie murmured. "I will again."

Because Ellen was restless and maybe because Anne Marie wanted to change the subject, the two of them went for a short walk around the park before the music started. As they left, Barbie saw that the little girl stuck close to Anne Marie's side. Being with so many people was probably overwhelming for a child. Barbie had to credit her friend; it couldn't have been easy to bring this child into her home, even for a short while.

In fact, Barbie thought Anne Marie seemed softer now, less cynical and more open. Being with such a vulnerable child, having to take responsibility for her, meant that Anne Marie was less focused on her own sorrows. Wasn't that what Elise kept saying? Doing something for someone else made you feel better about yourself.

The group of Irish singers was introduced, and the crowd instantly broke into applause. Ellen and Anne Marie hurried back to the blanket just as the performance began.

The singers, the fiddlers and dancers were thrilling, and Barbie loved every minute. The music was infectious. And the dancing—it was so vigorous, yet disciplined, too. Ellen sat through the entire hour mesmerized. She seemed to absorb the music, every note of it. When the performance was over, her face glowed.

"That was so good," she said, looking at Anne Marie and Barbie. "I want to sing like that someday. Do you think I can?" she asked plaintively.

"Yes," Anne Marie told her in a confident voice. "I'm sure you can."

People had started to leave the park. The exodus was slow moving, but Barbie wasn't in any hurry. Besides, her feet hurt. That was what she got for wearing designer shoes; she'd chosen them because they were the perfect complement to her black linen pants and green silk blouse. The sun warmed the day, and she'd left her raincoat open, the belt dangling at her sides.

As she and Anne Marie waited patiently for the crowd to thin, Barbie saw a flash of chrome from the corner of her eye. She turned to look and then caught her breath. She grabbed Anne Marie's elbow.

"It's him…" She could barely get the words out. Feeling self-conscious, she dropped her hand.

"Who?" Anne Marie asked.

Barbie couldn't tell her because she hadn't told anyone about her attraction to Mark Bassett, the man in the wheelchair. She looked again, just to be sure. He was alone, or appeared to be, apparently waiting for the crowd to disperse. Maneuvering his wheelchair would be difficult with so many people pressing in around him.

"You know someone here?"

"Not really." Barbie tried to calm the wild beating of her heart. This was an unexpected surprise, a bonus. She was pleased now that she'd taken care with her outfit and makeup.

If Mark had seen her—and she couldn't tell either way—he refused to acknowledge her. Barbie bit down hard on her lower lip to keep from raising her hand and calling out to him.

"Do you know that guy in the wheelchair?" Anne Marie asked.

"I…not exactly. I bumped into him recently." She didn't mention the part about emptying her soda in his lap.

"He's certainly a striking man."

He was. Barbie had trouble taking her eyes off him. The crowd had mostly disappeared by then and only a few stragglers remained.

"Can we go see Grandma Dolores soon?" Ellen asked.

Anne Marie smiled at the girl. "After we visit my mom, okay?"

Her patience with Ellen impressed Barbie.

"I think I'd better head out," Anne Marie said, glancing

down at her watch. "We're meeting my mother for a late lunch, and after that we're going to the hospital."

"Of course, no problem," Barbie told her. "I've got plans myself."

They left, which worked out well because now she was free to confront Mark. Barbie didn't have a single idea as to what she'd do or say once she reached him. She'd figure that out when the time came.

He'd managed to leave Freeway Park and was moving steadily down the sidewalk. Barbie raced after him, having some difficulty with her shoes. "Hello, again," she called out cheerfully.

He ignored her.

"Remember me?"

At her second attempt, Mark spun his wheelchair around. "What are *you* doing here?"

"I came to enjoy the music, just like everyone else."

"I didn't know there'd be a concert," he grumbled.

"In other words, you wouldn't have come if you had."

"Right."

"But you enjoyed it, didn't you?"

"No."

Barbie didn't understand him—and she didn't believe he hadn't been affected by the music. "Why are you such a grouch?" she asked.

"I like being a grouch."

"Yes, Oscar."

He frowned. "What?"

"Oscar the Grouch from *Sesame Street*." Her sons had often watched it when they were young. She planted herself directly in front of his wheelchair, blocking him off.

He wasn't amused.

She'd never been so rude in her life, but Barbie wasn't about to let him escape.

"What is it you want?" he demanded.

Now that he'd asked, she wasn't entirely sure. To get his attention, yes, but she couldn't admit that. "To talk, I guess."

He tried to wheel around her, but once again she hindered his progress. "I'm not interested in talking, nor am I the least bit interested in you."

Barbie sighed deeply. "That is *so* refreshing."

"I beg your pardon?"

She smiled down at him. "You wouldn't believe how many guys constantly hit on me. Not you, though, and yet we seem to like the same movies. You know, we might actually have something in common."

He wagged his index finger at her. "I'm on to your game. You and Tessa are in cahoots—you have to be. That's how you knew which movie I'd be watching last week. Well, that won't happen again."

Barbie felt her blood surge with excitement. "I wouldn't count on it. You can't tell me which movie to see or not to see."

He scowled back at her. "Don't count on me being there."

"That's no guarantee we won't bump into each other somewhere else," Barbie said, changing tactics. "We met here, didn't we? I think it must be fate."

"I think it's bad luck."

"Oh, Mark, honestly."

His scowl grew darker.

"Your niece seems fond of you," Barbie said conversationally.

His hands were on the wheels of his chair. "I'd like to get out of here if you don't mind."

"I wanted to talk, remember?"

"I don't."

"Fine." She raised both hands in a gesture of defeat. "Have it your way."

"Thank you," Mark said gruffly and as soon as she stepped aside, he wheeled past her.

Despite his dismissive tone, Barbie followed him. "Can I ask you something?" she began.

Mark disregarded her, apparently a habit of his. His speed was surprising and in an effort to catch up with him, Barbie was nearly trotting. Her heel caught on a crack in the sidewalk and she went flying forward, landing hard on her hands and knees.

"Damn!" she cried at the sudden sharp pain. Momentarily stunned, she sat back and brushed the grit from her hands. Blood seeped through her pants and tears smarted her eyes.

Mark stopped, then reluctantly spun around to face her. "What happened?" he asked, none too sympathetically.

"I tripped."

"Are you hurt?"

"Yes. Look, there's blood."

"Should I call 911?"

He was making fun of her, but Barbie didn't care. She peeled up her pant leg to examine her knee.

"That's what you get for wearing those ridiculous shoes." She let the insult pass.

"Do you need help getting up?"

"No, I can manage." When she scrambled to her feet, she discovered that she'd broken the heel off her left shoe. "Would you *look* at this?" she cried. "If you knew what I paid for these shoes, you'd be as outraged as I am."

"Next time don't go chasing after me," he said. "I'm not interested, understand?"

"Okay, fine," she snapped.

"Fine with me, too." He started to roll away from her.

Barbie sniffled and limped off. She'd made an idiot of herself and now she was paying the price. So much for this supposed bond between them. He wanted nothing to do with her. Well, she got his message, loud and clear.

Her progress was slow with her knee aching and her broken shoe.

"Miss, Miss."

Barbie turned to find a woman with a first aid kit in her hand. "I heard that you fell."

"Who told you?"

"A man in a wheelchair stopped in my store and said you might need help."

"Really." So Mark wasn't as hard-edged as he'd like her to believe. He *was* concerned about her but he didn't want to show it. "I'm okay. My pride hurts a lot more than my knee. It was my own fault."

"Are you sure I can't help you?"

Barbie thanked the woman with a smile. "I think I'll just go home." She'd call her mother for sympathy and then have a cup of hot tea.

"The man told me you'd probably say that. If you'll sit down, I'll take a look at your knee."

"I don't suppose you have any glue, do you?" she asked, holding up her broken shoe.

"No, sorry."

Barbie thanked her again and left, hobbling back to Blossom Street, where she'd parked her car. The injury to her knee was nothing more than a scrape but the blow to her pride would take much longer to heal.

Her one consolation was the fact that, despite everything, Mark had sent someone to check on her. It wasn't a
lot, but it was *something*. A tiny fracture in his resistance.
It gave her hope.

By Monday evening, Barbie's knee was healing nicely.
Although she didn't need to, she wore a huge bandage over
it and a short skirt, short enough to reveal her bandaged
knee.

Tessa was at the ticket window when Barbie approached.

"So, which movie should I see?" Barbie asked, the same
as she had the week before.

Tessa's dark brown eyes searched hers. "He isn't here."

"You mean not yet, right?"

"Uncle Mark's not coming, period."

"Why not?" Barbie couldn't have disguised her disappointment if she'd wanted to.

"He figured out that I was the one feeding you information." Tessa sounded as disgruntled as Barbie felt.

Because she was holding up the line, Barbie stepped
aside until there was a break.

"I'm sorry," Tessa murmured. "He told me he won't be
coming to the movies again and that I should make sure
you knew it."

"Oh," Barbie murmured. "Do you see him outside the
movies very often?"

Tessa shrugged. "Sometimes."

"Next time you do, tell him I think he's a coward."

Tessa's jaw dropped. "You're not serious."

"Yes, I am," Barbie insisted. "Tell him that for me."

She purchased her ticket, plus popcorn and a soda. Although she sat through the entire movie, she couldn't remember a single scene.

Fourteen

Monday evening Anne Marie put a meat-loaf-and-potato casserole in the oven. It was a favorite recipe of her mother's and one she hadn't made in years. The meat mixture baked with sliced raw potatoes, both covered in tomato sauce. Anne Marie had liked it when she was around Ellen's age and she hoped Ellen would, too.

As she closed the oven door, she noticed Ellen approaching the large oak desk where she kept the scrapbooking materials for her Twenty Wishes book.

"What's this?" Ellen asked, looking over her shoulder.

"My Twenty Wishes."

"Twenty Wishes," the girl repeated. "What are those?"

"Well, on Valentine's Day, my friends and I had a small party. We started talking about all the things we'd wished for in our lives and then we each decided to make a list."

"Just twenty?"

Anne Marie laughed. So far, coming up with twenty had been hard enough, and in fact, she was only halfway there. "This is fine for now. I'll think of more later on," she said. "In fact, I'm still working on my first twenty." She had a total of nine: the five she'd written earlier, plus her most recent additions.

6. Find a reason to laugh

7. Sing again

8. Purchase a home for me and Baxter

9. Attend a Broadway musical and learn all the songs by heart

She was considering a line dancing class, which was a wish she'd erased earlier. The St. Patrick's Day performance had inspired her interest in dancing again.

"The wishes don't need to be practical," Anne Marie went on to explain. "That's why they're called wishes instead of resolutions or goals."

"What do you mean?"

"Well, I don't necessarily expect them all to happen."

"If you don't expect them to happen," Ellen asked, regarding her quizzically, "then why are you writing them down?"

"Because they're *wishes*," Anne Marie said. Finding a pen, she added a wish she'd erased two or three times.

10. Travel to Paris with someone I love

That encompassed the essence of what she sought—love, adventure, new experiences.

Ellen stared down at the recently entered wish. "Can anyone make a list like this?"

"Of course." Anne Marie set the timer on the oven. They'd gotten into a routine, the two of them, during the past five days. It felt as if Ellen had been with her much longer. One obvious difference in her life was that Anne Marie now regularly cooked dinner.

Ever since she'd started living alone, she'd fallen into the habit of grabbing something quick and easy or skipping dinner altogether, which she could ill afford to do. But Ellen needed regular nutritious meals and a daily structure. With everything else in the girl's life in upheaval, Anne Marie could at least offer her that.

The phone rang and Anne Marie picked it up immediately before Call Display could even register the number. She was expecting to hear from Elise, whom she'd been trying to reach all afternoon. "Hello." She figured Elise wanted to share her news, which Anne Marie had already heard via the neighborhood grapevine. Elise had taken a part-time job working for Lydia at A Good Yarn.

"Anne Marie, it's Brandon."

"Brandon! It's great to hear from you," she said with genuine pleasure.

"I've been meaning to call you for a couple of weeks," he went on. "Melissa told me what she did. I can't believe my sister sometimes. And as for my father…"

"Don't worry, I'm fine." That was mostly true.

"You're sure?" Brandon pressed. "To be fair to Melissa, I doubt she realized how hard you'd take that business about Dad. And she was pretty devastated herself."

"Really, it's okay," Anne Marie lied, brushing off his concern. The last thing she wanted was to talk about her husband's indiscretion—or even think about it. She felt a rush of pain whenever she remembered and constantly guarded herself against the image of Robert with Rebecca. In his office, on the couch…

"You're *sure?*" he asked again. He didn't seem convinced.

"Yes. Positive." As much as possible she made light of the incident.

Her stepson hesitated a moment, then blurted out, "Let me take you to dinner tonight. I know it's short notice, but we could talk and—"

"I can't." She hoped he'd take her at her word, not force her to explain.

"Why not?" Brandon's voice fell with disappointment.

"I have a visitor."

Her announcement was met with a short silence. "Anne Marie, are you seeing someone?" he asked somberly.

"No, of course not!" The question amused her. "Melissa asked me the same thing."

"Of course not? Why say it like that? You're young and beautiful and—"

"I'm with a...friend."

"Ah, the mystery intensifies."

"It's not a mystery," she said, smiling at his teasing banter. "It's Ellen. She's eight and she's living with me for the next week or two."

"You have an eight-year-old living with you? Is she a relative of yours?"

"No, I met her through a nearby school—the Lunch Buddies program. Why don't you join us?" she said impulsively. "I just put a casserole in the oven and it won't be ready for another forty minutes."

"You made dinner?"

"Don't sound so shocked. I did a lot of cooking in my time."

"Okay, I'd like that. Thanks. Give me a few minutes to finish up here and I'll drive straight over. You're still living above the bookstore, right?"

"For now." She really did hope to purchase a house.

Once Ellen was back with her grandmother, Anne Marie had every intention of beginning her search.

"Brandon, one thing… Melissa's and my conversation…"

"Yes?"

"I don't want to discuss it, all right?"

He hesitated. "If that's what you want."

"It is," she told him, keeping her voice firm.

Anne Marie hung up the phone and turned around to discover Ellen perched on a chair at the kitchen table, staring blankly into space. She had the end of a pencil clamped between her teeth.

"Are you doing your homework?" Anne Marie asked.

Ellen shook her head. "I'm making a list of Twenty Wishes."

"Oh, really?"

Ellen nodded. "Do you want to hear what I have so far?"

"I would." Anne Marie pulled out the chair next to her and sat down.

"One," Ellen announced with great formality. "Plant a garden."

"What kind of garden?"

"Flowers," Ellen said. "I read the book you gave me about that garden, remember?"

Anne Marie smiled approvingly. Of course. On Sunday she'd given her a copy of the Edwardian children's classic, *The Secret Garden*. Ellen was an advanced reader and had no difficulty with comprehension. Occasionally she'd asked about the meaning of a word. She'd loved the idea of the walled garden, hidden from the world, and had instantly identified with the story's orphaned young heroine.

"Is there any other kind of garden than flowers?"

"Vegetables."

"You can grow tomatoes?" Ellen asked in an excited

voice. "I like tomatoes a lot, especially when they're warm from the sun. I like them with salt."

Anne Marie looked at her curiously. "Did you ever have a garden before?"

Ellen lowered her gaze. "No... Grandma Dolores told me about warm tomatoes with salt. I've never had one but I know they'd be really good because my grandma said so."

"I like tomatoes, too." Anne Marie closed her eyes at the memory of working in her garden at the house she and Robert had owned. The smell of earth, the sun warm on her back... "Last summer I grew tomatoes right here, on my balcony."

The child seemed thoroughly confused by that.

"It was a container garden because I didn't have any-where to plant an actual garden."

"What about corn?"

"That might be a challenge, but I'll check into it. If you like, we can plant seeds in egg cartons and then once your grandmother's home again, I'll help you clear a small space in her yard for your very own garden."

"Really?" The girl's face shone with uncomplicated joy. "A garden," she breathed.

"Anything else on your list?"

Ellen nodded. "I want to bake cookies with Grandma Dolores."

"I bet she'd like that."

"She always said we could, but then she'd get tired or she wouldn't be feeling well and we never got to do it."

Anne Marie slipped her arm around Ellen's shoulders. "When your grandmother's back from the hospital, she'll be feeling much better and have a lot more energy, and I'm sure she'll want to bake cookies with you then."

"Oatmeal and raisin are my favorites." Ellen set the pencil down. "I couldn't think of anything else."

"What about something whimsical?"

Ellen turned to her, expression blank.

"Whimsical means fanciful—a wish that's not…serious, I suppose you could say. Something lighthearted, just for fun."

The end of the pencil returned to Ellen's mouth. "Do *you* have anything whi-whimsical on your list?" she asked.

Good question. "Not yet. Let's think about it." She stood to get three plates from the cupboard.

"Like what?"

"Well…" Anne Marie murmured. She looked at the child, then walked over to her own list.

11. Dance in the rain in my bare feet

"What did you write?" Ellen asked.

Anne Marie told her.

Ellen started to giggle. "That's silly. Aren't you afraid your clothes will get wet? Or you'll get mud between your toes?"

"I wouldn't care, especially if I was dancing with someone I loved." She opened the refrigerator and removed a bag of romaine lettuce and other salad ingredients. Anne Marie occasionally made salad for dinner; she wasn't afraid to add unusual ingredients, like walnut bits, cranberries, raw green beans, Chinese noodles, sunflower seeds, pickle slices, beets… Her inventions weren't always successful—the chopped anchovies came to mind—but they were usually interesting.

For Ellen's sake, she chose more conventional makings of cherry tomato, shredded carrots, cucumber and green pepper. Then, because she couldn't resist, she added crushed pretzels, guessing Ellen would enjoy that.

As she and Ellen set the table with a white cloth and some leftover St. Patrick's Day napkins, Anne Marie explained who Brandon was and said he'd be coming over for dinner. Ellen seemed a little nervous about meeting him and, perhaps, about sharing their private time together.

There was a knock at the back door just as Anne Marie put the salad in the middle of the table. "That's Brandon," she said, walking to the door as Baxter barked excitedly.

Her stepson entered the small apartment, both hands behind his back. With a sweeping gesture, he produced a bottle of her favorite wine and a bouquet of flowers. He kissed Anne Marie on the cheek, then presented the flowers to Ellen. "You must be the lovely Ellen. These are for you," he said.

Ellen gave Brandon a tentative smile. "I like flowers."

"Are you going to thank Brandon?" Anne Marie asked.

"Thank you."

"You're welcome, Ellen."

Anne Marie found a vase and helped Ellen arrange her bouquet. Then, without being asked, Ellen opened the silverware drawer and counted out what they needed, while Anne Marie got two wineglasses and one for juice. When they sat down to dinner, Ellen said grace.

Brandon's eyes met Anne Marie's as he bowed his head, and he murmured "Amen." Ellen insisted on saying a prayer before all their meals. Her grandmother had taught her that and it always made Anne Marie wonder how the woman's two daughters, presumably raised the same way, had turned out so badly.

Brandon raved about the casserole. "This is *really* good."

"Secret family recipe," Anne Marie told him with a smirk.

"Will you give it to my grandma?" Ellen asked, scraping up the last of the casserole from her plate.

"If you want me to."

"I'd like it, too," Brandon added. "Hey, I'll give it to one of my girlfriends to make."

"Hey, make it yourself."

"Fine," he laughed. "I will."

They finished their wine; then Brandon and Ellen cleared the table, while she made a pot of coffee.

"May I go to my room and read?" Ellen asked. She'd just started the Laura Ingalls Wilder series and Anne Marie knew she was eager to return to *Little House in the Big Woods*.

"Yes, Ellen, you may."

They watched as Ellen retreated to her bedroom, Baxter close behind. Brandon turned to Anne Marie, leaning casually back in his chair. "You'd make a good mother," he said thoughtfully.

"Thanks," she said, but it was a moot point. If she was going to have a child, there had to be a father, and she was nowhere near ready for another relationship. In a few months she'd be thirty-nine and soon after that it would simply be too late. She had no intention of doing what a few women she'd heard of had done—get pregnant via a willing "sperm donor," a man who would play no role in their babies' lives.

When the coffee had brewed she filled a mug for Brandon and one for herself before joining him at the table.

"Have you talked to Rebecca yet? My dad's assistant?" he asked.

He certainly hadn't delayed in getting to the point, even though she'd explicitly said she'd prefer not to discuss it.

Anne Marie let the question slide for a moment as she busied herself with the cream and sugar.

"You don't have to tell me if you don't want to," Brandon said with teasing sarcasm.

She sighed, giving up. "The short answer is no. The long answer is I'm not sure I ever will. If she comes forward and acknowledges the child is Robert's...then I'll deal with it. Not before."

"I can understand that," Brandon said after a long moment. "I want you to know that Mel genuinely regrets what happened."

Anne Marie shrugged it off. "How is your sister?"

"We talk every now and then. I have to say she seems a lot more serious now. More mature, you know?" He frowned. "When I called her last week, she told me she's on the outs with Mom."

That surprised Anne Marie. As far as she knew, Melissa and Pamela were close. Robert's ex-wife lived in England, where she worked for an international hotel chain. According to Robert, her devotion to her career had led directly to their divorce. Pamela had accepted a position that involved frequent travel, even though Robert had asked her to wait until the children were out of school. She'd refused and left him and their family for months on end.

"What's wrong between Melissa and her mother?"

Brandon shrugged. "She wouldn't tell me. When I pressed the issue, she changed the subject. She obviously doesn't want to talk about it, but she made it sound like she's busy with school and she probably is."

"She's graduating this year, isn't she?"

Melissa was completing an MBA program; she then planned to follow in her mother's footsteps, moving into hotel management.

Robert had always been proud of his children, and he'd often said they were the only good thing to come out of his marriage to Pamela.

"Yeah, she should be done in June."

"Is she still seeing Michael?"

"As far as I know. He's a good guy. I like him better than any of the other guys my sister's gone out with. Some of them were...well, put it this way." He reached for his coffee again. "Melissa's made some strange choices."

Before Anne Marie could respond, Ellen stepped into the room, a pad and pencil in her hand. "Is having a goldfish a wish or a goal?"

"Well, it's a little of both, I'd say."

"Okay."

"I thought you were reading," she said.

Ellen looked down, a tendency she had when she was afraid she might be in trouble. "I was reading, but then I thought of another wish. I want twenty, the same as you."

"I only have eleven written down so far."

Ellen nodded. "Can I put dancing in the rain with bare feet on my list, too?"

"Sure." Anne Marie grinned. "Just remember, there's no need to rush. Think carefully about each wish."

"Okay." Ellen returned to the bedroom, muttering quietly to herself.

That interruption generated a series of questions about Anne Marie's Twenty Wishes. She didn't mind Brandon's interest; in fact she was grateful for the change of subject and explained in detail what she and the other widows were doing.

A half hour later, after Brandon had finished his coffee, he left. It was eight-thirty, time to get Ellen ready for bed.

"Grandma sounded tired when I talked to her this afternoon," Ellen said, sliding her nightgown over her head, thin arms raised.

"She'll be tired for a long time. Heart surgery takes a lot out of a person. She's going to need plenty of rest."

Ellen seemed distressed by that. "But—"

"You'll be able to go home to your grandmother soon," Anne Marie promised quickly. She received daily updates on Dolores's condition and everything was progressing exactly as it should. In two or at most three weeks, she'd be back in her own home, with a visiting nurse to look in on her. Ellen would be returning to the only stable life she'd ever known.

Pulling back the sheets, Anne Marie tucked the child into bed.

"Can we say our prayers?" Ellen asked sleepily.

"Of course."

"Should I say the words out loud or should I just say them in my heart?" Ellen murmured. Most nights she'd prayed in silence, mouthing the words as Anne Marie watched.

"What do you usually do with your grandmother?"

"She likes me to say them out loud."

"Then do it like that," Anne Marie said. The child's simple faith touched her, reminding her of a time when she, too, had prayed. Anne Marie couldn't remember when she'd stopped or why. She'd just…gotten out of the habit, she supposed.

Ellen studied her. "You're supposed to hold my hands and close your eyes. That's what Grandma Dolores does."

"All right." She clasped Ellen's hands in hers and shut her eyes.

Apparently she'd satisfied Ellen, because the youngster began to speak. "God, it's me, Ellen, again." She prayed for her grandmother and thanked God for her teacher and her friends and went through a long list of subjects, from hoping she'd do well on tomorrow's spelling test to thanking God for her new green raincoat.

Anne Marie didn't want to interrupt, but *she* was the one who'd supplied the coat, not God.

"And thank you most of all for Anne Marie, so I didn't have to go to a foster home and amen," Ellen whispered.

"Amen," Anne Marie echoed. Her knees had started to hurt and she rose awkwardly to her feet. On impulse she bent over and kissed Ellen's forehead. "Good night, sweetie."

"Good night."

About ten, she took Baxter for a five-minute walk, keeping the apartment in sight. When she got back, the phone rang; it was Elise Beaumont. "I wondered when we'd connect," Anne Marie said after her initial greeting.

"Sorry to call so late."

"That's okay."

"The last couple of times I stopped by the bookstore, you were busy."

"I know."

"I wanted to ask how the conversation with Rebecca Gilroy went."

"Oh." That question just didn't seem to go away. "I heard you're working for Lydia now," she said instead.

"Don't try to distract me. Have you spoken to Rebecca?"

Anne Marie didn't understand why everyone seemed to think it was her responsibility to confront the other woman.

"You *have* spoken to her, haven't you?"

"No." She had good reasons for not contacting the woman who'd been sleeping with her husband—reasons that were no one's business but her own.

Why would she *want* to talk to this woman, who'd likely given birth to Robert's child?

Fifteen

Anne Marie tossed and turned all that night, and when she got up at seven, she doubted she'd had even two hours' sleep. Whenever she started to drift off, she'd jerk awake, unable to escape the image of Robert and his assistant together, arms and legs entwined. Anne Marie had only met Rebecca Gilroy a few times but remembered her well. Tall and curvy, auburn-haired and in her twenties. As she struggled to sleep, all she could see was the other woman with her swollen belly. Pregnant.

With Robert's child.

Ever since the dinner with Melissa, Anne Marie had tried hard to keep busy, not to think, not to dwell on the pain that threatened to swallow her whole. But then it would come back, refusing to leave until she acknowledged it.

No, she wouldn't confront Rebecca Gilroy. She couldn't see the purpose of exposing herself to that reality if she could avoid it.

With Baxter on his leash, Anne Marie walked Ellen to the bus stop, where a small group of youngsters waited, her eyes smarting from lack of sleep. She took her dog home and did a few household chores before going down to the bookstore at ten and officially opening it.

Lillie was there at five after. As soon as she saw Anne Marie, she frowned. "You look terrible."

"Thanks," Anne Marie said wryly. "Good morning to you, too."

"Is something wrong?" Lillie asked.

"I didn't sleep very well last night."

"Anything I can do to help?"

"No, but thanks for offering." She wasn't going to discuss this with one more person, even a friend as caring and sympathetic as Lillie.

Anne Marie turned on her computer to do an inventory check while Lillie roamed the shelves. A little while later, she brought an armload of books to the counter; she was a voracious reader and usually purchased hardcovers. Anne Marie could count on Lillie to buy as many as ten books a month. Her most recent selection included a couple of romances. This was a switch; her friend tended to read mysteries and thrillers. Anne Marie added up her purchases, which Lillie paid for with a debit card.

"Have you spoken to Elise lately?" Lillie asked as she slipped her card back into her wallet.

"She called last night."

"Did she mention her Twenty Wishes?"

Elise and Anne Marie had chatted about a number of things; however no topic had stayed in her mind beyond the first one Elise had brought up. "Not really."

Lillie shook her head. "We really need to meet again and update one another. I've taken action and I know you have, too. Sharing our lists would be an encouragement, don't you think?"

Anne Marie wasn't convinced of that, but arguing about

it required more energy than she had. Lillie suggested a day and time, and Anne Marie agreed. "We'll meet at my house next Thursday, the twenty-seventh," Lillie said, consulting an elegant little calendar she pulled out of her purse.

Anne Marie agreed to that, too.

"Barbie told me you're looking after a young girl," Lillie said next. "That's wonderful!"

Anne Marie was beginning to feel guilty accepting all this praise. The fact was, had there been any other alternative for Ellen, she would've been grateful.

"My wishes are coming along nicely," Lillie said, continuing the conversation. "I'm taking this very seriously, you know. It was exactly what I needed." She sighed. "I find myself thinking more and more about the things I'd like to do, to experience." She placed one hand over her heart. "I have a sense of…of *expectation* that I haven't felt in years. It's like I've finally given myself permission to do what *I* want."

Anne Marie hadn't felt any of that. Most of her wishes had to do with recovering from Robert's death. To sing, to laugh, to dance. None of those had come to pass yet and in her current frame of mind, she wasn't sure they would.

Feeling obliged to say something, she said, "Did I tell you I bought scrapbooking supplies and a binder for my wish list?"

Lillie straightened. "You did, and I like the idea very much. I've been planning to do it myself."

"You should," Anne Marie urged. She didn't hold an exclusive on the idea.

"I think we'd *all* profit from making a Twenty Wishes binder, don't you?"

Anne Marie nodded with a tired smile.

Lillie left a few minutes later, carrying two large bags,

and the day crawled from that point on. Anne Marie could hardly make the effort to smile. She could've phoned Theresa to fill in for her but didn't. Ever since Ellen had come to live with her, she'd called on her three part-time employees again and again. Since her other two were college students, they were in class on and off during the day. She didn't want to take advantage of Theresa's kindness, although she would gladly have gone upstairs and crept into bed, craving the oblivion of sleep.

When the school bus dropped Ellen on Blossom Street, the girl dashed into the bookstore, her eyes sparkling. "I got an A on my spelling test!"

Anne Marie tried to show her how pleased she was and wondered if she'd succeeded.

Ellen didn't seem to notice her exhaustion. "Can I show my grandma?" she asked eagerly.

"I…"

"You said we could visit her again on Tuesday, remember?"

Unfortunately Anne Marie did. "Sure," she said, taking a deep breath. Too many promises made to Ellen had been broken, and she refused to be guilty of that herself. Robert had promised to take her to Paris one day. And he hadn't. He'd promised to love her and be faithful. He hadn't done that, either.

She allowed Ellen to bring Baxter down to the store, and the two of them curled up in one of the big chairs. Ellen spelled each of the words from her test for the Yorkie, who appeared to listen intently.

At four Steve Handley arrived. He usually worked from four to six Monday to Wednesday and four to eight on Thursday and Friday. He often closed for her, and Anne Marie trusted him implicitly.

As soon as she'd handed everything over to Steve, she, Ellen and Baxter retreated to the apartment. Not up to making dinner, Anne Marie heated yesterday's leftover casserole for Ellen, adding an apple and a store-bought oatmeal cookie. Her own appetite was nonexistent.

The child ate silently, then placed her dishes in the sink.

"Are you ready to go?" Anne Marie asked.

Ellen turned to face her, eyes wide and hopeful. "I *can* visit Grandma Dolores?"

"You certainly can." God would bless her for this, Anne Marie told herself.

Ellen raced into her room and hurried back with her spelling test clutched in one hand. All the way to the hospital Ellen talked excitedly, about Baxter's progress with his new tricks and how she'd almost spelled *puzzle* with one *z* and a hundred other things she planned to tell Dolores. Anne Marie felt wretched. She'd been so consumed by her own troubles that she'd failed to realize how desperately the child missed her grandmother.

Ellen needed reassurance that Dolores was on the mend and that everything would soon return to normal. Anne Marie wasn't the only one whose life had been disrupted. The child must feel so lost and adrift without her grandmother's love and guidance.

Anne Marie had kept in touch with Dolores Falk by phone, and she'd called the hospital every day for information on the older woman's condition. Dolores was improving at a steady rate. The last time she'd spoken with the head nurse, Anne Marie had learned that Dolores would be transferred from the hospital to a nursing facility for at least a week before she went home.

Anne Marie was fortunate enough to find a parking space on the street and decided to view that as a reward for thinking of Ellen's needs rather than her own. Holding the child's hand, she walked briskly toward the hospital's main entrance.

"Will Grandma be able to talk more?" Ellen asked.

On their first visit the previous Saturday Dolores had a tube in her throat that prevented her from speaking in anything other than a hoarse whisper. "The tube's out, so she should be able to talk normally again," Anne Marie explained.

Dolores had slept through most of that visit, and afterward Ellen had seemed quieter than usual. The contrast between the child who'd listened to the Irish singers and the child who'd walked out of the hospital later that afternoon was striking. Anne Marie had tried to tell her that Dolores was doing well, but all Ellen saw was a very sick woman.

"Your grandmother's going to be so proud of you for getting an A," Anne Marie told her now.

"I know," Ellen said solemnly.

They passed the gift shop.

"Should we bring her flowers again?" Ellen asked, looking at the floral arrangements displayed in the window.

"I'm sure the ones we brought on Saturday are still fresh." After the concert on Saturday, they'd purchased white tulips and yellow daffodils from Susannah's Garden, the flower shop next to the bookstore. Dolores had hardly seemed aware of the bouquet, which, given the circumstances, was understandable.

They walked directly to the elevator and Ellen pushed the button for the fifth floor, which was reserved for surgical patients. The doors opened in front of the nurses' station.

When they entered the room, Dolores was sitting up in bed, watching the television mounted on the wall. The flowers in their vase rested on the stand beside her bed. Although the room was a semi-private, she was the only patient. The moment she saw Ellen, Dolores's expression changed to one of rapture. "Oh, my little Ellen, my little love."

"Grandma! Grandma!" Ellen rushed toward the hospital bed with such enthusiasm she bounded into the mattress.

"Oh, Ellen, it's so *good* to see you." Dolores turned off the TV, focusing on her visitors, and held out both arms.

Anne Marie lifted Ellen up for a moment so she could gently hug her grandmother. She was moved almost to tears by the deep affection between them. This was love in its purest form. A child and her grandmother.

"I got an A on my spelling test," Ellen said, thrusting the paper at Dolores.

"Oh, Ellen! I'm so pleased."

"She studied hard," Anne Marie said.

"This was all the spelling words since Christmas, too."

"*All* the words?" Dolores's eyes widened with appreciation.

"Yup, and Stevie Logue and me were the only kids who got an A."

"That's excellent, honey." Dolores reached for her pitcher of water. "Ellen," she said, "could you do me a favor? Would you please go to the nurses' station and ask if I can have some more ice?"

The little girl nodded and took the pitcher, obviously gratified to be performing this important task for her grandmother.

"How's she doing?" Dolores asked urgently.

Anne Marie smiled at her. "Really well."

"I knew I could trust you," Dolores said as tears filled

her eyes. "I hadn't even met you, but I knew you were the one from everything Ellen had to say about you."

"I'm happy to help." Anne Marie discovered this was the truth, that it had *become* the truth.

"Ellen likes you."

"I like her, too."

"If anything happens to me…" Dolores continued, leaning forward to clasp Anne Marie's arm.

Shock bolted through her. "You haven't had bad news, have you?" Surely the medical staff would've told her if that was the case. Still, she wasn't family, and she didn't know how liberal the hospital's policies were in regard to nonrelatives.

"No, no, I'm doing well, according to the doctor," Dolores said.

"Oh, thank goodness!" Anne Marie couldn't hide her relief.

"But I'm not a new dishwasher." Dolores smiled, releasing her grip on Anne Marie. "That's what the young woman who operated on me said. I don't come with a guarantee that all my parts are going to work perfectly for the next five years."

"Of course not. No one does."

"But… I feel better than I have in months."

That definitely boded well.

"Still," Dolores said thoughtfully, "one never knows."

Anne Marie swallowed. She wondered if Robert had any premonition when he woke up that it would be the last day of his life. She wondered if he'd experienced any warning signs. Had there been any pain? Nausea? Tingling in his fingertips? Had his left arm ached? Did he assume the pressure in his chest was just heartburn? If she'd been living with him at the time, would she have recognized what was happening and been able to help?

Anne Marie didn't have the answers to any of those questions and they would forever haunt her.

"One never knows," she echoed bleakly.

"I gave birth to two daughters," Dolores told her.

"I know."

"I tried to be a good mother after their father left me."

"I know," Anne Marie said again.

Once more there were tears in the older woman's eyes. "I have no idea where I failed and there's no going back. Candace and Clarisse," she whispered. "Such beautiful girls. And now…"

"I understand." Anne Marie spoke soothingly, seeing how distressed Dolores was.

Dolores seemed to reach some decision. She turned to Anne Marie and took her arm again. Her eyes were fierce. "You have to *promise* that if anything happens to me you won't let Ellen go back to her mother."

"But it's not up to—"

"She's on meth," Dolores broke in. "The last time I saw her was in court. Her hair was falling out and her teeth were rotting in her head and she's barely thirty years old. My daughter is killing herself."

"You have sole custody of Ellen?"

"Yes. Promise me you won't let Ellen go back to her."

"I'm sure the Child Protective Services wouldn't—"

"Promise me," Dolores insisted, her hand tightening on Anne Marie's forearm.

"But I—"

"I won't rest until I know Ellen will be with someone who loves her. Promise me."

Anne Marie could see that it would do no good to argue.

"I promise." She suspected the state would never allow it, but she had to calm the woman down and there was no other way to do it.

Dolores relaxed her hold on Anne Marie's arm. "Thank you," she breathed.

"*You're* the one who's going to raise Ellen," Anne Marie said. "You're going to get well and Ellen will go home…"

"Clarisse." Dolores's voice cracked.

Anne Marie already knew the second daughter was in prison.

"She's as bad as her sister."

"I'm so sorry."

Dolores looked away. "Maybe I should've had tighter control of them when they were teenagers."

"I…"

"I did my best but it wasn't enough. They got in with a bad crowd and before I knew it, they dropped out of school and started doing drugs…"

"I'm so sorry." Anne Marie wished she could think of something else to say. Something more useful.

"The state might try to give Ellen to Clarisse once she's out of prison. Ellen can't go with her, either. Understand?"

"I won't let that happen." Anne Marie had no idea how she was supposed to prevent it, should the state make that decision. She decided not to worry about any of this, since Dolores would probably live for years and would be taking care of Ellen herself.

As though suddenly exhausted, Dolores closed her eyes and fell back against the pillow.

Just then Ellen returned, escorted by one of the nurses, who left right afterward. Ellen held the plastic pitcher filled with ice and carefully set it on the stand next to the flowers. "Is Grandma sleeping?" she asked in a loud whisper.

When Dolores didn't open her eyes, Anne Marie figured she'd either drifted off or was close to it. Their conversation had drained her of strength; she was, after all, recovering from surgery. And—perhaps even more of a factor—she'd been recalling the bitterest regrets of her life.

"I got ice," Ellen said.

"She'll thank you later," Anne Marie told the girl. "But at least you had a chance to show her your test. Didn't you see how proud she was of you?"

Ellen nodded reluctantly.

"We should let her sleep."

"Okay." Still Ellen didn't seem ready to leave. "Would it be all right if I sat with her for a few minutes?"

There was only one chair by the bed, and Anne Marie was sitting there. Soon Ellen had climbed onto her lap. The even rise and fall of Dolores's chest, the regular cadence of her breathing, lulled Anne Marie into closing her eyes, too.

She didn't know how long she'd been dozing there when her head slumped forward and she realized Ellen had cuddled up in her arms with one cheek pressed against her shoulder. The child's weight was warm and oddly comfortable, and she would've been content to stay that way for a while.

"Did Grandma Dolores tell you who my daddy is?" Ellen asked.

Anne Marie wondered what had prompted that question. "No…"

"Oh." She sighed with disappointment.

"Do you remember him, Ellen?"

"No." Ellen sounded so sad that Anne Marie wrapped her arm more securely around the girl's thin shoulders. "He's on my wish list."

"Your daddy?"

"Yes, I want to see him."

Dolores had said that Candace, Ellen's mother, probably didn't even know who the father was. Anne Marie didn't want to encourage Ellen to pursue something that would bring her more unhappiness. But as Dolores had also said, you never knew. The man just might make an appearance in the child's life when she needed him most.

"We can look on your birth certificate, I guess." Perhaps the school had a copy, although Anne Marie wasn't sure they'd show it to her.

"I have six wishes now," Ellen stated proudly.

Six wishes.

Six reasons to hope.

"Are you ready to go home?" Anne Marie asked. It was nine o'clock now, and she was surprised they hadn't been told that visiting hours were over.

"Okay."

Ellen climbed down from her lap. "Thank you for bringing me to see Grandma Dolores."

"You're welcome."

"Thank you for telling me about the wishes, too."

Anne Marie nodded. For some reason the gloom of depression had lightened and the image of Robert and Rebecca had receded. Holding this child in her arms made everything else seem less important, less immediate.

Dolores snored softly on. Anne Marie held Ellen's hand and flicked the switch, darkening the room, and they returned to Blossom Street.

Sixteen

Lillie Higgins was meeting Jacqueline Donovan, her dearest friend on earth, for lunch. She wore a beige linen skirt and a jacket that showed off the pearls David had bought her in Hong Kong. Lillie was well aware that some transgression had elicited her husband's generosity.

The three-strand necklace was a guilt offering. She didn't know what had happened while he was in the Far East—or with whom—and she preferred it that way. Her husband generally gave her expensive gifts when he felt remorseful about something. That *something* always involved another woman.

Lillie had rarely worn the pearls until after David's death. Now it didn't seem to matter. They really were lovely and it didn't make sense to hide them in a drawer. She had no reason to feel guilty, so she'd begun to wear them regularly.

As she fastened the matching pearl earrings the phone rang. Lillie hesitated, tempted to let it ring. But Jacqueline was usually ten or fifteen minutes late, so Lillie decided to take the call.

"Hello?"

"Ms. Higgins?"

Lillie instantly recognized the voice of Hector Silva, the service manager at the BMW dealership.

"Hello, Mr. Silva," she said, unable to disguise her pleasure.

"I hope you don't mind that I'm phoning you."

"On the contrary, I'm delighted." And that was the truth. She hadn't expected him to contact her, and this came as a marvelous surprise.

"I'm calling to thank you for speaking to Mr. Sullivan."

"I'm sorry, who?"

"Mr. Sullivan owns the dealership. You phoned and left a message about me and the good service you received."

"Oh, yes." Lillie remembered that now. "You went above and beyond my expectations, and I wanted Mr. Sullivan to realize what a valuable employee he has in you."

"Thank you again."

"Mr. Silva, please, I'm the one who's indebted to you."

"Hector," he said. "We agreed to use first names," he reminded her.

She smiled at the genuine warmth in his voice. "And I'm Lillie."

"I wanted to inform you, Lillie, that as a direct result of your comments I was named employee of the month for February."

"Which you deserved."

"I…ah…" He hesitated and seemed about to say something more. "I know it's not—" Again he paused, as if unsure how to proceed.

"Yes?" Lillie's heart was in her throat. It might be presumptuous of her, but she had the distinct feeling that he was about to suggest they meet again.

"I hope you have a pleasant day," he finished in a rush.

"You, too." She didn't bother to hide her disappointment. Then, hoping to encourage him and let him know she'd welcome an invitation, she added, "Was there anything else, Hector?"

Her question was followed by a long pause. "Not really."

"Oh." She swallowed.

"Calling Mr. Sullivan was very nice of you," he said, rushing his words again. "I hope you're enjoying your new car."

"Very much, thank you, Hector."

"Goodbye, Lillie."

"Goodbye."

He didn't hang up right away and neither did she. Lillie closed her eyes, willing him to speak, willing him to suggest they see each other again. He didn't, and after a short pause she heard him disconnect. Her heart sank about as far as it could go. Well, that was that, she supposed. It was probably for the best—although it didn't *feel* that way—but she had to be reasonable. His social status was too different from hers and financially they were worlds apart. Hector understood that even if she didn't.

If she had a relationship with him, her friends would think she'd lost her mind. Well, maybe she had. Maybe she was tired of all the pretense that surrounded her life. She'd loved her husband, but her marriage had been a sham. When David had his affairs, she'd politely turned her head and looked the other way. Lillie had carried the knowledge and the shame that the man she loved, and had been completely faithful to, treated his marriage vows as if they were merely suggestions.

She fingered the pearls at her throat. She remembered the night David had given them to her. He'd stood behind her as she sat at her dressing table and draped them around her neck. In that moment it was all she could do not to rip them off. Although David could well afford the pearls, their price had been too high.

She and Hector Silva were little more than acquaintances, but Lillie instinctively recognized that this man would never cheat on his wife. Unlike David, Hector was a man who took his emotional commitments seriously. Anyone might ask how she could possibly know this about a man she'd only met a few times. But Lillie knew. Call it intuition or whatever you wanted. She just *knew*.

Feeling melancholy, she sighed, removing the car keys from her purse. She wouldn't hear from him again.

Lillie left the house to meet Jacqueline Donovan at the exclusive Seattle Country Club. The two of them had been members for years. They'd worked on any number of charitable projects together and been co-chairs of the Christmas Ball more times than she could recall.

When the news came that David and Gary had been killed in the plane crash, the one person Lillie had turned to for solace and advice had been Jacqueline. Barbie had her own intense grief to cope with and her sons to comfort; those three had formed a closed circle in the weeks after the accident. Jacqueline had stayed by Lillie's side for days, helping her deal with the multitude of immediate decisions. Her love and concern didn't end there, either. Jacqueline remained her friend while others had drifted away. She was also the only person Lillie had confided in about David's affairs.

Lillie pulled up in front of the club building and was instantly greeted by a valet. He didn't give her a voucher. None was necessary. Every employee of the club recognized her and her new vehicle.

"Ms. Donovan arrived two minutes ago," the valet told her.

"Thank you, Jason," she murmured and headed inside.

Sure enough, Jacqueline sat at their usual table, glancing over the menu. She wore her hair in her customary French roll and had chosen a Venetian glass necklace in teal and gold that stood out against her black pants and jacket. She put down the menu and smiled.

"It's not like you to be late," she said when Lillie joined her. She'd already ordered a bottle of their favorite wine, a New Zealand sauvignon blanc that the club kept in stock primarily for them.

"I answered the phone on my way out the door," she said, reaching for the menu, although she practically had it memorized. Naturally, it didn't include prices. A bill would be mailed at the end of the month with the accumulated charges.

"Nothing important, I hope."

"Not really." Lillie considered mentioning Hector but quickly dismissed the thought. Of all her friends, she trusted Jacqueline most, and yet...

A waiter came to their table, and Lillie decided on the Oriental salad; Jacqueline ordered blackened scallops.

"So," Jacqueline said, swirling the wine in her glass. "What's new with your Twenty Wishes?"

The last time they'd met for lunch, Lillie had been full of enthusiasm about her list. She'd talked nonstop, extolling the idea and describing her wishes—starting with the red BMW.

"The widows are meeting next week. We're going to talk about our wishes and the progress we've made."

Jacqueline sipped her wine. "This is *such* a good idea. Ever since you told me about it, I've been planning to make my own list."

"You should," Lillie said, nodding vigorously.

"It's certainly given you a new lease on life."

"You think so?"

"I haven't seen you look this happy in years."

She wanted to say something, to explain that the Twenty Wishes weren't entirely responsible for this "new lease on life." But she couldn't; she had to accept that she wouldn't be hearing from Hector again. Ironically, he was the embodiment of her most longed-for wish—a decent, honorable man. A man she couldn't have. A wish she might never fulfill. The whole thing was just so hopeless.

"Actually, I've met someone." Lillie couldn't imagine what had made her say that. She wanted to snatch the words back the instant they left her mouth.

Jacqueline nearly tipped over her wineglass. "When? How? Who? You haven't said anything about this!"

"It's just that, well…"

"Yes?"

Lillie drew in a deep breath. "Before you get all excited, let me say this isn't anyone you know."

"He's not a member of the club?" Much of their social life revolved around the country club, although both had plenty of friends outside it.

"No."

"Why the big secret?"

"It isn't a big secret. I should never have mentioned it." Lillie could feel her face heating up. "Forget I said a word."

"No way! You're dying to tell me, I know you are. Spill it."

"I've never been on a date with him, so there's nothing to tell you."

Jacqueline frowned. "Why not?"

"For one thing, he hasn't asked and…and, well, I doubt he ever will, so there's no point in discussing this any further."

"He's younger, isn't he?"

"No! Wipe that silly grin off your face, Jacqueline Donovan. It's not like that at all. He's shy and I think he'd like to ask me out but he hasn't." She was saying more than she'd ever intended and desperately wished she'd never introduced the subject.

Jacqueline leaned back in her chair and a smile quivered at the edges of her mouth. "You should ask *him* out," she insisted.

"What?"

"I mean it. In our generation, the men always did the asking, but times have changed. If you're interested in this man—this stranger you refuse to tell your very best friend about—then all I can say is that you need to take the initiative."

Lillie stared across the table at her, and Jacqueline stared right back. "I can't!"

That went against every dictate of her upbringing. Ask Hector out on a date? It was a preposterous suggestion. An outrageous idea.

Jacqueline simply shook her head. "You *can* ask him, and you will. Or...or I'll do it for you."

At that Lillie giggled. "Don't be ridiculous."

"Why is that ridiculous? You're a lovely woman, Lillie, and a beautiful person besides. You deserve happiness. Isn't that what the Twenty Wishes are all about? Going after the things you want in life. Places to see, people to meet, experiences to live. Don't hold back now. Go for it!"

Could Jacqueline be right?

Without some kind of pledge from her, Jacqueline was never going to shut up about this. "I'll consider it." That was the best she could do for now.

"Good." Jacqueline nodded, obviously pleased.

Lillie relaxed, wondering how she could possibly approach Hector. Oh, for heaven's sake, what did she know about such things? If David was alive, she could've asked him. He was the one with all the dating experience. That thought produced a hysterical giggle that she tried, unsuccessfully, to swallow.

Jacqueline regarded her closely. "What's so funny?"

Embarrassed, Lillie shook her head. "You—saying I should contact my friend and ask him out." She waved her hand. "I was just thinking— Never mind."

"No, tell me," Jacqueline insisted.

So she did, and soon they were both laughing.

The waiter brought their lunch and automatically refilled their glasses.

"You're going to do it," Jacqueline said firmly, leaving no room for argument. She reached for her fork.

"I—"

"Yes, you are," Jacqueline returned. "You want to see this man, don't you?"

Lillie gave a barely perceptible nod.

"If you need me standing by to encourage you, then that's what I'll do."

Lillie felt a moment's hope. No, it was impossible. Even if she did find the courage, she didn't know what kind of outing to suggest. Perhaps a movie? Barbie seemed to be going to the movies a lot these days.

"You're looking serious now," Jacqueline said.

"He might refuse," she blurted out. "I might've completely misread him."

"So what?" Her friend shrugged as if this was an insignificant concern. "Nothing ventured, nothing gained."

"But…"

"Would you *stop*," Jacqueline said.

Lillie had yet to try a single bite of her salad. "You're right, you're right." She picked up her fork, then laid it down again. "The problem is, we don't have a single thing in common."

"Except for the fact that you're attracted to him and I assume he is to you."

"Jacqueline, I *am* attracted to him. I really am. I go to sleep thinking about him. I yearn for him…" Her face flushed with embarrassment.

"Have you analyzed what's so attractive about him?"

She knew the answer immediately. "Oh, yes—he's kind and gentle and honorable. He loves his children and I'm positive he was a faithful husband." Just talking about Hector was enough to bring tears of longing to her eyes.

"You want him?" Jacqueline whispered the question.

"Not the way you're thinking." This wasn't merely physical desire, although he was a good-looking man and late at night she'd fantasized about his mouth, his hands… What she felt was, above all, *emotional*—that need for true kinship, that recognition of another's soul. She tried to explain her feelings to her friend.

"This must be one helluva man," Jacqueline commented.

"He is."

"Then don't wait, Lillie," Jacqueline said earnestly. "I wasted too many years of my life before Reese and I…"

She let the rest fade, but Lillie knew what she meant. Jacqueline's marriage had been like her own. She and Reese had lived as strangers for years. Jacqueline had reason to believe her husband had a mistress, and as a result she'd moved into a spare bedroom. They'd remained stiffly polite, ignoring each other as much as possible in the privacy of their home, acting like a loving couple outside it. No one had suspected. No one knew the truth about them.

Except Lillie.

She'd been able to identify the signs because she'd lived the same scenario.

Then, shortly before David's accident, something

changed between Jacqueline and Reese. Almost overnight they set aside their differences and became lovers again. They'd even traveled to Greece on a second honeymoon. The love was back in their marriage and in their lives.

Lillie never learned exactly what had brought about the change, although she suspected that Tammie Lee, the Donovans' daughter-in-law, had something to do with it. When Paul had first brought home his young bride from Louisiana, Jacqueline had been horrified. Tammie Lee, with her southern drawl, wasn't the daughter-in-law she'd wanted.

Personally, Lillie had instantly liked the young woman. She was sweet and genuine and good-humored, even if she did talk about recipes for pickled pigs' feet and boiled peanuts.

It'd taken Jacqueline months to accept the idea of her only son married to Tammie Lee and then gradually, the relationship between the two women had undergone a shift. Not long after that, the relationship between Jacqueline and her husband had improved, too. She and Reese had clearly achieved some sort of reconciliation.

For a while Lillie had been jealous. She wanted the same happiness Jacqueline had rediscovered in her marriage. She'd hoped for that kind of turnaround in her own—but it never happened.

And yet, it wasn't too late for a change in her *life*. It wasn't too late to fulfill a wish...

She'd do it.

She'd defy her upbringing and find a way to ask Hector Silva on a date.

Seventeen

Monday morning Anne Marie was finishing up the sale of a hardcover novel for one of her favorite customers, Larry Barber, a retired accountant, when Lillie and Barbie entered Blossom Street Books. Mother and daughter had never looked better. In fact, Anne Marie caught herself staring. A transformation had taken place in both women and while it might not be apparent to anyone else, Anne Marie noticed. Trying to discern what was different about them, she decided it was a new sense of *life*. They seemed to shimmer with it.

They talked animatedly to each other while Anne Marie completed the sale.

As Larry signed the charge slip, Anne Marie smiled a warm welcome at her friends. He wasn't in any hurry to leave. Since his wife had died, he was lonely and came to the store for conversation with Anne Marie as much as he did for reading material. When business was slow, Anne Marie didn't mind. She knew what it was to be alone and to crave companionship. This morning, however, she was impatient to be with Lillie and Barbie.

Larry must have realized the other women wanted to

talk to her and, reaching for his purchase, thanked Anne Marie and headed out the door.

The minute he left, Barbie shimmied up to the counter. "I found a belly dancing class," she announced and threw her arms in the air as if she was about to give a demonstration.

"Belly dancing?" Anne Marie repeated. "You talked about that during our Valentine's get-together."

"It's on my wish list," Barbie informed her. "I'm so excited I can hardly stand it."

Lillie rolled her eyes playfully. "My daughter sometimes shocks even me."

Barbie waved off her mother's comment. "Oh, honestly, Mother, I've wanted to learn how to belly dance for ages."

"You never said anything to me."

"I know—I thought about it a lot, but it seemed so...oh, I don't know, silly, I guess. Then, when I read about a class at the Fitness Center, I decided to learn how to do this. I'm not putting it off any longer."

"That's great," Anne Marie said. She had an announcement of her own. "I signed up for a knitting class." On Saturday, Lydia had told her that the long-delayed beginners' class would start the following Wednesday at twelve-thirty.

"Is Elise teaching the class?" Lillie asked.

Anne Marie nodded. Elise had told her that working at the yarn store had been one of her wishes.

These lists of Twenty Wishes were influencing all their lives—and those of others, too. For instance, Elise's wish had been a solution to Lydia's problem of teaching too many classes. It seemed that every time Anne Marie went into A Good Yarn, Margaret was complaining that Lydia shouldn't be taking on as much as she did. Now Elise would fill in as sales help when necessary and teach three classes. In addition to the beginners' class, she'd be teaching a session on knitting with beads and another on felted purses.

For the moment, Anne Marie was content with the beginners' class. Once she learned the basics, she'd venture out into more complicated techniques and projects.

Already she could see that knitting was something she'd enjoy. At noon she'd go and choose her yarn for the first class, two days from now. Timing would be tight, since Anne Marie was still joining Ellen for lunch on Wednesdays, even though the girl was living with her.

"I was thinking I'd have everyone over for dinner," Lillie murmured, breaking into Anne Marie's thoughts.

She must have responded with a blank look because Lillie immediately said, "For our meeting? To discuss our wishes."

"Oh, right."

"Is Thursday still okay?"

"Yes…" Anne Marie returned with some hesitation. "But remember Ellen will be with me."

"That's fine," Lillie said.

"You're sure?" Anne Marie could probably find someone to watch Ellen if she had to.

"Of course she can come," Lillie was quick to tell her. "We'd love to have Ellen."

Anne Marie grinned, remembering how intently Ellen had worked at compiling her own list. "Did I mention Ellen's got Twenty Wishes, too?"

Mother and daughter shared a smile.

"My friend Jacqueline Donovan is making one, as well," Lillie added. "The minute I mention the idea to anyone, they decide to make their own. Jacqueline told me the first wish on her list is to ride a camel in Egypt and see the pyramids. She also wants to sleep under the desert sky."

"Jacqueline? Camping?" Barbie said incredulously. "That woman likes her luxuries."

"I know, that was my reaction, too." Lillie shrugged in amusement. "Who knew?"

"I guess it's like me and belly dancing," Barbie said. "It was in the back of my mind, just a vague…whimsy, I guess you could say, but it didn't enter my consciousness until I started working on my list of wishes. Sometimes I think we're afraid to admit we want certain things. Especially things that contradict the image we have of ourselves."

"Or the way others think of us," Lillie said.

"Right."

A customer walked in the door.

Lillie glanced over her shoulder and then back at Anne Marie. "Thursday night, then. Shall we say six?"

"I'm looking forward to it." And she was. Her list of wishes was growing and it wasn't as difficult to come up with ideas as it had originally been. All at once a whole world of wishes, of desires and possibilities, had opened up to her, ideas that had seemed beyond the scope of her imagination only a few weeks ago. Perhaps her heart had finally, gradually, begun to mend. She had fifteen wishes now.

12. Take a cake-decorating class and bake Ellen a huge birthday cake

13. Practice not-so-random acts of kindness at least once a week

14. Ride the biggest roller coaster in the world at Six Flags in New Jersey

15. Visit the Civil War battlefield in Gettysburg and then go to Amish country

That evening as Anne Marie put away the dinner dishes, Ellen sat at the kitchen table, doing her homework. Her ankles were demurely crossed, her entire demeanor intent.

Ellen had spoken with her grandmother before dinner, and so had Anne Marie. Dolores was regaining her strength. It wouldn't be long before Ellen could return to her home and all that was familiar.

"Do you need me to go over your spelling with you?" Anne Marie offered as she wiped the countertop.

"No, thank you."

"Don't you have a test tomorrow?"

"Yes, but I already memorized all the words," Ellen said proudly.

"On the very first day?"

Ellen nodded. "I did that after I took Baxter for a walk when I got home."

Anne Marie wasn't sure how Baxter would do when Ellen went back to her grandmother's. The eight-year-old had completely spoiled him. Every day after the school bus dropped her off, Ellen ran up the stairs to their apartment and lavished Baxter with love and attention. Anne Marie walked her dog twice every day and once in the evening. Now, however, Ellen took over for her in the afternoon. Anne Marie used to take him to the alley behind the store. Not Ellen. She paraded him up and down Blossom Street with all the ceremony of visiting royalty. Needless to say, Baxter loved their excursions.

Cody, Lydia's stepson, had recently come by with his dog, Chase, and the two dogs and children had quickly become friends. The dogs made quite a pair; Chase was a hefty golden retriever and Baxter was tiny by comparison. Like many small dogs, Baxter wasn't intimidated by the bigger dog's size, and the two of them marched side by side, looking for all the world like Laurel and Hardy.

In addition to Lydia, Ellen had made friends with several of the other business-owners. It wasn't uncommon for her to return with a carnation given to her by Susannah or a cookie from Alix at the French Café.

"Can I watch TV when I finish my homework?" Ellen asked, glancing up from her arithmetic.

"Okay." Anne Marie was looking forward to sitting down in front of the TV, too. She'd gone to A Good Yarn on her lunch break to buy the necessary knitting supplies. With the extra classes and increased business, the shop was now open six days a week. Elise had helped Anne Marie select her yarn and needles. The choices seemed endless, and after much debate, she'd decided on a soft washable wool in lavender to make a lap robe for Dolores Falk.

Because Anne Marie was so eager to learn, Elise had taught her how to cast on and showed her the basic knit stitch. To her delight, Anne Marie had picked it up without a problem.

An hour later, Anne Marie and Ellen sat together on the sofa, watching the Family Channel. Wanting to practice what she'd learned, Anne Marie took out the needles and a skein of yarn.

"What are you doing?" Ellen asked.

"Knitting," she said, adding "I hope," under her breath.

"Grandma Dolores used to knit."

Anne Marie nodded.

"She said she'd teach me."

Again Anne Marie acknowledged the comment with a

slight inclination of her head as she concentrated on casting on stitches.

"Is it hard?"

"Not really."

"Can I watch you?"

"Sure."

Ellen scooted closer and stared fixedly as Anne Marie attempted what Elise called a knitted cast-on. The term didn't mean anything to her; all she wanted to do was get stitches onto the needle.

"That's knitting?" Ellen said.

Anne Marie paused. "I think so."

Ellen removed her shoes and stood on the sofa to get a better view.

Suddenly she bounded off the sofa and dashed into her bedroom. She was back an instant later with a pad and paper.

"What's that for?" Anne Marie asked as the youngster skidded to a stop, barely missing the coffee table.

"My Twenty Wishes. I want to learn how to knit, too."

Anne Marie grinned at her. "How about if I teach you what I know?"

"You mean *now?*" The girl's eyes grew round.

"Why not?"

"Okay." Ellen leaped back onto the sofa, sitting close beside Anne Marie.

"According to Elise…"

"Mrs. Beaumont?"

"Yes, Mrs. Beaumont. There are actually only two basic stitches. The first is called the knit stitch and the second is a purl stitch."

"Okay," Ellen said again, nodding sagely.

"So far, I just know how to do the knit stitch. I'll learn how to purl in the first class."

"You haven't taken a real class yet?"

"No. I'm signed up, though."

"Oh."

"In other words, Ellen, I don't know all that much, but I'm willing to show you what I can do. If you like it, I'll take you to the yarn shop and let you pick out your own needles and yarn."

"Really?" Ellen was beside herself with excitement. "*Really?* Really?"

"Yes, really," Anne Marie responded, smiling.

For the next forty minutes, the television show was forgotten as Anne Marie showed Ellen what Elise had taught her that day. Ellen didn't catch on as easily as Anne Marie, but she was, after all, only eight.

Anne Marie was pleased with the child's determination to learn. Before the evening was over, Ellen was every bit as proficient as Anne Marie.

"I want to knit something for Grandma Dolores," Ellen stated. "Something pretty."

"What about a scarf?" Anne Marie suggested. She'd seen several exquisite ones at the shop. Elise had explained that these elaborate scarves had been knit using only the basic stitch she'd taught Anne Marie that very day.

"For her to wear to church," Ellen continued excitedly. "I'll give it to her when she comes home from the hospital."

"That's a very good idea."

Ellen finished the row and was about to start another when Anne Marie noticed the time. The evening had simply slipped away. It used to be that the hours she spent in the apartment moved so slowly she seemed aware of every passing minute.

"It's nine o'clock," Anne Marie said. "You should've been in bed half an hour ago."

"Is it nine *already?*" Ellen protested, but she couldn't hold back a yawn.

"I'm afraid so. We'll knit again tomorrow night," Anne Marie promised.

Ellen set down the needles and yarn and stumbled toward her room, yawning every step of the way.

"Call me when you're ready for your prayers, sleepyhead."

"Oh…kay."

A few minutes later, Ellen called out that she was ready. They followed the same routine as when Ellen lived with her grandmother, which meant that Anne Marie listened to the girl's prayers. She'd been saying them aloud for the last while.

Kneeling by the sofa bed, Anne Marie propped her elbows on the mattress, closed her eyes and bowed her head. Ellen's prayers didn't vary much. First, she asked God to help her grandmother get better. Then she asked Him to bless a number of people, Anne Marie and Baxter included, with lengthy descriptions of each. Finally, she gave thanks for the day's small triumphs. At the end of the seemingly interminable list, she said "Amen."

"Amen," Anne Marie echoed. "Good night, Ellen." She drew the covers more firmly around her and was about to get up when Ellen threw both arms around Anne Marie's neck and hugged her tightly. "Thank you for teaching me to knit."

"You're welcome," she said, hugging her back. Getting to her feet, she turned out the light, then tiptoed out of the room. As was her habit, she left the door slightly ajar.

It wasn't until Anne Marie had stepped into the hallway

that she realized something—this was the first time Ellen had actually hugged her. The night Anne Marie had gone to Dolores Falk's home, Ellen had fallen weeping into her arms, but that wasn't a real hug. Not like the one she'd just received.

Anne Marie stood right where she was and savored the moment. She felt loved and needed in a way she never had before.

It was like the return of warmth after the coldest winter of her life.

Eighteen

"**Y**ou came!" Tessa Bassett said with unrestrained glee when Barbie stepped forward to purchase her movie ticket. The teenager's face was flushed with excitement, and she leaned forward, lowering her voice. "He's here."

"Mark?" Barbie could hardly believe it. She hadn't expected this, but it shouldn't surprise her. Mark was definitely intrigued, even if he resisted her. Despite his hostility he hadn't really wanted to scare her off. Or maybe he was testing *her* interest. At any rate, Barbie saw the first substantial crack in that impervious exterior of his.

Mark was back. For that matter, so was she.

"He said he wasn't going to ever come on a Monday again—but now he has. I wanted to call you but I didn't know your last name, so I couldn't. I just hoped you'd be back and you are." This was all said in one breath. While she was speaking, Tessa slipped her the movie ticket and held out her hand for the money.

"What movie am I seeing?"

"A horror flick."

"Oh…"

"You don't like horror movies?"

"Not particularly."

"Oh." Tessa's face fell. "Do you want to see something else? You don't, do you? Because I think my uncle Mark likes you. Only he's afraid 'cause, after the accident, his wife divorced him and he's never heard from her again. You're the first woman he's even noticed since then."

Barbie stared at her, appalled. This ex-wife of his sounded like a shallow, selfish woman. Whatever happened to "for better, for worse"? Marriage vows didn't become null and void if one of the partners got sick or hurt. She knew without a second's hesitation that she and Gary would have stuck by each other, regardless of circumstances.

She sighed. "I suppose I could watch a horror movie," she said. "How bloody is it?"

Tessa grimaced, wrinkling her nose. "Real bloody."

"Are there dismembered body parts?" That was the worst, in Barbie's opinion.

Tessa nodded reluctantly. "But he came back! That's big."

Undecided, Barbie chewed on her lower lip. Tessa was right; neither of them had expected Mark to return. Barbie wasn't sure why she'd come—force of habit? Hope?

"Just go," Tessa urged. "Don't look at the screen. Close your eyes and plug your ears. That's what I do."

Other than the thought of having to watch the dispersing of gore and guts, choreographed to loud, pounding music, Barbie couldn't have said what was stopping her. So the movie wasn't exactly her choice. So what? She'd be with Mark and wasn't that the whole point of being here?

"Okay," she said with a deep breath. "I'll do it."

"Terrific!"

She just prayed she wouldn't have nightmares for the rest of her life.

"Let me know what happens, okay? With Uncle Mark, I mean," Tessa said. "My parents and my grandmother want to know, too."

"Okay." That meant the whole family was in on this, which was encouraging.

Barbie took her time, waiting until the last possible minute before slipping into the darkened theater. She purchased her popcorn and soda and lingered in the lobby until the show was about to start.

When she walked into the theater, the previews had already begun. She made her way to the row where Mark had parked his wheelchair, the same as usual. As she had previously, she sat one seat away from him.

He turned and stared at her in feigned surprise. "What are you doing here?" he whispered.

She could act as well as he could. "Oh, hello," she said brightly. "Is that you again?"

For a moment she suspected the hint of a smile. She turned back to the screen just in time to see an ax-murderer heave his weapon of death into a wall next to a trembling woman's head. Unable to stop herself, she gasped aloud and nearly dropped her popcorn.

"Frightens you, does it?" Mark asked in a far too satisfied tone. "Might I remind you these are only the previews."

"Yikes." She gritted her teeth.

Mark laughed, causing a woman behind him to make a shushing sound. *"Yikes,"* he repeated, lowering his voice. "Is that the best you can do?"

"Might I remind you I have sons."

"And you're a *lady*, right?" He spoke as if he intended that to be an insult.

"As a matter of fact, yes," she said stiffly. "I know all the words you do. I merely choose not to say them."

"I doubt it," he muttered, then settled back in his wheelchair to watch the movie, which was just getting started.

He gave every appearance of enjoying it, but as far as Barbie was concerned, this was torture. She'd always avoided being around when her sons watched horror DVDs with the bloodthirsty gusto of teenage boys. Now she squirmed in her seat, covered her face frequently and dashed out of the theater twice. It was even worse than she'd expected. Special effects being what they were, little was left to the imagination.

Barbie knew very well that Mark had planned this. He'd guessed—and guessed right—that she'd hate a movie like *The Axman Cometh* and had intentionally subjected her to an hour and a half of disgusting violence. The more she thought about it, the more irritated she became. And yet, she was determined to prove she could take it. Even if she couldn't.

After her second escape, when she'd hurried into the foyer to avoid watching another horrific scene, Mark leaned toward her and asked, "Are you going to finish that popcorn?"

"How can you possibly eat?" she snapped.

His grin seemed boyish as he reached for her bag and helped himself to a huge handful. Oh, yes, she thought grimly, he was enjoying her discomfort.

The movie wasn't actually all that long but it seemed to drag on for hours and hours and hours. The music, the tension, the blood, the *stupidity* was simply too much. By the time the movie ended, Barbie felt drained. The lights came up and the twenty or so viewers filed out of the theater. Mark stayed put and so did Barbie.

Finally she turned to him. "You did that on purpose, didn't you?"

"Did what?" he asked innocently.

Barbie wasn't fooled. She also decided that if this was a test, she'd failed. He knew she wanted to be with him, and because of that she'd endure this…this torture. She began to wonder if Tessa and her family had it all wrong. Maybe Mark wasn't attracted to her. Maybe he was just trying to punish her. Barbie began to mistrust her own intuition, her certainty that he reciprocated her interest. If he meant to signal that he didn't want her to bother him again, perhaps she should listen.

Fine. She would.

Barbie stood and, without another word, walked out of the theater.

Tessa, who'd been busy both times she'd fled into the lobby, was waiting for her.

"Well?" the girl asked anxiously.

"I don't care if I ever see your uncle again," Barbie said flatly.

Tessa's mouth fell open.

"What?"

"You heard me. He's rude and arrogant and…and…" She tried to think of a word that adequately described him. "Mean," she concluded. Making her sit through that debacle of a movie was downright mean.

"What did he say?" Tessa demanded, trotting alongside her.

"He didn't have to say anything. I got the message."

"Tell me," Tessa pleaded. "My mom and grandma are gonna bug me if I don't tell them what happened."

"Let me put it succinctly. Mark isn't interested. Period. If you think he is, then you and your family are sadly mistaken." Hearing his wheelchair behind her, Barbie whirled around to face him, ignoring the curious bystanders arriving for the next movie. "Isn't that right, Mark?"

Mark was silent.

"You like her, don't you, Uncle Mark?"

"I came to see a movie," he responded, his voice impassive. "If I wanted to find my perfect match, I would've gone online. She *is* right. I'm not interested."

Barbie tossed the girl an I-told-you-so look and stalked out. She was all the way to the exit when Mark called her name.

"What?" she asked angrily. "Don't worry," she told him before he could say a word. "I won't make the mistake of sitting next to you again—at any movie."

He blinked, then shrugged as if it made no difference to him. "Whatever."

Over the years, Barbie had come to hate that word and its connotation of teenage apathy. With as much dignity as she could gather, she continued toward the parking lot.

She was surprised when Tessa ran out of the building after her. "He didn't mean anything," she said breathlessly. "How would he know you hated scary movies? He just wanted to find out if you'd be willing to see something besides a romantic comedy. The least you can do is give him another chance."

"Why are you trying so hard?" Barbie asked. She was willing to accept that she'd made a mistake and move on. As attractive as she found Mark, she wasn't going to invite his rejection over and over again.

"You *have* to give him another chance," Tessa said.

"Why?"

Tessa paused, then answered on a heavy sigh. "Because my uncle Mark deserves to be loved." Her eyes pleaded with Barbie's. "This is new to him. He married his high school girlfriend and never loved anyone else and then she dumped him after the accident…" She gulped in a breath. "I'm positive he likes you—only he doesn't know how to show it."

Barbie hesitated. If anything about this entire evening astonished her, it was that Mark hadn't come outside and insisted his niece mind her own business. Delving inside her purse, she searched for a business card. "Okay, fine. Give him this and tell him the next move is his."

Tessa's face shone with eagerness as she nodded. "Great! Thank you so much. Thank you, thank you. You won't be sorry, I promise."

That remained to be seen.

Feeling wretched, Barbie did what she always did when she needed solace—she drove to her mother's house.

Lillie opened the door and immediately asked, "What's wrong?" Without delay she led her into the kitchen. "It isn't the boys, is it?"

Barbie swallowed hard and shook her head.

Hands on her hips, Lillie stood in the middle of her beautiful, gleaming kitchen. "Should I put on coffee or bring out the shot glasses?"

Barbie managed to smile. "This time I think I need both."

Lillie took a whiskey bottle from the small liquor cabinet in the kitchen, then started a pot of coffee. That involved first grinding beans, a production Barbie lacked the patience to bother with.

"So, tell me what happened," Lillie said when she'd made two Irish coffees. She sat on the stool at the counter next to Barbie and they silently toasted each other with the mugs.

"I saw Mark again."

Her mother nodded. "The man you met at the theater."

"Yes." She hadn't told Lillie much about him, and with

good reason. As soon as her mother learned he was in a wheelchair, she'd find a dozen reasons to dissuade her from pursuing him.

Barbie already knew a relationship with Mark wouldn't be easy. She'd done her homework. All right, she'd looked up a few facts about paraplegics on the internet. Even his anger with the world wasn't unusual. Until this evening, she'd assumed she was prepared to deal with it. Apparently not.

Lillie gestured for Barbie to continue. "And…"

"And he…he isn't interested."

Lillie cast her a look of disbelief. "That can't be true. You're gorgeous, young, accomplished—and a lovely person. Is something wrong with him?"

"Not really."

"He's not…"

"No, Mother, he's not gay. Or married." Barbie wondered how much more she should explain.

Lillie studied her and raised one elegantly curved eyebrow. "What aren't you telling me?"

Barbie should've known her mother would see straight through her prevarication.

Lillie's voice grew gentler. "What is it, honey?"

Barbie sighed. "If I tell you, I'm afraid you'll discourage me, and I don't think I could bear that just now."

For a long moment her mother didn't respond. "It's odd you should say that, seeing I have something I wanted to discuss with you and…and haven't, for the very same reason."

"What?" Barbie's curiosity was instantly piqued. She couldn't imagine her mother keeping anything from her. They were each other's support system, especially since David and Gary had died. But then, she'd never supposed she'd ever hide secrets from Lillie, either. Obviously they were both guilty of deception.

Lillie cleared her throat. "I... I recently met someone myself."

Barbie was stunned. "You haven't said a word."

Her mother avoided eye contact. "I'm afraid if I mention...my friend, *you'll* discourage *me*." She picked up her coffee and took a deep swallow. "This man I met—I believe we're both afraid of what others will think," she added. "Jacqueline urged me to ask him out, since he seems reluctant to approach me. But women of my generation don't do things like that. Yet I find the idea so appealing, I'm willing to put aside everything I've had ingrained in me all these years just for the opportunity to spend time with him again."

Lillie's cheeks were flushed and her hands trembled slightly as she raised the mug to her lips. It might've been the whiskey, but Barbie doubted that. There was more to this. Her mother was the most competent, composed woman she'd ever known and her being so flustered and unnerved over a man was completely out of character.

"Mom, you don't need to worry what I think."

"But I do. You're my daughter and, well...okay, I'm just going to blurt it out." Lillie straightened her shoulders. "He's the service manager at the car dealership."

Barbie couldn't help it; her jaw dropped. Her mother was attracted to a mechanic—a man with grease under his fingernails? Lillie Higgins, society matron, and a *mechanic?* Instantly warnings rose in her mind. This man must know that her mother had money. Lillie was lonely and vulnerable, easy prey. Her usual common sense had evidently deserted her, and she needed protection from this gigolo or whatever he was.

Barbie saw that her mother was waiting for her reaction, so she said, "I…see."

Lillie downed the last of her Irish coffee. "His name is Hector Silva."

This was as shocking as the fact that he was a mechanic. "He's Hispanic? Is he legal?"

"Yes! Of course! Hector's a citizen. He's decent and hardworking and kind." She hiccuped once, then covered her face. "This is even worse than I thought it would be," she moaned.

"No, Mom, really, I apologize. That was a stupid question. It's just… I don't know what to think." She'd assumed her mother couldn't surprise her; she'd assumed wrong. Of all the men who'd love to date her mother, Lillie had fallen for a mechanic?

Lillie dropped her hands. "I believe I know what you're trying to say," she said in a cold voice. "And I'm disappointed in you."

"I'm sorry," Barbie mumbled. But the image of her mother with this man refused to take shape in her mind.

Her mother motioned toward her. "It's your turn."

"But…"

"Tell me what the problem is with this Mark. Why you didn't want to say anything. Is he too old? Too young? Some kind of addict?"

"None of those." Like her mother, she squared her shoulders and expelled her secret in a single breath. "He's paralyzed from the waist down."

Lillie closed her eyes briefly. "Oh, Barbie."

It was just as she'd expected. Annoyed, she slid off the stool. "I knew it! I should've realized you'd react like this. I wish I hadn't said anything." Her annoyance turned to disillusionment and then just as quickly to pain. "You're the one person in the world I trust to understand me and all you can say is *Oh, Barbie?*"

"You weren't exactly a great encouragement to me, either," Lillie muttered.

"Oh, please. A mechanic? You want to ask a mechanic out for a date and you expect me to *cheer?*" All the frustration and anger of the evening burst from her. She stood with her hands knotted into fists at her sides. "You didn't tell Jacqueline who this man is, did you? What's the appeal? Do you think he'll be good in bed? Is that it?" Her own words shocked her, but not nearly as much as they did her mother.

Lillie stood frozen, her eyes wide with horror. Then she did something she'd never done in her whole life.

She slapped her.

Stunned into silence, Barbie pressed her hand to her cheek. Tears sprang to her eyes.

When her mother spoke, her voice shook with fury. "At least Hector could take me to bed."

Barbie gasped at the implication, grabbed her purse and shot out of the house. Over the years they'd quarreled— every mother and daughter did—but never anything like this.

A sick feeling engulfed her as she drove to her own house, less than two miles away. Pulling into the garage, she sat in her car and hid her face in both hands. The urge to break into heaving sobs of rage and pain and regret nearly overwhelmed her. But she refused to give in to the swell of grief, refused to allow the ugliness that had come between them to disintegrate her emotions any further.

Barbie didn't sleep that night or the next.

Nor did she speak to her mother. Ten times at least she

reached for the phone. Normally they spoke every day, often more than once. Now the silence was like a vast emptiness.

As far as Barbie was concerned, her mother owed her an apology. Lillie had struck her—her own daughter.

By the end of the second day, Barbie could hardly stand it. She missed her mother. She *needed* her.

The dinner for the widows' group was scheduled for Thursday night. Barbie was determined to go, but as Tuesday passed and then Wednesday, that resolve weakened.

This was ridiculous, she told herself. They'd both been at fault.

They'd both said things they regretted. It was time to apologize and put this behind them.

Late Thursday afternoon, a floral delivery truck parked in front of her dress shop just as Barbie was about to close for the day. The man carried in a huge floral arrangement from Susannah's Garden. This had to be a hundred-dollar order. It took up nearly half the counter space.

The driver handed her a clipboard, and Barbie signed her name as a rush of relief came over her. She didn't need to look at the attached card to know her mother had sent the flowers. Like her, Lillie was sorry. She was apologizing, trying to restore what they'd lost. Smiling, Barbie removed the small envelope and opened it.

She was wrong; Lillie hadn't sent the flowers.

Only one word was written on the card.

Mark.

Nineteen

Anne Marie and Ellen were both looking forward to dinner at Lillie's that night. Earlier, Anne Marie had called to ask what she could contribute to the meal.

"Nothing," her friend had insisted. "Just bring yourselves." As she replaced the receiver, Anne Marie thought that Lillie didn't sound like herself. Ever since they'd made their wish lists, Lillie's spirits had been high. But following their conversation, she wondered if she'd misread Lillie's feelings. Her voice had been flat, emotionless, devoid of her usual enthusiasm.

Anne Marie was afraid this dinner might be too much work for her. Later in the day she phoned Lillie again, to make sure everything was all right.

"Everything's perfectly fine," Lillie said, although her tone belied her words. "Actually, I'm really enjoying myself. It's been a long time since I've cooked for a dinner party." Anne Marie heard a timer in the distance, and Lillie told her she had to get off the phone.

Still, Anne Marie wondered. She sensed that something was off, but Lillie obviously wasn't going to tell her. All she could do was accept her word and hope that if there *was* a problem, it would soon be resolved.

The school bus rolled past the shop window and Anne Marie knew Ellen would appear in a few minutes.

"It's tonight, isn't it?" Ellen said happily as she bolted into the store. She released one strap and allowed her backpack to slip carelessly over her shoulder.

"Tonight's the night," Anne Marie concurred. Being invited to someone else's home for dinner seemed to be a new experience for the eight-year-old. Although Ellen had always displayed good manners, Anne Marie reviewed them with her, just to be on the safe side.

"I won't talk with my mouth full or interrupt the conver... conver—" she stumbled over the word "—the conversation."

"Excellent." Anne Marie smiled at her. "You can bring your knitting if you want."

At that suggestion, Ellen raced up the stairs to the apartment as if they were heading out the door that very moment. Such exuberance made Anne Marie smile again.

They were both making progress with their knitting. Anne Marie's first official class the day before had gone well. In teaching Ellen, she'd learned more about the basic knit stitch than she'd realized. After school on Tuesday, Anne Marie had taken Ellen to A Good Yarn and allowed her to purchase yarn and needles of her own. Lydia had chatted with Ellen for quite a while; by now, as Lydia said, the two of them were old friends. That evening, after the dinner dishes and Ellen's homework, they'd sat side by side, helping each other. Anne Marie couldn't avoid reflecting that this was something she'd never had the chance to do with her stepdaughter. Even as a ten-or eleven-year-old, Melissa had rejected all her attempts to work on projects together, whether it was reading or baking or gathering autumn leaves for a scrapbook. Whatever Anne Marie suggested was deemed "stupid" or "boring." The memory had produced a sadness she found hard to forget.

In the knitting class, Anne Marie had learned how to purl and she had about three inches of the lap robe finished. Ellen was half done with the scarf for her grandmother; the girl had a good eye for color and had chosen a soft pink yarn and a peach. The combination was lovely. They were colors Anne Marie would never have thought to put together.

Lydia had praised her color choice, too, and Ellen glowed with pleasure at the compliment.

"Are you bringing your Twenty Wishes binder?" Ellen asked now.

"Yes, I think so."

Ellen slipped her knitting into her backpack. "Should I bring my list?"

Anne Marie hesitated, a little worried that Ellen might inadvertently dominate the conversation. "Maybe next time, okay? For tonight I want you to sit and listen."

"Okay." Running up the stairs with her backpack, Ellen collected an excited Baxter for his walk, the requisite plastic bag tucked into her jeans' pocket.

At four, Steve Handley came into the shop for his shift. Anne Marie didn't have time to shower, but went upstairs to refresh her makeup. The day was overcast, so she decided to put a forest-green knit vest over her cream-colored long-sleeved blouse.

Ellen was modeling the new denim skirt Anne Marie had bought her when the phone rang.

"Want me to answer?" Ellen asked.

Anne Marie hesitated. "Let me check who it is first." She glanced at the phone as caller ID flashed Melissa's name and number.

Instinctively Anne Marie backed away. She still hadn't recovered from her last conversation with her stepdaughter. Another heart-to-heart might just finish her off.

The phone rang again and then again. After the fourth ring, voice mail came on. Anne Marie listened to the brief message. Melissa identified herself, then said, "Call me," without explaining why.

"Anne Marie?" Ellen spoke tentatively, staring up at her with worried eyes.

"Hey," she said, forcing some enthusiasm into her voice. "I thought we had a dinner date. Are you ready?"

Ellen nodded eagerly.

"Me, too. Let's go."

On the short drive to Lillie's, they sang camp songs. Or rather, Ellen sang. Anne Marie *tried* to sing and once again her voice sounded as if someone was strangling her. After the first few lines, she stopped and simply listened. Ellen truly was gifted and she loved to sing. After the first song, she immediately started a second one—"This Little Light of Mine," a song she told Anne Marie she'd learned in church.

Which reminded Anne Marie that one thing she hadn't done was take Ellen to church. It wasn't part of her normal practice, not that she had anything against religion. Although, at the moment, she didn't exactly feel God had dealt her a fair hand. Yet she realized that if she was going to maintain the routine Ellen had with Dolores, she should probably be taking her to Sunday-school class.

Just as Ellen's song came to an end, Anne Marie pulled up outside Lillie's house. This was the first time she'd been invited here. She parked in the circular drive, gaping at the sprawling Tudor-style house, which must have seven or eight thousand square feet. The outdoor lighting revealed a sweeping, verdant lawn and, closer to the house itself, an arrangement of flower beds filled with tulips of all colors, daffodils and delicate narcissus.

"Wow," Anne Marie whispered.

"Does Mrs. Higgins live in a castle?" Ellen asked in a hushed voice.

"It seems so."

Barbie arrived then, pulling into the drive behind them, and they all walked into the house together, followed a moment later by Elise. As soon as Barbie greeted her mother, Anne Marie could tell that something was amiss, although both Barbie and Lillie struggled to hide it. Instead of the usual camaraderie, the teasing and joking, they were stiffly polite with each other.

They must've had an argument or a falling-out. No wonder Lillie had seemed upset.

Lillie had arranged a small buffet with everything on a sideboard in the formal dining room. The buffet started with a selection of cheeses, olives, brie-stuffed dates and three different salads—a seafood pasta, a Caesar with homemade croutons and a fruit salad. For the entrée, Lillie presented them with ricotta-filled chicken breasts and scalloped potatoes.

Elise shook her head. "My goodness, Lillie, you must've been cooking for days."

"Mother is a tremendous cook," Barbie said quickly.

Lillie turned to her daughter. "Thank you. I enjoy spending time in the kitchen—it takes my mind off other concerns."

The comment seemed to be directed at Barbie, whose cheeks flushed as she looked away.

Anne Marie helped Ellen prepare her plate and then served herself. The five of them assembled around the table, which seated twelve. Anne Marie noticed that Lillie didn't have much of an appetite; for that matter, neither did Barbie. They barely seemed to touch their meals. Anne Marie, Ellen and Elise, however, savored every bite.

Conversation was general at first, with everyone asking Ellen about school and which classes she liked best. Reading, spelling and math, she'd answered, providing examples of what she'd recently learned.

"Speaking of classes, did you sign up for belly dancing?" Anne Marie asked Barbie.

Barbie jerked her head up, apparently caught unawares. "Belly dancing?"

"You said it was one of your wishes."

"Oh, yes. No, I haven't. Not yet at least. I will, though… probably." She sat straighter in her chair, chasing the food around her plate before she set her fork aside.

"What else is on your list?" Elise asked her.

Barbie reached down for her purse and withdrew a sheet of paper. "I started a binder like Anne Marie but left it at home this morning. I have my list here, though."

"I left my binder at home, too. At Anne Marie's house," Ellen said in a comforting voice as if to reassure Lillie's daughter.

"You know, I thought skinny-dipping would be fun."

"I've always thought that would be fun, too," Anne Marie murmured. She'd forgotten all about it until now.

Ellen tugged at her sleeve and when Anne Marie bent close, the girl whispered, "Is skinny-dipping a new diet? Grandma Dolores talked a lot about diets."

Anne Marie wasn't sure how to answer. "It's, uh, something like that."

For the first time that evening a smile tweaked the edges of Barbie's mouth. "I *am* going to do it."

"Do what?" Elise asked as she and Lillie entered the

dining room with dessert—platters of brownies, cookies and tarts.

"Skinny-dipping."

"Barbie!" her mother gasped.

"At night, Mother. In what you'd call a controlled environment."

"In the moonlight," Elise added softly. "Maverick and I—" She stopped abruptly and her face turned bright pink.

"You and Maverick went skinny-dipping?" Barbie asked.

"It was years ago…" She paused. "Well, to be honest, it happened shortly after we reunited." Elise shook her head fondly. "That man was full of crazy ideas."

"No wonder you loved him so much," Barbie whispered.

"Oh, I did, I did. I regret all the years we wasted. Maverick wouldn't let me talk about my regrets, though. He said we had to make up for lost time and we did everything in our power to squeeze thirty years of life into three." The expression on her face showed both happiness and loss and was almost painful to watch.

Anne Marie's eyes filled with tears, and she stared down at her binder. "What about you, Lillie?" she asked, wanting to draw attention away from Elise so the older woman could compose herself.

"You first," Lillie insisted, offering Ellen some dessert. The girl studied the platter carefully and chose a blueberry tart.

Anne Marie smiled, then glanced down at her binder again. The sheet she'd turned to had a picture of the Eiffel Tower. "I want to go to Paris with someone I love."

"That's so nice," Barbie murmured.

Anne Marie didn't mention that this was one of Robert's promises. She'd felt the lure of France, of Paris in particular, from her high school days, when she'd taken two years of

French. Robert had spun wonderful stories of the adventures they'd have…someday. It was always in the future, always around the corner. Next month. Next season. Next year. And whenever they made tentative plans, his job interfered.

She tried to dismiss the thought. Her life was her own now and if there was happiness to be found, it was up to her to seek it. She couldn't, wouldn't, rely on anyone else ever again.

Because she'd loved and supported her husband, Anne Marie had never complained. Now it became clear that she'd lived her entire marriage based on tomorrow—on well-intentioned promises, directed toward the future.

"I believe you talked about that one before," Elise reminded her. "It must be important to you."

"It is."

"What's stopping you?"

"I don't want to go alone."

Ever practical, Elise said, "Okay, it's not just about seeing Paris. It's also about falling in love."

"Yes, that's true. I want to be in love again."

"Good."

"I do, too," Lillie said quietly. Her gaze drifted down the table to her daughter.

Anne Marie was shocked to see tears glistening in Lillie's eyes. "I have Twenty Wishes but only one is important," Lillie said next. "None of the others means a thing without the first."

"What's that?" Elise asked. "As if I can't guess."

Lillie smiled briefly at Elise's remark. "I want to fall in love again," she said, "with a man who's honorable. A man respected by his peers. A man of principle who values me as a woman… A man who'll be my friend as well as my lover." A tear rolled down the side of her face. "I have lived most of my life trying to please others. I don't think I can do that anymore."

"Nor should you," Barbie said. "You deserve to find that man, Mom."

Lillie's voice shook. "So do you."

"I know."

Then to everyone's astonishment, Barbie burst into tears. "I'm so sorry, Mom, so sorry."

"I am, too."

Lillie pushed back her chair and a moment later, mother and daughter were hugging each other, weeping together.

Anne Marie looked at Elise, who shrugged. Once again Ellen tugged at the cuff of her blouse. "Why are they crying?" she asked in a loud whisper, leaning toward Anne Marie.

"I'm not sure."

"Will they be okay?"

Anne Marie placed her arm around Ellen's shoulders. "I think so," she said.

As quickly as Lillie and Barbie had burst into tears, they started to laugh, dabbing their eyes with the linen napkins, smearing their mascara and giggling like teenagers.

Ellen began to giggle, too. Soon Elise joined in. After a while she got up and carried her dinner dishes into the kitchen and set them on the counter.

Anne Marie collected her plates and Ellen's and did the same thing. This evening had been cathartic for all of them in some way. Except for Ellen, but Anne Marie knew the experience had been valuable for her, too.

Before she left she picked up her binder and as she shut it, her gaze fell on the Paris postcard she'd glued next to the cut-out picture of the Eiffel Tower.

One day she *would* go to Paris—and she wouldn't go alone. Because the love of her life would be with her.

Twenty

When the official-looking woman in the no-nonsense suit walked into Blossom Street Books, Anne Marie knew she was the same one who'd called earlier in the day. She'd introduced herself as Evelyn Boyle, a social worker from Washington State Child Protective Services. She'd sounded calm, professional and reassuring; otherwise Anne Marie might have been alarmed. She had the paperwork Dolores Falk had given her before the surgery, and Ellen and Anne Marie spoke with Dolores frequently.

She didn't understand why a social worker was involved now. In a few days, Dolores would be released from the care facility and Ellen would return to her. If the state was concerned about Ellen, it was too little, too late.

"You must be Ms. Boyle," Anne Marie said as she stepped around the counter. Thankfully Theresa, who worked Friday afternoons, had arrived a few minutes earlier.

"And you must be Anne Marie." The social worker came forward and thrust out her hand. "Please call me Evelyn."

Despite the woman's tranquil demeanor, Anne Marie was nervous.

"Is there someplace private where we could visit?" Evelyn asked.

"Sure." Anne Marie momentarily left her and walked over to Theresa, who eyed her speculatively.

"Is everything all right?" Theresa whispered.

"It's fine," she whispered back. In slightly louder tones, she added, "I'll be upstairs if you need me."

Theresa nodded.

Anne Marie led Evelyn up the narrow stairway to the apartment. Now that Ellen was more comfortable living with Anne Marie, she'd left a pair of rubber boots on the steps. Anne Marie grabbed them on her way up the stairs.

Baxter stood there waiting for her, tail wagging wildly. He cocked his head to one side, as though curious about her unexpected appearance. After she'd paid Baxter the required amount of attention, he sniffed the social worker's shoes, then returned to his bed in a corner of the kitchen.

Without asking, Anne Marie walked to the stove and put on water for tea. Evelyn pulled out a chair at the table, then set her briefcase on it and withdrew a yellow legal pad.

"How did you know Ellen was staying with me?" Anne Marie asked. She assumed Dolores hadn't told Social Services, which meant it was either the hospital or someone from Woodrow Wilson Elementary, probably Helen Mayer.

"I received a call from Ellen's school," Evelyn said, confirming Anne Marie's guess as she dug around the bottom of her purse for a pen.

Anne Marie stood with her back to the kitchen counter, hands behind her. "Ellen's grandmother wrote a statement that gives me full guardianship of Ellen while Dolores is recuperating." How legally binding that scribbled, almost illegible document was remained uncertain. Considering how desperate the poor woman had been for someone, anyone, to look after Ellen, she would've signed the girl's care over to practically anyone.

"I gather you were originally supposed to have Ellen for only a few days."

"Yes." Anne Marie wanted to say more but restrained herself. In instances such as this, the less said the better. "Dolores made me promise Ellen wouldn't go into a foster home."

Evelyn Boyle glanced up. "There are many excellent foster homes in this area."

"I'm sure there are…"

"But in essence, Anne Marie, Ellen is already in one."

"I'm someone Ellen knows and trusts," Anne Marie said quickly.

"That's true. It's exactly what I mean. You *are* her foster mother." Evelyn waited a moment. "I do understand the situation correctly, don't I? You and Ellen are not related in any way?"

"That's correct," she responded. But the question hovered in the air, swirling up doubts and fears.

The teakettle's whistle offered a welcome respite. Anne Marie concentrated on pouring water into the pot. She covered it with a cozy and set it in the middle of the table to steep while she got two matching cups and saucers.

Her good dishes were packed away in the storage unit, and the apartment cupboard was filled with mismatched place settings. It had never bothered her before, but it did now. Logically she knew that Social Services wouldn't pull Ellen from her care because her dishes didn't match. Still, Anne Marie discovered that she didn't want to take *any* chances.

She poured two mugs of tea, hating the way her hand trembled.

"I should tell you I stopped by the school before I drove over here."

Anne Marie couldn't decide if that was reassuring or not. "Did you speak to Ellen?"

"I did," Evelyn said as she reached for the sugar bowl and added a heaping teaspoon. "She had nothing but wonderful things to say about you. She told me about your visits to her grandmother and how you've bought her several pieces of clothing. Have you been to the house recently?"

"Twice," Anne Marie replied. "Ellen needed some of her stuff, and I told Dolores I'd check on the place for her."

"Excellent. I'm sure she'll appreciate that."

Some of the tension seeped away.

Evelyn raised her cup. "Is it true you taught Ellen to knit?"

"Actually, we sort of taught each other. Ellen's knitting a scarf for her grandmother and I've started a lap robe. The various colors don't match and Dolores won't be able to wear one near the other. Mine's a shade of lavender and Ellen went with a peach and pink combination. It's really lovely. I mean, who would've guessed…well, I suppose that isn't important." Anne Marie knew she was rambling and forced herself to stop. And yet, she couldn't resist bragging about Ellen's accomplishments.

Pushing back her chair, she hurried into the other room and got Ellen's scarf, still on the needles. "Look how even her stitches are," she said, displaying the child's efforts. "My own aren't half as neat. Ellen loves to knit and she's already taught three of her friends. Her teacher was so impressed she thought it might be a good idea for the whole class to learn."

Evelyn nodded approvingly. "Ellen's teacher mentioned that to me. She said knitting will help the children with math concepts and learning patience. It'll also give them a sense of achievement. I think it's a terrific idea."

"Really?" Anne Marie couldn't hold back a smile.

"When I spoke to Ellen, she also told me something about Twenty Wishes. What's that?"

"Ah…oh, it's nothing."

"Not according to Ellen. She has a book she drags to and from school in her backpack."

Anne Marie didn't realize Ellen brought it with her. "She does?"

"From what I understand, half the class is making lists as well."

"Oh…" Anne Marie took a sip of her tea. "A group of my friends and I decided it would be fun, that's all." She didn't want to explain anything beyond that; it was too complicated and too private.

"I love it," Evelyn said, her enthusiasm unmistakable.

Anne Marie's gaze shot toward the other woman. "You do?"

"Why, yes. In fact, I immediately started thinking about what I'd put on my own list."

Anne Marie relaxed a little.

"When I spoke to Ms. Peterski, she said there's been a marked improvement in Ellen in the last three weeks. Her grades have always been good but she had problems in other areas. Her social skills have vastly improved and she's making new friends and reaching out to others."

Anne Marie nodded. Although she had no personal reason to feel such overwhelming pride, it was difficult not to.

"Ellen is happy, too. This arrangement has obviously worked out well," the social worker said.

"She's an easy child," Anne Marie told her. True, it had

taken them a few days to find their footing, but they'd adjusted to living together with surprisingly few problems.

"Yes, she's done very well," Evelyn murmured.

"Did Ellen tell you she taught Baxter—my dog—to roll over?" Anne Marie asked. Ellen had worked with the dog for weeks and had only recently accomplished that goal.

"As a matter of fact, she did," Evelyn said with a glance at Baxter, who snored softly in the corner.

"I believe I mentioned that I spoke to the staff at the nursing facility where Dolores Falk is currently residing, didn't I?" Evelyn continued.

In her nervousness, Anne Marie didn't recall. "I'm not sure. Dolores tells me she's recovering nicely. She said she'd be released sometime next week. Wednesday, she thought."

Ms. Boyle hesitated before responding. "I understand Mrs. Falk is making excellent progress. She confirmed that you and Ellen visit frequently. And she waits every day for that brief telephone chat with her granddaughter."

"We see Dolores as often as we can."

"I'm aware of that, and I applaud your conscientiousness."

"Three to four times a week," she added. She made the effort to fit those visits into her schedule because she appreciated how important it was for Ellen—and, of course, Dolores.

"Very good."

"Thank you. I'm doing my best."

Evelyn sipped her tea. "I can see that, and the proof is in Ellen. Her teacher's delighted. Ms. Mayer, the school counselor, sang your praises, too."

This conversation wasn't nearly as difficult as Anne Marie had feared it would be. She was beginning to relax.

"Getting back to Mrs. Falk…" The words hung in the air like an unanswered question.

"Yes?" Anne Marie put down her cup.

"Did I hear you say she's going to be released next week?"

"Yes. Ellen and I were by on Wednesday after school and Dolores said she'd talked to one of the nurses about it."

"I'm afraid that's wishful thinking on Mrs. Falk's part," Evelyn said.

"What? How do you mean?"

"I spoke with the doctor's office as well as the head nurse."

A chill raced down Anne Marie's spine. "She's going to be all right, isn't she?"

"Oh, yes," Evelyn assured her. "The healing process is coming along well. But don't forget she had major heart surgery."

"Yes, of course." Fortunately there didn't seem to be any significant complications.

"However..."

"Are there problems with her recovery?"

"Not exactly problems."

"What is it, then?"

Mrs. Boyle's hand lingered on her cup and she ran her index finger along the rim. "Unfortunately it will be some weeks before she'll be able to return to her own home."

"Weeks?" Anne Marie repeated. This was a shock and she knew Ellen would be terribly disappointed.

"I'm sorry."

"How...many weeks?" Anne Marie asked, wondering how she'd explain this to Ellen. "Can you tell me how much longer it'll be before Dolores can go home?"

"I'm not a physician."

"What did the doctor say?"

"Two weeks."

"That's what I was told," she said. "But you mean an *additional* two weeks, right?" Anne Marie exhaled slowly.

"Yes. Are you okay with that?"

"Definitely. I'm just afraid this is going to be upsetting for Ellen. The child loves her grandmother very much."

"I know."

"Ellen's been marking off the days until she can move back in with Dolores."

"I understand this will be a setback for the child. I also understand that it's far and above what you agreed to when Ellen came to stay with you," Evelyn said. "If you feel it's too much, I could probably find a temporary home for Ellen."

"That would upset her even more," Anne Marie said, dismissing the offer out of hand. "It was difficult enough for Ellen to be separated from her grandmother. Placing her in another completely foreign environment would be doubly traumatic."

"I couldn't agree with you more."

At least they saw eye to eye on that, Anne Marie thought with relief.

"Then you won't mind keeping Ellen for another two weeks?"

"Of course I don't mind." Any other option wasn't worth considering.

"In that case, I'd like to leave some forms for you to complete."

"What kind of forms?" Anne Marie didn't like the sound of this.

Evelyn took a sheaf of papers out of her briefcase. "Since Ellen's been with you for more than two weeks already and is likely to remain for an additional two, I'd like you to apply for your license."

"My license for what?"

"To be Ellen's foster parent," she said as if this was perfectly logical.

An automatic objection rose in her throat, but Anne Marie bit down on her tongue rather than argue. The best thing to do was to appear compliant. However, she had no intention of becoming a foster parent. What was the point? By the time she finished applying, Ellen would be back with her grandmother and it would be irrelevant.

"Thank you," Anne Marie said, accepting the papers.

She stood and took the teapot and cups to the sink. "I appreciate your coming by," she said, since the interview was clearly over.

"My pleasure."

Baxter got up from his dog bed and walked them to the stairs, as though that was one of his prescribed duties. He stood silently at the top while the two women climbed down.

Anne Marie was saying goodbye to the social worker when she noticed a lone figure in the overstuffed chair, her head drooping, hair half-covering her face. The woman appeared to be asleep. Anne Marie glanced at her again, and suddenly realized who she was.

Her stepdaughter, Melissa Roche.

Twenty-One

As if aware of Anne Marie's scrutiny, Melissa opened her eyes and sat up, looking self-consciously around. Anne Marie wished now that she'd returned her phone call. Even from a distance, she could see that Melissa was in distress.

For the moment she ignored her and accompanied Evelyn Boyle to the door. She thanked her for the visit and agreed to read over the paperwork—and read it was all Anne Marie intended to do. Evelyn obviously didn't want to remove Ellen from her temporary custody any more than Anne Marie wanted to let the child go.

She had to admit she felt ambivalent about this latest information concerning Dolores. On the one hand, she knew Ellen would be disappointed; on the other hand, she herself wasn't unhappy about the girl's extended stay.

By the time Evelyn had gone and Anne Marie turned back to the shop, Melissa was standing uncertainly beside the chair. She seemed to be waiting for Anne Marie.

Anne Marie spoke with Theresa for a few minutes about some special orders, then walked toward her stepdaughter. "Hello, Melissa."

"You didn't return my phone call. I left a message."

"I was out last night. I didn't get in until late."

Melissa seemed confused. "You're not dating anyone, are you?"

Why would she ask that question again? Anne Marie couldn't even *think* about another relationship so soon after losing Robert. "No. I was with a group of women friends, although that isn't really any of your concern," she said brusquely. "I intended to call back this evening." Actually, Melissa had phoned more than once. Caller ID had shown three calls, all from her stepdaughter, although she'd left only the one message.

"Could I buy you lunch?" Melissa asked in a surprisingly tentative voice.

"Thank you, but I've already eaten."

Melissa blinked as if she hadn't expected that despite the fact that it was nearly two in the afternoon.

"The truth is, I'm not eager to visit another restaurant with you."

Melissa blanched. "I said I was sorry about that."

Anne Marie nodded. "Yes, you did."

"And I am, I really am! Sometimes I do stupid stuff. I don't know why I thought I should tell you what I saw. Brandon about bit my head off. He said—well, never mind."

Anne Marie could see this wasn't going to be a quick visit, so she motioned for Melissa to sit down again, then took the chair next to hers. The shop wasn't busy and Theresa was handling what business there was without a problem.

The two women sat silently for several seconds. Anne Marie was determined not to speak first. After all, Melissa had sought *her* out. She was the one with the agenda and frankly, Anne Marie was curious as to what it might be.

"Brandon said he came by a little while ago."

"Yes." She didn't elaborate.

"He said there's a child living with you."

"It's a temporary situation."

Melissa acknowledged the comment with a slight nod. "He said that, too, and that—Allie, is it?"

"Ellen."

"He said that Ellen's a real sweetheart."

"She is." Anne Marie wished Melissa would get to the point. "But I'm sure you aren't here to discuss my child-care activities."

"No," her stepdaughter agreed, fidgeting nervously with her hands. "Did Brandon tell you Mom and I aren't getting along?"

"He mentioned it."

"Mom's really upset with me."

"Is there any particular reason?"

She responded with a shrug. "Several, actually. For one thing, it doesn't look like I'll be able to graduate on time."

"Melissa!" Anne Marie couldn't help the gasp of shock. Robert had bragged about Melissa's making the Dean's list; Anne Marie doubted that the problem, whatever it was, had anything to do with her grades.

"I... I dropped out of school."

Anne Marie's mouth fell open. "But...why?" she asked incredulously.

Melissa didn't answer.

Anne Marie saw that the younger woman's eyes had filled with tears. Gazing down at her hands, Melissa murmured something Anne Marie couldn't quite hear.

"I beg your pardon?"

Melissa raised her chin. She inhaled and then said more loudly, "I'm pregnant."

Anne Marie sagged against the back of the chair. "Pregnant," she repeated, doing her best to hide her stunned surprise.

"Mom is furious with me."

Anne Marie could well imagine. Pamela had big plans for her daughter. Melissa's career path had been paved very nicely by her mother, who worked in upper management for an international chain of hotels based in London. According to Brandon, Pamela had secured a middle management position for Melissa as soon as she received her MBA. With the position came the opportunity to live in England.

"She wants me to get rid of it—that's how she put it. To have an abortion."

Anne Marie hardly knew what to say. She couldn't believe Pamela wanted to "get rid of" her first grandchild. Robert would've been horrified by that, she thought.

"The baby is your boyfriend's? Michael's?" Anne Marie asked as she tried to sort through her own emotions.

Melissa nodded.

"What does he want you to do?"

Melissa closed her eyes. "I... I haven't told him yet."

Leaning forward, Anne Marie clasped Melissa's hand.

Sobbing, her stepdaughter held on tightly. "I broke up with him."

In her fear and panic, Melissa suddenly seemed very young to Anne Marie. "Michael has a right to know," she whispered gently.

Melissa sniffed piteously. "I realize that, and I will tell him. It's just that... Everything's so messed up, and I'm not sure what to do. I didn't tell him because I was afraid he'd try to influence me one way or the other, and I didn't want that."

"So you broke off the relationship?"

Melissa bit her lip. "Stupid, wasn't it?"

Uncertain how to respond, Anne Marie squeezed her hand.

"I've never missed my dad more than I do right now. I'm so confused, and my mother's so angry with me."

"What does she say?" Anne Marie asked.

"She emails me two and three times a day with what she calls advice, except it reads more like a court order. I made a mistake, according to Mom, but that mistake doesn't need to screw up the rest of my life. She told me to make an appointment at one of those clinics and terminate the pregnancy before it's too late. She said if I lose this chance to work in England, I'll always regret it—that I'll never get a chance like this again."

Anne Marie had to struggle to keep from saying what she thought of that advice.

"She made it sound like I wouldn't regret making a hasty decision about my baby. I don't think I can do it, Anne Marie." The tears made wet tracks down her pale cheeks.

"What do *you* want?"

"I don't know," she whispered, still clutching Anne Marie's hand. "The thing is, I talked to a lady at the Pregnancy Crisis Clinic, and there are a lot more options than I thought."

"Don't you think you should explore all your options before you make such an important decision?"

"That's just it," Melissa sobbed. "I only have a few more days while it's still legal to have an abortion."

"How far along are you?"

"Over three months." She pulled her hand free and scrabbled in her purse for a tissue. "At first I didn't believe I could possibly be pregnant. I mean, I've never had regular periods, anyway, and there wasn't any reason to…to think I might be. Michael and I used protection and, well, apparently it wasn't a hundred percent effective, because here I am." She gestured weakly, then wiped her nose.

"You've been to a doctor?"

She looked away. "Not yet. But a technician at the pregnancy clinic did an ultrasound and I actually saw my baby move."

"Have you talked to your friends? Or Brandon?"

Melissa shook her head. "No one knows, other than you and my mother. I just couldn't face anyone else."

"How can I help you?" Anne Marie asked, wondering why Melissa had turned to her. But the reasons for her stepdaughter's change of heart didn't matter, Anne Marie told herself. She would do whatever she could.

"I need... I need someone who can help me decide."

Melissa had difficulty making decisions; that was clear, since she'd made a number of spectacularly bad ones. But perhaps some of them could be reversed.

"Okay," Anne Marie began, taking a deep breath. "First, I don't see that there's any reason to drop out of school, especially this close to graduation."

"I know. That was just as stupid as breaking up with Michael, wasn't it?"

"Do what you can to get back on course for graduation. Your father would've wanted you to complete your education."

Melissa nodded; she seemed to appreciate the advice. "Several of my professors have asked to talk to me, so I don't think that'll be a problem."

"Good."

"What about my mother?" Melissa asked, looking anxiously at Anne Marie.

"This is your decision, not hers."

She nodded again, as if she needed to be reminded of that. "If I don't go to England..."

"Why can't you go?"

"Mom said I couldn't have the job unless I aborted the baby."

"I'm sure she doesn't mean that," Anne Marie said. "The news shocked her, that's all." She remembered Robert confessing that he'd gotten Pamela pregnant before they were married. Apparently she was afraid her daughter would repeat her own mistakes by marrying too young—and in Pamela's view, marrying the wrong man.

"I should tell Michael right away, shouldn't I?"

"That would be a good idea." Anne Marie could see this was something Melissa wanted to do. "The two of you can talk it over together. Do you love him?"

"Yes, but… A friend told me she saw him with someone else." She paused, tears running unchecked down her face. "If he loved me, he wouldn't be dating again so soon, would he?"

"Who knows why men do anything?" Anne Marie asked, hoping to inject a bit of humor into the conversation.

Melissa responded with a wobbly smile. A moment later, she whispered, "Thank you, Anne Marie. I never thought I'd turn to you for anything and now I feel you're the only person I can talk to."

There'd been a time, a long time, when Anne Marie would've done anything to win her stepdaughter's approval. Little did she realize it would come after Robert's death.

They hugged and arranged to meet for lunch the following week. As they broke apart, Anne Marie recognized that Melissa wanted to say something else. She looked away and then back at Anne Marie, her eyes intent.

"I *am* sorry about the last time we met—you know that, right?"

Anne Marie nodded.

"Have you…?" She didn't complete the thought, almost as though she was weighing the advisability of even asking.

"Have I what?"

Melissa shrugged. "Contacted Rebecca? Have you asked her about the…baby?"

"No." Anne Marie kept her voice as flat as possible.

Her stepdaughter accepted that without further comment. With a wave and a "See you next week," she headed for the door.

Anne Marie waited until Melissa had left the bookstore before she collapsed onto the overstuffed chair and pressed one hand over her eyes. This nightmare that had become her life just wasn't going away. *She* was the one who wanted a child.

Not Rebecca.

Not Melissa.

Anne Marie.

Her longing for a baby had led to her separation from Robert—a desperate attempt to impress on him how serious she was. Not that it had done her any good. Instead, Robert's personal assistant now had a baby, most likely his, and his daughter had turned to Anne Marie for advice about an unwanted pregnancy.

But there was no baby for her.

No love, either.

She sensed someone at her side and opening her eyes, found Theresa standing there. Her employee rested one hand on Anne Marie's shoulder.

"Bad news?" she asked.

Forcing a smile, Anne Marie shook her head. "That was Robert's daughter."

Knowing the history between them, Theresa stared at her. "Melissa? Is she okay? Are *you?*"

"She…she misses her father."

So did Anne Marie, even more than she'd thought possible.

Twenty-Two

On Monday evening Barbie purposely stayed away from the movies. It wasn't easy, but she felt she had no option. Last week she'd left her business card with Tessa; now Barbie felt the next move had to come from him.

In a way Mark *had* made the next move by having flowers delivered, although she considered that an indirect, even cowardly approach. The flowers were a lovely gesture, but she'd been looking for more—like an apology or an invitation to meet again. By ordering the floral arrangement he'd managed to communicate his interest, yet keep his pride intact.

Maybe…the gesture *was* enough. For the moment.

She recognized what he was trying to tell her. He'd made a move in this elaborate game of theirs; the next one was hers.

She knew a little more about him after a Google search. He was an architect with an independent practice and lived in a downtown condo he'd designed himself.

Barbie felt encouraged by his interest. No, she was ecstatic. Still, she had to restrain herself, not let him have the upper hand. She decided she'd return to the movies again, but not right away.

Tuesday afternoon, she thought she'd register for the belly dancing class being held at the Seattle Fitness Center. This was her first trip here, and she was surprised to find an Olympic-size pool, along with a huge gymnasium and several activity rooms. As she walked down the hallway to the office, she passed a shop that sold workout clothes, swimsuits and other exercise paraphernalia.

After filling out the paperwork and paying her fee, Barbie began to leave the building, feeling positive and determined. She was making her wishes come true. Smiling to herself, she rounded the corner and stopped abruptly as a man in a wheelchair moved toward the pool.

Mark Bassett.

Coincidence? Fate? Barbie wasn't about to question it. Her heart felt as if it had shot all the way up into her throat. Without conscious thought she did an about-face and headed back, toward the shop. Within five minutes, she'd purchased a swimsuit and towel. Gaining entrance to the pool was a bit more difficult; before she was allowed to swim, she had to buy a six-month fitness membership. She slapped her credit card down on the counter, impatient to get into the water before Mark.

He *had* to believe this meeting wasn't staged—which, in truth, it wasn't. Okay, so her showing up at the pool might be a bit manipulative, but when life presented you with an advantage, you had to grab it with both hands.

Barbie changed into the swimsuit, a sleek blue one-piece, in the women's dressing room and walked out as though she was strolling along a Caribbean shore. The suit, thankfully, was a perfect fit. She squared her shoulders and silently thanked her mother for every lesson she'd taken at that expensive charm school.

Using the railing, she lowered herself into the water and cringed at the temperature. Her own swimming pool was kept at a comfortable eighty-five degrees. This was eighty, eighty-one maximum, and in her opinion downright cold.

When she'd entered the pool area, the attendant had explained that this was the adult lap swim. As soon as she got into the water, Barbie realized these noontime swimmers were serious about their workout. They wore goggles and bathing caps, and to her they resembled nothing so much as a bunch of insects with their smooth shiny heads and large round eyes.

Barbie refused to allow her hair to get wet. She needed to go back to work right afterward, and she couldn't arrive with dripping hair.

The minute she broke away from the side of the pool, another swimmer streaked past her, quickly followed by a second. It was quite apparent that no one appreciated her rather lazy form of breaststroke.

A third swimmer went by, kicking wildly, splashing her face and hair. Barbie swallowed a mouthful of chlorinated water and choked violently. She felt like she was about to cough up her tonsils. So much for making a sophisticated appearance.

She muttered a curse, treading water for a moment while she caught her breath. When she could breathe normally again, she wiped the water from her eyes. She'd given up even trying to keep her hair dry.

As she finally reached the other end of the pool, she saw Mark hanging on to the side, watching her. Clearly her antics were a source of amusement to him. His gaze found hers and he actually smiled.

Mark had *smiled* at her!

Since her hair was already ruined, Barbie stopped worrying about it and started swimming for all she was worth, face fully in the water. Her mascara was probably running, too, but she no longer cared.

Mark was waiting for her.

"Fancy meeting you here," she said, hoisting herself up on the side of the pool. She gave him what she hoped was a dazzling smile.

"Yeah, some coincidence."

"Come here often?" she asked.

"Every day."

"Me, too," she lied. "I can't believe we've never run into each other before."

"Every day?" He arched his eyebrows in disbelief. "Since when?"

She wasn't fooling him, so she might as well own up to the truth. "Since today."

He not only smiled at that, he laughed. The sound was deep, pleasant to the ear. She had the impression that he hadn't done a lot of laughing in the last few years.

"I come here to swim," Mark told her. "Keep up if you can."

"Hey, you're going to have to catch *me*," she shouted after him.

That was a joke if there ever was one.

Mark took off and with impressive upper body strength sliced through the water. His ease and grace were mesmerizing. Barbie didn't make the slightest effort to catch up with him. When he'd passed her twice, he stopped, waiting for her in the deep end. By then, Barbie had swum two laps and was too exhausted to swim anymore. Her breath came in shallow gasps. She grabbed the edge of the pool and felt her heart pounding hard against her ribs.

"Are you going to tell me why you're really here?" he asked.

"Belly dancing."

"I beg your pardon?" He sounded incredulous, and she wondered if he thought she was making fun of him.

"I signed up for a belly dancing class."

"At the Fitness Center?"

Propping her elbow on the ledge, Barbie pushed the hair away from her face. "Just as I was leaving, I saw you and had the overwhelming urge to take a dip."

"You're a member?"

"I am now."

Almost everyone had left the water. Barbie looked around, astonished to discover that only the two of them were still in the pool. When she glanced back at Mark, she saw him frowning.

"Why?" he asked.

Barbie didn't know how to answer him. "Don't *you* feel it?" she asked him instead. Judging by his puzzled expression, he either didn't understand or didn't want to, so she continued. "That first night in the theater… I've never experienced anything like it."

"You're imagining things," he snapped.

"No, I'm not." She wasn't going to let him lie to her, let alone himself. The attraction between them was too intense to ignore.

"I realize you're not happy about this," she whispered. "You've made that pretty obvious."

"Then leave me alone."

"I wish I could," she said, "but I just…can't." She hadn't meant to reveal so much, but the words slipped out before she could stop herself. Their eyes met, and she could see the warring emotions inside him.

Using his free arm, he reached for her and slid his hand behind her neck and then slowly, as if fighting her every inch of the way, he brought his mouth to hers. He gave her ample opportunity to pull back.

She didn't.

Barbie wanted his kiss, hungered for it. She opened her mouth to welcome him, and then she was crushed in his embrace, arms and legs entwined, mouths joined.

Their kiss was better than she ever would have dreamed. They abandoned the effort to stay afloat and started to sink. Clinging to each other they sank far below the surface, their mouths straining, searching, devouring.

By the time they broke the surface again, Barbie was gasping for air. Because his legs were paralyzed, Mark needed to move his arms to remain afloat. All Barbie needed to do was kick her feet.

The sheer exhilaration of his kiss overwhelmed her. But he didn't seem to share her enthusiasm. His look was fierce, angry…afraid. He glared at her in much the same way he had the evening they'd first met.

"That was wonderful," she said reverently. It was very different from any sensual experience she'd shared with Gary, and she felt no guilt, no regret. Only gratitude.

He didn't respond.

"Mark?" His name was a soft plea on her lips. She couldn't bear it if he said or did something to destroy what she'd found to be an intensely moving experience.

Without speaking he kissed her a second time, and they sank into the clear blue water, wrapped in each other's arms. After a moment, they bobbed to the surface again.

Mark released her and Barbie sagged breathlessly against

him, her head on his shoulder. It'd been so long since a man had held her or kissed her...

"I don't think this is a good idea," he whispered, but even as he spoke the words, he caressed her wet hair. He was braced against the side of the pool and she held on to him.

"It's a brilliant idea! Stop arguing with me." The sheer joy of being in his arms rang in her voice.

"Barbie—"

She shushed him with a kiss. "I mean it. Stop arguing."

He laughed again, the sound echoing in the cavernous room.

"I'm turning into a prune," she said, "and I love every second of it and all because I'm with you."

"You're very beautiful," he murmured.

"Even with wrinkled skin and mascara running down my face?"

"If you only knew..." Then, seeming to reach some kind of decision, he slowly exhaled. "Listen, Barbie, this is all very flattering, but—"

She interrupted him again, kissing him full on the mouth, using her lips and tongue to steal his very words. After coming this far, she didn't plan to let him get cold feet and a cold heart now.

His eyes were still closed when she broke off the kiss.

"You don't know what you're letting yourself in for. You—"

"I won't tolerate a man making decisions for me. If you think I'm going to allow you to decide what I do and don't know, then you're sadly mistaken."

The edges of his mouth quivered with the effort of suppressing a smile. "So you know everything there is to know about my disability."

"Of course I don't."

He ignored her response. "You read a few things on the internet and you think you know it all."

"Well...okay, I read a few things."

His eyes narrowed. "Like what?"

A flush rose in her cheeks. "Mainly, I was interested in how we'll make love."

Mark gasped—or perhaps it was a groan, she couldn't tell which. "You're getting way ahead of yourself."

"Probably," she admitted."But that's what I was most curious about."

His face somber and apprehensive, he smoothed a wet tendril from her cheek. "I should tell you... I haven't... since the accident."

"Then it's about time." Barbie couldn't believe they were having this conversation. Even more unbelievable was the fact that she could speak so openly and boldly about love-making with a man she barely knew.

Mark held her gaze a long moment. "Where do we go from here?"

"Where do you want to go?"

A smile twitched his lips. "Now, that's a leading question if I ever heard one."

She slapped his shoulder. "What I mean is we should probably get to know each other a little better."

"Must we?" he asked with pretended chagrin.

"Yes!"

"We can't go to bed first and ask questions later?"

"I'm not that kind of woman." Although considering the way he kissed, she might think about converting.

"I was afraid of that."

"You swim every day?"

"Every day," he assured her. "You too, right?"

"Right." This schedule change was going to take some

adjustment. "Except Monday and Wednesday, when I'll be in my belly dancing class. Okay, I'll swim two or three times a week."

"Right."

"I could meet you afterward." Her staff was going to be putting in a lot of extra hours. That wasn't a problem; Barbie had been planning to give them more hours, anyway.

"You're sure about this?" Mark didn't seem convinced.

"I'm positive and if you ask me once more, I'll—"

"If you want to punish me, all you have to do is press that perfect body of yours against mine."

"That's nice to know." She moved closer and slid her right leg between his thighs. Her breasts brushed his chest as she spread eager kisses along his jaw.

"I suggest you stop now," he muttered. "There's a seniors' class coming in soon."

"Can't. I'm thanking you."

"For what?"

"The flowers you sent." She wouldn't have found the courage to confront him this afternoon if he hadn't made that move.

Mark went very still. "I didn't send you flowers."

"But...the card had your name on it."

He muttered something she couldn't completely hear; she caught the gist of it, though. Mark's sister or perhaps his mother was responsible for that bouquet.

"So, you *didn't* send the flowers," she confirmed.

Mark wound his fingers into her hair and dragged her mouth to his. "Let's just pretend I did."

Barbie was more than willing to do exactly that.

Twenty-Three

Lillie Higgins stared at the phone, then groaned in frustration and turned away. This should be easy. Everyone seemed to think there was nothing to it. But try as she might, Lillie couldn't make herself call Hector.

In desperation, not knowing how else to manage this, she'd contacted the dealership instead, with a list of imaginary complaints about her car. The receptionist she spoke with made her an appointment for Thursday morning at ten. By the time she arrived at the service department, her stomach was tied up in knots a sailor couldn't untangle.

A man she didn't recognize came out to discuss the trouble her car had supposedly been giving her.

"Could you explain again what the problem is?" he asked, studying his clipboard.

Lillie had a panicky moment before she remembered what she'd told the receptionist yesterday when she'd made the appointment. "There seems to be a hesitation…"

"Coming from a full stop?" he asked, glancing up from his notepad.

"Yes, that's it. From a full stop."

"How often has this happened?"

She didn't want to overplay the situation. "A couple of times."

He jotted that down. "Just twice."

"No, more. Four or five times." Her hands were clammy and her mouth had gone dry and she had the most compelling urge to turn tail and run. If she hadn't handed her car keys over to the mechanic, she would've made an excuse and left before she looked like an even bigger fool.

He wrote something else on the chart.

"This won't take long, will it?" she asked.

"Not at all," he assured her.

Inside the waiting area, Lillie got a cup of coffee from the machine and picked up that day's paper. Although she'd come for the express purpose of seeing Hector again, now she prayed she wouldn't. How could she possibly explain what she'd done?

Lillie liked to think of herself as mature and sensible. Never in all her life, not even as a teenager, had she indulged in such a ridiculous deception over a man. Her face burned with mortification. She'd lied about her car—told an outright lie in a futile effort to see Hector Silva again.

Fifteen minutes later, the receptionist came to tell her that her vehicle was ready. She immediately went to pay the bill but found there was no charge. Eager to be on her way, Lillie hurried out of the building to the lot, where her car was waiting for her.

She nearly stumbled when she saw Hector standing next to it.

"Lillie," he said, his smile warm. "I've personally checked out the car and I can't find anything wrong with it. I thought if we took a drive, the problem might reappear and I could analyze it."

The offer to spend time with him was tempting, but

she'd frittered away enough of his morning. "If you say it's in fine working order, then I'm sure it is. I trust you."

"I wouldn't mind, Lillie."

"Hector." Her face shone as brightly as a lighthouse beacon. "There's nothing wrong with my vehicle," she said, making a spontaneous decision. "I apologize. I shouldn't have wasted your time." The most important thing at the moment was getting away with her dignity—or what remained of it—intact.

Hector nodded. "We don't need to test your car, then?"

"We don't."

He opened the driver's door for her, and she climbed in. Her hand trembled as she inserted the key in the ignition. The door was still open.

"Do you…have you ever gone bowling?" The words came at her in a rush.

"Bowling?" she repeated, frowning. "Oh, sure, of course." This must be a day meant for lies. In her entire life, she'd never even stepped inside a bowling alley.

"I know it's short notice… I hope you don't mind my asking…"

"I don't mind." How eager she sounded. Her heart did a silly dance while she tried to disguise her excitement at his invitation.

"Tonight?" he asked.

"Yes."

"Six?"

"Okay." She mentally reviewed her closet filled with Misook and St. John suits. What did one wear bowling? Barbie would know.

Barbie would help her. Then she realized she couldn't tell Barbie.

Not yet. Later maybe, after she'd gone out with Hector.

He grinned. "Perhaps we should meet there?"

"That's fine." *Anywhere* was fine.

With a verve that was almost boyish, he shut her door, but not before giving her the address of the bowling alley. "I'll look forward to seeing you this evening," he said.

"Yes." Lillie didn't know if she was going to dissolve into tears or giggles. Either way, her actions today had been embarrassing—but she didn't care.

She was going to see Hector tonight, and they wouldn't be talking about cars, either.

That evening, thanks to her navigation system, Lillie located the bowling alley and got there at ten minutes to six. She wore beige linen slacks and a soft teal cashmere sweater with a floral silk scarf around her neck. Earlier in the afternoon, she'd purchased tennis shoes and white cotton socks. With her makeup she'd gone for a light, natural look, and she'd worn her hair neatly tied back. Every detail of her appearance had been closely scrutinized.

Hector, dressed in a suit and tie, was waiting outside the entrance, and when he saw her, his eyes lit up. Lillie knew exactly how he felt, because she felt the same happiness at seeing him.

As she approached, he held out his hands to her, and for a moment neither of them spoke. "Thank you for agreeing to meet me."

"Thank you for asking me." A little worried, she glanced at his suit. He looked as if he was about to attend a wedding. Lillie hadn't realized bowling was such a formal sport. "Should I change my clothes?"

Hector shook his head. "No, no, you look perfect."

"But you're wearing a suit…"

His cheeks reddened slightly. "My daughter said I should never have suggested bowling. She said you must think me a buffoon. Would you care to dine with me, Lillie? I apologize if I offended you by offering to take you bowling. It's been many years since I invited a woman out. I don't know how such things are done now."

All Lillie really wanted was to be with Hector. It didn't matter to her if they were in a five-star restaurant or knocking down pins in a bowling alley. "Hmm. That's quite a decision."

"Shall we have coffee and then decide?"

She nodded. "That's an excellent idea."

Next they needed to figure out where to have coffee. They chose the café in the bowling alley, since that was the simplest alternative. Hector led her to a booth in the corner. The menu was shaped like a bowling pin and the salt and pepper shakers were empty beer bottles. Lillie was enchanted.

He slid into the booth across from her as she glanced happily around. The atmosphere reminded her of a fifties diner, the kind of place where the day's special was a double bacon cheeseburger with greasy fries. When she read the chalkboard, she saw that the special here was actually two cheese enchiladas with rice and beans.

Hector raised his hand and the waitress brought coffee.

Lillie leaned forward. "There was nothing wrong with my car." She'd told him as much earlier, but she wanted him to understand the reason for her pretense.

"Oh, I knew that all along."

"You did?" That made it even more embarrassing. "I wanted to see you again," she said bluntly.

Hector spooned sugar into his coffee. "I wanted to see you, too."

"But you didn't phone, you didn't ask… My daughter

and my friends urged me to contact you. They say that's how it's done nowadays."

"You *didn't* call me."

She avoided eye contact. "I wasn't sure how. I've never called a man—well, other than a professional or a friend."

"My daughter said if you agreed to see me after tonight, it would be a miracle. She crossed herself when I told her I invited you to go bowling."

Lillie laughed. The cheerful clatter from the bowling alley made her curious and she noticed that everyone seemed to be having fun. "I have another confession to make."

"Two confessions in a single night?"

"Two," she said with a smile. "I've never been bowling."

This didn't appear to surprise him, either. "Would you like to learn?" he asked.

"Only if you're going to be my teacher."

From across the table he grinned at her and she was mesmerized. He'd captured her imagination and her senses with his unfailing courtesy, genuine charm and with his kindness.

When they finished their coffee, Hector procured them a lane, fitted her with rented shoes, and then proceeded to show Lillie how to bowl.

By the end of the evening, Lillie had to admit she hadn't laughed this much in twenty years. It was gratifying—and completely unexpected—to discover that she had a certain knack for the sport. What they both found nothing short of hilarious was the fact that her ball rolled at the speed of an earthworm. She'd release it just the way Hector instructed, return to her seat and wait while the bowling ball slowly but surely trundled down the narrow lane. After what seemed like minutes, the ball would connect with the pins. They'd fall lazily over, one at a time, almost in slow motion, knocking into one another.

People stopped to watch when the ball finally made contact and the pins started to tumble. Once she managed to knock down nine pins, and the people in the next alley actually broke into applause.

Hector—who was obviously an accomplished bowler, as his succession of strikes made clear—claimed he'd never seen anything like it. Apparently, no one else had, either. The place was growing crowded, and Lillie was unaccustomed to all the attention, which embarrassed her. All she could do was laugh.

And when she laughed, Hector did, too.

In the last frame of their final game, Lillie achieved her first strike. It took nearly a minute for all the pins to fall and when the last one spun around and around and eventually toppled, she jumped up and down like a schoolgirl. Hector hugged her and then self-consciously stepped back.

After that, they turned in their bowling shoes and balls. She could hardly remember a time she'd enjoyed more. When they left the lanes, it seemed the most natural thing in the world for him to take her hand.

"Are you hungry?" he asked, dangling his suit jacket over his shoulder.

"Famished."

"I am, too. Do you have a favorite restaurant?"

"Yes, I do," she said and smiled over at him. "It's right here."

"Lillie, please allow me to take you to a real restaurant."

"This one looks real."

He hesitated. "My daughter suggested Gaucho's. She said they have an extensive wine list and a pianist who plays classical music."

"Are you planning to wine and dine me?"

"Yes, it's what you deserve. I want only the best for you."

It was such a sweet gesture, but she couldn't let Hector spend that kind of money. Besides, she wasn't dressed for anyplace formal. "I'd love some cheese enchiladas," she told him.

Hector squeezed her fingers. "If you insist, but if my daughter asks, please tell her the choice was yours, not mine."

"Rita?"

"Yes. Before I left this evening, she gave me a long list of things I should and shouldn't do. When I dated my wife, it was nothing like this." He stopped abruptly. "I don't mean to imply…"

"I know," she assured him. "I feel just as nervous as you."

"Really?"

She laughed. "You mean you can't tell?"

"No." He seemed genuinely surprised. "I have a confession to make."

"You?" Well, she'd already made two of her own.

"When I look at you," he said in a low voice, "I forget to breathe."

She wondered if he realized the effect his words had on her—or that she felt the very same way.

"Me, too," she whispered. She might have said more but a booth became available and they slid inside.

They each ordered the enchiladas and lingered over coffee, chatting until after one in the morning. Only when Lillie couldn't hold back a yawn did Hector suggest they call it a night.

He walked her to her car, which was one of the four or five still in the parking lot. The entire time Lillie prayed

Hector would want to see her again. When he didn't mention it, she was sure this would be their one and only date.

"I had a lovely evening," she said, fumbling for her keys.

"So did I."

"Thank you for everything." She opened the car door and got in.

He nodded, stepping away as she started the engine.

Lillie's heart was in her throat.

"Saturday," he blurted out just as she was ready to drive away.

"Pardon?"

"Would you like to attend a lecture at the museum with me this Saturday?"

The relief was so overwhelming, she nearly broke into tears. "That would be wonderful, Hector."

Wonderful didn't begin to describe it.

Twenty-Four

Wednesday afternoon, the sun was shining and the wind off Puget Sound was warm. This was a perfect spring day, and Anne Marie suddenly realized she felt…good. She'd almost forgotten what that was like. The comfort of the sun, the freshness of the breeze, the company of others—they all contributed to her sense of well-being. Most of all, though, she felt a contentment she hadn't experienced since before her separation from Robert.

She'd just finished a knitting class with Elise Beaumont. Three other women had signed up, and the session had been fun, with plenty of banter as Elise reviewed their work.

While she was at the yarn store, Colette Dempsey came by with her infant daughter. At first Anne Marie had been afraid that seeing her friend with the baby would be painful; it wasn't. Even though the world seemed to be full of surprise pregnancies and secret ones, too, she managed to distance herself from destructive emotions like envy.

She found she could genuinely delight in Colette's joy. They talked for an hour, and the visit passed with barely a ripple of pain.

Anne Marie was saddened by the news that Colette and

her husband, Christian, would be moving to California at the end of June for business reasons. Christian owned a successful importing firm and would be opening a second office in San Diego.

She recalled that only a year ago, Colette had been a widow like her, and that was something they'd had in common. But Colette had been hiding a pregnancy and she'd struggled with a painful dilemma that had been dramatically resolved.

Nothing dramatic had happened to Anne Marie in the last two months. Nothing had really changed, either; certainly not her circumstances, other than the fact that Ellen was living with her but that was only a temporary situation. The only difference was in Anne Marie's attitude.

She still had to make an effort to maintain that attitude. Her Twenty Wishes had helped, because she now felt she had some control over her emotions. Doing something for someone else—Ellen—had, without a doubt, made the biggest difference.

To be honest, avoiding the question of Rebecca Gilroy had helped, too. One day soon, she'd ask who had fathered her son. But not until she felt ready to accept the answer.

After her knitting class, Anne Marie did a few errands and then collected Baxter so the two of them could meet Ellen's school bus. The girl's spirits had been low since she'd learned that her Grandma Dolores wouldn't be home as quickly as they'd hoped.

Anne Marie decided a leisurely walk, maybe stopping somewhere for something to eat, might improve Ellen's mood. As she waited on the street corner, the big yellow bus rumbled down Blossom Street. When it stopped and Ellen hopped out, Baxter strained against his leash, whining excitedly.

"How was school?" Anne Marie asked.

"Good."

The noncommittal reply was typical. Generally it wasn't until later in the evening, usually over dinner, that Ellen began to talk more freely. She appeared to need time to assimilate the day's events and perhaps figure out how much to share.

"I thought we'd take Baxter for a walk together."

"Okay."

Ellen rarely showed much enthusiasm when Anne Marie suggested an outing. She revealed her pleasure in other ways. Anne Marie suspected she was afraid to let anyone know she was happy about something, for fear that the object of her happiness would be taken away.

"If you want, you can leave your backpack in the shop with Theresa."

"Okay." Ellen raced ahead and Anne Marie watched her employee place the heavy bag behind the counter. A minute later, Ellen was back.

"You ready?" Anne Marie asked.

"Ready."

Baxter certainly was. Her Yorkie pulled at the leash; apparently Anne Marie wasn't walking briskly enough to satisfy him. The dog had places to go, territory to mark and friends to greet, especially the friends who kept special treats just for him.

"Let's walk down to Pike Place Market and have dinner at one of the sidewalk cafés," Anne Marie said. "Does that sound good?"

Ellen shrugged. "I guess so."

"Or would you rather go down to the waterfront and get fish and chips?"

Ellen didn't seem to have an opinion one way or the other. "What do you want?"

Anne Marie had to think about it. "Pizza," she finally said. "I haven't had it in ages."

"What kind?"

"Thin crust with lots of cheese."

"And pepperoni."

"Let's see if we can find a restaurant where we can order pizza and eat outside."

"Okay."

On a mission now, they trudged down the steep hill toward the Seattle waterfront. Pike Place Market was a twenty-minute hike, but neither complained. Baxter didn't, either, although this was new territory for the dog. Once they reached the market, Anne Marie picked him up and cradled him in her arms.

Ellen and Anne Marie strolled through the market, where they watched two young men toss freshly caught salmon back and forth for the tourists' benefit. Ellen's eyes grew huge as she gazed at the impromptu performance. When they left the market building, the little girl slipped her hand into Anne Marie's and they walked down the Hill Climb stairs to the waterfront. Baxter was back on his feet by then, taking in all the fascinating smells around him.

"Have you ever been to the Seattle Aquarium?" Anne Marie asked when the building came into view.

"My class went."

"Did you like it?"

Ellen nodded eagerly. "I got to touch a sea cucumber and it felt really weird and I saw a baby sea otter and a real shark."

She'd liked it, all right, if she was willing to say this much. After investigating several stores that catered to Seattle tourists, Anne Marie located a pizza place. While they waited for their order, they sipped sodas at a picnic table near the busy waterfront. They both ate until they were stuffed and still had half the pizza left over.

"Shall we save it?" Anne Marie asked. Ellen agreed. It seemed a shame to throw it out, but she suspected that if they brought it home, it would sit in the refrigerator for a few days and end up in the garbage, anyway.

Anne Marie carried the cardboard box in one hand and held Baxter's leash in the other. They'd just started back when Ellen noticed a homeless man sitting on a bench, his grocery cart parked close by. Tugging at Anne Marie's arm, she whispered something.

"What is it?" Anne Marie asked. "I couldn't hear you."

"He looks hungry," Ellen said a bit more loudly. "Can we give him our pizza?"

"What a lovely idea. I'll ask if he'd like some dinner." Impressed with Ellen's sensitivity, Anne Marie gave her the leash and approached the man on the bench.

He stared up at her, disheveled and badly in need of a bath. Despite the afternoon sunshine, he wore a thick winter jacket.

"We have some pizza," Anne Marie explained, "and we were wondering if you'd like it."

The man frowned suspiciously at the box. "What kind you got?"

"Well, cheese and—"

"I don't like them anchovies," he broke in. "If you got anchovies on it, I'll pass. Thanks, anyway."

Anne Marie assured him the pizza contained no anchovies and handed him the box. He lifted the lid and frowned. "That's all?" They'd gone about a block when the absurdity of the question struck her. She started to giggle.

Clearly puzzled, Ellen looked up at her.

That was when Anne Marie began to laugh, really laugh. Her shoulders shook and tears gathered in her eyes. "That's all?" she repeated, laughing so hard her stomach ached. "And he didn't want anchovies." Why she found the man's comments so hilarious she couldn't even say.

Ellen continued to study her. "You're laughing."

"It's funny."

"That's on your list, remember?"

Anne Marie's laughter stopped. Ellen was right. She wanted to be able to laugh again and here she was, giggling hysterically like a teenage girl with her friends. This needed to be documented so she pulled out her cell phone and had Ellen take her picture.

Then she dashed back and piled all the change and small bills she had—four or five dollars' worth—on the pizza box.

Another wish—an act of kindness. The man grinned up at her through stained teeth and rheumy eyes.

It came to her then that she was *happy*.

Truly happy.

Deep-down happy.

Anne Marie had felt good earlier in the day, but that was the contentment that came from a sunny day, seeing old friends, spending a relaxing hour with her knitting class.

Granted, her newly formed optimism had a lot to do with these feelings. But her unrestrained amusement was something else—the ability to respond to life's absurdities with a healthy burst of laughter.

It meant the healing had begun, and she was well on her way back to life, back to being herself, reaching toward acceptance.

When they returned to the apartment, it was still light

out. Ellen had a number of small tasks to perform. She watered the small tomato, cucumber and zucchini seedlings they'd planted in egg cartons last Sunday. Once Ellen was home at her grandmother's, Anne Marie would help the girl plant her own small garden. They'd already planted a container garden on Anne Marie's balcony, with easy-care flowers like impatiens and geraniums.

As soon as she'd finished the watering, Ellen phoned her grandmother. Anne Marie spoke to the older woman, too.

"I don't know why these doctors insist on keeping me here," Dolores grumbled. "I'm fit as a fiddle. Ready to go home."

"It won't be long now," Anne Marie told her.

"I certainly hope so." She sobered a bit. "How's Ellen doing? Don't whitewash the truth for me. I need to know."

"She misses you."

"Well, of course she does. I miss her, too."

Anne Marie smiled. "Actually, she's doing really well."

Dolores Falk sighed expressively. "God love you, Anne Marie. I don't know what Ellen and I would've done without you."

The praise embarrassed her. She was the one who'd truly benefited from having the child.

When Ellen had done her homework, the two of them knit in front of the television. Ellen had completed the scarf for her grandmother and started a much more ambitious project, a pair of mitts. After an hour's knitting, she had a bath and put on her brand-new pajamas. She crawled into her bed. Prayers were shorter than usual that night, since Ellen was especially tired, and then Anne Marie read to her. They were now on the third "Little House" book and rereading these childhood favorites gave Anne Marie great pleasure. Ellen fell asleep listening.

When Anne Marie got down from the bed, Baxter hopped up to take her place.

The small apartment was quiet now, and a feeling of peace surrounded her. As always, she kept the bedroom door partially ajar for Ellen, who was afraid of the dark.

Tiptoeing down the hallway to her own bedroom, Anne Marie opened her binder of Twenty Wishes. She wanted to document the fact that she'd laughed. As Ellen had said, that was, indeed, one of her wishes.

She turned the pages in the binder and reviewed her list. She added a few more.

16. Go to Central Park in New York and ride a horse-drawn carriage

17. Catch snowflakes on my tongue and then make snow angels

18. Read all of Jane Austen

Lillie and Barbie had both said they wanted to fall in love again. Anne Marie wasn't sure she did. Love had brought her more grief than joy. She'd loved Robert to the very depths of her soul, and his sudden death had devastated her.

Then to learn he'd had an affair with his personal assistant… The betrayal of it still felt like a crushing weight.

Anne Marie closed her eyes at the pain.

"Stop it," she said aloud. "Stop it right now."

She felt suddenly angry with herself. It was as if she'd set out to dismantle the positive attitude she'd so carefully created and destroy all the happiness she'd managed to find by thinking of everything that had gone wrong. No, she wouldn't do it; she refused to let herself reexamine the pain of the last months.

Turning a page, she looked at the picture of the Eiffel Tower.

Someday she'd go.

Someday that wish, too, would be fulfilled.

Twenty-Five

Anne Marie entered the small neighborhood park at the end of Blossom Street, where she walked Baxter every morning. Her stepdaughter sat on a bench waiting for her.

The weather had taken a turn for the worse since Wednesday, when she'd gone to the waterfront with Ellen and Baxter. This afternoon the sky was overcast and the scent of rain hung in the air.

Melissa had suggested they have lunch in the park. Anne Marie appreciated not having any reminder of their last restaurant meeting.

"Hi," Melissa said as Anne Marie sat down beside her.

"Hi." Strange—after years of avoidance, they were now seeking each other's company. Anne Marie was curious about what Melissa had decided since they'd last talked.

"I'm having yogurt for lunch," Melissa announced. "I don't even like it, but Michael says it's good for me and the baby."

Anne Marie took out a tuna sandwich she'd slapped together that morning. "You told Michael, then."

Melissa peeled off the foil top on the yogurt container and discarded it in her sack. "I went to see him right after you and I met, just like you said, and I'm glad I did." She paused. "He was definitely shocked."

"No more than you were."

"True." She grew quiet. "He didn't believe me at first."

This angered Anne Marie on her stepdaughter's behalf. "Why not?"

"Remember I was the one who broke up with him, and I hurt him pretty badly. I should never have done that. I should've told Michael right away."

"We all make mistakes," Anne Marie said. She'd certainly made hers. Late at night she sometimes wondered if she'd been wrong to give Robert an ultimatum, if she should've tried to work things out in a different way.

"I could see he wanted to talk to me, but he was scared I'd hurt him again, so he kept looking away." Melissa's voice became more animated. "I kept asking him to look at me and he wouldn't."

It must have been terribly frustrating. "What did you do?"

Melissa appeared to be studying her yogurt, but Anne Marie could see she was smiling. "I kissed his neck."

"His neck?"

"Michael's a lot taller than I am and that's as far as I could reach. I said I loved him and that I was sorry. I put my arms around him and told him the reason I broke up with him was because I was afraid." She unwrapped the plastic spoon "To tell you the truth I was even more scared then. My friend, the one who told me she'd seen Michael with someone else, had some other news, too, and I was sure I'd lost him for good."

"What news?"

"She said she'd seen him in a jewelry store, looking at diamond rings."

"For this other girl?"

"No, but I'm getting ahead of myself."

"Okay, go back. Tell me what happened when you told Michael about the baby."

Some of the happiness left Melissa's eyes. "Like I said, he didn't believe me. He thought I was making it up, which made me so mad I almost walked away. I'm glad I didn't, though."

"But why would he even think that?"

Melissa shrugged. "He didn't trust me, and I can't blame him." She met Anne Marie's eyes. "I said I'd never make anything like this up and to prove it I showed him the ultrasound I got from the pregnancy center."

"I'll bet that got his attention."

Melissa laughed. "It sure did. He nearly fainted. All he could do was look at that little picture of our baby and walk around in circles. He was so pale I thought he was going to pass out. It took him a few minutes to get used to the idea, and then he asked me what I intended to do. I said that was why I'd come to see him. I felt this was a decision we should make together."

Anne Marie nodded. She didn't speak, not wanting to interrupt the flow of Melissa's story.

"One thing I did, which I regret now, was to tell him that Mom wanted me to get rid of the baby. Michael got really, really upset. Basically I'd already decided that there are so many other options, an abortion would be my last resort."

Although she didn't remember Michael from the funeral, Anne Marie felt warmly disposed toward him, sure she'd approve of this obviously responsible young man.

"He said a baby needs a mother and a father," Melissa went on, "and naturally I agreed because I believe that, too." She dipped her spoon into the yogurt and put it in her mouth. "Do you want to know how bad my sense of timing is?" she said a moment later.

Anne Marie grinned at her wry tone. "I can't wait to hear."

"The night I broke up with Michael was the very same night he was going to propose to me. He had an engagement ring in his pocket and everything. The diamond he'd been buying when my friend saw him was for me. *And* the other girl was just a study partner."

"Oh, Melissa."

"We've been seeing each other practically every night. Oh, and I'm back in school." She smiled confidently. "You can bet he's doing all his studying with *me* now."

"That's great! But there's something I need to know. Are you going to marry Michael?" She knew marriage was what Robert would've wanted for his daughter.

"Yes. Yes, I am. But I'm getting ahead of myself again."

Anne Marie took the first bite of her sandwich. Robert would've been thrilled at the prospect of grandchildren. That was always his excuse when he refused to consider having a baby with Anne Marie. He said he didn't want children and grandchildren the same age. Nor, he claimed, did he want his children to be mistaken for his grandchildren.

But it was useless to review their arguments now. What she recalled most strongly was Robert's anticipation of his children's children. Unlike Pamela, he would've been thrilled with the news of this baby.

Apparently Pamela had yet to be won over. But Anne Marie had to assume it wouldn't be long before the baby stole his or her grandmother's heart.

"As soon as I talked to Michael, we decided to get engaged," Melissa said. "Then I called my mother." Melissa frowned. "Unfortunately, it wasn't a pleasant conversation."

"How did you tell her?"

"I tried to be positive. I told her I'd discussed the baby with Michael and right off, that upset her. Mom said the decision was mine and mine alone, and by dragging him into it I was only complicating what should be a simple decision."

"Oh, dear…"

"You know," she said slowly. "I've never seen this side of my mother before. She's totally convinced I should take that job and move to England."

"You still could, I guess."

She nodded. "But I'm not sure I ever really wanted a job in London. Mom keeps telling me what a fabulous opportunity this is, the chance of a lifetime and all that. But it would mean leaving Michael and I don't want that, baby or no baby."

"Couldn't he come with you?" With Pamela's resources, it might be possible to get Michael employment, as well.

"No. He's going to work in his father's carpet business. He'll eventually take over the company. It isn't like he could just pack up and follow me to another country. He'd like to go to Europe one day, but Seattle is home."

That made sense to Anne Marie.

"I don't think I ever realized how much Mom had her heart set on me joining her in the corporate world."

Anne Marie could understand Pamela's disappointment. Her marriage to Robert had disintegrated when Pamela accepted a position that often took her out of the country. The arrangement had suited Pamela and, although Robert was involved in his own career, he loved his children and willingly looked after their needs. Pamela cared about her kids, too, of course, but she had her own vision of what was best for them. Whether they actually agreed with that vision seemed irrelevant to her.

"I'm sure your mother's afraid you might be repeating her mistake—or what she sees as one," Anne Marie said as gently as she could. She didn't want to suggest the marriage had been a mistake, although in retrospect it probably was.

"She started yelling at me and said I'd regret this for the rest of my life."

Pamela's temper was legendary.

"I asked her if she regretted having Brandon and me and she said…" Melissa swallowed hard. "She said if she had to do it over again, she wouldn't have had either one of us because we've done nothing but let her down."

"She didn't mean that! She *couldn't* mean it." Anne Marie was horrified by such a cruel remark, even if Pamela had lashed out, unthinking.

"I know," Melissa said in a small voice. "Afterward she emailed me and apologized, but she still said she wanted no part of the wedding."

The wedding. Melissa and Michael were going to have a wedding. Of course they were.

"Will you come to our wedding?" Melissa asked tentatively.

"Absolutely! I wouldn't miss it for anything."

Melissa smiled, and Anne Marie saw tears in her eyes. "I still can't believe this, you know," she muttered.

"What your mother said?"

"No, me coming to you for advice. And support. A year ago, even three months ago, I would never have done that. I… I thought I hated you."

"Let's try to forget all that, okay?"

"I blamed you for the divorce, although I know it wasn't

your fault at all. Brandon and I had a long talk about you, and he's helped me figure things out. Emotions can become habits," she said haltingly as she wiped her eyes. "But habits can be changed."

There was a silence, and Anne Marie found herself blinking back tears of her own. "Can I help with the wedding?" she finally asked, diverting the subject from herself and their painful past.

"You'd do that?"

"I offered, didn't I?"

"Well, yes, but I never expected… I didn't think you'd have time."

"I'll make time." Anne Marie *wanted* to help Melissa. The possibility filled her with hope and a kind of exultation. For nearly thirteen years her relationship with her stepdaughter had been nothing less than turbulent. Then, for reasons she didn't completely understand, it had begun to change.

"I wasn't going to tell you, but…"

"Tell me what?" Melissa glanced at her suspiciously.

"I'm taking knitting classes and I bought yarn for a baby blanket."

Melissa smiled tremulously. "You did that for me?"

"I'm going to be a stepgrandma, aren't I?"

Melissa nodded, and tears coursed down her cheeks unrestrained. "I can't believe how wonderful you've been to me." Melissa reached for her hand and squeezed it. "Thank you, Anne Marie," she whispered.

Anne Marie put aside her half-finished sandwich. "Ellen picked out the yarn," she said, clearing her throat. "It's a variegated one with yellow, pink, pale blue and lavender." Anne Marie was eager to start. As soon as she'd finished the lap robe for Dolores, she'd knit the blanket for Melissa and Michael's baby. Her stepgrandchild.

"I'll treasure it. And please thank Ellen. I hope I can meet her soon." Melissa used a napkin to mop her face as she spoke. Except for her reddened eyes, she looked as beautiful as ever.

"We'll arrange something," Anne Marie said. "Now, have you and Michael set a date?"

"July twelfth."

It was almost the middle of April. That didn't leave them much time, especially with Melissa and Michael both graduating from college in the next month.

"You're reinstated in your classes, but what about the work you missed? Have you caught up?"

"Yes, Mom," Melissa said with a laugh.

Anne Marie was beginning to feel like a parent, or rather Melissa was *letting* her feel like one. Melissa's stepmom. Darn it, she loved how that felt.

Robert would be so proud of them. This was what he'd always wanted for her and Melissa. How sad that it hadn't happened until he was gone. Somehow, though, she had the feeling he knew and approved.

"Your father would've wanted you to get your degree," she murmured.

"I know," Melissa said.

"Okay, let's discuss the wedding."

Melissa sighed. "It's a bit overwhelming. We have no idea where to start. Michael's mother said we should set a date and get the minister first, but I don't know any."

"I do."

"Really?"

"Sort of. Alix Turner, who works at the French Café, is

married to a minister. Would you like me to get his phone number for you?"

Melissa nodded. "That would be great."

"What about your dress?" Anne Marie asked.

Another deep sigh. "I haven't even thought about that yet."

"I'll do some research—a friend of mine owns a dress shop, and if she doesn't have what you need, she'll know someone who does. Then I'll make an appointment with Alix over at the French Café so we can check out a catering menu and look at wedding cake designs."

"You're sure you have time for all this?"

"For you, Melissa, yes," Anne Marie told her. "Ellen will help, too. It'll be good to get her mind off her grandmother."

"Thank you," Melissa whispered with a watery smile.

She might not ever be a mother, Anne Marie realized, but she was a stepmom and she'd make a wonderful grandmother for Melissa's baby.

She'd learned two things from Melissa. The habits of a lifetime *could* be changed. And family could come about in the most unexpected ways.

Twenty-Six

When Barbie approached the ticket window at the movie complex, she was pleased to note that Tessa was handling sales again that night. As soon as she'd advanced to the front of the line, Tessa broke into a huge smile.

"Uncle Mark left a ticket for you."

Barbie hesitated. "He bought my ticket?" So far, they'd met at the pool four times for the adult lap swim session—and that was it. Although they'd kissed that first day in the water, they hadn't since. Not for any lack of desire, at least on Barbie's part. But the circumstances weren't ideal; their privacy the first time hadn't been repeated, and she wasn't interested in giving the seniors' swim class an eyeful.

"It's a *date*," Tessa said, as if she needed to clarify.

"Please tell me we're not seeing another horror movie."

"No," Tessa assured her. "It's a courtroom drama. Lots of talking. You don't have to worry about being scared out of your wits."

But Barbie *was* scared. She'd fallen for Mark and fallen hard. The wheelchair didn't frighten her, but the man who sat in it did. Their relationship wouldn't be easy and the realities of a future with him were intimidating. Yet the strength of her attraction overcame her doubts.

He was slowly letting her into his life, and that thrilled her. As was her custom, she purchased popcorn and a soda and entered the theater.

"Howdy," she said as she slipped into the seat directly beside Mark's.

"Hi." He didn't look in her direction.

"Thanks for the ticket."

"My pleasure."

She tilted her bag of popcorn in his direction and he took a handful. "As Tessa pointed out, this is like a real date."

"Aren't we both a bit old for that nonsense?"

"I certainly hope not," Barbie said. "My mother has a male friend and *they're* dating."

"You make it sound like high school."

"Does it feel like that to you? In some ways it does to me." In good ways. She woke each morning with a sense of happy expectation. Mark was in her thoughts when she drove to the dress shop and then at noon when she dashed to the fitness center. He'd never asked for her phone number, which she would willingly, gladly, have given him. It would've been sheer heaven to lie in bed and talk to him on the phone, like she had with her high school boyfriend. And then with Gary…

"Yeah, it feels like high school." Mark snorted. "In all the stupid ways."

"Mark!"

"I'm not a romantic."

"No!" She feigned shock. "I never would've guessed."

"I'll be honest with you," he said, his voice clipped. "I don't expect this to last."

"You're obviously an optimist, as well," she teased.

Mark still wouldn't look at her. "I don't know what you expect to get out of this relationship, because I haven't got much to give."

"Would you stop?" This little speech of his sounded rehearsed.

"Let me finish."

"All right, have your say and then I'll have mine." She tilted the popcorn in his direction again.

He stared at it. "I can't eat very much of that."

"Why not?" He *had* eaten it earlier, so it wasn't a food allergy.

"I have a lot of limitations, Barbie. For instance, I can't eat whatever I want."

"Few of us can eat whatever we want. You know what? Everyone has limitations. Okay, so yours are more obvious than some people's. But I have several of my own, which I'm doing my best to keep under control."

"Let me guess." He pressed his index finger to his lips. "First, you have one hell of a temper."

She laughed outright at that. "How kind of you to remind me."

"What I'm trying to say," he continued, "is that this relationship is doomed. You apparently get some kind of emotional kick out of flirting with me, and that's fine. It's good for the ego, and mine's been in the gutter so long that this is a refreshing change. But I'm not a fool. A woman like you can have any man she wants."

"Mark, I—"

"I don't mean to be rude here. However—"

"Why not? It hasn't stopped you in the past."

He grinned. "True. Just let me finish, okay?"

She motioned with her hand. "Be my guest."

"This is the way I figure it. For reasons beyond my comprehension, you're attracted to me."

"Is it a one-way attraction?" For the sake of her own ego, she needed to find out. "Answer this one question and I promise I won't interrupt you again."

He raised his eyebrows. "You already know. You pretty much turn me inside out every time I see you."

Barbie clasped her hands, still clutching the bag of popcorn. "Do I really?"

"Barbie, please, you're making this difficult."

"Okay, sorry." But her heart was leaping with joy.

"Listen, for whatever reason, you feel safe with me. I'm not a threat to you. I don't know what went on in your marriage, and frankly, I don't want to know. Whatever happened then or since has really rattled you. So a guy in a wheelchair's a safe bet. Fine. The truth is, I can't seem to forget you and I'm tired of fighting my attraction to you."

"For your information, I had a very good marriage." Barbie wasn't sure where all this talk was leading. "I think you're looking for an excuse to avoid a relationship with me."

"Listen," he said again, exhaling slowly.

"You're ignoring what I just said."

For the first time he glanced in her direction. As soon as he did, his eyes softened. "Okay. For now I'm willing to do things your way."

"For now?" She wasn't sure what that meant either. "Could you explain that?"

He sighed loudly. "We play this by ear. When you want out, you get out. Don't prolong it. Do me a favor and just leave, okay?"

Barbie had to think for a moment. "What about you?"

"If I want out, then I need you to respect my wishes in the same way that I intend to respect yours."

That sounded fair. Still, she hated the idea of planning their breakup. "Can't we just take this one day at a time?"

He didn't respond.

"One *date* at a time?" she said and then leaned over and kissed his ear, running the tip of her tongue over the smooth contours and nibbling on his lobe. "One kiss at a time?"

"Yes," he said, his voice husky with desire. "I told you earlier—you turn me inside out."

The theater darkened, and the previews started. Barbie put her popcorn and soda on the floor at her feet. To her surprise and delight, Mark reached for her hand and entwined their fingers. She leaned closer and a few minutes into the movie, rested her head on his shoulder.

Mark snickered softly. "Like I said, it's high school all over again."

"I don't care if it is or not."

In response, he raised their clasped hands to his lips and kissed the back of her hand. A chill of pleasure slid down her spine.

At the end of the movie, she walked next to his wheelchair as they left the theater. She half expected him to ask her out for coffee. The movie might be over, but that didn't mean their evening had to be. When he didn't suggest it, she did.

"I can't tonight." He didn't offer an excuse.

"Perhaps another night, then." She did her best to hide her disappointment.

"Perhaps."

"Will you call me?" she asked.

"When?" He didn't seem pleased by the prospect.

"Tonight before you go to sleep."

He frowned. "Barbie."

"It's a simple request. If you can do it, fine. If not…if not, I'll lie awake all night wondering why you didn't phone."

"Just like high school."

"Yes." She wasn't about to deny it.

He muttered something she couldn't quite decipher and from the gruffness of his voice, she figured she was better off not knowing. "Give me your phone number," he growled.

"Thank you." Reaching inside her purse for a pen and pad, she wrote out her home number and tore off the sheet.

Mark crumpled it and stuffed it in his shirt pocket. "If you're loitering here because you expect me to kiss you, don't. I never kiss in public."

She didn't remind him that he'd kissed her at the pool and at the theater. "Want to go someplace private, then?"

He shook his head. "I'll take a rain check on that."

"Okay." What she'd learned from their brief conversation before the movie was that Mark was as terrified as she was. He didn't *want* to be attracted to her. He'd rather chase her away, only he hadn't succeeded in that. Yes, he desired her, but he wouldn't risk any kind of dependence on her. Insofar as he was willing to get involved, he wasn't letting her any too close. She had a mental image of a heavily armed guard standing watch over his heart.

Several hours later, Barbie lay on her bed, waiting for Mark's call. It was almost eleven before the phone finally rang.

"Hello, Mark."

"Hi." His voice was impatient. "I phoned like you asked me to. Now what is it you want to know?"

She hadn't actually thought the call required a purpose. "What are you wearing?"

"I'm on to your game! You're asking me that because you want me to ask *you* the same question."

"I'm wearing an ivory silk gown."

"Short?"

"No, full-length. What about you?"

"I'm not saying," he muttered. "I don't understand the point of this, and I'm not interested in silly games."

"I want you to want me," she said. "That's all."

"That's *all?*" She heard him snort disbelievingly. "You don't need to work nearly this hard."

"That's very sweet."

"It wasn't meant to be."

"Mark," she whispered, nearly purring his name. "Loosen up. We hardly know each other. I thought we could use this time to talk, to get acquainted."

He didn't say anything for maybe ten seconds, although it felt more like ten minutes. "What do you want to know?" he asked again.

"What do you do?" She already knew, but wanted him to tell her, anyway.

"I'm an architect." He didn't elaborate or describe any of the buildings he'd designed. Nor did he say where he worked or where he'd gone to school or anything else regarding his professional life. Barbie was beginning to understand him. The less he revealed about himself, the less likely she was to hurt him.

"I have twin sons," she said, moving the conversation into more personal realms.

"Identical?"

"Yes. My husband was killed in a plane crash three years ago."

"I know. You aren't the only one who uses the internet.

Both your husband and your father worked for a huge per-fume conglomerate. You never said anything about that."

"Why should I? Mom and I don't really have anything to do with the company."

"You do smell good most of the time."

"*Most* of the time?" she flared.

"Chlorine isn't one of your better scents."

"I'll have you know you're the only man in the world who could get me into a public swimming pool. I live in mortal fear that my hair's going to turn green in that over-chlorinated water and it'll be entirely your fault."

"Then don't come."

"Uh-huh. And miss getting splashed by you? It's the highlight of my week!"

He laughed, and in her mind she saw the mercenary who stood guard over his feelings lay down one weapon in his arsenal.

They spoke for two hours. Before they said good-night, Mark admitted he'd been in bed a full thirty minutes before he phoned. He wouldn't have called at all, he said, if not for the fact that he couldn't sleep. Every time he closed his eyes, the thought of her waiting in bed taunted him until he couldn't tolerate it anymore.

On Thursday afternoon, after her belly dancing class, Barbie met her mother for lunch. Lillie had already ar-rived at the upscale hotel restaurant and was reviewing the menu when Barbie joined her. Lillie did an immedi-ate double take.

"My goodness, you look wonderful! I know it's a cliché, but you're positively glowing."

"It's just sweat. This belly dancing is hard work."

"No, it's more." Lillie set the menu aside. "Is it that…man?"

"His name is Mark and yes, now that you mention it, he and I have been talking."

"You really like him, don't you?"

Barbie was crazy about him, but she wasn't ready to let her mother know that. She didn't want to ruin their lunch; so far, Lillie had been accepting of the situation and Barbie wanted it to stay that way.

"I didn't come to talk about Mark. I want to know how things are developing between you and Mr. Silva."

Lillie smiled, her eyes warm. "If I tell you something, you have to promise not to laugh."

"Mom, I won't laugh."

"We've been bowling twice in the last week."

"Bowling?"

"I'm good at it."

"My mother's a bowler. I'm calling Jerry Springer," Barbie teased.

"Oh, stop it," Lillie said and blushed.

"All you do is bowl?"

"Oh, heavens, no. We've gone for long walks and we attended a lecture at the Seattle Art Museum and signed up for a Chinese cooking class."

"What I mean is, has he kissed you?"

Lillie lowered her eyes. "Yes. We might be over sixty, but we aren't dead."

"That's for sure." In fact, her mother looked more alive than she had in years. "I think this is great!"

"What about you and Mark?"

There wasn't much to tell. "We've talked for the past three nights." Mark had confessed he generally didn't enjoy chatting on the phone. Still, they'd talked nearly two hours every time. Gradually, he was opening up to her and he became as engrossed in their conversations as she did.

When Barbie returned from lunch that afternoon, a large floral arrangement had been delivered. "Who sent the flowers?" she asked.

"Don't know. The card's addressed to you," one of her employees announced.

Eagerly she removed the small envelope and tugged out the card. Mark had written his name, together with a short note. *This time the flowers really are from me.*

Twenty-Seven

The big day had finally come. Dolores Falk was going home after nearly a month away, first in the hospital and then a nursing facility. According to her physicians, the heart surgery had been a complete success and Dolores had many good years left.

Certainly Anne Marie had noticed a definite improvement in the older woman. Every day Dolores seemed to regain more of her strength and her spirit. She was as eager to get home as Ellen was to join her there.

Thursday morning at breakfast, Ellen talked incessantly about moving back with her grandmother. The instant she got home from school, she ran upstairs to pack her bag. Anne Marie could hear her telling Baxter that she'd visit him soon. Ellen had him repeat the tricks they'd practiced—rolling over and playing hide-and-seek with his tennis ball—a few times for good measure. "So you won't forget," she told him sternly.

Anne Marie drove the child to her old neighborhood. "Remember, your grandmother's been very sick," she cautioned her.

"I know. I won't do anything to upset her," Ellen promised.

She glanced at the girl sitting in the passenger seat, the dog on her lap. "You can come see Baxter whenever you want," she said.

"Can I see you, too?"

"Of course."

"Will you still be my Lunch Buddy?"

Ellen must've asked the same questions ten times since they'd been told that Dolores was being released. "Of course," she said again.

"Goody." And then as if she'd almost forgotten something important, Ellen added breathlessly, "What about Lillie and Barbie and Mrs. Beaumont? What about Lydia and Margaret and Susannah and Theresa?" she asked. "Will I be able to visit them, too?"

"I'm sure that can be arranged." Her friends and neighbors didn't know yet that Ellen was moving back with her grandmother. As soon as they heard, they'd send their love to Ellen, and to Dolores.

"I'll still knit every day," Ellen assured her. She had a knitting bag now, the same as Anne Marie's. Young as she was, the child had proven to be an adept knitter.

"Me, too," Anne Marie said. She'd finished the lap robe for Dolores earlier and had given it to her during their most recent visit; she'd completed Melissa's baby blanket, as well. For her third project she planned to knit Ellen a sweater and had chosen a simple cardigan pattern. The girl had picked out a soft rose-colored yarn. Ellen was working on a pair of mittens. She wanted to knit Anne Marie a sweater but Lydia had wisely suggested she knit one for Baxter first and then try a larger project. Ellen had agreed.

As she neared the street where Dolores lived, Anne Marie examined the neighborhood more closely than she had before. It consisted of mostly older homes, many of them in ill repair. Now Anne Marie couldn't help wondering if this was a safe place for Ellen—or Dolores for that matter.

It'd been weeks since she'd seen the Falk home, which seemed even shabbier and more run-down now that she really looked at it. The front porch tilted, indicating the foundation had eroded on one side. The roof had a plastic tarp over part of it. Funny, Anne Marie hadn't noticed that before. The yard needed some serious attention; the flower beds sprouted weeds and a lone rosebush struggled for survival, choked off by the encroaching lawn. A pang went through Anne Marie at leaving Ellen here. Yet, this was her home...

"After we say hello to your grandmother, I'll need your help carrying in the groceries." Before heading over to Dolores's house, Anne Marie and Ellen had picked up some necessities. She didn't think Dolores would be up to a trip to the grocery store anytime soon.

"Okay," Ellen agreed. She'd already put Baxter in the back and unfastened her seat belt.

With a smile, Anne Marie watched Ellen dash out of the car and fly across the yard. She threw open the front door, then barreled inside. By the time Anne Marie entered the house, she found Ellen in her grandmother's arms, both of them a little teary. For an instant Anne Marie felt like an intruder.

Dolores Falk looked up at Anne Marie. "I can't thank you enough for taking care of my girl."

"I was glad to do it," Anne Marie said simply.

Holding on to her grandmother, Ellen said, "Anne Marie's still going to be my Lunch Buddy and she said I can see Baxter anytime I want. We're growing seeds and she taught me to knit and we knit every night after dinner when I'm finished my homework."

Dolores had heard about Ellen's knitting at least a dozen times. The child was more animated today than Anne Marie had ever seen her.

Breaking away from her grandmother, Ellen raced toward the hallway. "I want to see my room!"

"I didn't have an actual bed for her at my place," Anne Marie explained. "She slept on a pull-out sofa." She wished now that she'd purchased a bed for Ellen, but it hadn't seemed logical at the time. She couldn't possibly have known the girl would be with her a full month.

Obviously fatigued, Dolores sank into her recliner. "I'm just so grateful for everything you did."

"I'm going to miss her." The apartment, tiny though it was, would seem empty without her.

Ellen tore back into the living room. "Should we bring my clothes in now?"

"Sounds like a plan," Anne Marie said briskly. For a moment she'd forgotten about Ellen's bags and the groceries. "We got a few things we thought you'd need for the first couple of days," she told Dolores. "Enough to last until you can get to the grocery store."

Dolores seemed about to weep. "God bless you."

Anne Marie shrugged off her appreciation and, with Ellen at her side, returned to her vehicle. Baxter, lying in the backseat, didn't seem pleased to be left out of the action.

"Can I take Baxter for a walk?" Ellen asked as she pressed her nose to the car window.

"Help me first and then you can take him. Just be sure his leash is secure."

"Okay."

They collected Ellen's various bags, unloaded the groceries and brought everything inside. Anne Marie sorted through the cartons of milk and juice, the vegetables, cereal, cheese and bread, and organized them as logically as she could so Dolores wouldn't have any problem locating what she needed.

"Is there anything else I can do for you?" she asked Dolores once Ellen had come back with the dog.

"No, no—you've done far more than I would've thought to ask."

Anne Marie moved toward the front door, reluctant to leave. "Ellen, finish your homework, okay?"

"I will."

"See you soon," Anne Marie said, trying to swallow the lump in her throat.

"Okay." Ellen hugged Baxter goodbye, then ran across the living room to throw her thin arms around Anne Marie, holding tight. Her shoulders trembled with her sobbing.

"Hey," Anne Marie said, bending down. "This is your home, remember? You're back with your Grandma Dolores. Isn't that great?"

"Yeah, but…" Ellen sniffled. "I'm going to miss you."

"I'll miss you, too, but we'll see each other often."

"You promise?"

"I promise, and I always keep my promises," Anne Marie said. "You know that, right?" She rubbed Ellen's back gently as the child nodded. "In fact, why don't I stop by tomorrow evening to see how everything's going?" Glancing over at Dolores, she asked, "If that's okay with your grandmother?"

"That would be just fine," Dolores said.

Anne Marie left a few minutes later. As she drove away from the bedraggled little house, she experienced an overwhelming sense of loss. For one wild moment, she felt a compelling urge to turn back. She couldn't imagine what she'd say if she did. Ellen belonged with her grandmother; Dolores deeply loved this child. *So did she.* Anne Marie realized it with a shock that galvanized her.

She understood now that what she'd seen as affection, caring, a feeling of responsibility—all emotions she'd readily acknowledged—added up to one thing. *Love.*

She loved this little girl and wanted to be part of her life for as long as she could.

"Well, Baxter," she murmured, sighing loudly. "It's just you and me again."

Her Yorkie, who'd been sitting up in the backseat, turned in a circle several times, then dropped down. He curled up, nose to tail, and Anne Marie thought he seemed as despondent as she was.

When she reached her quiet apartment, she roamed from room to room, feeling restless. Dissatisfied. Living here was only supposed to be a temporary situation. The apartment was empty when she'd separated from Robert and it had seemed the logical place to live while they sorted out their differences. It really was time to look for a house, a home for her and Baxter. She might see if she could find one in the same area as Ellen, a fixer-upper she could keep for a while and then sell for a nice profit.

As she moved into the kitchen to prepare a sandwich, Anne Marie stopped abruptly, recognizing something about herself. She was different than she'd been a month ago. She'd gradually changed into a woman who could make her own wishes come true. A woman who was ready to move on with her life. This was the gift Ellen had given her. She'd opened Anne Marie's eyes to the many ways she'd been blessed, despite her losses, and the many possibilities that still existed.

Preparing for bed, she paused in the doorway to Ellen's room. The bed was a sofa again, and Baxter had nestled on the cushion and gone to sleep, as if he expected the little girl to return.

The room was neat and orderly. Nothing of Ellen remained, and yet Anne Marie felt her presence. Many a night she'd stood right here, watching Ellen sleep. That ritual would come to an end now. But she couldn't be sad about it because Ellen was where she wanted and needed to be, with the grandmother who adored her.

"Sleep tight, sweetie," she whispered, then went to her own room to read before turning out the light.

Twenty-Eight

Lillie was as nervous as a bride the night before her wedding. Hector was coming to pick her up and bring her to his place for dinner. They'd seen each other a number of times, but this was different.

Hector had invited her to his *home*.

Lillie felt as if she'd passed some test, and that the invitation to visit his home was Hector's way of saying he trusted her and was willing to reveal more of his life.

When the doorbell rang, she pressed her hand over her heart and took a deep breath before walking to the front door and opening it. As always Hector was punctual.

"Good evening, Lillie," he said, bowing his head slightly. "I hope you had a pleasant afternoon."

"No. I mean, yes, I had a lovely afternoon." Rather than explain her initial response, she gathered up her sweater, made of silver-blue cashmere, and her purse.

She'd agonized over whether to ask him in, self-conscious about her wealth and her luxurious house. But it wasn't an issue, since he immediately asked if she was ready to leave.

After she'd locked her door and set the alarm, he led her to his car, parked in her driveway. His manners were impeccable as he escorted her and made sure she was comfortably seated. His courtesies came from a soul-deep regard for others, a true considerateness; she knew that with absolute certainty. This was nothing as superficial as charm. It was a mark of respect.

"I hope you're hungry," he was saying once he'd joined her in the vehicle.

Lillie was far too nervous to be hungry. "I've been looking forward to this all day," she told him.

He glanced over at her, his dark eyes intense. "I have, too."

Her stomach pitched. From the first moment they'd met, he'd had an unprecedented effect on her. She felt things with him that she hadn't felt before. David had never shared much with her; he'd been what her women's magazines now referred to as "emotionally inaccessible." His affairs were part of that, of course. It wasn't until after his death that she'd recognized how withdrawn she'd become through the years. There had been a price to pay for ignoring his betrayals, for turning a blind eye to his shortcomings as a husband and lover. The price had been much higher than she'd realized. Only now was she beginning to understand how repressed her feelings had become. She'd learned to subdue her own emotions as well as her expectations.

Hector was talking about dinner, and she shook off her pensiveness.

"You made everything yourself?" she asked.

"My daughter offered advice."

Hector and his daughter seemed to be especially close. Like everything else about this man, she found that endearing—and she couldn't help comparing it to David's relationship with Barbie. At first he'd been disappointed not to have a son, but Barbie had quickly wrapped him around her little finger. He'd accepted Lillie's inability to have other children and lavished his attention on his daughter. David could be generous and loving; he'd certainly shown Barbie that side of himself. But Lillie considered him both uncommitted and morally weak in his emotional life. Yet he'd been a scrupulously honest businessman... She supposed that was a result of his skill at "compartmentalizing," which men were said to be good at, again according to her magazines.

"I need to mention something about my home," Hector said, looking straight ahead as he concentrated on traffic. "I don't live in a fancy neighborhood."

"I understand that."

"Your home is beautiful, Lillie."

"Hector, are you telling me you're ashamed of your home?" she asked bluntly.

"No, I'm not."

"Then please don't apologize for it."

"You apologized for yours, remember?"

She had. She'd feared that once Hector saw her opulent home, the differences between their financial situations would discourage him. She'd been wrong. He wasn't easily intimidated. At least, she didn't think so until he'd brought up the subject of his own neighborhood.

"People might talk about us, Lillie," Hector added. "However, Rita's aware that I'm seeing you and has been most supportive."

"My daughter has been, too." Lillie didn't mention their initial conflict and the painful few days that had followed their disagreement.

"I haven't told my sons about you yet."

"Oh?"

"They might not be as understanding as Rita."

Lillie glanced at him. "Will their opinion make a difference?" she asked.

He didn't answer right away. "I would like to tell you it
wouldn't. The truth is, I don't know. My family is important and I trust that my children love me enough to want to
see me happy. And you, Lillie, make me happy."

"Oh, Hector." His sincerity touched her heart. "You
make me happy, too," she whispered in return.

Hector reached for her hand.

As soon as they turned onto Walnut Street, Lillie knew
instantly which home was his. The yard was beautifully
maintained, the flower beds splashed with brilliant color.
When he pulled into the driveway of the house she'd
guessed was his, it was all Lillie could do not to congratu-
late herself.

Hector helped her out of the car and led her to the front
door of the white-painted two-story house. The first thing
she saw inside was a multitude of family pictures. They
covered the walls and the top of the piano. The wall next
to the stairs was another gallery of photographs. Lillie's
gaze went to a portrait of Hector and his deceased wife.
Angelina, maybe fifty in the picture, had been a slender,
elegant woman.

"These are my children," he said, pointing to college
graduation photos of his daughter and his two sons. "This
is Manuel," he said, tapping the picture of his oldest son.

"The attorney," Lillie murmured. The young man in the
cap and gown, proudly displaying his diploma, had serious
eyes and a fierce look. Lillie could picture him in a courtroom vanquishing his opponent.

"Luis," he continued, tapping one finger on the next
photograph.

"The doctor." Unlike his brother, Lillie observed, Luis

had gentle eyes that reminded her of Hector's. "He looks the most like you."

"Yes," Hector said. "Angelina and I always knew he'd work in the health field. From the time he was a little boy, he wanted to help anyone in pain."

Yes, this son was most like his father.

"And Rita," Hector said, going down the line of photographs.

His daughter was a true beauty who resembled her mother. There was an engaging warmth in her smile.

"She's lovely," Lillie whispered. "I'm sure she's a popular teacher."

The smells coming from the kitchen were enticing, and suddenly Lillie felt ravenous. Once she'd torn her gaze from the photographs, she noticed that Hector had set the dining table with his best dishes; a small floral centerpiece sat in the middle.

"What's for dinner?" she asked.

"You'll see." He escorted her into the dining room.

"What can I do?"

"Nothing. You're my guest."

"Hector, I *want* to help."

He hesitated but finally agreed. "If you insist. You can cut the bread."

"You never did tell me what you're serving."

"It's a classic Mexican dish," Hector teased as he opened a drawer and pulled out a bread knife. "It's spaghetti. My daughter gave me the recipe. She even went to the store with me and chose the ingredients."

"You didn't need to go to all that trouble," Lillie said, although she was flattered that he had. "We could eat potato chips and it would taste like ambrosia to me because I'm here with you."

Hector grinned, then took a step closer. "I have been lonely for a long time," he said in a low voice.

Lillie had spent most of her marriage being lonely. "I have, too," she told him.

For just a moment it seemed that he was about to kiss her. Their first kiss had been the evening they'd attended the Frida Kahlo lecture at the Seattle Art Museum. At the end of the evening, he'd dropped her at home; he'd declined coffee but walked her to the door. It'd been an awkward moment and by unspoken agreement they'd each leaned forward and kissed. Lillie was eager to repeat the experience. Their kiss had been polite, almost chaste, but very satisfying...

"I'm just reheating the sauce," he said, wielding a large wooden spoon.

"Hector?" Lillie drew in a deep breath before plunging ahead.

The way she said his name seemed to alert him to the fact that she had something important to say.

"Yes?"

"I want you to know..."

"Yes, Lillie?"

"When it feels right to you, I hope you'll kiss me again." She didn't want him wondering—or worrying—about what her response might be.

"Thank you." His eyes sparkled with delight. "I shall keep that in mind."

She picked up the bread knife and carefully sliced the loaf of French bread, arranging the pieces neatly on a serving plate.

After stirring the sauce, Hector boiled the spaghetti noodles; when they were ready, he placed them inside a beautiful hand-painted ceramic dish. Next he poured the meat-and-tomato sauce over the noodles. The salad, waiting in the refrigerator, was already mixed. Lillie put it on the table, along with the bread.

Hector opened a bottle of red wine that he told her Rita had recommended. Then he seated her at the table and sat across from her.

They toasted each other, touching glasses, and began the meal. She discovered that Hector preferred his food spicier than she did but he'd made the sauce fairly mild, adding chili peppers to his own. Another example of his thoughtfulness.

In the beginning their conversation was tentative. But it wasn't long before the hesitation dissolved and they found any number of topics to discuss. They agreed on political issues and surprisingly had enjoyed some of the same films and novels. Hector bragged about his grandchildren and she told stories about her grandsons. The conversation flowed naturally from one subject to the next as they lingered over their wine. Afterward, despite Hector's protests, Lillie helped with the dishes. Her shoes hurt her feet, so she took them off and tucked a dish towel into her waistband as she moved effortlessly around his kitchen.

Hector put on some easy-listening music from the '70s, and soon they were dancing about the room, twirling and laughing. He kissed her once, twice, and it was as natural as breathing. His touch left her with the most inexplicable urge to weep. Rather than allow him to see the effect his kisses had on her, she buried her face in his shoulder.

Hector released her and they both went back to cleaning the kitchen, dancing around each other as they did.

He was about to kiss her again when the back door opened and Manuel walked inside. Lillie recognized him from his photograph. "Dad, I need to borrow your—" He stopped abruptly. "Dad!" he barked, shouting to be heard above the music.

Instinctively Lillie stepped closer to Hector. He leaned over to turn off the CD player on the counter, and the resulting silence was almost shocking.

Hector straightened, putting his arm around Lillie's waist. "Son, this is my friend, Lillie Higgins. Lillie, this is Manuel."

Manuel nodded politely in her direction but addressed his father. "I didn't realize you had a woman friend."

"Your father's told me quite a bit about you," Lillie said, feeling guilty although she wasn't sure why.

"Funny, he hasn't said a word about you." Manuel gave her a cold look.

Hector placed one hand on her shoulder and spoke gently. "If you'll excuse me, I will talk to my son privately." He ushered Manuel out of the room.

She nodded and finished wiping the kitchen counter. She rinsed and wrung out the cloth, then draped it over the faucet and removed her makeshift apron. Slipping on her shoes, she stood in the kitchen and waited for Hector.

Manuel left without saying anything else to Lillie and she could see from the look in Hector's eyes that the conversation hadn't gone well. "I'm sorry," she whispered and walked into his arms.

"I'm the one who owes you an apology," he murmured, holding her close. "My son was inexcusably rude."

"What did he say?" she asked.

Hector shook his head, obviously unwilling to repeat what his son had said. Lillie closed her eyes and remembered Barbie's immediate response when she'd told her she was interested in a man who worked for a car dealership.

"Give him time to adjust to the idea," she urged.

"Perhaps that's the best thing to do."

He took Lillie home soon after that; they were both quiet during the drive. When they reached her house, Hector walked her to the door. She thanked him for dinner, they kissed goodnight and then he left. Not until she was inside did she realize that he hadn't asked to see her again.

Lillie felt sick.

This was the end; she was sure of it. His family and their opinion mattered more to Hector than his own happiness. Even if he was torn, and she knew he was, Hector would appease his children rather than fight for a relationship with her.

When she didn't hear from him the next day or the day after that, Lillie decided to make this as painless as possible for them both. She wrote him a letter.

She'd only intended to write a brief note but by the time she finished she'd written three full pages. She described her list of Twenty Wishes and said that one of her wishes had been to meet an honorable man. She'd found that man in him.

In the last paragraph she explained that she had no desire to damage his relationship with his children and felt it was best that they not see each other again.

With tears in her eyes, she dropped the letter off at the post office. After a quick phone call to Barbie, she booked a trip to the coast.

Twenty-Nine

Anne Marie was fortunate enough to nab a spot in the Woodrow Wilson parking lot. She was back to the routine of Lunch Buddy dates and had brought Baxter with her for this visit.

Yesterday, when Ellen and Anne Marie had spoken, the eight-year-old had told her how much she missed her canine friend.

Bringing Baxter today was a surprise, and Anne Marie could hardly wait to see the child's face light up.

The transition from Anne Marie's home to her grandmother's had gone smoothly. Anne Marie wished she could say Ellen's departure had been as straightforward for her. The apartment just wasn't the same without Ellen; it was still too quiet, too empty. Her life felt that way, too. The child had found a vulnerable space in her heart, and Anne Marie had discovered how much she craved love. She wanted to give it as well as receive it.

Of course, she was in regular touch with Ellen and would continue to be so. She'd already arranged a trip to Woodland Park Zoo for that Saturday. Anne Marie was looking forward to it and she knew Ellen was, too. Dolores needed the break and seemed to appreciate Anne Marie's interest in the girl.

Ellen's grandmother was a pitiable woman. She blamed herself for what had become of her two daughters, and all the love in her heart was reserved for her only granddaughter. Dolores lived for Ellen. Since she'd been released from the hospital, Dolores had told Anne Marie that she'd searched for more than a year before she'd found Ellen. Once she did locate the child in the California foster care program, it had taken nearly another year to convince Child Protective Services to grant her custody of the little girl. Ellen had been with her grandmother for three years now, and the older woman had given her the security she so desperately needed.

As Anne Marie headed into the school, with Baxter on his leash, she saw Helen Mayer, the counselor, hurrying toward her.

"I can't tell you how grateful I am that you're here," Helen said. "The woman who answered the phone at the bookstore told me you were on your way."

"Is something wrong? Is Ellen okay?"

"Please—come into my office."

With a growing sense of panic, Anne Marie picked up Baxter and followed Helen into the building. She couldn't imagine what had happened, but all her instincts said it was bad.

The counselor waited until Anne Marie was inside her office, then closed the door and walked slowly to her desk. She sat down and turned to look at Anne Marie.

Tension twisted Anne Marie's stomach as she lowered herself into a chair. "What is it?" she asked, placing Baxter on the floor near her feet.

"We received word this morning that Dolores Falk died sometime last night."

Anne Marie gasped and covered her mouth with her hand. "Did… Ellen find her?"

"Apparently she overslept because her grandmother didn't wake her for school. According to what I learned, she made her own breakfast and decided to let her grandmother sleep. On her way to school she met a neighbor who inquired about Dolores. Ellen explained that her grandmother wasn't feeling well and that she was still in bed. A short while later, the neighbor went to check on her and when she couldn't rouse Dolores, she called 911."

At least the child was spared the trauma of discovering the body. Anne Marie thanked God for that. But this probably meant Ellen didn't know yet.

"Is she here?" Anne Marie knew how hard Ellen would take the news. Although she dreaded telling her, Anne Marie thought she was the best person to do so. Poor Ellen.

"I'm afraid not," Helen Mayer said.

Anne Marie barely heard her. "I'll make arrangements to get her things and bring her home with me." She wondered if Dolores had made funeral arrangements; she'd have to find out.

After burying Robert, Anne Marie had some experience in such matters. The staff at the funeral home had been both kind and respectful. Anne Marie would like them to handle the arrangements for Dolores, too, if that was possible.

"I don't think you heard me," the other woman said. "Ellen isn't at school."

Anne Marie stared at her, uncomprehending. "Where is she then?"

Helen Mayer placed her hands on the desk and leaned

forward. "About an hour ago, Child Protective Services took her away."

The words hardly made sense. "What? What do you mean they took her away?"

"I mean they came to the school, told us Ellen's grandmother had died and that they had to find a home for her."

"But…"

Helen Mayer gestured helplessly. "The only other relatives Ellen has are her mother, who has relinquished all parental rights, and her aunt, who is apparently incarcerated."

Anne Marie was well aware that Ellen had no one else. That was the very reason the child had come to live with her while Dolores was hospitalized.

"She's been placed in a foster home."

Anne Marie couldn't believe it. "Already?"

"Yes. I realize it's a shock. I tried to contact you but you didn't answer your cell. The woman at the bookstore said you'd be here soon."

Anne Marie felt disoriented but she had to focus on Ellen. The girl must be terrified. She had to get to her, reassure her that everything would be all right. "I have the name of the social worker assigned to her. She gave me her business card."

"What are you going to do?" Helen asked.

"I'll bring Ellen back to live with me." There was no question about that.

The counselor sighed with relief. "I'm so glad to hear it."

Anne Marie was on her feet, ready to take action. She committed half a dozen traffic violations in her rush to get back to the bookstore. She prayed she hadn't thrown out the social worker's card. In her agitation she couldn't even recall the woman's name.

With Baxter at her heels, Anne Marie ran up the stairs.

Heart pounding, she stood in the middle of her kitchen while she tried to remember where she'd put the woman's card.

Suddenly she remembered. She hurried into her bedroom and jerked open the top drawer of her nightstand. Yes—it was there, and the woman's name was Evelyn Boyle. She collapsed onto her bed and grabbed the phone.

Her hand trembled as she punched out the number. She listened to an automated system that requested the extension, which Anne Marie dutifully supplied. The phone rang five times before Evelyn's voice mail came on.

"This is Anne Marie Roche," she said. "I'm calling about Ellen Falk. Please contact me at your earliest convenience." She gave three phone numbers—home, work and cell— afraid the woman would give up too easily if she couldn't reach her on the first try.

The waiting was intolerable.

Anne Marie paced, she cleaned out drawers, then paced some more. When she couldn't stand it any longer, she drove to Dolores's house. The place was locked up. The neighbor who'd found her said the coroner's office had already removed the body. No one knew anything about Ellen or where she might be. Anne Marie gave the woman her numbers, desperate to learn whatever she could.

When her cell phone finally did ring, it was after four and Anne Marie nearly ripped it out of her purse in her haste.

"This is Anne Marie Roche," she said, the words tumbling over each other.

"Anne Marie, this is Evelyn Boyle returning your call."

"Where's Ellen?" she cried. The child must be frantic. Anne Marie was close to panic herself. Ellen needed her and Anne Marie needed to be with Ellen.

"It's unfortunate, but the only thing I could do was place her in a temporary foster home. It's a short-term solution until I can find a permanent home for her."

"I'll take her," Anne Marie blurted out. "Bring her to me."

"I wish I could. If you recall, when I visited the bookstore I suggested you apply for a license to become Ellen's foster parent. I didn't hear from you after that."

Anne Marie wanted to kick herself for not following through. Had she been able to look into the future, of course, she would've started the paperwork that very day. How was she to know? Dolores had been doing so well.

"I promised Dolores Falk that Ellen would never go back into the foster care system. What can I do now? How long will it take to be approved?" Her fear was that the paperwork would still take months. By then, Ellen might have been moved any number of times. Ms. Boyle had said the home where she was currently placed was temporary, which implied that Ellen would be transferred soon.

She remembered Dolores Falk telling her it had taken a year to find Ellen once she'd learned she had a granddaughter, although Anne Marie didn't know how much of that time had been spent searching in other states.

"We can have a background check done on you in twenty-four hours."

"Then Ellen can come and live with me?"

"Yes. We want what's best for Ellen and I feel that's you."

The relief was enough to flood her eyes with tears. "Thank you. Thank you."

The social worker explained the process. Anne Marie tried to pay attention but her mind kept darting off in different directions. One thing that did register was that there'd be a home study, which hadn't been scheduled yet. The apartment, small as it was, hardly seemed suitable. That would mean an immediate move. Anne Marie didn't care. She'd do whatever was necessary.

"If everything checks out, I should be able to deliver Ellen to you sometime tomorrow afternoon."

Anne Marie tried to recall any possible blemish on her record. She had a speeding ticket, but thankfully, nothing of real importance.

All the next day, Anne Marie waited. The tension was almost more than she could bear. She left three messages for Evelyn Boyle, wanting to make sure there weren't any problems with her background clearance. The social worker didn't return any of the calls.

Had Anne Marie known where Ellen was staying, she would've driven there and parked outside the house.

When she hadn't heard anything by five o'clock on Thursday afternoon, Anne Marie was positive something had gone wrong. She'd been useless the entire day, too nervous and jittery to concentrate.

Just as she was about to give up in despair, the door to the bookstore opened and Evelyn Boyle came in with Ellen at her side.

Ellen looked at Anne Marie and burst into tears as she bolted toward her.

Anne Marie fell to her knees, her arms open for Ellen.

They clung tearfully to each other. "You promised, you promised," Ellen sobbed against her shoulder. "You said— you said…"

"It's all right," Anne Marie whispered, brushing Ellen's hair. "You're here now, and no one's going to take you away from me."

Ellen sniffled. "Grandma Dolores went to live with Jesus."

"I know."

"I don't have anyone who loves me."

"I love you, Ellen," Anne Marie whispered, tears streaking her face. "You're going to be my little girl from now on."

"I can live with you?"

Anne Marie couldn't speak, so she just nodded.

"I don't have to go back to the foster house?"

"No, not ever again."

Still sobbing, Ellen tightened her arms around Anne Marie's neck. "Everyone I love goes away."

"Not anymore, Ellen," she promised. "Not if I can help it."

"I loved my mommy and she...she did bad things and she left me and then Grandma Dolores d-died and then you left me."

"I didn't leave you," Anne Marie insisted. "I would never leave you."

They continued to hold each other until Baxter started to bark at the foot of the stairs. Anne Marie released Ellen who ran to open the door. The dog immediately did a dance of joy at the sight of his friend.

Wiping the tears from her face, Anne Marie stood to find Evelyn watching her.

"I believe we have a good placement for Ellen," she said, her own eyes moist.

Anne Marie wasn't going to make another mistake. "I've decided I don't want to be Ellen's foster parent."

A look of shock broke out across the other woman's face. "I beg your pardon?"

"I want to adopt her," she said. "I want to make Ellen my legal daughter." The child was already her daughter in every way that mattered. It was time to make that official.

Thirty

"**M**om," Anne Marie said, speaking softly into the receiver. It was late Monday evening, and Ellen had just gone to sleep. The poor kid still wasn't sleeping well, so Anne Marie didn't want to risk waking her. Every night since Dolores's death, Ellen had ended up crawling into bed with Anne Marie and crying herself to sleep. The girl had suffered yet another loss. Being taken out of school, informed that her grandmother was dead and then shuffled off to a foster home hadn't helped.

"Anne Marie?" her mother murmured. "My goodness, I haven't heard from you in weeks. Is something wrong? There must be if you're phoning me this late."

"I should've called earlier." Handling the funeral arrangements and looking after Ellen had kept her busy. But the truth was, it hadn't occurred to her to contact her mother until that night.

Even now she hesitated, fearing her mother's reaction once she learned that Anne Marie was going to adopt Ellen. Her mother had made her disapproval known when she decided to marry Robert. She'd been equally negative when Anne Marie purchased the bookstore. Laura wasn't a risk-taker and she'd been convinced that Anne Marie would be throwing away her investment. She generally believed in living a cautious, conventional life, although she wouldn't have put it in those terms.

Despite her mother's reactions in the past, Anne Marie felt compelled to seek her out. Perhaps it had to do with becoming a mother herself…

Might as well just blurt it out. "I thought I should tell you that you're about to become a grandmother."

A strained silence followed her announcement.

"You're…pregnant?" Once again, Laura Bostwick's reproach was evident. "I know you want a baby, Anne Marie, but I don't think you have any idea what life's really like for a single mother. Oh, dear…"

"It isn't… I'm not—" Anne Marie didn't get the opportunity to explain before her mother interrupted her.

"If you don't mind me asking, who's the father? No, don't tell me. Obviously there's a problem, otherwise you would've married him. You *aren't* secretly married, are you?"

"No, I—"

"I don't need to know any more about him. He's married, I suppose?"

"Mom!"

"Sorry, sorry. I said not to tell me and then like a fool I ask. It's none of my business. Well, you're going to have a child. When are you due?"

"It's a bit more complicated than that," she began.

"For heaven's sake, you haven't done anything stupid, have you?"

"What do you mean?" Anne Marie asked, a little taken aback.

"Artificial insemination, that's what. I heard about it at

the hairdresser's. Apparently a lot of women are using artificial methods to get pregnant. Please don't tell me you went to one of those fertility clinics and—"

"Mother, I'm *adopting*."

She'd finally shocked her mother into total silence.

"Remember Ellen Falk?"

"Who?"

"I was her Lunch Buddy. You met her the Saturday before St. Patrick's Day. We had lunch with you." Surely her mother hadn't forgotten.

There was another silence. Then Laura said, "Let me see if I have this straight. This second-grade girl you agreed to have lunch with once a week is the one you're going to adopt?" Her mother sounded incredulous.

"Yes, Mom. She came to stay with me, remember?"

"Well, yes, and I told you I thought it was rather nervy of that girl's grandmother to call you in the middle of the night."

"Dolores Falk died."

This information appeared to unsettle Laura. "Oh... dear. That is a shame."

"Ellen doesn't have anyone else," Anne Marie said.

"You're fond of the child?"

"I love her as though I'd given birth to her myself," Anne Marie confessed. "I've already talked to the social worker and asked to be considered as Ellen's adoptive mother." She closed her eyes, certain her mother would discourage her, as she had with every important decision Anne Marie had ever made, from the school she'd chosen to the man she'd married.

"Oh, Anne Marie..."

She waited for it.

"I think that's a wonderful thing to do."

Her jaw fell so fast and hard, Anne Marie was surprised she hadn't dislocated it. "You…think I'm doing the right thing?"

"My dear girl, you're old enough to decide what you want to do with your own life. If this child means so much to you, then by all means bring her into the family."

As far as Anne Marie could remember, this was the first time in her adult life that her mother had supported her choices. She didn't understand it, other than to assume the child had won over her mother's heart in the hour or two they'd spent together.

"There won't be any legal problems, will there?" Laura went on to ask.

"I don't know." Evelyn Boyle had to do a search for Ellen's birth certificate and find out who was listed as the father. He would need to be contacted and given the opportunity to state his wishes.

Anne Marie was pretty sure Ellen's biological father didn't even know she existed. But if Evelyn managed to track him down… He could decide to declare his parental rights and Anne Marie would have no option but to relinquish Ellen. The thought made her feel ill.

"What about her biological mother?"

"She gave up all rights to her daughter three years ago when Ellen went to live with her grandmother."

"Does that mean the mother can't change her mind?"

"It's too late for that. Anyway, if it wasn't for Dolores, Ellen might've been put up for adoption years ago."

"Oh."

"The social worker was encouraging." The fact that Ellen was living with Anne Marie and that they'd so obviously bonded was a hopeful sign. However, the issue of Ellen's biological father still had to be resolved.

Anne Marie suddenly remembered something. "The wishes."

"I beg your pardon?" her mother said. "Stop mumbling, Anne Marie. How many times do I have to tell you? Speak up."

"Sorry, Mom. I was just thinking out loud."

"What was that about wishes? That's what you said, isn't it? It certainly sounded like *wishes*."

"Ellen has a list of wishes. Twenty wishes." Anne Marie had no intention of referring to her own list or those of the other widows. Her mother would no doubt throw scorn on the idea or dismiss it as childish.

"Children do that sort of thing," her mother said, confirming her suspicion. "I wouldn't give it any mind. I suppose she wished for a mother and father?"

"No, no...nothing like that." Then, because she felt she had to explain after bringing it up, she said, "Ellen wants to meet her father."

"Every child wants that. My guess is she's well rid of him."

The rest of the conversation made no impact on Anne Marie. A few minutes after she ended the call, she wandered into Ellen's tiny bedroom and watched the child as she slept, one hand flung out and resting on the dog, who was cuddled up close beside her. The poor kid was exhausted and seemed to be lost in her dreams.

Earlier, in between working at the store and looking after Ellen, Anne Marie had called the school. She'd updated Helen Mayer, who'd cheered when Anne Marie told her about adopting Ellen. She'd even offered a character reference should any be needed in the adoption process.

Anne Marie was just afraid the proceedings might not get that far.

On Saturday morning, three days after Dolores's death, they'd visited the funeral home and arranged for a small private service. A short obituary written by Anne Marie appeared in the paper. Several neighbors stopped by on Sunday to pay their respects.

The house was a rental property and Anne Marie had until the end of the month to get it cleaned out and ready for the next tenants.

That afternoon, with a few friends gathered around, Anne Marie and Ellen had laid Dolores Falk to rest. Throughout the service, Ellen stayed by Anne Marie's side. She didn't weep, although her eyes filled with tears more than once. Afterward, they'd returned to the apartment alone.

"I think Grandma Dolores was ready to live with Jesus," Ellen had said calmly as she reached for her knitting bag. She seemed to find solace in knitting.

"What makes you say that?"

She'd glanced up. "I saw it in her eyes. She told me she was tired."

Anne Marie had thought her heart would break.

Late Tuesday afternoon, Anne Marie and Ellen were in the apartment, planning a visit to Dolores's house to sort out what to keep and what to give away, when the phone rang. It was Cathy in the bookstore. "The social worker's here to talk to you. Should I send her up?"

"Yes, please." Evelyn Boyle had said she'd hoped to attend the memorial service the previous day; she'd also said she had a court date and wasn't sure how long that would last.

Anne Marie waited anxiously for her at the top of the stairs.

"How did everything go yesterday?" Evelyn asked, taking the steps one by one.

"It was very nice." Several of Dolores's neighbors had attended, and Helen Mayer from the school had been there, too, along with Lydia, Elise and Lillie. Dolores had requested that her remains be cremated; Anne Marie and Ellen would receive the ashes at a later date.

"I'm so sorry I couldn't be there."

Anne Marie bit her lip until it hurt. "Do you have news?"

"I do." The middle-aged woman paused on the landing and placed her hand over her heart. "Stairs are God's way of telling me I'm not getting any younger."

Anne Marie resisted the urge to shake her by the shoulders and demand to know what she'd learned. "Come in, please," she invited, doing her best to disguise her nervousness.

The social worker stepped into the kitchen. Ellen sat at the table knitting, with Anne Marie's notes for the disbursement of Dolores's belongings scattered about. "My goodness," Evelyn murmured, "who taught you to knit so well?"

"Anne Marie," Ellen said without looking up. "I'm sorry, Ms. Boyle, but I can't talk now. I'm counting stitches."

"Perhaps you could move into the living room so Ms. Boyle and I can chat. Okay?" Anne Marie said.

"Okay." With the ball of yarn under her arm, Ellen carried her wool and needles into the other room and, Anne Marie hoped, out of earshot.

Evelyn pulled out a kitchen chair and sat down as Anne Marie gathered up her notes and put them in a loose pile. Evelyn placed her briefcase on the table and opened it, then ceremoniously removed Ellen's file.

Anne Marie sat across from her. Waiting...

"I located a copy of Ellen's birth certificate and the father is listed—"

Anne Marie's heart slammed hard against her ribs. She hadn't expected this. "You have a name?" Okay, she'd deal with it. No matter what, Anne Marie would find a way to be part of Ellen's life and she didn't care what it cost.

Evelyn frowned. "If I'd been allowed to finish, you would've heard me say that Ellen's father is listed as unknown."

"That means…" Anne Marie was too excited to complete the question.

"It means that as far as the State of Washington is concerned, you're free to adopt Ellen Falk."

"Thank you," Anne Marie whispered, her throat thickening with emotion. "Thank you so much."

"Have you said anything to Ellen?"

Anne Marie hadn't felt she could until she had all the facts. "Not yet."

"Then let's tell her now." The social worker called out to the eight-year-old. "Ellen, would you please join us in the kitchen?"

Ellen immediately came inside and sat down in the chair next to Anne Marie.

"Hello, Ellen."

The child regarded the social worker suspiciously. Anne Marie didn't blame her; it was Evelyn Boyle who'd taken her out of class and uprooted her entire life with the news of her grandmother's death.

Hoping to reassure Ellen, Anne Marie leaned over and gently touched her arm.

"What would you think if Anne Marie became your mother?" Evelyn asked. "Would you like that?"

Ellen didn't answer right away. Then she turned and looked at Anne Marie. "Would I call you Mom?"

"If you wanted," Anne Marie said. "Or you could call me Anne Marie. Whatever you prefer."

"Could I have play dates with my friend Cassie if you were my mom?"

"Yes, of course." Anne Marie remembered the day of the school concert, when she'd been approached by the mother of Ellen's friend about a possible exchange of play dates.

Ellen looked from Anne Marie to the social worker. "Would it mean no one could ever take me away again?"

"No one, not ever," Anne Marie promised.

Ellen shrugged. "I guess it would be all right."

"You *guess?*" Anne Marie teased. "You guess?"

Ellen's face lit up with a huge smile. "I'd like it a whole lot."

"I would, too," Anne Marie told her.

Ellen bounded out of her chair and threw her arms around Anne Marie's neck.

"Wonderful," Evelyn whispered. "This is just perfect. It's cases like this that make everything else worthwhile." She opened the file again. "I have all the paperwork with me. Be warned, though, the process will take about six months."

Anne Marie didn't care how long it took. The paperwork was a mere formality.

She already had her daughter, and Ellen had her mother. Nothing would ever come between them again.

Thirty-One

"Tell me where we're going," Mark said, wheeling his chair alongside Barbie on 4th Avenue. They'd left Seattle Fitness and, after some pestering on her part, Mark had agreed to join her. She refused to allow his mood to taint this lovely May afternoon. The sun was shining, and she was in love. Mark loved her, too, although he wasn't ready to admit it yet.

"It's a secret. But we're going to meet a couple of my friends first," she explained. He knew that and had already agreed. "Stop acting so cranky."

He was quiet for a moment. "You might not have noticed, but I don't do well with most people."

"I promise you'll like Anne Marie and Ellen."

"What makes you so sure?"

"Mark, please, we've been through this." She found it difficult to hold back a smile.

"You cheated," Mark grumbled. "You lured me here under false pretenses, telling me you had a surprise for me."

"I do have a surprise for you," she said, ignoring his protests. "Besides, a deal is a deal."

Mark slowed his pace. "I might be in a wheelchair, but..."

"A wheelchair doesn't have anything to do with this." They'd struck a bargain, and she was going to ensure he

kept his part of it. She'd promised him dinner and an evening for just the two of them—after he'd met her friends.
She hadn't told him yet that dinner would be at her house.

"You don't play fair," he muttered.

"Doesn't matter. You agreed."

"Might I remind you that you had your legs wrapped
around my waist at the time?"

"Oh, did I?" She loved being in the pool with Mark, especially when they had the entire area to themselves. It was
never more than ten or fifteen minutes at the end of a session, and it didn't always happen. But when it did… The
water seemed to free him, allowing him to show his need
for her in ways he never would while sitting in his chair.
They played in the water, teased and kissed and chased each
other. Gradually, the barriers Mark had erected against her,
against the world, were coming down.

"These are two of your gal pals who also have a list of
Twenty Wishes, right?"

"Right. Anne Marie has a list and I believe Ellen's got
one, as well."

Mark still wasn't satisfied. "But why do I have to meet
them?"

She sighed. "Do you need a reason for everything?"

"Well, yes, I do," he said with a chuckle. "That's just
how I am."

"I don't understand why you're making such a fuss."

"Okay, okay, but at least tell me where we're going now."

"If you *must* know," she said, and smiled down at him,
"we're meeting them at a Burger King." She'd been looking
forward to introducing him to Anne Marie for quite a while.

He frowned. "I don't eat fast food."

Barbie knew Mark was a real stickler about his diet. For
one thing, he had to be careful about his weight.

"We aren't eating there. I'm making dinner at my place."

Mark's frown deepened. "I can't get into your house," he muttered.

"Mark," she said, coming to a halt. "Would I invite you if you couldn't get your wheelchair into my home?"

He studied her closely. "You have a ramp?"

She nodded.

His eyes revealed his shock. "You're serious about us. You must be, if you're going to all this trouble."

"Are you finished arguing with me now?" She started walking again and had gone several feet before she realized he hadn't budged. "Are you coming or not?"

Slowly, he wheeled toward her. "You really know how to get to a guy."

"I'm happy you think so." The joy that coursed through her was enough to send her dancing through the streets.

When they reached the Burger King restaurant, Barbie held open the door. As soon as they were inside, Ellen skipped toward her. "Barbie! Barbie—" She stopped abruptly when she saw Mark.

"Ellen, this is my friend Mark."

"Hello," Ellen said and solemnly held out her hand, which Mark shook. "I saw you before."

"Did you? Where?"

"At the St. Patrick's Day party in Freeway Park."

"Did I see you?"

Ellen shrugged. "You were watching Barbie."

That wasn't the way Barbie remembered it. "You were?"

"You didn't even watch the singers," Ellen elaborated, studying Mark. "The whole show, all you did was look at Barbie."

Mark shifted uncomfortably and was saved from having to respond by Anne Marie who'd just joined them.

"You must be Mark," she said. "Barbie's told me about you."

"Has she really?" He twisted around to stare up at her.

"She's only said the most flattering things," Anne Marie told him with a grin.

True, Barbie thought; she hadn't made a secret of how she felt about Mark.

"We're just finishing our meal." Anne Marie led them to the table littered with the remains of their dinner. They'd evidently ordered hamburgers and fries.

"Anne Marie and I signed up for karate lessons," Ellen explained, her excitement unmistakable.

"Karate?" Barbie repeated. "How come?"

"It's on my list."

"And I decided I might as well join her," Anne Marie said.

"We already had one lesson. We're going to the karate place right after we have our drinks." She pointed at a carton of chocolate milk.

"Karate, huh? I wouldn't want to meet either of you alone in a dark alley," Mark teased. "I can picture it now. You'll warn me off by telling me you've had two—count 'em, two—karate lessons. I'll be shaking in my boots."

Ellen giggled.

Barbie noticed that Mark was grinning, too. He so rarely showed any emotion, and it pleased her to know he liked her friends. But then, she'd predicted that he would.

Mark turned to Anne Marie. "You're the one who started this Twenty Wishes business."

"Four of us—all widows—came up with the idea together," Anne Marie said.

"Do *you* have any wishes?" Ellen asked him.

"Yes, indeed," Mark said. "Several."

"Have you ever made a list?"

"I can't say I have, Ellen. Do you recommend it?"

"Oh, yes," Ellen returned seriously. "It's helpful if you have a real list. Otherwise you might forget."

"That's true," Mark concurred.

"Your heart has to let your head know what it wants," the child added.

"You sound very wise for one so young," Mark said, raising his eyebrows. "Where did you learn this?"

"Anne Marie told me. It's true, too. I didn't even know how much I wanted a mom until I put it on my list of Twenty Wishes."

"You wrote that down?" Anne Marie asked, apparently surprised by this revelation.

Ellen nodded, her eyes downcast.

"You never showed me that."

"I know," the girl said. "I wrote your name in pencil beside my wish 'cause if I could choose my own mom, I wanted you."

Anne Marie slid her arm around Ellen. "If I could have any little girl in the world, it would be you."

"Anne Marie's adopting Ellen," Barbie explained for Mark's benefit.

"We'd better scoot." Anne Marie smiled. "Like Ellen said, we're on our way to karate."

"Karate Kid and Mom, the sequel," Barbie joked.

"After that, we're going to see Melissa and help her work on wedding plans," Ellen said excitedly.

"That's my stepdaughter," Anne Marie told Mark.

"I might get to be in the wedding! Melissa said she needs a little girl to help serve the cake and Anne Marie said what about Ellen and Melissa said she thought that was a good idea."

"I think it's a grand idea myself." Barbie knew the difficult relationship Anne Marie had with her stepdaughter and was delighted by the way things had changed.

They left, and Barbie sat down in one of the chairs vacated by her friends. "So," she murmured, "you only had eyes for me last March, huh?" She reached for a leftover French fry and dipped it in ketchup.

Mark avoided her gaze. "I didn't think you'd let that pass."

"That was just the third time we met." If it took all night, she'd force him to admit how he felt about her.

"And?"

"And you're crazy about me," she insisted.

"I already told you I'm willing to go along for the ride, however long it lasts." His voice didn't betray a hint of sentiment.

"Monday-night movies."

He shrugged casually. "Sure."

"Lap swims on Tuesday and Thursdays."

He sloughed that off, as well. "We could both use the exercise."

"Dinner at my house tonight."

He hesitated. "Sure. Why not?"

Barbie took a crumpled hamburger wrapper and smoothed it out. Then with the ketchup-dipped fry, she drew a heart. "What am I getting out of this relationship?" she asked in conversational tones. "So far, I seem to be the one doing all the giving."

Mark tensed. "I've asked myself that from the start. I told you anytime you want out, all you need to do is say the word."

"Just like that?" she asked and snapped her fingers.

"Just like that," Mark echoed, snapping his own.

"No regrets?"

"None," he assured her.

"No explanations?"

He shook his head.

"No looking back, either."

"Not on my end."

"What if that isn't enough for me?" she asked.

His face tightened and his eyes went hard. "Let's clear the air right now."

"Fine by me."

"Exactly what do you want from me?" he demanded, none too gently.

Taking the same French fry, she scribbled out the heart. This discussion wasn't one she'd intended to have and yet she couldn't stop herself. Her pulse raced. She was afraid that by pressuring him for a response she'd put everything on the line. She'd chosen the one sure way to lose Mark.

"I'm not sure what I want," she replied, unable to look at him.

"Yes, you are," he countered, "otherwise we wouldn't be having this conversation."

"My list of wishes…" she said, and her voice faltered.

"Oh, yes, those Twenty Wishes you and your friends have." His tone had a mocking quality, which made her furious.

"You might think they're silly, but they're not!" she insisted.

"I didn't say they were," he said calmly. He could be so difficult to talk to sometimes. Squaring her shoulders, she met his eyes. "Okay, I'll tell you what I want."

"Good. I was hoping you would."

He wouldn't like this. The truth would probably scare him off. Still, it was a risk Barbie had to take. "I want to be loved," she said. There, it was out.

"By me?" he asked.

"You're the one I love." She might as well go for broke, and he could either reject her right now or accept her.

For a long time Mark didn't say anything, and when he did, regret weighted each word. "I don't want to love you," he said slowly.

So that was how it was going to be.

Barbie swallowed painfully. Hard as it was, she'd rather

he was honest. "Thank you for not leading me on," she managed to say through quivering lips. She stood up to leave.

Mark caught her hand. "I don't *want* to love you," he repeated, "but I do."

"You love me?" She could hardly believe it, yet she knew it was true. He let his love shine from his eyes and his fingers tightened around hers.

"I have practically from the first moment I saw you at that theater."

"You tried to kick me out, remember?"

"That's because you scared me to death," he said wryly. "But regardless of what I said or did, you wouldn't go away."

She offered him a shaky smile and sat back down, dragging her chair close to him, their knees touching.

"Then before I knew it," Mark muttered, his eyes closed, "I was dreaming about you."

Barbie savored every word.

"For the first time since the accident, I'd wake up each morning with a sense of…hope. I'd go to the movies and hope you'd stay away and at the same time, I'd hope you'd show up—and then I'd curse myself for being so stupid. Acting like that, I was just looking for more heartache."

Breathless, Barbie didn't trust herself to speak. This was everything she'd craved, everything she wanted to hear.

"I'm grateful you came into my life," Mark said and all his intensity was focused on her. "I can't say it any plainer than that."

"You mean *forced* my way into your life, don't you?"

He laughed and then grew serious again. "You want my heart? You've got it, Barbie. You've had it all along." Then he did something completely out of character. Reaching for the paper crown left behind by a birthday group, he placed it on his head and leaned over to kiss her.

Barbie leaned back and stared at him as a chill raced

down her arms. With tears blinding her eyes, she held both hands to her lips. Despite all her efforts, she doubled over and started to weep.

"Barbie?" Mark touched her back. "What's wrong?"

She straightened and noticed that the paper crown sat crookedly on his head. *Her wish.* She'd wanted to be kissed by a prince. She'd known it was a ridiculous request—yet it had been fulfilled.

Mark was her prince. He loved her.

And she loved him.

Slipping her arms around his shoulders, she hugged him with such exuberance she nearly toppled his wheelchair. "I'm going to love you for the rest of my life."

"I certainly hope so," he muttered. "Now do you think we can get out of here?"

"What's the matter? Is the aroma of those burgers getting to you and weakening your resolve?"

"The only thing getting to me is you. I think it's time you showed me what you learned on the internet."

Her eyes widened. Mark didn't need to remind her what she'd looked up weeks ago.

All she needed to know was that he loved her.

As much as she loved him.

Everything else they'd figure out with a little inventiveness and a lot of time.

Thirty-Two

Thursday afternoon, Anne Marie waited for her pulse to slow before she called Robert's office. Even after nearly two years, the number was ingrained in her memory.

Anne Marie knew she finally had to see Rebecca Gilroy. She didn't want to show up without warning, so she'd decided to phone Robert's assistant and make a formal appointment first.

She had to know the truth before she could put this behind her—or at least in perspective.

Was the child Robert's? If so, she wondered why Rebecca hadn't come forward. Robert's son deserved part of his estate, was entitled to an inheritance. Despite the circumstances, that was only right.

Her heart in her throat, she made the call. A moment later, she heard Rebecca's voice.

"This is Rebecca Gilroy. How may I help you?" The young woman, now presumably an assistant to one of the other partners, sounded businesslike and professional.

Anne Marie took a deep breath. "Hello, Rebecca," she said, speaking quickly. "It's Anne Marie Roche, Robert's wife."

Rebecca's tone softened instantly. "Anne Marie, of course. How are you?"

"Better." Which was true. "What about you?"

"Busy."

Anne Marie couldn't tell if this was a brush-off or an indication that Rebecca couldn't speak now.

"I won't keep you then," she said, following the other woman's lead. "I was hoping we could get together soon. Would that be possible?"

"You and me?" Rebecca didn't bother to conceal her surprise, or her reluctance.

"Could we meet for lunch? When it's convenient for you…"

"Well, I suppose lunch would work. How about tomorrow?"

A strange calm settled over Anne Marie. A day from now she'd know the truth, whatever it might be. She'd make this as painless as she could for all involved. Two months ago, when Melissa had told her about this, she'd wanted to hate Robert's assistant, to view her as the manipulative other woman. She still tended to see Rebecca as a gold digger who saw her big chance when Robert and Anne Marie separated. And yet…she'd never approached the family for child support.

Rebecca suggested a small, upscale restaurant close to Pike Place Market. Anne Marie knew it well; Robert had taken her there on a number of occasions. It catered to businessmen who wanted privacy to conduct negotiations over lunch or dinner—and the deals they negotiated obviously weren't all business.

Rebecca said it would have to be an early lunch and asked if eleven-thirty was okay. Anne Marie agreed.

Rebecca must know why Anne Marie had called her. The

choice of restaurant told her so. Anne Marie tried not to imagine the younger woman and Robert at the dark corner table, the one he used to reserve for their intimate lunches.

On Friday Anne Marie arrived at eleven-fifteen, fifteen minutes early. Theresa had promised to substitute for her at the bookstore for the rest of the day. In an effort to pack as much into one free afternoon as she possibly could, Anne Marie was going shopping with Melissa after lunch.

The wedding plans consumed every free moment Melissa had and much of Anne Marie's time, as well. Unfortunately Melissa's mother continued to shun her, but Anne Marie believed that once the baby was born, Pamela would have a change of heart. How could she *not* love her very own grandchild?

The hostess led Anne Marie to a quiet table near the window. The restaurant typically wasn't busy until noon and she appreciated the privacy. So far, only one other table was filled, with three men and a woman engaged in some intense discussion. Anne Marie ordered iced tea while she waited. She nervously squeezed lemon into the tea as she rehearsed her remarks.

Rebecca got there right at eleven-thirty and was escorted to the table. "Hello again," the other woman greeted her. She pulled out the chair across from Anne Marie.

What struck her all over again was how very young Robert's assistant was. Young and lovely. Her hair was a rich auburn, shoulder-length and naturally thick. She wore an olive-green skirt and matching jacket with a white silk blouse. An antique cameo—a family heirloom? a gift from Robert?—was pinned at her throat.

"Thank you for taking the time to join me," Anne Marie said, keeping her voice neutral.

Rebecca didn't respond; she opened the menu and scanned it, saying, "Perhaps we should order first."

"Good idea," Anne Marie said, eager to do anything to delay this uncomfortable conversation. "By the way, this is on me."

"That's not necessary," Rebecca said with cool politeness, "but thanks."

Anne Marie amended her assessment of Rebecca Gilroy. She might be young and vulnerable-looking, but she had a self-confidence that wouldn't have been out of place in someone much older.

When the waitress came to take their order, they both chose a soup and salad combination.

"I expect you're here to discuss what happened between Robert and me," Rebecca said, leaping headfirst into the conversation Anne Marie had been avoiding—until today.

"Yes."

"I thought so." Rebecca kept her eyes lowered and toyed with the spoon, belying the confidence she'd shown just moments before.

"Did Robert lead you to believe we were divorced?" Anne Marie asked bluntly.

"No."

"Had you been…physically involved before the two of us separated?"

Rebecca shook her head. "No. We…we weren't actually involved at all."

"What do you mean?"

"Well, physically—as you put it—we were." Rebecca shrugged. "I knew the two of you were going through some difficulties and that you were working toward a reconciliation. Mr. Roche didn't share much of his personal life with me, or anyone else for that matter. I learned you were living apart quite by accident."

"I see." Her own fingers moved to the silverware. She caressed the tines of the fork as she listened.

"We were both working lots of extra hours."

The muscles in Anne Marie's throat tightened, in nervous anticipation of what Rebecca was about to tell her.

"It was a bad time emotionally for us both. I'd recently broken up with my boyfriend, and I knew you and Robert weren't living together anymore."

That was no excuse for what they'd done! Anger and pain raged within her, but Anne Marie dared not let either emotion show.

The waitress chose that moment to bring their meals. The soup, tomato basil, smelled delicious and was accompanied by a Caesar salad with homemade croutons. Anne Marie waited until Rebecca reached for her spoon before she did.

"As I was saying," Rebecca said, picking up the conversation. "Both Robert and I were at a low point in our lives."

"And spending a lot of time together," Anne Marie added.

"Yes."

"So it was…natural for you to be attracted to each other." She shrugged again. "I suppose."

Any appetite Anne Marie might have had vanished.

"I'm not proud of what happened," Rebecca said, "and I believe Robert was…ashamed of it."

"How long did this affair last?" Anne Marie didn't know what had prompted the question other than the fact that she was obviously looking for more pain. "How…many times did you—"

"Does it matter?" She stared down at the table.

Well, yes, it does, she wanted to say but didn't. That night she and Robert had slept together, shortly before his death—was he still involved with Rebecca then?

"Afterward everything changed between us," Rebecca was saying. "We'd had a great working relationship and that was completely ruined by the affair. We tried to keep it quiet and except for that one time when Melissa walked in on us, I don't think anyone knew."

She lowered her head and Anne Marie could see that this was as embarrassing for Rebecca as it was for her.

Rebecca raised her head. "I'm surprised Melissa told you. That's how you found out, isn't it?"

"She…she was very upset."

"Robert was, too. He was mortified. His biggest fear was that you'd learn the truth."

That news was of little comfort. "Had…did he…"

"Did he what?" Rebecca pressed.

It was increasingly difficult even to speak. "Did he see other women? Were there others?" As his personal assistant, Rebecca was in a position to know.

Her hesitation said it all.

"How many?" She would never have believed it. She felt shocked, *grieved,* that she'd misjudged him so completely.

"One, I think," Rebecca admitted reluctantly. She seemed unwilling to divulge any more.

"Please," Anne Marie said urgently. "I need to know."

"He had me make a reservation at a hotel by the ocean under a different name."

"Redford?" she asked.

Rebecca's gaze widened. "You know about her?"

Her throat muscles relaxed. "That was me. Us. We… played this game." A smile came and went, tinged with humor and relief. Memories of their getaway weekend immediately came to mind. Happy, playful memories that were in stark contrast to what she'd just experienced.

"Okay, well, like I said, that's the only other time. And it turns out he *wasn't* cheating on you."

"Thank you," Anne Marie whispered, and she meant it.

"I should tell you that the night Melissa caught us was the last time." She paused. "Deep down, I know that if we could do everything over again, neither of us would've done it." Her eyes held Anne Marie's. "I'm not just saying that, either. It's the truth. If Robert were here, he'd agree."

"Was there…" The moment had come, and still Anne Marie couldn't make herself ask the question. "Did he ever tell you why we'd separated?" she asked, taking another route to the question that burned in her heart.

Rebecca looped a strand of thick auburn hair around her ear. "Actually, we didn't talk about you very often."

That made sense. "Robert was a private person," Anne Marie murmured.

"Yes, he was."

"I wanted a baby," Anne Marie said.

Rebecca looked away. "I didn't know that. I guess Robert didn't want another child."

"No. He…he was opposed to starting a second family and I felt that if I could show him how important this was to me, he'd change his mind."

"But you were getting back together," Rebecca said.

Anne Marie suddenly realized something. She knew why Robert had left after that night they'd spent together. He'd been gone in the morning, and the callous way he'd simply disappeared without a word or even a note had devastated her. For the first time, Anne Marie understood why he'd done it. Robert had been overcome with guilt. He was sorry about the affair with Rebecca. He'd probably wanted to tell her and ask her forgiveness, and at the last second he'd backed down. She assumed the affair was over by then; if not, she felt certain he would've ended it.

"You had a baby," Anne Marie said without flinching.

"A son. I named him Reed."

"Is the baby's father—is this Robert's child?" The question was out at last. Much as she feared the answer, she needed to know.

"Robert's?" Rebecca repeated, looking stunned. "No!"

"No?"

"Of course Reed isn't Robert's! Oh, my goodness, that's what this lunch is all about? You thought I'd had Robert's child. No, no, no. Reed's father is my ex-boyfriend. Denny cheated on me and I found out the same week I discovered I was pregnant. I should've explained. The only reason I slept with Robert was because I was trying to hurt Denny. It was just so twisted and stupid."

"Denny knew about Robert?"

"Yes."

"And he knows about Reed?"

"Of course, and so far he's been a good father."

"You're getting married?"

"No way! I'm not an idiot. If Denny couldn't keep his pants zipped before the wedding, he won't afterward. I'm seeing someone else now."

"Oh." Anne Marie had to resist hugging the other woman and thanking her for not giving birth to Robert's son.

"You must've heard about Robert and me and then learned I was pregnant and thought—"

Anne Marie nodded. "That's exactly what happened."

"But if that was the case, don't you think I would've contacted his attorney? I mean, Reed would've been a legal heir once paternity was established."

"I wondered why you hadn't."

"Well, it was for a very good reason. Reed isn't Robert's son."

Anne Marie's heart soared with relief and, even more than that, with joy.

"I didn't know Robert all that well," Rebecca told her. "But I know one thing about him—he loved you."

"He loved *me*," Anne Marie said.

"He did," Rebecca concurred with a smile.

That was all that mattered. Robert wasn't going to win any Husband of the Year award. The pain of his betrayal would always be with her but *he'd loved her*. It was what she'd known all along, despite the doubts and the mistakes they'd both made.

Yes, that was all that mattered.

The past wouldn't change.

But the way Anne Marie saw the future would.

Thirty-Three

Lillie estimated that it'd been three weeks since Hector had received her letter. She hadn't heard from him, and after all this time, she didn't expect to. The last thing she wanted was to cause problems between Hector and his children.

After mailing the letter, Lillie had spent a week by the ocean and found solace. The ocean had always been her escape. Whenever she learned about another of David's affairs, she'd booked a visit to her favorite ocean resort. She'd gone there three or four times every year, often enough that she had her own room, and the staff knew her by her first name. Although it'd been well over three years since her last visit, she'd been greeted warmly. Her regular room was ready and waiting for her.

She'd regained her emotional equilibrium walking along the beach. Every morning, she'd strolled in the sand, letting the waves lap against her bare feet, thinking, meditating, praying. After a while, the ache would gradually diminish as she was reminded that her worth as a woman, as a human being, didn't depend on David. His actions couldn't demean her. Her husband, sad though it was to admit, was a man without honor.

When she returned from the ocean, Lillie carefully sorted through the mail, searching for a response from Hector. There was none. She'd hoped he'd answer her note, although she hadn't really expected it.

On Monday, the twelfth of May, Lillie spent the morning working in her garden. She loved her Martha Washington geraniums, and with the rhododendrons in full bloom and the azaleas as well, her garden had never looked better. Her neighbors hired landscape specialists and Lillie had a company that performed the more demanding physical tasks, such as mowing. The flower beds, however, were her domain. Her personal joy.

At noon, she took a break and went inside for a glass of iced tea. The mail had been delivered and, as she drank, she leafed through the few advertisements and set the bills aside. A hand-addressed envelope caught her attention.

She didn't immediately recognize the writing. Curious, she opened it to discover an invitation to a retirement party for Hector Silva.

Lillie read it twice.

The party was planned for that very evening and when she studied the handwriting a second time, she realized the envelope had been personally addressed to her by Hector. She recognized his penmanship from the work order on her car.

All the necessary details were there. Date. Time. Place.

Lillie inhaled sharply. The party would be held at the dealership at seven that night, and she had every intention of attending.

By six forty-five, Lillie was dressed in a semiformal knee-length linen dress with a cropped jacket. Barbie phoned just as she was about to walk out the door and Lillie explained where she was going.

"I was *sure* Hector would be in touch," her daughter said in that gleeful way of hers when she knew she was right. "Have a wonderful evening, Mom."

"I will," Lillie promised.

They spoke for a few more minutes and then it was time for Lillie to go. Although she was nervous, she had a strong intuition that this was going to be one of the most magical evenings of her life. Happiness spread through her and she felt so light it was as though she could float.

When Lillie arrived at the dealership, the retirement party was in full swing. The showroom floor was decorated with banners and balloons, the counters spread with bottles of champagne and trays of lovely hors d'oeuvres. Surrounded by his children, customers and coworkers, Hector didn't see her right away. As soon as he did, his eyes flew wide open and he said something to his daughter, whom Lillie recognized from the photographs she'd seen in his home. Hector broke away from the group and hurried toward her.

"Lillie." He held out both hands.

"Hello, Hector."

"I'm so pleased you came." His gaze seemed to devour her, and she couldn't doubt the sincerity of his words.

Her own eyes were equally hungry for him. "Thank you for the invitation, and congratulations on your retirement." Words hardly seemed necessary. All she wanted to do was stare at him.

"Thank you." His hands firmly clasped hers. Then, as if he'd forgotten himself, he asked, "Can I get you some champagne?"

"I'd like that."

But Hector didn't need to leave her. Rita, his daughter, brought over a champagne flute and offered it to Lillie.

"I'm Rita," she said unnecessarily.

"You're as lovely as your pictures," Lillie said as she accepted the flute and impulsively hugged his daughter. Rita hugged her back, her expression welcoming.

"This is Andy, my fiancé," she said, introducing the man at her side. "Dad wasn't sure you'd come. I told him you would."

"I don't think I could've stayed away if I'd tried," Lillie confessed.

Hector stood close by as his two sons, Manuel and Luis, walked toward them, their progress hindered by the crowd. Manuel studied Lillie, his eyes devoid of emotion; that, to her way of thinking, was an improvement over the hostility he'd shown at their previous meeting. A lovely red-haired young woman—obviously pregnant—was with him.

"You came," Manuel said, not bothering with any form of greeting.

"Manuel," Hector warned in low tones. "I won't have you disrespecting Lillie."

His oldest son conceded with a nod. "Welcome, Ms. Higgins," he said. He introduced his wife, Colleen.

"Thank you, Manuel. Nice to meet you, Colleen. Both of you, please call me Lillie."

"This is my son Luis," Hector said, gesturing toward the second young man.

Luis and Lillie exchanged a friendly greeting under Hector's watchful eye—and Manuel's.

"You made my father very happy by accepting his invitation," Manuel told her when Luis had drifted off to talk to someone else.

"He made me happy by sending it to me."

Manuel gave her a tentative smile.

Lillie smiled back. She hoped that in time the two of them could be friends.

"We're all going to dinner after the party," Hector said, leaning closer. "Can you join us?"

Lillie readily agreed.

"Allow me to introduce you to my friends," Hector said and led her away. As they moved from one group to another, she became even more aware of how greatly he was respected and loved. His coworkers told story after story about Hector, embarrassing him since he was a modest man. Lillie enjoyed every word. If she needed confirmation that this man was everything she'd imagined, then she received it tonight, many times over.

The party started to break up at about eight-thirty. She'd remained at Hector's side, either clasping his hand or with his arm about her waist. There could be no doubt that they were together.

At the Mexican restaurant a little later, Lillie met more members of his family. A brother and sister, nieces and nephews, various in-laws. The table seated at least thirty, and the names flew past her, although she made a determined effort to remember each one. She sat between Hector and Manuel.

Music and laughter filled the room. Children ducked under the table and raced around the chairs while their parents—Hector's nieces and nephews—did their best to contain them. Although Hector introduced Lillie to everyone in his extended family, it seemed they already knew her. They accepted her without question and seemed genuinely pleased to make her acquaintance.

When the food arrived, it was served family style. Manuel passed Lillie the first dish, holding the heavy platter of rice while she helped herself. Next came *chilaquiles*, which seemed to be some kind of tortilla casserole, followed by corn tamales, chili rellenos and another dish Lillie didn't hear the name of.

"My father's in love with you," Manuel said quietly.

"I beg your pardon?"

"He showed me your letter. You love him, too, don't you?"

Lillie could see no reason to deny it. "Very much."

"He's a man of strong feelings," Manuel said. "His family is important to him."

"I know." That was the reason she'd decided to break off the relationship; she refused to place Hector in the impossible position of choosing between his family and her.

Manuel acknowledged her statement. "Yes. He was willing to give you up for our—*my* sake."

"He already had." She couldn't resist asking, "Can you tell me what changed?"

Rita slapped her brother's arm. "Hey, Manuel, what's the holdup here? You're supposed to be passing the food."

"Sorry." Manuel handed the dish to his sister.

"I've never seen my father this miserable," Manuel informed Lillie. "Even when Mom was ill, the entire family counted on our father to keep up our spirits and he did. He nursed Mom, cared for her, held her when she breathed her last and loved her to the very end."

"He still loves her." Lillie blinked hard as tears welled up in her eyes. This was how she wanted to be loved.

"After Mom died it was Dad who held our family together. Don't misunderstand me—he grieved for our mother. But her death was also a release from terrible pain. Dad understood that better than anyone. He was lonely and lost but he found ways to cope. Through work, family— and now you."

Mesmerized by Manuel's words, Lillie passed plate after plate without serving herself.

"After receiving your letter, my father wept." Luis, who'd been listening avidly, spoke from across the table while Hector was busy talking to a nephew on his other side.

"He…did?"

Manuel frowned at him, but he acknowledged Luis's words. "It's true." He paused to take a gulp of his Corona. "I knew then that you were no ordinary woman," he resumed, "and that I'd made a mistake. If my father loves you, then I need to be willing to look past my own prejudices and give you a chance, as well."

That did it. Tears spilled down her cheeks. "Thank you, Manuel."

He nodded and passed her another dish.

Lillie wondered why Hector had waited so long to reach out to her. As if reading her thoughts, Manuel added, "Rather than repeat what happened with me, Dad decided he needed to let the family know. So he went to everyone and explained that he'd met someone very special."

No wonder his family behaved as though they already knew her.

"My fear was that you'd break his heart," Manuel murmured. "Unfortunately my attitude toward you was what did that. I hope you can look past our rather…difficult beginning and start again."

"Of course," she said and when the next dish was handed to her, she scooped up a huge helping of *chili conqueso* and placed it on Manuel's plate before serving herself.

Manuel grinned and then winked at her.

After dinner, the music began, and Hector took Lillie's hand and led her onto the dance floor. "You and Manuel seemed to be deeply involved in conversation," he said as he turned her into his arms.

"Hmm." She leaned her forehead against his and closed her eyes, grateful that this was a slow number.

"He apologized?"

"He said you loved me."

Hector exhaled noisily. "I never expected to fall in love a second time and certainly not like this."

"I didn't, either. Blame the wishes if you want."

"Your Twenty Wishes?"

"I wrote that I wanted to be loved by an honorable man."

"You are loved, my Lillie. By me."

"I love you back."

His hold on her tightened briefly. "Manuel still has doubts that it'll work out between you and me."

"At least he's agreed not to interfere."

Hector nodded. "He said he'd be willing to wait and see—after he told me there's no fool like an old fool."

"Shall we be foolish together?"

Hector laughed. "I was hoping you'd say that."

Lillie lifted her head. "Are we a pair of fools, Hector?"

"I can't think of anyone I'd rather be foolish with than you, my Lillie."

"Me, neither."

With their eyes closed, they continued dancing until the music ended. When the last note faded, they reluctantly broke apart in order to applaud politely. To Lillie's astonishment, the entire Silva family had formed a circle around them and started to clap.

Lillie blushed profusely and Hector laughed.

It was a relief when the musicians began again. This time, his family joined them on the dance floor. The mariachi music was lively, punctuated by slow, plaintive songs.

Hector and Lillie danced every dance and stayed until the restaurant was ready to close.

Hector drove them back to the dealership, where Lillie had left her car. There, in the shadows, he kissed her. Lillie slipped her arms around him and leaned into his embrace, letting her actions tell him of all the love in her heart.

"How did you know I'd come to the party?" she asked.

"I prayed you would."

"And if I hadn't?"

"Then I would have come to you. Most men don't find a love this good, this pure, once in a lifetime—let alone twice. I wasn't letting you go, Lillie, not without a fight."

"But you already had," she reminded him.

"No," he said swiftly. "I needed time to regroup and to reason with my son. You were always with me, always in my heart." He took her hand and pressed her palm against his chest. "You inspired me, my Lillie."

"I did?"

"Yes. I have my own list of Twenty Wishes now."

"Really?"

"Oh, yes." He paused to kiss her again. "And every one of those wishes is about you."

Thirty-Four

The small chapel adjacent to the Free Methodist Church off Blossom Street reverberated with the traditional wedding march as Brandon Roche escorted his sister down the center aisle.

Standing in a pew at the front of the chapel, with Ellen at her side, Anne Marie felt her heart swell with joy. When Melissa walked past her, she turned to look at Anne Marie and mouthed the words "Thank you."

Robert would've been so proud of them, she thought, not for the first time. So proud and so delighted by the change in their relationship. For all the pain his betrayal with Rebecca had caused, it had a positive—if inadvertent—effect. It had brought Anne Marie and Melissa together.

Anne Marie gazed after her stepdaughter. The wedding was small, with only a maid of honor and best man. As promised, Ellen would serve wedding cake at the reception, a role to which she attached great importance.

Melissa looked lovely in her pale pink floor-length dress. A halo of flowers adorned her head, with flowing white ribbons cascading down her back, and she carried a small bouquet of white roses. The pregnancy was just starting to show.

Anne Marie's one disappointment was Pamela. It would've meant so much to Melissa if her mother had relented enough to attend her wedding. Unfortunately, she remained upset and angry, and Anne Marie couldn't help thinking she should have put her daughter's needs ahead of her own feelings. But then, Pamela hadn't come to Robert's funeral, either, although her children could have used her support. Anne Marie hoped they'd eventually be able to resolve their differences.

With the maid of honor and the best man, both close friends, standing beside them, Melissa and Michael approached the young minister. Jordan Turner, Alix's husband, would be performing the ceremony. He'd agreed as long as Melissa and Michael were willing to participate in marriage counseling classes. Even with all the busyness of college graduation, the couple had gone to every session, which boded well for their marriage, Anne Marie thought.

When the ceremony began, Ellen leaned forward, absorbing every word. This was her first wedding and she didn't want to miss a single detail. Anne Marie had enjoyed watching Ellen line up her dolls and stuffed animals the night before and then carefully choose two—a Barbie and a panda—to march down the makeshift aisle. Later, Anne Marie had found her at the kitchen table writing furiously in a tablet.

"What are you doing?" she'd asked.

"I'm putting a new wish on my list," Ellen explained. "I'm going to have a big wedding with lots of people and a dress with lace and pearls and a long veil."

"What about your husband?"

Ellen chewed on the end of her pencil. "He'll be handsome."

"Is that important?"

The eight-year-old considered her response carefully. "I want to marry a man who's handsome on the *inside,* too," she'd said.

"And if he's good-looking on the outside, that would be a bonus, right?"

"Right," Ellen had said.

Now as Melissa and Michael exchanged their vows, Ellen studied them attentively, dreaming of her own wedding one day.

Anne Marie gazed protectively at this child who would legally become her daughter. The greatest desire of her life was to be a mother and that wish had been fulfilled—but not in the way she'd expected.

As the ceremony continued, Anne Marie felt Dolores Falk's presence. The older woman had nurtured the child to the best of her ability. She'd given her love and security. In the end, Ellen's grandmother had handed her over to Anne Marie.

Anne Marie believed Dolores had recognized that the two of them belonged together, that they needed each other. Once the bond between them was established, and Anne Marie had promised to keep Ellen if anything happened to her grandmother, Dolores had been able to die in peace, knowing Ellen would be loved and cared for by Anne Marie.

Anne Marie placed her hand lightly on Ellen's shoulder. The child joined fervently in the applause when Jordan Turner pronounced Michael and Melissa husband and wife.

"This is so nice," Ellen whispered as the music crescendoed. Then Melissa and Michael walked back down the aisle together, their arms linked and their faces bright with joy.

"It is lovely," Anne Marie agreed, struggling to hold back tears. It wasn't only Dolores Falk's presence she felt, but Robert's, too. She knew Melissa felt him there, as well.

"What happens next?" Ellen stared up at Anne Marie with wide, curious eyes.

"Now we go to the wedding reception."

"Oh, goody! When do I serve the cake?"

"Not till later on."

The reception was at a restaurant on Lake Washington. Lillie had secured the banquet room, and Melissa's friends had decorated it and prepared everything for the small reception. Anne Marie had volunteered to help and Melissa was grateful but said she'd already done so much. Besides, her friends had everything under control.

When they arrived, Anne Marie could see that was true. The room, which was separate from the main part of the restaurant, had a sweeping view of Lake Washington. Sailboats with their multicolored spinnakers glided across the choppy waters. A lush green lawn sloped from the restaurant down to the waterfront, bordered by rows of blooming perennials. Double-wide French doors opened onto a stone patio.

Because the day was overcast, Melissa and Michael had decided to hold the reception indoors. Lillie had chosen the perfect location, Anne Marie thought gratefully.

The room itself was strung with white streamers, twisted from the center of the ceiling, where a large paper wedding bell hung. The streamers fanned out in every direction. White and silver balloons were tied behind each chair.

The cake, topped with the traditional bride and groom, sat on a table with an array of gifts surrounding it. Alix

Turner had baked and decorated it herself. The restaurant had supplied an elegant buffet, for which Brandon, Anne Marie and Michael's parents had split the expense.

Entering the room with her husband, Melissa looked radiantly happy.

"It's hard to think of my little sister as married," Brandon said, claiming the chair next to Anne Marie and Ellen. "Mom's going to regret not flying over for the wedding."

Anne Marie nodded. Pamela would have to accept that Melissa had her own path to follow. "In time I believe she will."

"Who?" Ellen asked, then added, "Is this for adult ears or kids' ears?"

Brandon laughed outright. "It's for adult ears."

"Okay."

He grinned at Anne Marie.

The buffet line formed, and after they'd filled their plates and sat down again, Michael's parents, Jim and Paula Marshall, joined them.

"This turned out to be such a lovely wedding," Paula said, watching her son with pride. "I wasn't sure what to expect. What is it with children these days? So much happening at once. Michael graduated from college, married and a father-to-be. It's enough to make my head spin."

Anne Marie agreed. "I didn't know what to knit first, a baby blanket or a garter for her wedding."

"You knit?" Paula asked with real interest.

"I'm only just learning. I've been taking classes."

"It was one of our wishes," Ellen told her gravely.

Anne Marie explained and marveled anew at the changes in Ellen since the child had come to live with her. When they'd first met, only three months ago, the youngster had barely spoken a word. These days it was difficult to get her to stop.

"Have I introduced you to Ellen?" Anne Marie asked Jim and Paula and tucked her arm around the child's waist. "This is my daughter, Ellen Falk."

"I'm getting a new name soon," Ellen said, looking at Anne Marie.

"A new name?" Paula repeated. "What do you mean?"

"I'm adopting Ellen," Anne Marie said, "and when I do her last name will be Roche, the same as mine."

"Congratulations to you both," Jim said, sampling the lobster salad.

"Anne Marie's going to be my new mother," Ellen said amicably. "I have an old one, but my grandmother told me my real mom couldn't take care of a little girl, which is why I get a new one. I'm glad my new mother is Anne Marie."

The conversation moved on to pets when Ellen lovingly described Baxter, now "our" dog, and lauded his intelligence. The Marshalls contributed stories about their own badly behaved but much-loved dog, Willow. Everyone laughed a great deal, and Anne Marie was thrilled that Ellen responded so naturally and well to adult company.

Halfway through the reception, Lillie Higgins and Hector Silva came in. Anne Marie had met Lillie's friend a couple of times previously. He was everything Lillie had promised and obviously adored her.

"I'm sorry we're late," Lillie began as she approached Anne Marie.

"It's my fault," Hector said. "My oldest grandson had a soccer game and wanted me there to see him play."

"Can I play soccer, too?" Ellen asked.

Anne Marie nodded. "Should we see about signing you up?"

"Yes!" Ellen clasped her hands, her expression rapturous. "And I want to join Girl Scouts."

"One thing at a time, Ellen," Anne Marie said gently. She didn't want to squelch the child's enthusiasm, but didn't want her overwhelmed by too many activities, either. She already took karate lessons and if she added soccer *and* Girl Scouts to that, there wouldn't be enough time just to sit and read or knit or play imaginative games with her dolls.

"I got your message," Lillie said. "Have you found a house yet?"

"No, but I'm starting to look." However, Ellen had expressed hesitation about moving, and Anne Marie planned to go about this slowly and cautiously. She hoped to find a neighborhood close to the school; with all the upheaval in the child's life, Anne Marie wanted to keep her there.

"I'll have a real bedroom, too," Ellen said.

"And a real bed," Anne Marie added. Ellen hadn't complained once about sleeping on the fold-down sofa in the tiny apartment. One of her first purchases would be a bedroom set for Ellen, with a matching dresser, bookcase and computer desk.

She looked forward to getting her own things out of storage. She'd delayed for a long time, preferring to live in the small apartment rather than move. Her fear was that the household goods that had belonged to her and Robert would trigger too many memories.

A few months ago, Anne Marie hadn't felt strong enough to deal with the past. Her grief had been too raw, too close to the surface. She'd purposely kept the furniture in storage, convinced she'd never find the courage to sit at the table where she'd shared so many meals with her husband. Every item, everything she'd so carefully packed away, was linked to Robert.

But the memories of her life with him no longer tormented her. Even knowing of his betrayal, she continued to love him and always would.

Michael and Melissa ceremonially cut the first slice of cake, and Melissa beckoned to Ellen.

"Can I serve cake now?" Ellen asked, eyeing the slices Melissa's friends were placing on colorful plates. "Is it time?"

"Looks like it," Brandon said. They stood up and headed for the table, where the plates had been set out.

"Aren't you going to throw the bouquet?" Alicia, the maid of honor, asked Melissa.

"Oh, my goodness, I almost forgot." Melissa turned her back to her group of friends and hurled the bouquet over her shoulder.

Anne Marie hadn't been part of that group. She didn't mean to participate, but when the bouquet shot directly at her, she instinctively grabbed it.

"Anne Marie!" Melissa cried, laughing delightedly. "You caught the bouquet!"

Ellen squealed with excitement, a plate of cake in each hand.

"This means," Melissa told her, "that Anne Marie will be the next one to get married."

"I don't think so." Anne Marie tried to pass the bouquet to one of Melissa's college friends, who refused to take it.

"Don't be so sure," Melissa chided good-naturedly. "You never know when love's going to tap on the door."

Frankly, Anne Marie wasn't interested in falling in love again. She had everything she needed for happiness. Ellen was part of her life now, and she'd made peace with the past. She had Blossom Street Books. Her eyes fell on Lillie and Hector, and she immediately added dear friends to her list of blessings.

"Look," Ellen said, tugging at her sleeve. She pointed at the French doors.

Music swirled in from the piano player in the nearby bar.

Anne Marie bent down. "What am I supposed to be looking at?"

"It's raining."

It was more of a mist than rain but Anne Marie didn't point that out. "Yes?"

"Your wish," Ellen reminded her.

What wish?

Then Anne Marie remembered.

Taking Ellen's hand, she walked out to the small patio. With the music playing softly in the background, they removed their shoes and stepped onto the wet grass.

Ellen slipped one arm around Anne Marie's waist and together they spun 'round and 'round.

"We're dancing barefoot in the rain." Ellen giggled.

Throwing back her head, Anne Marie giggled, too.

The music grew louder and their movements became more sweeping as the rain fell and people gathered at the open doors to watch them.

She saw Brandon giving them a thumbs-up and Michael and Melissa waving. Lillie and Hector smiled.

Anne Marie Roche had made Twenty Wishes and they'd brought her love.

Epilogue

The courtroom was crowded as Anne Marie and Ellen waited patiently for their turn to come and stand before the judge. When their names were called, Anne Marie stepped forward with Ellen beside her. Evelyn Boyle, Ellen's social worker, moved to the front of the court.

Judge Harold Roper read over the paperwork, which included a home study and background check. This was actually a formality; Child Protective Services had already approved the adoption. The months had passed quickly. They'd moved into their new home, and Ellen was a third-grader now, getting top marks in her classes.

"So, Ellen, you're going to have a new mother," Judge Roper said.

"Yes, Judge," Ellen answered politely.

"Your Honor," Anne Marie whispered.

"Your Honor," Ellen repeated.

She placed her hand in Anne Marie's and edged closer to her side.

"Congratulations," the judge said and signed his name at the bottom of the document.

"That's all there is?" Ellen asked in a whisper.

Anne Marie was surprised herself. "Apparently so."

Anne Marie's mother wept noisily at the back of the courtroom. The next name was called, and Anne Marie and Ellen hugged and left the room. Laura Bostwick continued to sob, dabbing at her eyes with a tissue as they walked out into the hallway. The heavy door closed behind them.

"Are you sure you can't come to the party, Mom?" Anne Marie asked.

"I'll come by later if that's okay."

"Of course. I want you to meet my friends."

Catching her off guard, Laura awkwardly hugged Anne Marie. "You're going to be a wonderful mother."

"Thanks, Mom."

"My name is Ellen Roche," Ellen announced to a guard who strolled past.

"That's a nice name," the uniformed man told her.

"Ellen Dolores Roche," she said. "Dolores was my grandmother's name. She's with Jesus now."

The man smiled at Anne Marie and kept on walking.

"This is my new mother," Ellen called after him. "She loves me a lot."

"Ellen," Anne Marie murmured. "He's busy."

"I just wanted to tell someone I have a new name," she whispered, lowering her head.

"Would you like to tell Barbie and Mark?"

The girl nodded eagerly. "Lillie and Hector, too?"

"They'll all be at the party."

"What about Mrs. Beaumont and Lydia and Cody and all my friends from Blossom Street?"

"They wouldn't miss it."

"Melissa and Michael, too?"

"Yes." This shouldn't be news to Ellen, who knew all about the party at Blossom Street Books after court.

But Anne Marie understood. Ellen was happy and excited, and she had to express that happiness. She mattered to all these people, belonged to their community as Anne Marie did. Her daughter… Anne Marie's mind came to a sudden halt.

Ellen was her *daughter.*

Her *daughter.*

Unexpected tears gathered in her eyes.

"Anne Marie?" Instantly Ellen was concerned. "Are you okay?"

"Yes—I'm just happy."

"Like Grandma Laura?" she asked.

Anne Marie squeezed her hand. "Just like Grandma Laura."

By the time they got to the bookstore, it seemed the entire street was there to celebrate. Susannah from the flower shop had come, but could only stay briefly. She brought a number of small floral bouquets to commemorate the adoption and a pretty pink corsage for each of them to wear.

Soon after their arrival, Alix Turner carried in a tray of freshly baked cookies, compliments of the French Café. Lydia and her sister, Margaret, came over in turns, so as not to leave the store unattended. They'd brought several bottles of champagne for the adults—Veuve Clicquot, of course—and sparkling lemonade for the kids. Lydia's husband, Brad, dropped in later, bringing their son, Cody. Michael and a heavily pregnant Melissa showed up, too, and Ellen was doubly excited.

"It's going to be a girl, right?"

"Right."

"Can I be her big sister?"

"I'm counting on it," Melissa said. She was due anytime and Michael remained close to her side. They didn't stay long as they had a birthing class to attend, their final one before her due date.

Theresa, Cathy and Steve, her part-time employees, helped serve, and Ellen mingled with the crowd, reminding everyone that she had a new name and a new mother.

Late in the afternoon, both Evelyn Boyle and Anne Marie's mother stopped by, but could only stay for a few minutes.

"We were thinking of holding a mommy shower for you," Barbie said around five o'clock. Almost everyone had come and gone by this point. The ones who remained were the original members of the widows' group—with the addition of Mark and Hector. It was hard to believe nearly a year had passed since that bleak Valentine's evening, when they'd started their lists of Twenty Wishes.

She'd completed her list last spring.

19. Karate classes with Ellen

20. To live happily ever after

Twenty wishes, nearly all of them a reality now.

Anne Marie had found a pair of red cowboy boots in a secondhand store for a fraction of the cost. They fit perfectly and she wore them often.

Then one Sunday in July, shortly after Anne Marie had begun attending church with Ellen, she'd spontaneously sung a hymn. She was well into the second verse before she remembered that she couldn't sing anymore and yet here she was... Now not a day went by without her belting out one song after another.

Anne Marie's gaze fell on Barbie, who sat next to Mark, holding his hand.

Anne Marie had met him only half a dozen times, but Barbie had spoken of him often enough to make her feel as if she knew him.

"When we made our lists of wishes, did you ever dream it would come to this?" Elise asked, joining the circle of friends.

"We haven't talked about our lists recently," Lillie said, sitting in the overstuffed chair with Hector standing behind her, his hands on her shoulders. "Has anyone completed any wishes lately?"

"I have," Elise said, looking down at her plastic glass of champagne. "I've set up a charitable foundation in memory of Maverick."

"Elise, that's wonderful!"

The older woman struggled to hide her emotion. "That's not all. I took my two grandsons on a hot-air balloon ride. That was something Maverick and I always intended to do. We put it off—and then it was too late."

"Was it as exciting as you thought it would be?" Anne Marie asked.

Elise smiled warmly. "Even better than I imagined. When I closed my eyes, I could almost feel Maverick's arms around me again," she said in a low voice. "It was the most thrilling sensation to be that high above the ground. He would've loved it."

"I completed one of my wishes, too," Barbie volunteered.

"Which one?" Lillie asked.

Eyes dancing, she glanced at Mark. "I went skinny-dipping."

Lillie frowned. "I have a feeling you weren't alone."

Barbie giggled like a schoolgirl. "As it happens, I wasn't."

Mark shifted uncomfortably in his wheelchair. "I believe that falls under the heading of too much information."

"You went with *Mark*." Lillie feigned shock.

Barbie laughed and leaned over to kiss his cheek. "I'm not telling."

Mark couldn't quite restrain a smile.

"What about you, Anne Marie?" Barbie asked, diverting attention away from her and Mark.

"I'm about to accomplish one of my most heartfelt wishes."

"About to?" Hector asked. "I thought the adoption was finalized this afternoon."

"It was, and Ellen's now my daughter in the eyes of the law. But this is another wish." She opened her purse and removed a thick envelope and showed it to the group.

Ellen dashed over to her side. "Can I tell everyone?" she pleaded.

"Go ahead," Anne Marie told her.

"Mom," she said, and looked at Anne Marie. "Is it okay to call you Mom?"

"Absolutely."

"Mom bought tickets for us to fly to Paris for our first Christmas together."

"Paris," Elise repeated slowly. "What a perfect idea."

Anne Marie slipped her arm around Ellen. "I'm going to Paris with someone I love."

Barbie's eyes were soft. "That's just beautiful." She glanced at Mark, who grumbled something about not getting any ideas. She ignored him and reached for the brochure Anne Marie handed her.

"Barbie, I'm warning you right now, I'm *not* going to Paris." Mark hesitated. "Go if you like. I'll even encourage it. But I'm staying right here."

"Yes, Mark."

"I mean it, Barbie."

"I know you do." Apparently she had no intention of arguing with him. "I'm perfectly capable of traveling to Europe for two weeks on my own."

"Two weeks?" Mark said, frowning. "That long?"

"It would hardly be worth my while to travel all that way for less than that."

Mark groaned. "Why do I have the feeling that I'm going to be staring up at the Eiffel Tower and wondering how I got there?"

Everyone smiled.

Ellen walked over to where Anne Marie was sitting and climbed onto her lap. "One of my wishes came true, too," she told the group.

"Which one was that?" Hector asked kindly.

"I found a mom," Ellen announced. "I thought Anne Marie would just be my Lunch Buddy but now she's my mom. Forever and ever."

"Forever and ever," Anne Marie repeated.

It was a solemn moment, broken only by Ellen's happy shout. "Hey, Mom! You have to start a *new* list of Twenty Wishes now, don't you?"

Anne Marie smiled. This truly wasn't the end but a new beginning for them all.

* * * * *

THE TWENTY-FIRST WISH

To
Candi Jensen
in gratitude for San Francisco yarn crawls,
wine on your back porch
and, best of all,
your friendship

One

April 22

Today I sign the papers on our new house! I'm excited and exhausted and feel completely out of my element. I have so much still to do. I should've been finishing up the packing or cleaning the apartment before the movers arrived. But no. Instead, I sat down and began to knit. What was I thinking? Actually, knitting was *exactly* what I needed to do. Knitting always calms me, and at this point my nerves are frayed. I haven't moved in years and I'd forgotten how stressful it can be. Usually, I'm organized and in control, but today I'm not (even if I look as though I am). On the inside—and I don't mind admitting this—I'm a mess.

Mostly, I'm worried about Ellen. My ten-year-old has already had so much upheaval in her life. She feels secure in our tiny apartment. And it is tiny. It was just right for one small dog and me, but I never intended to stay here so long. When I moved into this space above the bookstore it was with the hope—the expectation—that Robert and I would reconcile. But the unthinkable happened and I lost my husband to a heart attack. After his funeral I remained here because making it from one day to the next was all I could deal with.

Then Ellen came into my life and it was obvious that two people and a dog, no matter how small, couldn't live comfortably in this minuscule space, although we managed for more than a year. I did make an earlier offer on a house but that didn't work out.

After bouncing from foster home to foster home, Ellen had ended up with her grandmother, who died when she was eight. So Ellen needed stability. She'd endured enough without having a move forced upon her so soon after the adoption.

In retrospect, I'm grateful that first house deal fell through, since it would've happened too fast for Ellen—although I was disappointed at the time. Even now, Ellen feels uneasy about leaving Blossom Street, although I've reassured her that we aren't *really* leaving. Blossom Street Books is still here and so is the apartment. The only thing that'll be different is that at the end of the workday, instead of walking up the stairs, we'll drive home.

Sitting in the office of the Seattle title company, Anne Marie Roche signed her name at the bottom of the last document. She leaned back and felt the tension ease from between her shoulder blades. As of this moment she was the proud owner of her own home. Today was the culmination of several months of effort. She smiled at the two sellers who sat across the table from her; they looked equally happy.

"Is the house ours now?" Ellen whispered as she tugged at the sleeve of Anne Marie's jacket.

"It is," she whispered back.

A few years ago Anne Marie had merely been going through the motions. Robert, her husband, had died, and she'd found herself a widow at the age of thirty-eight. She had no one in her life who loved her, no one she could love. All right, she had friends and family and she had her dog, Baxter, a Yorkie—admittedly a special dog—but Anne Marie needed *more,* wanted more. She'd craved the intense, focused, mutual love of a spouse, or a child of her own. Then she'd met Ellen through a volunteer program and they'd grown close. When Ellen's grandmother, Dolores, who'd been raising the girl, became seriously ill, Anne Marie had stepped in—at Dolores's urging. She'd taken over as the girl's foster mother and, after Dolores's death, adopted her. Dolores must have known she was reaching the end of her life, and when she saw how attached Ellen and Anne Marie were, she'd been able to die in peace, confident in the knowledge that her granddaughter would be safe and, above all, loved.

"You can cross finding a house off your list of twenty wishes," Ellen said, referring to the list Anne Marie had compiled with a group of widowed friends the year she'd met Ellen.

The child's straight brown hair brushed her shoulders, with a tiny red bow clipped at each temple. Her eyes were wide with expectation—and a little fear. Anne Marie hoped Ellen would quickly adjust to her new home and neighborhood, although Ellen kept insisting she liked her old one just fine.

"We want you to be as happy in this home as we've been," Mr. Johnson, the previous owner, said. With a great deal of ceremony he and his wife handed the house key to Anne Marie. The Johnsons, an older couple who'd lived there for more than twenty years, planned to move to Arizona to spend their retirement near friends.

"I'm sure we will," Anne Marie said. She'd looked at a number of places and this was the first one that felt right, with its large backyard and spacious rooms. Ellen would be able to go to the school she currently attended, which Anne Marie considered a bonus.

She would do whatever she could to ensure that the transition would be a smooth one for her daughter. Ellen had made friends on Blossom Street, people she visited almost every day, and she could continue doing that. Her favorite stop was A Good Yarn, Lydia Goetz's store. Both Anne Marie and Ellen had learned to knit, thanks to Lydia.

"You *promise* I'll like the new house as much as Blossom Street?" Ellen asked with a skeptical frown.

"You're going to love having a big bedroom."

"I like my old bedroom," she said, lowering her head.

"Yes, but you'll like this one just as much." This was a conversation they'd had a number of times already. "And Baxter's going to enjoy racing around that big backyard, chasing butterflies."

The hint of a smile touched Ellen's face, and Anne Marie put her arm around the girl's shoulders. "Everything's going to be fine," she said. "You'll see."

Ellen nodded uncertainly.

Now that the paperwork had been completed, Anne Marie thanked the title agent, who'd been so helpful. With the house keys safely inside her purse, she stood and reached for Ellen's hand. "Mel's taking us out for a celebratory lunch," she said on their way out the door.

"What's *celebratory* mean?"

"It means we have something to celebrate, and that's our brand-new home." New to them at any rate. She raised her voice to show how pleased she was that this day had finally arrived.

"What about Dad?"

"We'll see him later." Over the past few months, Anne Marie's relationship with Tim Carlsen had become…complicated. He was Ellen's biological father and hadn't known he had a daughter until after Anne Marie had adopted her. Tim had connected with Ellen through a long and indirect process. Anne Marie had reluctantly—very reluctantly—granted him permission to visit Ellen. Thankfully, Tim, who'd acknowledged his problems with drug and alcohol abuse, was now clean and sober. He'd turned his life around several years before, unlike Ellen's biological mother, who was still incarcerated. She'd surrendered her parental rights, which had made it possible for Anne Marie to adopt the child. It was only after Anne Marie saw how much Tim loved his daughter that she'd softened toward him. All too soon, a rosy, and completely unrealistic, picture had formed in her mind—the three of them together, as one happy family.

Then Tim had dropped his bombshell and that dream had been blown to smithereens. He was engaged to Vanessa, a woman he'd met at his AA meetings. Anne Marie had felt incredibly foolish even entertaining the notion of the two of them as a couple.

Shortly afterward she'd met Mel through her friend Barbie. He was a widower, the same age Robert would have been—close to twenty years older than Anne Marie. Mel was a comfortable person, easy to be with, unthreatening and undemanding. He got along well with Ellen, too. They'd been dating for a few months, and while it wasn't a steamy romance or an exciting one, she was content.

Mel's attention had helped soothe her ego after the letdown she'd experienced with Tim. The ironic part was that shortly after she'd started seeing Mel, Tim and Vanessa had parted ways. After her disappointment with Tim, Anne Marie wasn't willing to make her heart vulnerable to him again. She'd made that clear and he'd accepted her decision. She let him see Ellen, however. Her daughter loved being part of her father's life and looked forward to spending time with him.

"Where's Mel taking us to celebrate?" Ellen asked as they rode the elevator down to the ground floor. There was a light drizzle outside, not unusual for April in Seattle. It wasn't heavy enough to warrant an umbrella, but damp enough to curl Anne Marie's naturally wavy hair.

"We're meeting him in Chinatown," Anne Marie answered.

"We're having Chinese?"

This was Ellen's all-time-favorite food. "Can I order chow mein with crispy noodles?" she asked.

"I'm sure you can." How thoughtful of Mel to remember Ellen's preference for Chinese cuisine. He really was a good man; she doubted there was anything he wouldn't do for her if she asked.

"What about almond fried chicken with extra gravy?"

"You'll need to discuss that with Mel." Once out on the sidewalk, Anne Marie took Ellen's hand again, and with their heads bowed against the cold and the wind, they hurried toward the restaurant.

Mel was already there and had obtained a booth. A large pot of tea with three small ceramic cups rested in the center of the table. Anne Marie was grateful Mel had thought to order it.

He stood as they approached and leaned forward to kiss Anne Marie's cheek.

"Hello, Pumpkin," he said to Ellen.

"Hi, Punky," she returned with a giggle. Where Ellen had come up with that name for Mel, Anne Marie had no idea. Maybe her version of "pumpkin"? In any event, Anne Marie appreciated their relaxed, friendly relationship.

When the waitress arrived, they ordered far more food than they'd ever manage to eat.

While they waited for their lunch, Mel made conversation with Ellen. "This is perfect weather for Baxter to wear that sweater you knit him," he said.

Ellen had made her own list of twenty wishes, and learning to knit was one of them. Fortunately, Lydia's yarn shop was only a couple of doors down from the bookstore, and Lydia had encouraged Ellen's first efforts. With practice, Ellen had improved to the point that she was able to complete a sweater for Baxter.

"After lunch, would you like to show Mel the house?" Anne Marie prompted. She wanted Ellen to feel good about this move. Ellen had gone with Anne Marie to view various houses and had found something wrong with each one. It finally dawned on Anne Marie that Ellen simply didn't want to leave Blossom Street, which she should've realized from the start. The little girl wouldn't say so directly but she came up with convenient excuses to reject every home they'd seen—until this one. If Anne Marie had been more experienced as a parent she might have caught on earlier. But Ellen's resistance was the main reason she'd put off the search after the first deal fell through.

"Do you want to see the house?" Ellen asked Mel, sounding hesitant.

"I'd enjoy that, especially if you'd give me a personal tour."

Ellen glanced at Anne Marie.

"Mel would like you to show him around," Anne Marie explained.

"I can do that," Ellen said, revealing her first enthusiasm for their new home. "I know every room. Did Mom tell you I have a big closet of my own and my bedroom faces the backyard, so I can look out my window and watch Baxter? He likes to chase birds and butterflies and bugs. I won't have to take him for walks anymore because there's a fence… I can just open the door and let him go out."

"True, but it's still a good idea to keep an eye on him," Anne Marie reminded her. "*And* to take him for walks."

Ellen nodded.

"I'll bet there are lots of kids your age in the new neighborhood," Mel said.

Anne Marie hoped that was the case, although she hadn't seen any.

Ellen toyed with her fork and plate, moving the fork around the plate's circumference. "I like my old neighborhood best," she muttered.

"But it's a retail one," Mel said.

Ellen looked quizzically at Anne Marie.

"He means there are shops on Blossom Street instead of houses."

"I *like* shops. I have friends there. Susannah lets me help her with the flowers in Susannah's Garden. Last week I stood out front of her store and gave away pink carnations. Baxter was with me."

"That was fun, wasn't it?"

Ellen nodded again. "And Alix sometimes brings me leftover croissants from the French Café across the street."

Laughing, Anne Marie brought her head close to Mel's and added, "That doesn't happen often because they sell out of croissants almost every day."

"I like them warm so the jelly gets runny on them," Ellen said. "Mom puts them in the microwave for me in the morning."

"I'll have to try that," Mel told her. "Sounds good."

"Lydia and Margaret are my friends, too." Ellen continued to list her favorite people on Blossom Street.

"Lydia owns A Good Yarn," Anne Marie pointed out to Mel.

"Yeah, I remember," he said.

"Lydia and Mom taught me to knit, and we knit every day, don't we, Mom?"

Before Anne Marie could respond, their food arrived. The conversation lagged as they passed around the serving plates. Mel asked for chopsticks, but Anne Marie and Ellen used forks—although Ellen proclaimed that she wanted to try chopsticks *next* time. She was just too hungry today.

"You have lots of friends, don't you?" Mel asked Ellen.

Mouth full, the girl nodded eagerly.

"But they're all adults. Do you have any friends from school on Blossom Street?"

After a short pause, Ellen said, "Cody and Casey, but they're older and they go to a different school than me."

Anne Marie could see that Mel was trying to help Ellen see all the possibilities that awaited her in her new home. She thanked him with a smile, and he clasped her hand beneath the table.

Half an hour later, when they couldn't eat another bite, Mel asked for the bill. Carrying their leftovers, Anne Marie and Ellen walked to the parking garage for their car. Mel drove to the house on his own.

Anne Marie and Ellen got there before him and after parking in the driveway, Anne Marie unlocked the front door, conscious that this was the first of many times. The inside looked different now that it was empty of furniture. The Johnsons had left the house meticulously clean, the floors scrubbed and polished and the walls freshly painted and unmarked.

Mel showed up soon afterward. "What a lovely house," he commented, stepping inside. He paused in the doorway to survey the hall and the living room.

"Come," Ellen said, grabbing his hand and tugging him toward the hallway. "My bedroom's this way."

"What about your mom's?" he asked, looking back at Anne Marie over his shoulder.

She nearly burst out laughing.

"Mom's across the hall from me," Ellen told him.

"*Directly* across the hall," Anne Marie said pointedly. Although they'd been dating for several months, their relationship hadn't gotten physical—not beyond kissing, anyway—although Anne Marie sensed that Mel was interested in taking it further.

While Ellen showed him the bedrooms and the other areas of the house, she put the leftover Chinese food in the otherwise empty refrigerator. The official move was the next day—Saturday morning. The movers would take care of the furniture, while friends and family had volunteered to bring over the boxes. Anne Marie hoped to get Ellen settled before the end of the school year, which would give her a chance to make friends in her neighborhood this summer.

She heard Ellen and Mel clattering down the hallway, their footsteps echoing.

"Do you want to see the kitchen?" Ellen was asking Mel.

"Of course. Will you cook me dinner one night?"

"I don't cook that good without Mom helping me."

"I bet she'd do it if you asked."

"Do you like macaroni and cheese?" Ellen asked. "I can make that in the microwave. It comes in a box."

"Ah..." Mel met Anne Marie's look as he entered the kitchen.

"I think Mel would be thrilled with whatever you cooked," she inserted smoothly, smothering a laugh when Mel rolled his eyes.

"I'll eat anything you decide to serve me," Mel agreed.

"Okay." Ellen nodded seriously. "A boy in my class brought chocolate-covered ants to school last week."

"Chocolate-covered ants?" Mel repeated.

"I didn't eat any," Ellen said, then explained, "There weren't enough for everyone."

"That's a shame," Mel said with obvious insincerity, although Ellen didn't seem to notice.

Ellen was about to say something else when the doorbell chimed.

Anne Marie shrugged, answering Mel's unspoken question. "I'm not expecting anyone," she said. It seemed a bit early for the neighbors to be introducing themselves. However, this could be a visit from a political candidate, as an election was coming up soon.

Ellen beat her to the door and threw it open. Even before Anne Marie could see who'd come calling, her daughter announced, "It's Dad!"

Anne Marie cast Mel an apologetic look. "Hello, Tim," she said cordially, standing behind Ellen.

"Hello." He smiled at his daughter. "How's my girl?"

"Good." Ellen beamed happily, always excited about seeing her father.

Tim gazed at Anne Marie, as if seeking confirmation that everything really was fine. His smile had a curious effect on her, which she did her best to ignore. She stood in the doorway, blocking his entry. "What can I do for you?" she asked politely, praying Mel would stay in the kitchen until Tim left.

His timing was bad. Mel already had a problem with Tim's coming around as much as he did, and Anne Marie didn't want him to think Tim stopped by whenever he felt like it. That wasn't the case; he generally made arrangements well in advance. Thank goodness, because she tried to keep the two men apart as much as possible.

"I can only stay for a few minutes," Tim said. "I came over to drop off a small housewarming gift."

"Oh." Anne Marie felt properly chastised—and a little embarrassed.

"Can I come in?" he asked.

"Oh—of course." She stepped aside to let him in as Ellen held the screen door, not hiding her delight.

Two

April 22

Mom says I'll get used to my new house, but I won't. I keep telling her I like it right here on Blossom Street. Lydia said I'd have a big room all to myself and a closet, and that I'll make new friends. But I like my old friends. I don't want new ones. Baxter doesn't want to move, either. I told my dad I'd rather stay here and he said I might not like the new house now but I will later. He said I'd still have my friends on Blossom Street. Mom said that, too... I'm not sure she really wants to move, either, because she's been knitting a lot and she knits real slow when she's worried about something. She doesn't think I pay attention but I do.

Tim decided he shouldn't have come to the house—not yet. Ellen had said Anne Marie was signing the final papers that day, so it was probably too soon. In their visit the previous weekend, he'd spent a lot of time reassuring his daughter that the move would be a good thing. He wondered how successful he'd been.

More than anything, Tim wanted to help Ellen make a comfortable transition to her new neighborhood. He'd picked up a plant for the yard, which he'd set on the porch. But the housewarming gift was just an excuse, and Anne Marie had seen through it right away.

Anne Marie.

He'd blown it with her, handled the situation between them poorly. His AA sponsor had repeatedly emphasized the importance of honesty, but Tim had been afraid that if he told Anne Marie he was engaged to Vanessa, she wouldn't let him see Ellen. Because his daughter meant everything to him, Tim had been afraid to take that risk. He'd have had to be blind not to see that Anne Marie was falling for him but he hadn't acknowledged it. Instead, he'd delayed telling her the truth, which was a passive—and dishonest—way of encouraging her.

Knowing her better now, Tim understood that Anne Marie would never have used the fact that he was involved with someone else as a pretext for keeping his daughter away from him. The irony was that his engagement hadn't lasted very long once Ellen—and Anne Marie—became part of his life.

Tim could hardly bear to think of his troubled past, his wasted years. Thank God for his family's support. It'd been an act of tough love for his parents to step back and allow him to self-destruct. As a parent himself, he knew that couldn't have been easy. But when he'd finally hit bottom, his family had been there, waiting. His mother and father were the first ones to offer him guidance and practical help.

They'd gotten him into a rehab center and from that moment on he hadn't looked back. He'd been sober ten years now. It was while he was trying to make restitution to the people he'd hurt that he learned he might have a child.

The discovery had shocked him, thrown him into a tail-spin. That day was the closest he'd come in all those years to taking a drink.

Just after he'd entered rehab, Candy, the woman he'd been living with, had attempted to contact him. He'd ignored her phone calls once he became aware of them. He wasn't permitted to receive any outside calls while in rehab; the only reason he even knew she'd tried to reach him was the multiple messages she'd left on his cell phone. When he got his cell back, he deleted each one without listening. Candy belonged to his old life and he was starting fresh.

Later, she'd written him, but Tim wanted nothing to do with her, so he'd tossed out the letter, unopened and unread.

Not once did he suspect she might be pregnant.

Nine years later...he'd sought out Candy's mother to repay the money they'd stolen from her in order to buy booze and drugs. Back then, all Candy and Tim could think about was the next hit, the next drink. Time melded together, hours, days, weeks. Often he didn't know or care where he was or who he was with, as long as he could get drunk or high.

After rehab, Tim had wanted to repay the old woman and apologize. If he was ever going to become the man he hoped to be, that meant restitution. So he went to see Candy's mother. What he found was the house empty and listed for sale. The next-door neighbor told him Dolores had recently passed away.

Then she'd added that the granddaughter Dolores had been raising had gone to live with a woman called Anne Marie.

A granddaughter, aged nine.

A chill had gone through Tim at those words. The timing was too coincidental to discount. That very minute he'd known. This granddaughter, this little girl, was *his* little girl.

His daughter.

Tim hadn't slept that night or the following one. Thankfully, the neighbor knew Anne Marie's full name, and after a couple of days to sort out his feelings and consider his options, he'd contacted her at the bookstore.

At first Anne Marie assumed Tim wanted to take Ellen away from her. The thought had actually crossed his mind. Ellen was his flesh and blood, so he should be the one to raise her. But he'd consulted an attorney and discovered he had no legal rights where Ellen was concerned.

Candy had signed away her parental rights, and the grandmother had stepped in. More shocking yet, Tim learned he wasn't even named on the birth certificate. After the old lady's death, Ellen became a ward of the state; when Anne Marie adopted her, he lost any chance of raising her, although a blood test proved that she was indeed his child.

It'd taken weeks of gently, carefully, proving himself to Anne Marie before she allowed him into their lives. The funny, wonderful part was that Ellen seemed to recognize almost from the first that he was her father. In fact, before he could tell her, she asked him outright.

He'd been so tongue-tied he hadn't been able to answer.

"I knew it," she'd said, and smiled happily. He'd nearly dissolved into tears. So much for being manly and in control of his emotions.

That night Ellen showed him her list of twenty wishes. She explained that Anne Marie and her widowed friends had each made a list, so she had, too. One of her wishes was to meet her father, and now she had. She'd thrown her arms around his neck, hugging him tight.

From then on, Tim's relationship with Vanessa had gone steadily downhill. He realized it must've been hard on her to see him develop a relationship, no matter how innocent, with another woman. His sponsor had advised him to tell Anne Marie about Vanessa. He'd tried a couple of times and then, coward that he was, kept his trap shut. He *couldn't* lose Ellen. By then he was completely captivated by his daughter and refused to take the risk.

Then Vanessa had gotten drunk. After three years of sobriety, this awkward situation with Anne Marie had proved to be too much for her. Vanessa's second slip followed shortly thereafter, when Ellen broke her arm. Tim could see where this was going. Vanessa couldn't deal with such a complex relationship. That second slip was compounded by a third.

Tim broke off the relationship entirely, and frankly, he was glad he'd done it. Once he'd made that decision, he made another. He wanted to get involved with Anne Marie—only he was too late. By then she'd started dating Mel and was no longer interested in him.

He couldn't blame her.

Tim had met Mel a number of times and clearly the older man considered him competition. If that was the case, Tim didn't see it. Anne Marie was always polite but distant; whatever chance he'd had with her was over.

"You brought us a gift?" Ellen asked, looking eagerly around.

"Ellen," Anne Marie chastised her softly.

"It's a plant," Tim said. "On the porch."

"Thank you."

He heard the reserve in Anne Marie's voice. He stuck his hands in his pockets and was about to make his excuses and leave when Ellen asked, "Do you want to see the house? I gave Mel a tour. I can give you one, too."

Tim looked at Anne Marie, seeking her approval before he agreed. She nodded slightly.

"I'd like that very much."

His daughter closed the screen door behind him.

He trailed her into the living room and stopped when he saw Mel standing there, arms crossed. The other man didn't need to say anything to convey the fact that he wasn't keen on Tim's presence at the house.

"Hello, Mel," he said. He offered his hand, and Mel accepted.

"Good to see you again," Tim said, although that was an exaggeration.

"You, too." Mel's returning comment lacked sincerity, at least in Tim's opinion.

"This way, Daddy," Ellen said, grabbing his hand. "I want to show you my bedroom."

Tim followed his daughter to one of the closed doors. Ellen opened it and spread her arms wide. "See how big my room is?"

He stood with his hands on his hips. "Where do you want your bed?" he asked, relieved that she seemed more enthusiastic about the house.

"By the window."

Clearly she'd given the matter some thought.

"Then I can stand on it and watch Baxter play in the yard."

"Good idea."

"And my dresser will go over here." She bounded to the far side of the room to show him.

"Where are you going to put all your books?" The ten-year-old had more books than any kid he knew, which made sense since Anne Marie owned a bookstore.

"Mom's buying me my own bookcase and I want to keep it over there." She pointed at the wall across from the window.

Ellen was a bright child who loved to read; he was pleased

she enjoyed books as much as he did. Tim had been a voracious reader from the time he was old enough to hold one in his hands. That wasn't the only interest he shared with his daughter and Anne Marie. They all seemed to love playing board games and being around the water, to name two.

He and Ellen spoke for a few more minutes and Tim knew he should leave. As it was, he'd trespassed on Mel's time with her and Anne Marie.

"So when's the big moving day?" he asked once he'd joined the others.

"Tomorrow," Anne Marie said.

"Need help?"

"Not really."

He doubted she'd be interested in any assistance from him but had wanted to ask, just in case.

"A big truck is coming for the furniture," Ellen said, "but all our friends from Blossom Street are helping us move the boxes."

"I've got muscles." Tim bent his elbow and flexed his biceps. "See? I can lift boxes, too. Many hands make for a lighter load," he said, misquoting a saying he didn't quite remember. "Or something like that."

"Can Dad help us move?" Ellen asked excitedly.

"I don't think so, Pumpkin," Mel answered.

Tim recognized the other man's mistake even before Mel did. Mel apparently hadn't realized that Anne Marie didn't like anyone else speaking for her.

Which was no doubt why she'd changed her mind about allowing him to be involved.

"The more helpers we have, the less work," she said.

"*I'll* be here," Mel said, as if that would make all the difference.

Anne Marie ignored his remark. "If you're available, Tim, Ellen and I gladly accept your offer," she said. "Thank you."

"Just tell me what time and I'll be there." He resisted the urge to gloat. It would be poor sportsmanship, so he didn't, but he certainly felt like it.

Mel narrowed his eyes. "What might be more helpful is if you took Ellen for the day," he suggested. "She'll get in the way—"

"I want to be with my friends," Ellen protested, interrupting him.

"I want Ellen with me," Anne Marie said emphatically.

"What about Baxter?" Mel asked, a bit irritated now. "Surely you don't want the dog underfoot? Maybe Tim could take him."

"I've already arranged for someone to look after Baxter." Anne Marie obviously wasn't pleased with the way Mel had taken control. Tim hadn't known her long but he was well aware of her capable nature—and her independence.

"I should've known you'd be on top of things," Mel said, apparently trying to make amends, although his compliment sounded grudging.

An awkward silence stretched between them. Ready to leave, Tim reached inside his pants pocket for his car keys. "I'd better get back to the office before my dad wonders where I am." Tim worked as a broker at his father's insurance agency.

"Yes, good idea," Mel said.

"Mel," Anne Marie whispered.

Taking the hint, Mel stepped forward. "It's time I left, as well."

Anne Marie and Ellen walked them both to the door. "Thank you for lunch, Mel. That was a special treat."

"Thank you," Ellen echoed.

"Would you like to take the leftovers home?" Anne Marie asked.

"No, you and Ellen keep them." Then, with a sideways look at Tim, Mel announced, "Ellen's favorite is chicken chow mein with crispy noodles."

So that was how it was going to be. Mel was telling Tim he knew more about his daughter than Tim did. Tim felt his anger rise, but before he could respond, he inhaled a deep, calming breath and let the comment pass.

"Thank you, Tim, for the rhododendron," Anne Marie said next. "I'll plant it right away."

"I'll plant it for you," Mel said.

Apparently, Mel was a slow learner, Tim thought. By now he should know better than to leap in and answer for Anne Marie.

He could predict her response.

"No, thank you, Mel. I'll do it." Anne Marie cast them both a warning look.

"Bye, Daddy. Bye, Punky," Ellen said.

Mel's face lit up triumphantly. He turned and started toward his car. Tim had parked behind him.

"She calls me Punky," he said as they headed down the driveway together.

"Punky," Tim repeated, suppressing a laugh. "Where did she come up with that?"

Mel shrugged. "I don't know. I didn't ask."

Not to be outdone, Tim said, "Ellen has a special name for me, too."

"Oh?" Mel didn't look as though he believed him.

"She calls me Daddy."

With that, Tim opened his car door, slipped inside and drove off.

Three

Moving day. I'm so thankful for all the friends who offered to help. I've been talking to Ellen about this move for weeks, describing it in positive terms. Yesterday evening, when I tucked her into bed at the apartment for the last time, I compared the move to starting a new knitting project. Even though it can be exciting and fun, it's a little scary, too. There's a lot of work involved and sometimes you make mistakes, but when you're finished you have something that didn't exist before. Something beautiful. This was an analogy Ellen could understand. We've both completed our current knitting projects, so we'll begin new ones. The timing's perfect. A new house. A new neighborhood for Ellen to explore. And a new knitting project.

"Ellen," Anne Marie called, walking from room to room in their small apartment. "Where are you?"

"Here, Mom." Ellen emerged from her bedroom, dragging her backpack.

Anne Marie knew Ellen had placed her most precious items inside the backpack instead of entrusting them to a box for someone else to transport. She had her knitting and her list of twenty wishes, along with a framed photograph of her grandmother and a book of poems Tim had given her. From the obvious weight of the knapsack, she'd stuffed other things in it, as well. Anne Marie hadn't checked; she was busy enough doing her own last-minute packing.

"Tim's here," Anne Marie told her. Of all the friends who'd offered to help, he was the first to arrive.

After knocking once, he'd let himself into the apartment. "How are my girls this morning?" he asked cheerfully. He held a take-out coffee in one hand and wore blue jeans and a sweatshirt with the Mariners logo on the front. Both Tim and Ellen enjoyed baseball and declared themselves to be diehard Mariners fans.

"Girls?" Anne Marie repeated, one eyebrow cocked.

"How's my *girl?*" he corrected, and seemed rather amused with himself.

"Daddy!" Ellen raced to her father as if she hadn't seen him in at least a month rather than the day before.

After setting his coffee on the kitchen counter, Tim caught Ellen and lifted her up for a hug.

Anne Marie looked away. She was happy Ellen had found her father and grateful for the affectionate relationship between them. Still, moments like this were hard to watch for reasons she couldn't—or didn't want to—identify. Finding him had been one of the girl's wishes, which had prompted Anne Marie to allow the former addict into their lives. She could tell he genuinely loved the child.

"I brought my truck," Tim said when he'd put Ellen back on the floor. "I can start taking down boxes if you like."

"Can I ride over to the new house with you?" Ellen asked.

"That's up to your mom."

Anne Marie appreciated the fact that he'd acquiesced to her authority. "Fine by me. The others will be here any minute."

She had plenty of volunteers—so many she'd had to turn some down. Her stepchildren, Melissa and Brandon, and Melissa's husband, Michael, had offered, too. But they lived quite far away these days and she didn't want to inconvenience them.

In her usual organized fashion, Anne Marie had carefully planned the move. She'd decided her friends would transport the boxes before the hired movers showed up. Whatever didn't fit in Tim's truck would go in their individual cars. With Lydia's husband and family helping, Winter and Pierre from the French Café, plus Tim and his truck, Anne Marie thought it would only take one trip. They'd have lunch while the movers hauled the furniture from the apartment to the house, and after the truck had left, her small crew of friends would place the boxes in the appropriate rooms.

Tim sipped his coffee. "Where's...?" He didn't finish his question.

"Mel is stopping by after lunch. He had an appointment with a couple of out-of-town clients this morning." Mel owned a thriving architectural firm and often met with clients on weekends.

She held her breath, waiting for some derogatory retort from Tim, which never came. She was relieved he'd kept his opinion to himself. Honestly, those two men could be as bad as junkyard dogs, so intent on challenging each other. Anne Marie sometimes felt like a scrap of food they were competing for. Her one hope was that Ellen didn't sense the undercurrents between Mel and Tim. If she did, she hadn't said anything.

"Alix has Baxter for the day," Ellen explained to her father, obviously missing her adored dog.

"That's good, don't you think?" Tim asked.

Ellen shrugged. "I guess."

"He might get lost or stepped on by someone if he was here. And you know Alix will take great care of him."

"Alix and Jordan promised to bring him to the house this afternoon," Anne Marie said. "Then Baxter can help you unpack your bedroom."

Ellen nodded, but it was plain to see that she wasn't happy to have Baxter with someone else, even someone she knew and trusted.

Within ten minutes, the Goetz family arrived. Brad, Cody and Casey ran energetically up the stairs; Lydia hadn't been able to leave the store, as Saturday was one of her busiest times. Soon, with Anne Marie doling out instructions, they hauled boxes down to Tim's truck. Pierre and Winter followed five minutes later.

"Winter won't be lifting anything," Pierre said.

"Pierre," she muttered under her breath, looking slightly embarrassed.

Her husband replied in French. Anne Marie had been to France and had taken a few lessons, but he spoke far too quickly for her to understand. The one word that leaped out, though, was *bébé*.

"You're pregnant?" Anne Marie clapped her hands in delight. "That's fantastic!"

Winter smiled. "We just found out last week."

His expression proud, Pierre slipped his arm around his

wife's waist. "We're due in early December," he said. "Just in time for Christmas," he added with a grin.

"Congratulations!"

Winter elbowed her husband. "We weren't going to say anything until after the first trimester, but apparently Pierre forgot about our agreement."

Again he replied in French, and whatever he said made Winter laugh and hug him. "I should've known it would be too hard for him to keep quiet. He said he can't resist telling everyone because he's so excited."

"As he should be."

"Since Pierre doesn't want me to lift anything, I'll volunteer to prepare lunch."

Anne Marie had planned to purchase pizza or chicken wings, but she certainly wasn't turning down Winter's offer. "That would be wonderful."

"Okay, let me go back to the café and get started. Sandwiches okay?"

"Your sandwiches? Better than okay!"

Soon after Winter had left, Lillie and Hector came up the stairs. Anne Marie had met Lillie and her daughter, Barbie, through the reading group she'd held at the bookstore. They were both widows and had compiled their own lists of twenty wishes. Shortly afterward, Lillie had met Hector. They were dissimilar in superficial ways but alike in the ways that mattered and had fallen in love. Anne Marie assumed they'd eventually get married.

"We're here to help," Lillie said, "even though we're not on the official duty roster." She wore a man-size faded blue shirt with the sleeves rolled up past her elbows and jeans with white tennis shoes. Nevertheless, she looked as elegant as she always did. "Oh, Barbie and Mark send you their best," she added. Barbie, who owned an upscale dress shop, had recently married Mark Bassett, the man she'd met around the same time Lillie and Hector had begun their relationship.

"Shall we begin?" Pierre said. "*Allons-y.* Or in English, let's go."

Anne Marie wanted to do her share of the physical work, but she was needed to supervise and direct traffic. With so many people helping it didn't take long for everything to be loaded. Winter had coffee and pastries delivered from the café and during their break, Ellen sat next to Tim, keeping her backpack close to her side.

Since they had a quiet moment, Anne Marie asked Tim, "Would you mind looking after Ellen next weekend?"

"Sure. I don't have anything planned."

"Mel is taking Mom to see *Jersey Boys* at the 5th Avenue Theater," Ellen informed him.

"Oh." His gaze held Anne Marie's. "I'll be happy to stay with Ellen."

"Thank you. I—"

Her cell phone chirped and she glanced quickly at call display. Seeing that it was Mel, she walked over to the kitchen sink, turning her back to Tim and the others.

"Hi," she said in a low voice.

"Hi. How's everything going?"

"Great. We're on a break. The boxes are all loaded and ready to go, and once the van shows up I'm out of here."

"Listen, it looks like this meeting might go longer than I realized. I can't tell you how bad I feel about letting you down."

"Mel, please, we've got lots of people. You aren't letting me down. There's no reason to apologize. I understand."

"I'll come as soon as I can."

"Yes, but take all the time you need with your clients."

"Okay." His voice was regretful. "I'll see you later, then." When she shut off her phone she could feel Tim's eyes on her. She didn't explain the call; it simply wasn't his business.

Once they'd all headed over to the house and the moving van arrived, the rest of the morning passed in a blur of activity. While the two professional movers carried the furniture inside and set it in the various rooms according to Anne Marie's instructions, Winter came over with lunch. The small work party sat on blankets spread out on the lawn and enjoyed their soup and sandwiches—croissants with tuna, smoked salmon and turkey fillings.

Tim brought Anne Marie a small container of cream of mushroom soup, which she refused. "No, thanks. Don't have time." She continued to direct the movers.

"Save it for later."

"Okay." She was hungry but she had more important things to deal with.

When the movers were finished, her friends unloaded the boxes, piling them in their designated rooms.

"Can Baxter come home now?" Ellen asked when they were done for the day.

Anne Marie phoned Alix and Jordan, who drove to the house with their infant son—and the dog—half an hour later.

"Baxter!" Ellen crouched down and held out her arms. The Yorkie didn't need any encouragement; he ran toward Ellen at top speed, leaped into her waiting arms and licked her face frantically.

Soon the only volunteer left was Tim. Alix and Jordan went home. Brad had to take Cody to baseball practice and Casey wanted to be dropped off to spend time with Lydia's mother at the assisted-living complex. The girl had grown close to her adoptive grandmother, which Anne Marie knew would benefit them both. Hector and Lillie had plans with his family that afternoon and Pierre had to go to work. Anne Marie thanked them all. She'd been blessed with generous friends. Exceptional friends.

Ellen had gone to her room; Tim lingered. "Anything you need me to do?" he asked.

She shook her head. She'd prefer it if Tim wasn't around when Mel arrived.

"Baxter!" Ellen suddenly yelled. Looking upset, she dashed out of her bedroom. "Where's Baxter?"

"I thought you put him outside," Tim said.

"I did, but he isn't in the backyard!"

"You didn't let him inside, did you?" Tim asked Anne Marie.

"No. He must be in the yard," she said. "There isn't anywhere else." He was probably asleep under the apple tree and Ellen hadn't noticed.

The three of them hurried into the yard.

Baxter was nowhere to be seen.

Tim walked along the fence and squatted down to examine it, concentrating on the side that led to the alley. He raised his head and waved at Anne Marie.

She ran over. "What?" she asked fearfully, her heart pounding as she crossed her arms over her chest. She knew what he was about to tell her.

"Looks like he dug a hole under the fence."

"Baxter!" Ellen wailed. "We *have* to find Baxter."

Tim tried to soothe her plaintive cries as he hugged his daughter tight. "We will, sweetheart," he murmured. "Don't you worry, we'll find him."

Four

April 23

Baxter's missing! We have to find him. I want my
Baxter.

"We have to go after him!" Tim could hear the panic in
Anne Marie's voice. Ellen had run back outside, clutching
the dog's leash.

"He couldn't have gotten far," Tim said. "You two go
search for him and I'll stay here in case he comes back."

Anne Marie seemed uncertain. Normally she liked to be
in charge but she'd gone pale and was obviously as upset
as Ellen.

"Go," he urged. "He's got to be close by. He's probably
confused and can't find his way back."

His own thoughts were tumbling over each other. Some-
one could easily take a dog as cute and friendly as Baxter.
Or maybe he'd tried to return to the familiar territory of
Blossom Street; Tim had heard of such things.

Ellen herself felt that Blossom Street would always be
her real home. The apartment represented safety and se-

curity to her and she couldn't yet imagine feeling that way anywhere else.

"Come with me," Anne Marie said, decisive now as she reached for Ellen's hand. "We'll find Baxter."

"Of course you will," Tim confirmed, hoping his words lent them both confidence.

"He's wearing the green sweater I knit him," she whispered. "And his collar."

Anne Marie nodded. "Yes! And he has all his tags."

"That'll make it easier to locate him," Tim said. "People won't forget seeing a cute dog wearing a green hand-knit sweater—plus he's got ID. Just you wait. He'll be home in no time."

While Anne Marie and Ellen scoured the neighborhood, Tim went inside the house. Baxter might have gone into one of the still-empty rooms and fallen asleep.

He did a thorough walk-through of the house, checking every closet and behind every door.

No Baxter.

He returned to the backyard and once again walked all the way around. Still no Baxter. When he examined the hole beneath the fence, he found a piece of green fuzz. So, as he'd guessed, Baxter had slipped through that hole. He got a board from the garage and immediately blocked the escape route.

When he'd finished, Tim started pacing. He regretted now that he hadn't gone with Anne Marie and Ellen. He couldn't tolerate this anxiety, and his fears, for Ellen in particular, tormented him.

When his cell phone rang, he grabbed it so fast it nearly sprang out of his hands. Some quick juggling saved it from falling onto the lawn. "Hello," he said loudly, certain it must be Anne Marie with news.

"You sound mighty eager to hear from me." Mel, and his tone was sardonic.

Tim's shoulders sagged with disappointment. "What do you want?" he asked, not bothering to disguise his dislike of the other man. Actually, Mel was all right, and in other circumstances they'd probably get along fine. But, in his opinion, the fiftysomething architect was too old for Anne Marie. Then again, she seemed to prefer older men; her husband, Robert, had been about the same age. This could all be a lost cause, he reminded himself, feeling even more discouraged.

"I called to talk to you," Mel told him.

"How'd you get my number?" Tim demanded.

"Why are *you* in such a bad mood?"

Tim sighed; he was taking his frustration out on Mel. "Okay, I apologize. What's the problem?"

"No problem, and in answer to your question—"

"What question?"

"How I got your phone number."

"Yeah?"

"From Anne Marie."

Anne Marie? That didn't make sense.

"A few weeks ago her battery was dead, and Ellen was with you, so she borrowed my phone. Your number's on my call log."

"Okay." He remembered the occasion, since Mel's number had come up on *his* phone. "This isn't a good time," he said. "I'll tell Anne Marie you called." Maybe. Mel considered Tim competition, as well he should. And vice versa… Tim had ruined his chances with Anne Marie, but he was working hard to win her back, although that was difficult with Mel in the picture.

"Is she around?" Mel asked, disregarding Tim's comment.

"No," he said curtly. "Baxter's missing."

Mel exhaled audibly. "Oh, great. I suppose Anne Marie and Ellen are in a real panic."

"They're looking for him now. I'm waiting at the house in case Baxter comes back here."

"So you're still there. I thought you would be," he said cynically, "especially since I got delayed."

"Listen, I really don't have time for this. Like I told you, Baxter's lost and Anne Marie and Ellen are out looking for him."

"When did the dog go missing?"

Tim glanced at his watch. "Thirty minutes ago, maybe forty." It felt much longer.

"Who let him get out?" Mel asked in an accusatory voice, as if Tim was personally responsible for what had happened.

"No one," he snapped, allowing his irritation to show. "Baxter either dug a hole under the fence or found it there."

"Shouldn't someone have been keeping a closer eye on him?"

"Yes, probably, but the deed is done. There's no point in looking for someone to blame."

"Poor Ellen," Mel said kindly.

Anne Marie wouldn't take the loss of her pet lightly, either. Increasingly on edge, all Tim wanted was to get off the phone. "What can I do for you?" he asked brusquely. "I don't want to tie up the line in case Anne Marie needs to get hold of me." And why was Mel calling him in the first place?

"It's about Anne Marie," Mel said, his voice serious.

"What about her?" Tim could almost feel what was coming.

"She's dating me, not you. Do you understand?"

"Oh, I understand, all right." Tim didn't even try to keep the derision out of his voice.

"I know she had feelings for you at one time, but that's over. I'm in the picture now."

"And you're telling me this why?" What went on between him and Anne Marie was none of Mel's business, nor was her relationship with Mel any of his.

Tim started to pace the lawn once more, the phone still pressed to his ear.

"I don't like the fact that you hang around Anne Marie and Ellen so much."

"Fine, whatever. But you need to understand something, too, Mel. Ellen is my daughter and I have every intention of being part of her life. Nothing you say or do is going to change that."

"I have no objection to you being part of Ellen's life."

"Big of you." This time his words dripped with sarcasm.

Mel disregarded his slight. "I just felt it was a good idea for the two of us to clear the air."

"The air is already clear," Tim said. He clenched his fist at his side. "The only reason I see Anne Marie is because of Ellen. If it wasn't for my daughter, I wouldn't be anywhere near her." In fact, if it wasn't for Ellen, he wouldn't even know Anne Marie.

Just as he turned the corner of the house, he came to an abrupt halt as he almost walked straight into Anne Marie. One glance at her face, and he knew she'd heard every word of his last statement.

"I have to go." Not bothering to explain further, he snapped his cell phone shut.

"Daddy! We found Baxter!" Ellen dashed toward him, clutching Baxter's leash, the dog at her heels.

Tim had been too unnerved to even notice them. Anne

Marie held his gaze, her eyes narrowed and filled with—was that pain? He opened his mouth to speak and realized that anything he said now would only make matters worse.

"Daddy, guess what?"

"What?" he asked, without looking in his daughter's direction. His focus was on Anne Marie as she blinked rapidly, then turned and walked into the house.

"I met a girl named April and she lives down the street. I met her at the flower shop. Baxter was with her."

Tim started toward the house, wanting to at least *try* to talk to Anne Marie.

"April's my age, too."

"That's nice, sweetheart."

Ellen grabbed his shirt. "That's not all."

"You mean there's more?" Obviously excited, Ellen smiled up at him. Although his heart was racing with dread, he gave the girl his full attention.

"She has a dog, too."

"Named Baxter?"

"No, silly! Her name is Iris and she's a Yorkie, just like Baxter."

"You have a new friend and so does Baxter," he said, pleased for his daughter and worried about Anne Marie at the same time.

"April wants me to teach her how to knit."

"That's great. I need to talk to your mother now, all right?"

"Okay. April's going to ask her mother if she can come over and help me finish unpacking my bedroom. She likes books, too."

Tim hugged his daughter, grateful that she'd found a new friend. He hurried toward the house, leaping up the front steps. "Anne Marie?" he called when he didn't see her.

She came into the hallway, her arms crossed. "You don't need to explain. You made it fairly evident that your only interest is in Ellen, and I accept that."

Tim shook his head. "Not true."

"Who was that, anyway? Vanessa?"

"I haven't seen Vanessa in months. We're finished. It was Mel."

Her eyes widened in shock. "Why? Was he looking for you—or me?"

"I told him I'd pass on the message that he phoned," Tim said, skirting the truth but not lying, either. Not exactly.

Tim struggled to find a way to tell Anne Marie that he cared for her as well as Ellen. He wanted to confess how foolish he'd been not to recognize his own feelings. Now that he had, it seemed too late.

"Tim, listen, it's okay," she said. "Ellen loves you and you love her. I won't stand between you. Our daughter is all that matters, and what goes on between the two of us isn't important. Now, if you'll excuse me, I need to unpack."

"Can I help?" He didn't want to leave. In fact, he was willing to do just about anything to stay.

"No." She marched to the door and held it open for him. "Thank you for everything you did today. I appreciate it, but I want you to go now."

He nodded. Without further argument, he walked to the door—and then hesitated. "Can we talk about this?"

"No." Her denial was flat.

He nodded again, although he wished he could explain that hurting her was the last thing he wanted to do. Every time he was with Anne Marie, he realized how important she was to him. He'd learned a lot about life in his AA meetings, a lot about himself, too. He knew better, but he'd let his pride take over. Mel had gotten to him and he'd lashed back—with unintended consequences. Serious consequences.

He had the distinct feeling that he'd just ruined whatever chance he might still have had with Anne Marie.

Five

April 25

My friend Lydia Goetz once told me there are two
kinds of knitters in the world. Those who find tangled yarn a challenge and will spend hours restor-
ing it and those who'd rather throw out the whole
thing than deal with the mess. I haven't quite decided
which type I am. What I will say is that I feel like my
life's a tangled mess but instead of knotted yarn it's
my emotions. I thought I was over Tim. Completely
over him. I assumed nothing he said would have the
power to hurt me. I was wrong. When I heard him
say the only reason he had anything to do with me
was because of Ellen I actually stopped breathing. I
was incapable of drawing in air—it hurt that much.
It still hurts, and that angers me even more. I have
emotionally removed myself from him.

Monday afternoon, Anne Marie walked back from the
French Café where she'd had lunch. As she crossed the
street she saw that Lydia was inside A Good Yarn. The

shop was technically closed on Mondays, but Lydia was often there catching up on paperwork.

What she needed, Anne Marie told herself, was a talk with a good friend, and there was no better friend than Lydia Goetz.

Walking all the way through the bookstore, she came out in the alley behind the yarn shop. She knocked at the back door and a moment later, Lydia unlocked it, smiling when she saw Anne Marie.

"Do you have time for a cup of tea?" Anne Marie realized she sounded wistful.

Lydia's shoulders relaxed. "I was just thinking that. Come on in."

Anne Marie followed her through the back of the store where boxes of yarn waited to be unpacked.

"How did the move go?" Lydia asked.

"So smoothly I could hardly believe it. I really appreciate Brad's and the kids' help."

"They loved it, especially Casey. She's been moved from one family to the next all her life and never had more than a suitcase. She found it…interesting that two people could accumulate so much stuff."

Anne Marie groaned. "That's not the end of it, either. I have an entire storage unit that still needs to be emptied." The move to the apartment three years earlier was only meant to be temporary.

While she was married to Robert, Anne Marie had left over a disagreement regarding children. She'd wanted a family and, as the father of a grown son and daughter, he hadn't. When neither of them was willing to budge, they'd separated. To be fair to Robert, Anne Marie had agreed to no kids when she'd married him. Over the years, however, her feelings had changed.

Unfortunately, Robert had remained adamant. No children. When they'd reached that impasse, she'd moved into the small apartment above the bookstore—her way of letting her husband know she was serious. She wanted a family. Children of her own.

Then Robert had a heart attack and was gone, and with him, her dream of bearing a child. It was while she'd been dealing with her grief that she'd met several other widows; one Valentine's night, they'd made those lists of twenty wishes.

As one of her wishes—to do something for someone else—she'd volunteered at the local grade school and been paired with Ellen. Although she was doing well academically, Ellen had been extremely shy. Anne Marie became her "lunch buddy," and that was how everything began, how both their lives had been transformed.

Lydia filled the kettle and plugged it in, then reached for her knitting. "Well, I'm glad it all went well."

"Tim was a big help, too," Anne Marie commented, mesmerized by the way her friend knit, gracefully weaving the yarn around the needles, creating what appeared to be a child's sweater, one knit in the round from the top down.

"I heard Tim was there, but Mel didn't show up."

"He was with clients," Anne Marie explained, wondering what her friend knew.

"Casey likes Tim. She said his red truck was cool."

Anne Marie remembered how eager Casey had been to ride with Tim and Ellen on the way to the house. Tim had agreed, which thrilled Ellen, who admired the older girl.

"We had a scare Saturday afternoon when Baxter went missing," she said, "but it actually worked out well."

Lydia looked up in alarm. "Missing? You got him back, right?"

The kettle whistled and she set aside her knitting.

As she took two mugs from the cupboard and poured hot water over the tea bags, Anne Marie clarified her remark. "Ellen and I were out looking for Baxter and, yes, we did get him back—thank goodness. We also came across a flower shop and a bakery."

Lydia brought the tea to the small table, along with sugar and milk. "It sounds just like Blossom Street."

Anne Marie thanked her for the tea, added milk, then sat back. "Well, not *exactly* like Blossom Street, but close enough for Ellen to realize her new neighborhood isn't so different from her old one. She made a new friend, too— the girl who actually found Baxter—and, as it happens, April has a dog. Another Yorkie."

"You couldn't have arranged that more perfectly if you'd tried," Lydia said with a smile.

"I know." Anne Marie stared down at her tea. "Anything new on Blossom Street?" Ellen wasn't the only one who was going to miss living here. She'd still be working here, but— despite what she'd told Ellen—it wasn't quite the same.

"I saw Bethanne Hamlin on Saturday—and she had news."

"Oh? What?" Anne Marie sipped her tea. Bethanne frequented the yarn shop and was a good friend of both Lydia and Anne Marie. She ran a highly successful party business that she'd started shortly after her divorce and often visited the bookstore.

"Bethanne told me that Andrew and Courtney Pulanski are engaged."

"That's wonderful! When's the wedding?"

"Mid-July."

Anne Marie had never met Courtney, although she'd heard plenty about her. Bethanne's son, Andrew, and Courtney had been dating for several years; they'd met in their senior year of high school, after Bethanne and Courtney had taken one of Lydia's knitting classes.

"Bethanne's knitting Courtney a pair of beaded fingerless gloves for the wedding. I special-ordered the yarn," Lydia told her. "Cashmere."

"She's such an accomplished knitter," Anne Marie added. "I'm sure the gloves will become a family heirloom."

"Me, too," Lydia said.

Anne Marie put down her cup. She searched for a way to broach the subject that had been weighing on her mind all weekend. She'd unpacked boxes late into the night on Saturday and fallen into bed exhausted. Tired though she was, she'd been unable to sleep.

All thanks to Tim Carlsen.

"Did anything else happen on Saturday?" Lydia asked after a moment of silence.

"You could say that."

"Between you and Tim?"

Anne Marie's head shot up. "How'd you know that?"

Lydia shrugged, her smile sympathetic. "Call it a lucky guess."

Anne Marie exhaled slowly and picked up her tea, needing something to do with her hands. "I overheard a conversation he was having on his cell. As it turned out, he was talking to Mel, although he never really said why—other than to pass on the message that Mel called." She paused. "At first I thought it might've been Vanessa."

"The woman he was engaged to?"

Anne Marie nodded. "He told Mel the only reason he had anything to do with me was because of Ellen."

"Ouch." Lydia winced, not even attempting to minimize the hurt his words had inflicted.

Anne Marie looked away rather than reveal how upset she was.

"Why would he say this to Mel?"

"All I can think is that Mel phoned to clear the air. When I talked to him later, he didn't mention it. But he and Tim are constantly goading each other. It's ridiculous."

"So Mel decided to set matters straight?"

"Apparently."

"And I assume Tim was basically assuring him he had no interest in you," Lydia said.

"That seems to be the case."

"And that upsets you?"

More than Anne Marie ever dreamed it would.

"You still care about him, don't you?"

"No." Her denial was quick and emphatic. "How could I after everything he's said and done?"

"How could you?" Lydia repeated, then leaned forward and pressed Anne Marie's hand. "Well, first of all, the two of you have a strong bond in Ellen. She means the world to you both."

"True."

"He's hardworking, funny, sincere and darn good-looking."

All of that was accurate enough, especially the good-looking part. Tim was an attractive man; it wasn't as if Anne Marie hadn't noticed. When they'd first started seeing each other—while he'd been engaged to Vanessa and she hadn't known it—they'd had such fun together. He'd been wonderful to her and to Ellen. They'd gone on several outings, the three of them, and she'd grown close to Tim. He was easy to talk to, and before she realized what was happening, she'd fallen for him and fallen hard. She'd never let him know that, although he'd probably guessed.

The one and only time Tim had asked Anne Marie out to dinner without Ellen had been to tell her about his relationship with Vanessa.

The news had shaken her badly. When she'd had the opportunity to meet the woman who was going to become Ellen's stepmother, it had gone poorly. Vanessa, who'd taken an instant dislike to Anne Marie, had made her as uncomfortable as possible.

When Tim had announced that his relationship with Vanessa was over, it was too late. Anne Marie couldn't— wouldn't—trust him again. She wasn't willing to give him a second chance. She'd assumed that she'd completely recovered from her infatuation with Ellen's father. And then she'd overheard Tim talking to Mel... His revelation had distressed her more than she would've expected.

Okay, she'd admit that her relationship with Mel wasn't passionate, but it was comfortable and pleasant. He was a widower, and they had a great deal in common.

"Is Tim dating anyone else now?" Lydia asked, breaking into Anne Marie's musings.

"Pardon?" she asked, looking up, mesmerized again by the graceful movements of Lydia's hands. As a distraction she took a sip of her tea.

"Tim? Is he seeing someone else now that Vanessa's out of the picture?"

"I don't think so." But she hadn't known when he was involved with Vanessa and he was even less likely to discuss his dating life with her now.

"What does your gut tell you?" Lydia asked.

"That it was a mistake to let Ellen see him."

Lydia stared at her long and hard. "You don't mean that."

Anne Marie sighed. "No, I don't. Ellen's become a different child since she met Tim and learned he's her father." The painfully shy, reticent little girl had blossomed before Anne Marie's eyes. Tim's love had a lot to do with that transformation. Ellen's eyes lit up every time she saw her father.

"In my opinion—and this *is* just my opinion—you need to acknowledge that you still have feelings for him."

Anne Marie opened her mouth to ardently object—and then hesitated. If nothing else, the incident on Saturday proved how much she continued to care about Tim, despite all her efforts not to. For months she'd buried her feelings for him, not realizing how ineffective those attempts had been.

"I'm dating Mel now." *Mel* was her future, not Tim.

"Mel," Lydia murmured.

"Yes, Mel. He's generous and…and kind and sweet." She knew she was trying too hard to convince Lydia.

"Yes," Lydia agreed softly. Holding Anne Marie's gaze, she said, "But he isn't Tim Carlsen."

"Tim couldn't care less about me. By his own admission, the only reason he has anything to do with me is Ellen." Her voice cracked and she struggled to hold on to her composure.

Lydia glanced up from her knitting and, again, leaned forward to press her hand over Anne Marie's. "Don't be so sure. I've seen the way he looks at you."

Six

April 26

Something's wrong with Mom. I don't think she likes
the new house and I think she misses the apartment.
I thought I'd hate living away from Blossom Street,
but I don't. April isn't in my class, but we go to the
same school. I didn't know that. She said I could sit
with her on the bus and I promised to teach her to
knit. Mom gave me a pair of needles and some yarn
and I'm going to show April. I told her it feels awkward at first but it won't take long to figure it out.
She thought it was great that I knit Baxter's green
sweater. She wants to knit one for Iris and I told her
she could, but she should start with something easier.
She's going to knit a pot holder for her mom. I knit
one for my mom and she really likes it.

"Can April stay for dinner?" Ellen asked Anne Marie the
minute they walked in the door Monday night. Her daughter
and her new friend had played at April's house after school

that afternoon. The two girls had been inseparable since they'd met on Saturday.

Anne Marie was delighted Ellen had made a friend so quickly. Even better, they attended the same school, although they had different teachers. They'd become instant friends, the way kids did at that age.

"Ah…" Anne Marie had no idea what to prepare. "Sure, April can have dinner here, as long as it's all right with her mom and dad."

"It is," Ellen told her. "We already asked."

Anne Marie did a thorough search of her kitchen cupboards. She'd gone to the store and stocked their shelves, and she could cook any number of dishes—but she couldn't decide on even one. That showed how depressed she was; she wasn't capable of making such a simple decision. Of course there was always the old standby. "How about macaroni and cheese?"'

"We had that for lunch," Ellen called back.

Well, the freezer was her next option. She was about to check it when her cell phone buzzed. Sorting through the packages of frozen food, she answered it.

"Hello."

"What are you two doing for dinner?" Mel asked.

"I don't know yet. Why?"

"I thought I'd stop by and take you and Ellen out to eat."

"Thanks, but I don't think that'll work. Ellen invited her new friend over."

"She has a new friend already?"

"She does. April lives down the street. She found Baxter on Saturday, which is when we met her."

"Why don't I bring dinner?"

This was an offer too good to refuse. "Sounds great. What do you have in mind?"

Mel chuckled. "How about if I pick up one of those roasted chickens with all the fixings?"

"Thanks!" Mel was so thoughtful—and he'd just solved the problem of tonight's dinner.

"I figured you must be exhausted after last weekend."

"I am." The move had taken more out of Anne Marie than she'd realized. That, and what she'd learned about Tim's feelings toward her.

As soon as she'd closed her cell, she walked down the hall to Ellen's room, where the girls were playing with Baxter and Iris. "Mel's coming by with dinner. He's bringing chicken. Would you two set the table?"

Ellen and April exchanged a glance. "Who's Mel?" April asked.

"He's my mother's boyfriend," Ellen replied.

"I thought Tim was your mother's boyfriend," April said, cocking her head.

"He used to be but he isn't anymore. It's…complicated."

"Yeah, grown-ups can get that way," April said sagely.

Smiling, Anne Marie returned to the kitchen.

By the time Mel arrived with dinner, the table was set. They all sat down together with Baxter and Iris settled underneath, content after their own meals.

"Anyone miss me on Blossom Street?" Ellen asked Anne Marie. She reached for a chicken leg; April took the second one.

"Lydia sends her love. Oh, and Bethanne was in the yarn store on Saturday and guess what? Andrew and Courtney got engaged."

Ellen's eyes brightened and she waved the chicken leg. "Can I be in their wedding? I want to be the flower girl!"

"That's not something you ask," Anne Marie explained.

"You wait to be invited. But Courtney has several nieces and nephews your age."

Ellen put the chicken leg back on her plate and sighed with disappointment. "I *love* weddings."

"I know you do."

"I was in a wedding once," April said. "But I was only three and I don't remember it. My mom has pictures, though. I was supposed to sprinkle rose petals down the church aisle but I ate them instead."

Anne Marie and Mel laughed.

"Let's play weddings after dinner!" April said excitedly. "We can be wedding planners like on TV."

"Okay!"

Conversation flowed smoothly during the rest of the meal. They talked about television shows and upcoming movies, and Anne Marie appreciated Mel's lack of condescension, his good-humored patience with the girls. Afterward, they asked to be excused and tore back into Ellen's bedroom, while Mel and Anne Marie lingered over coffee.

"Thank you for bringing dinner," Anne Marie said.

"I wasn't here to help with the move like I'd planned. It's the least I could do."

"Mel, I understood. You had a business meeting."

"I know, but I felt bad about letting you down and then there was all that angst over Baxter. I should've been here instead of—"

He didn't need to complete the sentence; she knew he meant Tim. Rather than pursue the subject she let it drop. Her conversation with Lydia had stayed in her mind all afternoon. Anne Marie didn't *want* to have feelings for Tim. Mel was good with Ellen, so considerate and caring, and she needed to concentrate on her relationship with him.

He helped her clear the table and was about to kiss her when Ellen dashed into the kitchen. "Hurry!" she cried.

"Hurry?" Anne Marie repeated, noting the disappointed look in Mel's eyes. "Why?"

"Come and see," Ellen said urgently.

"See what?"

"The wedding. Come on!" She wore a white sundress and a lace-trimmed pillowcase as her veil.

Anne Marie dried her hands on the dish towel and followed her daughter down the hall. Mel came, too. Standing in the doorway of Ellen's bedroom, she leaned against the door frame, Mel beside her.

"These are the church pews," April said, gesturing at the books laid across the carpet in two even rows, with a center aisle wide enough for Ellen to walk down.

"Who's the groom?" Anne Marie asked.

"We haven't decided yet," Ellen said. "Baxter's going to be the best man, though." The girls had affixed a black ribbon to the dog's neck to resemble a bow tie. However, he didn't look pleased with his role.

"What part does Iris play?" Anne Marie asked April.

"She's the maid of honor."

"Of course. I should've guessed."

"We need someone who can sing the wedding march," Ellen said. "We're wedding planners so we have to arrange it. April and I don't know the words. All we know is 'Here comes the bride.'"

Anne Marie was about to tell them she couldn't sing it, either, when the doorbell rang.

"That must be April's mom," Anne Marie said. But even before she opened the front door she knew it wasn't. Her intuition told her it was Tim.

The way Mel felt about him would make this awkward.

Mel, nothing! Her *own* feelings were as tangled as any yarn she'd ever snarled. She didn't want to face him, not yet. She hadn't had time to absorb what she'd learned or the hurt he'd caused her. Still, her heart seemed to speed up as soon as she saw him and she was instantly annoyed with herself.

"Hello again," she said without any warmth, standing on the other side of the screen door, which she kept closed, aware of how rude she was acting, yet unable to stop.

"Hi." He held the handlebars of Ellen's bike. "I brought this back. It had a flat tire."

Anne Marie continued to leave the screen door shut. "I didn't know you'd taken it."

"I promised to repair it for Ellen."

Mel came up behind her, placing a possessive hand on her shoulder.

Ellen joined them, wearing her white dress but having discarded her "veil." "My bike's fixed already?" she squealed. "Thank you, Daddy!"

"I did it this afternoon," he said, smiling at his daughter. "Where would you like me to put it?"

"In the garage," Anne Marie told him.

"Come and see the wedding," Ellen said. "April and I are wedding planners. Baxter's the best man but he keeps running off. We couldn't decide who should be the groom. Will you, Daddy?'"

"Ah, sure," he said, but Anne Marie sensed his hesitation.

She opened the screen door, walked down the steps and over to the garage, which was located behind the house. Mel went with her; she could feel his disapproval every step of the way. No one spoke, which made this all the more disconcerting.

"Will you tell Ellen I'll play groom some other time?" Tim asked once he'd finished securing Ellen's bicycle.

Anne Marie crossed her arms against the evening chill. Thankfully, Tim realized she didn't want him there.

"That would probably be best," she murmured.

"I agree," Mel added.

Anne Marie could have done without his comment but didn't bother to object. At least he wasn't contradicting her opinion or her request.

Tim had started to leave when the back door flew open and Ellen came out. "We're ready," she shouted. "April and I are going to hum the song 'cause we don't know the words." She dashed toward Tim and grabbed his hand.

Tim threw Anne Marie an apologetic glance as he walked slowly toward the house.

"I've been meaning to talk to you about Tim," Mel said, not hiding his irritation.

"About what, exactly?"

"Well, for one thing, he turns up far too often. Do the two you have a parenting plan?"

"Not…really." At this point their agreement was pretty loose.

"That might be something to consider," Mel said. "Tim seems to think he can come by anytime he pleases. For obvious reasons, that's not a good idea."

Anne Marie turned back to the house. She didn't ask what those obvious reasons were, but she had to admit Mel was probably right. However, she wasn't in any mood to hear it. If she limited Tim's access to Ellen, he'd assume she was punishing him because he wasn't interested in her. "Can we talk about this later?"

Not waiting for his reply, she hurried inside. The instant she did, she was greeted by the sound of the girls giggling delightedly. Unable to resist, she had to look for herself.

Sure enough, Tim had taken on the role of the groom.

He wore Ellen's black velvet hair bow clipped to the top button of his shirt.

"We need a preacher," Ellen said. "Mel, will you be the preacher?"

Mel shook his head. "Trust me, Ellen, I wouldn't make a good preacher." The ten-year-old's face fell with disappointment.

"What about your mom?" April suggested.

"She can't," Ellen insisted. "Mom's the bride."

"Oh, right."

Anne Marie opened her mouth to protest but no one noticed. Wasn't *Ellen* the bride? *She* most definitely wasn't willing to pretend to be Tim's bride. "Hold on, you two—"

"I'll be the preacher," Ellen volunteered, ignoring Anne Marie.

"You'll need a Bible."

"Got it." Ellen stood on tiptoe to get her children's Bible from the top bookshelf.

"Can girls be preachers?" April sounded unsure of this.

"Girls can be anything they want," Anne Marie assured her firmly. Despite her discomfort, she couldn't let a comment like that pass unanswered.

"Even a firefighter?"

"Even a firefighter," Anne Marie said.

Now that she'd resolved that issue, Anne Marie seemed to lose control of the situation. She was handed a plastic flower and the pillowcase was pinned to her hair as a makeshift veil. As the two girls hummed "Here Comes the Bride," Anne Marie carefully marched down the aisle between the rows of books. Holding her Bible, Ellen went to stand in front of Tim. Mel remained in the background, looking disgruntled and ill at ease.

When Anne Marie reached Tim's side, he tucked her

arm in the crook of his, staring straight ahead. The best man had returned but clearly hadn't understood his role. He stretched out on the floor, knocking over several "pews." Iris, the maid of honor, peered out from under Ellen's bed.

With great ceremony, Ellen opened the Bible. In formal tones she began, "Dearly beloved, we are gathered together this evening in the presence of God and these witnesses to join together—"

April leaned close to Ellen. "What's *beloved* mean?" she asked.

"You can't ask questions during the wedding," Ellen told her friend.

"Okay. Sorry." But April didn't sound contrite.

Anne Marie quickly whispered the definition as Ellen frowned.

The ceremony took only a few minutes and by the time they'd finished Anne Marie and Tim both found themselves grinning. Ellen's performance—complete with sweeping gestures—was worthy of an acting award. Anne Marie had gradually relaxed enough to enjoy the charade.

The only person who didn't appear the least bit entertained was Mel. He stood out in the hallway, wearing a frown.

Shortly after the "vows" were exchanged, Tim kissed Anne Marie on the cheek, then pulled out his wallet.

"What's the money for?" Ellen asked when he removed a dollar bill.

"The groom always pays the preacher."

Ellen raised her hand to stop him. "Give the money to the poor."

"I'm poor," April said, and held out her palm.

"No, you aren't," Ellen retorted. "Wedding planners make *lots* of money."

"I guess you should put your money away," Anne Marie said with a shrug.

Grinning, Tim did as she suggested. When he glanced up he apparently caught sight of Mel. "I'd better go." He bent down to hug Ellen farewell.

"You need to thank your father," Anne Marie said.

Ellen wrapped her arms around Tim's neck. "Thank you again for fixing my bike and for being the groom and for everything," she said in a breathless voice.

"You're welcome, sweetheart."

"Can we go bike riding again soon?"

"Sure. I'll set a time with your mother."

When Anne Marie escorted him to the front door, Tim held her look for a moment, then raised his eyes to meet Mel's, who stood directly behind her. "Does next Saturday work for you? I can pick Ellen up around ten."

"We have plans for Saturday," Mel inserted without allowing Anne Marie the opportunity to respond.

She ignored him. "Saturday morning will be fine, Tim. I'll have Ellen ready by ten."

His expression uncertain, Tim nodded. "Okay. See you then."

"Bye," she said, closing the door. Neither man had addressed the other again. She took a deep breath to compose herself, then turned deliberately to Mel. "What was that about?" she snapped.

Mel didn't pretend not to know what she meant. "I've told you. I don't like the idea of Tim spending so much time with you and Ellen. Besides, we did discuss going for brunch."

She was in no state to deal with his insecurities and frankly she was a little unsettled by the make-believe wedding. "I think you might be making an assumption regarding our relationship, Mel. We're good friends—"

"Friends?" he repeated, breaking in. "We've been dating exclusively for the past six months. Correction, *I've* been dating *you* exclusively. And yet Tim is still in your life."

"Ellen's his daughter!"

"That doesn't mean *you* have to be involved with him."

Anne Marie expelled her breath and walked into the kitchen. They had to lower their voices, otherwise the girls might hear. "I don't want to argue about Tim."

"I don't either, but I need to find out where I stand with you. Just tell me flat-out—am I wasting my time here? I know you cared about Tim at one point."

"That's over," she said immediately. "I told you before."

"Is it, Anne Marie?"

"Yes…" But she didn't sound nearly as emphatic as she wanted to.

"I think that tells me everything I need to know."

Anne Marie felt terrible.

Calling goodbye to the girls, Mel started toward the front door. She stopped him. "Don't go," she whispered, her hand on his forearm.

He hesitated.

"Please."

Mel exhaled slowly as though undecided.

Anne Marie slid her arms around his middle and hugged him close. Mel was solid and warm, and she knew exactly where *she* stood with *him*. Tim was like shifting sand, not to be trusted. Eventually her heart would align itself with Mel's.

Seven

April 27

I've made a decision. I'm going to ignore my feelings
for Tim and concentrate on Mel. Once I do that, my
heart will follow. Ever since last Saturday I've been
miserable. Well, no more. I refuse to get emotionally
involved with Tim again. He's good for Ellen and she
loves him. I can't and won't keep him away from his
daughter. However, I think Mel might be right. We
need to establish a parenting plan. We need an agreement between us. Now that I've settled that in my
own mind, I want to start a new knitting project. I'd
like to make something for Courtney's wedding. I'm
sure Lydia will have a few ideas.

Wednesday afternoon Tim phoned Anne Marie at the
bookstore. "I hope I didn't cause a problem between you
and Mel when I came by the other night," he said.

"Why would that be a problem?" she asked, unwilling to
mention her argument with Mel. "It wasn't a big deal, and

Ellen loved the fact that you went along with her wedding-planner fantasy."

"I've often wondered what it would be like to be married. I just never expected to have a dog as my best man."

Despite herself Anne Marie laughed. "As I recall, he fell asleep during the ceremony. Some best man he turned out to be."

"You don't have any room to talk. Your maid of honor wouldn't come out from under the bed."

"True."

After a brief silence, Tim said, "Is Ellen there?"

"She met up with Casey Goetz after school, but she's due at the bookstore soon. Any particular reason you're asking?"

"Would you mind if I took her to Lake Wisdom? My parents recently bought a cabin there, and since it's such a sunny afternoon, I thought she might enjoy a boat ride."

The weather was unseasonably warm for April, and Anne Marie knew Ellen would love an outing like that. "I'm sure she'd be thrilled." They discussed the fact that Ellen would need a life vest if she went out on the water, then chatted amicably for a few more minutes.

"I'll pick her up at the store in half an hour."

"Okay."

Anne Marie glanced at her watch; it was now three-thirty.

As usual, Tim arrived precisely when he'd said he would. He had on jeans and a light jacket and wore a Mariners baseball cap. It was hard not to stare, to appreciate how handsome he was, but Anne Marie resisted.

"You ready, Ellen?" he asked.

She bounced off her chair, slammed her book shut and nodded. "Can Mom come, too?"

"I wish she would," Tim said.

Anne Marie automatically shook her head. "I'd like to, but I need to be here."

Teresa, who worked with her, was quick to weigh in with her opinion. Too quick. "We've had a slow afternoon." She looked at Tim and explained, "It's generally slow the first sunny day of spring. Besides," she added, turning to Anne Marie, "I thought you were supposed to take Wednesdays off." Anne Marie tried to give herself a midweek break but she'd gotten out of the habit.

"You'd be welcome," Tim said, encouraging her.

"*Please* come, Mom." Ellen folded her hands in a prayerful gesture. "You *always* have to work. I want you to go to the lake with us."

Anne Marie wanted to enjoy the sunshine, too, but she hesitated. She hadn't talked to Mel since Monday night, and while they'd parted on good terms they'd each felt unsettled by their disagreement. If he were to learn she'd gone to the lake with Tim, he'd be justifiably upset.

Tim opened his eyes wide and folded his hands like Ellen's. With both of them gazing at her in supplication, she couldn't refuse. Her one hope was that Mel wouldn't find out about this. "Oh, all right," she said, giving in.

Ellen hooted and jumped up and down, clapping.

"I'll have to stop at the house and change clothes," Anne Marie told them. "I can't very well go out on the water wearing this." She motioned at her white pants and pink jacket.

"We have time," Tim said with a boyish grin.

Once she'd driven home, changed her clothes and packed a few things for Ellen, it was close to four-thirty. "I need to be back before seven," she said as she slid into the front seat next to Tim. That wasn't strictly true, but she had an evening of paperwork planned. And imposing a time limit gave her at least the illusion of control.

"You will be," he promised as he started the engine.

The drive to the lake took another thirty minutes. He turned off the main road to a secluded one, then eventually drove down a dirt track that led to the water's edge. A rustic log cabin was nestled among tall fir trees. She saw two wooden rockers on the front porch; they looked comfortably worn, as though many conversations had taken place there over the years, many sunsets watched. The pristine lake was glass-smooth with the sun reflecting on the surface of the water, which was a deep greenish blue. Another cabin could be seen on the other side.

"Oh, Tim, this is lovely," Anne Marie said. "It's so peaceful."

"Mom and Dad have wanted a summer place like this for years and they finally found exactly what they were looking for."

"Can we go out in the boat now?" Ellen asked. After strapping on her vest, she raced down to the dock.

"Wait for us," Anne Marie called.

A boat ride had sounded like a simple thing when Tim first mentioned it. Anne Marie couldn't remember the last time she'd been in one—or one that small, anyway. Tied to the dock, the rowboat bobbed gently on the lake. Anne Marie wasn't sure how she was supposed to climb in and out.

"I'll help you," Tim said, as though reading her mind. "You have nothing to fear—I was a Cub Scout."

"Not a Boy Scout?"

"No, I didn't pass the test."

"Oh, great."

He chuckled. "I'm a natural on the water. I've been doing this for years."

"So you say."

"It's all right, Mom," Ellen said, clasping Anne Marie's hand. "I can swim—I'll save you."

Tim got in first, then helped Ellen lower herself into the boat. Anne Marie went last. She sat on the edge of the dock and gingerly eased herself in, sighing with relief once she was safely seated.

"Ready?" he asked.

"Yeah!" Ellen shouted. "Let's go!"

It soon became apparent that Tim was as comfortable on the water as he'd claimed. He rowed with regular, even strokes, and the boat seemed to glide effortlessly across the lake.

"See that cabin over there?" he asked, pointing to the one Anne Marie had noticed earlier.

"I see it," Ellen told him, shading her eyes from the sun.

"There's a story about the people who used to live in these two cabins, ours and that one."

"Oh?" He had a twinkle in his eyes, and Anne Marie was convinced he was about to make up some wild tale.

"Years ago, these cabins were owned by rival families. The Krugers and the Livermores."

"Krugers and Livermores?" Anne Marie repeated. "Like the Montagues and Capulets? Or the Hatfields and McCoys?"

"Something like that."

"What's *rival* mean?" Ellen asked.

"They competed with each other," Tim explained.

"Were they friends?"

"Rivals can be friends, but in this case they weren't."

"You mean like Mel and you?" She looked from Tim to Anne Marie.

"Sort of," Anne Marie said, saddened that her daughter was aware of the antagonism between Mel and her father.

"If one family bought a boat, then the other family did, as well," Tim went on as if he hadn't heard Ellen's last statement. "The two husbands were employed by rival companies, so when one family purchased a cabin on this side of the lake, the second family bought land and built a larger cabin on the other side."

"Is ours bigger?" Ellen asked.

"We have the smaller house," Tim said.

"Oh." Ellen seemed disappointed.

"As it happened, both families had teenage children. The Krugers had a daughter named Dani and the Livermores had a son, Scott, who was the same age as Dani."

"I feel a romance brewing," Anne Marie said.

"You're right." Tim directed the comment to her. "Dani and Scott were both out on the water one afternoon when Dani's canoe tipped over."

"This story isn't going to have an unhappy ending, is it?" Anne Marie asked.

"No way," Tim said, pulling rhythmically on the oars. "This is a romance, remember?"

"Mo-om, let Dad tell the story."

"Okay, okay, continue." Anne Marie gestured toward Tim.

"Seeing that Dani was in distress, Scott paddled over and rescued her."

"And the Kruger family was so grateful the rivalry ended," Anne Marie concluded.

"Nope. The Kruger family blamed Scott for causing Dani to fall out of the canoe."

"Didn't Dani defend him?" Anne Marie asked.

"She tried, but her family refused to listen. The Krugers disliked the Livermores so much that if there was any kind of mishap, the Livermores were automatically to blame."

"That's ridiculous," she muttered.

"I agree."

Ellen patted Anne Marie's knee. "Shh, I want to find out what happened."

"Would you like the short version or the long one?"

"Short version," Anne Marie insisted. "Definitely the short version."

"Okay," Tim said. "They lived happily ever after."

"Who did?" Ellen demanded. "I want the long version 'cause I don't know who married who."

Anne Marie groaned and glanced up at the sky. "Tim, honestly. All right, give us the long version."

"That night," he began, "Dani snuck out of the house and got in the canoe and paddled over to Scott's place. She woke him up and apologized for the way her family had reacted. They should've been grateful and they weren't. Dani wanted him to know she appreciated what he'd done."

"Did she kiss him?" Ellen asked excitedly.

"Not that night, but then they started meeting every night in the middle of the lake. They'd sit under the moonlight and talk."

"They did fall in love, though, right?"

"It wouldn't be a romance if they didn't. Except neither of their families wanted them to be together."

"Did they get married?"

"They did eventually—and guess what?"

"What?" Ellen echoed.

"The Krugers and the Livermores became the best of friends. Dani and Scott now have three children. Let me see." Tim squinted into the distance. "I believe their oldest daughter is around your age."

"That *is* a romantic story," Anne Marie said, mainly

grateful that no one had drowned in the middle of the lake during a midnight tryst.

They spent an hour on the water, the most pleasant, peaceful hour Anne Marie could remember in a long while.

"I'd better get you back to shore if I'm going to have you home before seven," he said. He sounded as reluctant as Anne Marie was to leave the tranquility of this special afternoon.

"Oh, yeah—I should be back by seven." Only she didn't want to leave. The temptation to stay on the lake was almost overwhelming. The sun felt warm on her shoulders; she'd finally begun to relax. Ellen yawned and rested her head against Anne Marie's leg. "Maybe we could stay a bit longer…"

"You're sure?" Tim asked, slipping the oar into the smooth water.

Anne Marie nodded. Eyes closed, she raised her face to the sun, reveling in the warmth of late afternoon. The birds chirped, the water rippled, and she could feel a light breeze on her face. She didn't immediately realize they'd stopped moving. When she opened her eyes, she saw Tim sitting there motionless, both oars suspended above the water.

"Is everything okay?" she asked.

"No."

He sounded uncharacteristically serious, and she tried to lighten the situation—whatever it was—with humor.

"Don't tell me there's a monster in this lake that's going to come out of the water and swallow us whole."

"Not to my knowledge."

"Then what's wrong?"

"Nothing." He set the oars in the water again and headed toward the cabin as if he were taking part in a race. Their speed was in stark contrast to the easy, tranquil quality of their earlier ride.

Once they'd reached shore, Tim secured the boat and hopped onto the dock. He helped Ellen up and then Anne Marie. "It's time I got you back," he said curtly.

Anne Marie had no idea what was going on. Taking her cue from him, she settled Ellen in the backseat while he stowed their belongings in the trunk. The inside of the car was warm and cozy, and Ellen closed her eyes, dozing off within minutes. Anne Marie got into the car; so did Tim. He braced his hands against the steering wheel.

"Tim," she whispered, not wanting to disturb Ellen. "What's wrong?"

"You don't want to know."

She placed her hand on his knee, preventing him from starting the engine. "Actually, I do."

"Really?" He turned and looked at her, his eyes holding hers.

Anne Marie wasn't sure who moved first. But the next thing she knew, Tim had his arms around her and his lips were on hers.

This wasn't a soft exploratory kiss—it was hot and hungry, moist and openmouthed, as if they were intent on absorbing each other completely. The kiss went on and on until Anne Marie broke away, breathless.

"Ellen," she whispered for fear her daughter would wake and find them like this.

"I tried to warn you…" Tim whispered back. His shoulders heaved and he clutched the steering wheel with both hands.

Anne Marie leaned against the back of the seat and closed her eyes, making a determined effort to catch her breath. "Wow," she gasped, hardly aware she'd spoken.

Tim snickered softly. "You can say that again." He was silent for the next few minutes. "Now what?" he finally asked.

Anne Marie blinked. "What do you mean?"

"The way I see it, we have two choices."

"Only two?"

He didn't respond to the question. "We can overlook what just happened…" he began.

"Or?"

"Or we can explore it further."

"Ellen's in the backseat."

"I didn't mean this minute." His gaze bore into hers. "You're the one who has to decide what you want, Anne Marie. The decision is yours."

It suddenly occurred to her what that kiss was all about. And it wasn't because he was attracted to her. He'd said as much. Anne Marie closed her eyes once more and pushed aside the exciting sensations that cascaded through her. His touch was thrilling—wonderful—but she couldn't trust him. He'd taught her painful lessons in the past and she'd be a fool to ignore them.

"You didn't need to do that, you know," she said stiffly.

He frowned. "What are you talking about?"

"You kissed me just now because you're afraid of what I might do."

"Might do?"

"Don't worry, Tim. I'll never block your access to Ellen. She's your daughter and she loves you. But I also know that if it wasn't for Ellen you wouldn't have anything to do with me. And I'm fine with that."

"Anne Marie, listen—"

"No, please, I don't want to hear your excuses. Mel suggested the two of us set up a parenting plan and I think that's a good idea. You don't need to flatter me with attention and kisses, Tim. We understand each other without playing games."

His frown darkened. "You honestly believe that's what the kiss was about?"

She didn't say anything.

He waited for a moment, then started the engine. "Your silence is answer enough."

He was angry and upset with her. Perhaps it was best this way.

In fact, she knew it was.

Eight

April 27

I saw Mom and Tim kissing this afternoon! They
didn't know I wasn't really asleep. They kissed real
hard and I was hoping maybe they might want to get
married for real. April and I could be their wedding
planners! But then something happened, only I don't
know what because Mom and Tim both got quiet. I
tried to listen, but I couldn't understand what they
were talking about.

When we got home, Mom said she's going to knit
something for a bride named Courtney, who's marrying the son of her friend Bethanne. Mom's going to
talk to Lydia, and I want to come along. I want to knit
something for a bride, too, except I want Mom to be
the bride, just like April and I planned.

When Anne Marie and Ellen returned from Lake Wisdom, there was a message on her home phone, which had
been installed Tuesday, and on her cell.

A message from Mel.

Anne Marie listened to both with more than a twinge of guilt. While she'd been necking like a teenager with Tim in his car, Mel, the man she was dating, had tried to reach her.

She waited until Ellen was down for the night before she called him back. "Hi," she said. She knew it sounded tentative—and guilty. She had to resist the urge to apologize for kissing Tim.

Mel instantly picked up on her agitation. "Are you okay?" he asked.

"Yes... So what's up?"

"Actually, I phoned for two reasons," he said.

"Oh?" She paced the kitchen as she held the phone against her ear.

"First, to apologize for the other night. I overreacted with Tim."

"It's all right, really," she rushed to tell him. Even discussing Tim casually was dangerous. "I understand. It was unfortunate, but it's over and best forgotten."

"I guess I'm jealous," Mel continued, oblivious to everything she'd said. "There were a dozen better ways to handle the situation. I behaved badly. I hope you'll excuse my little temper tantrum."

"Mel, it's over," she said again. "Forgotten." Now, if she could forget Tim's kisses just as easily.

"You're far more forgiving and generous than I deserve."

If he didn't stop soon, she was going to burst into tears and confess that she'd spent the afternoon with Tim and had succumbed to his charms, of which there were many.

"Secondly, I called to remind you about Friday night."

"Friday?" Her memory had gone completely blank—no doubt understandable in the current situation. She stopped pacing, frowning as she tried to remember.

"We have tickets to see *Jersey Boys.*"

"Oh, right!" Anne Marie had been ecstatic at the opportunity. Her husband, Robert, had loved the Four Seasons, and she knew many of their songs by heart.

"You mean you *had* forgotten?"

"Oh…momentarily." Tim had agreed to watch Ellen, which meant she'd be seeing him again soon…in front of Mel. This was guaranteed to be uncomfortable. "But I'm looking forward to it."

His voice lowered seductively, tenderly. "And I'm looking forward to spending time with you."

Another bolt of guilt struck her. Mel was a gentleman and a romantic, and she was an idiot to let Tim anywhere close to her heart.

"Everything's okay between us, then," Mel went on to say.

"Oh, yes, everything's just fine." She resumed her pacing.

"Good." How relieved he sounded.

"I'm glad you called me back," he said next. "I was beginning to worry."

"Why would you worry?"

"It's after ten."

Anne Marie couldn't very well admit why she hadn't been home earlier.

"Teresa at the bookstore told me you'd gone out for the afternoon," Mel said.

"Yes, Ellen and I…spent time together." Thank goodness Teresa hadn't told him everything.

"That's great. Ellen's a terrific kid."

"She is," Anne Marie said, and felt the pressing urge to get off the phone before she slipped up.

It took another five minutes to extricate herself from the conversation. She tried not to be obvious about wanting to end the call and hoped she'd succeeded. Her pacing continued even after she'd hung up.

Stupid, stupid, stupid! What was she thinking, letting Tim and Ellen talk her into going to the lake—and so soon after her resolve to remove him from her thoughts! She was courting temptation and she knew it. Oh, she hadn't realized they'd end up kissing again or that...that she'd feel his allure—again. She shook her head. She was smarter than this.

Her relationship with Tim had, from the very beginning, been problematic. She'd had to frequently remind herself that he was a recovering alcoholic and drug addict. He'd been sober and clean for a long time, but that didn't change the basic fact: he had all the personality traits of an alcoholic, even if he didn't drink.

Before she'd allowed Tim into their lives, Anne Marie had done extensive research on alcohol and drug addiction. She felt it was necessary to know what they were facing before she agreed to let Tim see his daughter.

Legally, he had no right to Ellen and Anne Marie believed it was her duty, her moral obligation, to protect Ellen from any psychological harm he might inadvertently inflict.

She went to bed that night feeling confused, angry with herself...and intent on counteracting any damage she'd done to her relationship with Mel.

The next day, as she'd feared, Tim contacted her. He showed up at the bookstore, but the minute he walked in she pretended to be busy.

He approached the service counter and greeted her with a smile that could have melted a glacier. "How's it going?" he asked.

She looked up, and returned his greeting with a tight smile, despite her determination not to display the slightest hint of emotion. "Very well, thanks."

"Do you have time for a lunch break?" he asked. "We don't need to go far. I checked, and the soup at the French Café is spicy black bean, which Ellen told me is one of your favorites."

It didn't matter what Winter was serving, Anne Marie wasn't going to have lunch with him. "Sorry, I can't leave the shop, but thanks, anyway."

Out of the corner of her eye she saw that Teresa was about to say it was perfectly fine; she'd watch the store. Anne Marie sent her a warning glare, and Teresa instantly shut her mouth.

To distract Tim, Anne Marie came out from behind the counter and placed a book on its shelf. "Oh, and did you remember you offered to look after Ellen on Friday night?"

"Tomorrow?"

"Yes. Mel's taking me to *Jersey Boys*."

He was silent for a moment. "It must've slipped my mind, but it shouldn't be a problem."

"If it is, I can ask April's mother… That might work even better now that I think of it. I'd like to set up a babysitting exchange with her."

"I said I'd do it," Tim said. His mouth thinned. "We'll get dinner and go to a movie."

"Okay, then." She walked over to another shelf, dismayed when Tim followed her.

"I thought we should discuss this parenting plan you mentioned."

"Yes, but now isn't the best time to do that."

"Well, whenever it's convenient. Just let me know." Still, he lingered. "So, everything's fine between you and Mel?"

"Oh, yes," she said, glancing over her shoulder as she spoke. Then, since she'd practically melted in his arms less than twenty-four hours earlier, she felt the need to add, "I hope you'll look past what happened at the lake because I'd like to forget the entire incident."

"If that's what you want."

"I do." She turned to face him, and he boldly met her eyes.

"Unfortunately, I'm not finding it that easy." He paused, his silence heavy with meaning. "Those kisses were pretty...revealing, Anne Marie."

She laughed off his comment and lowered her voice. "Okay, so I'm human. You're hot and so are your kisses— I'll admit it. But when I realized what it was all about, I came to my senses."

"You really believe I'd manipulate you like that?" He stiffened and his shoulders arched back, as though he was flinching from a physical attack.

"I...believe you love Ellen and will do whatever it takes to ensure that she stays in your life," she said evenly, moving about the store, straightening a book here, adjusting a poster there.

Tim trailed behind her.

"It happened before, Tim. What else am I to think?" Then, hoping to lighten the conversation, she murmured, "Don't get me wrong, our kiss was...nice." She shrugged carelessly. "I find your company enjoyable. Who wouldn't?"

"But you'd rather spend time with Mel?"

She wasn't sure she could pull this off much longer. "Let's put it this way. Mel and I have been dating for months. We get along beautifully and he's good to Ellen."

Tim shoved his hands in his pockets. "You get along with me, too, and I'm crazy about Ellen."

"This is obviously some kind of competition between you and Mel."

He glared at her, eyes narrowed and lips tensed. Anne

Marie could see that it was taking all the self-control he possessed not to explode in anger. "This all goes back to not telling you about Vanessa, doesn't it?"

Anne Marie felt the heat of embarrassment invade her face. Even her ears started to burn. "Yes, I suppose it does."

"Shakespeare sure got it right," he muttered.

"Shakespeare got a lot of things right. Which particular one are you referring to?"

"Hell has no fury like a woman scorned."

Anne Marie blinked. "First," she snapped, unable to resist correcting him, "that wasn't Shakespeare. It was William Congreve, a Restoration playwright. And second…if this is what you want to think, then you're free to do so."

"I'm not going to argue with you, Anne Marie. So you remember your literary references better than I do. Congratulations. Kudos to you. But say what you like—we both know what happened at the lake was real. Real for me and real for you. If you want to tell yourself I have some twisted ulterior motive, then go ahead."

Clenching her fists, she blurted out, "I made a fool of myself over you." She glanced anxiously at Teresa, who was at the other side of the store, although still within hearing distance.

"And you love turning the tables on me now."

"No." She wanted that to be perfectly clear.

He shook his head. "I've never lied to you. Never," he said emphatically.

"Fine, if that's what *you* want to tell yourself. However, I feel that a lie of omission is still a lie." She couldn't help it; her arms began to flail about and her voice rose. "You let me build up this romantic fantasy and then after months— yes, *months*—you conveniently remember to mention that you're engaged." This whole scene was mortifying, but her anger and sense of betrayal overcame her embarrassment.

"What was I supposed to do?"

"What were you supposed to do?" she mimicked in singsong fashion. "Well, telling the truth comes to mind. Couldn't you see that I was…attracted to you?"

"Yes. Anne Marie, I saw it and I agonized over it. Listen…" Tim walked away from her, then returned. "I realized how you felt—but I was afraid that if I said anything, you wouldn't let me see Ellen."

"You don't have a very high opinion of me, do you?"

"I didn't know you. My daughter, a daughter I'd only just found out about, had been taken away from me. I was left without any legal recourse. I had one opportunity to win you over and I—"

"Are you telling me you deliberately led me on?" This was too much!

"No! Now you're purposely distorting everything I say."

The frustration they were both feeling was almost more than either of them could take. Tim had raised his voice to match hers.

"It might be best if we had this conversation some other time," she said quietly, afraid their argument was keeping customers at bay. Several people had entered the store, but hadn't yet ventured beyond the displays near the front.

"Good idea." He whirled around and stormed out.

When Tim had left, Anne Marie began to shake. She placed her hands on the nearest bookshelf and slowly exhaled. She took several deep breaths, trying to control her emotions.

Teresa approached her. "Are you okay?" she asked tentatively.

"No."

"I'm sorry."

Anne Marie nodded. She simply couldn't respond to Teresa's sympathy, afraid she might burst into tears.

"Do you know who you remind me of?" Teresa asked.

"No." Furthermore, Anne Marie didn't care.

"My husband and me. That's the way we fight, too, but then we always make up afterward. You and Tim will reconcile and it'll be really good when you do. Mark my words."

Anne Marie was too upset to even think in terms of reconciliation. Not knowing what to expect, she made contingency plans for Ellen for Friday night. April's mother was available to fill in, if necessary.

As it turned out, Anne Marie didn't need her. Tim arrived soon after she and Ellen got home.

Ellen let him in, with Baxter dancing excitedly around them both.

"How're you doing, sweetheart?" he asked his daughter. "Hi, Baxter."

He hugged Ellen, then straightened when he saw Anne Marie. Holding her gaze, he intentionally resumed speaking to his daughter. "I understand we have a date tonight."

"A date?" Ellen said, sounding pleased.

"I'm taking you out for dinner and a movie."

"Do I get popcorn, too?"

"As much as you want."

Ellen grinned at Anne Marie. "Don't worry, Mom. I'll eat my vegetables at dinner."

"Good girl." Anne Marie felt bad about her argument with Tim earlier and took a hesitant step into the room. Mel would be here any minute, however, and with Ellen still standing in the hallway, she couldn't talk to Tim about what had happened. And really, what was there to say? All she knew was that the lump in her throat had stayed with her all afternoon.

"When will you have Ellen back?" she asked.

His eyes refused to meet hers. "Nine, nine-thirty. Depends on how late the movie ends and traffic afterward."

"Okay... I don't expect to be home before ten-thirty or eleven."

He nodded. "Ready to go, Ellen?"

"Yes!" She ran to grab her sweater—one Lydia had knit for her with a Yorkie on the back.

Tim opened the screen door.

"Have fun, you two," Anne Marie said. She scooped the dog into her arms and raised one hand in farewell.

"You, too." Tim paused, looking at her. "I mean that," he said, his voice low enough so only she could hear.

He seemed to be saying he regretted their argument as much as she did. Anne Marie wanted to believe that. Her lip quivered and she bit it hard, unwilling to give way to tears. "Thank you," she whispered.

He nodded and then, head down, walked out the door.

Mel appeared soon after Ellen and Tim had left. He kissed Anne Marie's cheek, then slid his arms around her, saying, "I adore Ellen, but it's been too long since it was just the two of us." His peck on the cheek had surprised her. She'd anticipated a real kiss, had actually hoped for one. She wanted to have strong feelings for Mel.

"Yes," she agreed. "It's been ages." She rested her head on his shoulder. She felt content in his embrace. Comforted. Unfortunately, there were none of the sparks she'd experienced with Tim, none of the heady rush of emotion. Mel was gentle, kind, honest. He would never mislead anyone.

In a word, Mel was *safe*. Anne Marie needed safe and so did Ellen.

The production of *Jersey Boys* proved to be everything Anne Marie had read and more. The music brought back memories of Robert, of dancing and laughing with the husband she'd loved, but unlike a few years ago, those memories offered more happiness than sorrow and deepened her enjoyment of the play. The story itself was the classic American tale of opportunity and success and the cost of fame.

"Thank you," she said when he'd driven her home, "for a lovely, lovely evening." Mel's arm was around her shoulders.

A sense of dread settled over her, dissipating her pleasure and her serenity, when she saw Tim's car parked out front. She felt Mel stiffen.

"I'd forgotten Tim had Ellen for the night," he said.

Anne Marie merely nodded, and Mel, apparently, had nothing more to say on the subject of Tim.

He escorted Anne Marie to the front door, but to her disappointment didn't seem eager to stay. "Coffee?" she suggested, hoping he'd accept...yet hoping he wouldn't.

"No, but I'll see you in."

Anne Marie wasn't fooled. Mel didn't want to abandon her to Tim and frankly she was just as glad. If she was alone with Tim they might start talking again. They might kiss again, and if they did, she'd be lost...

Tim came to the door, almost as if he'd been waiting for her, longing for her return. He smiled—until he saw Mel. He looked away, immediately removing his jacket from the hall closet.

"Welcome home," he said as he pushed his arms through the sleeves.

"Thank you. How did everything go with Ellen?"

"We had a great time." Tim nodded once in Mel's direction. "Good to see you, Mel."

"You, too, Tim."

Both men were being polite in the extreme.

Without another word, Tim let himself out, closing the door quietly behind him.

Nine

April 29

None of my plans for dealing with Tim have panned out. In fact, everything seems to have backfired. I resolved to put him completely out of my mind, but all I do is think about him…and about the possibility of him, Ellen and me together. I know how foolish that is, but I can't make myself stop. It's definitely time to pay Lydia a visit and start a new project. If ever I needed a distraction, it's now. I wonder if doctors realize how therapeutic yarn can be…

Not surprisingly, Anne Marie spent a sleepless night. On Saturday she was scheduled to work half a day at the bookstore. Ellen accompanied her, planning to visit her friends along Blossom Street—Lydia and Alix and Susannah and others—with Baxter in tow.

As they drove into town that morning, Anne Marie lost count of the number of references Ellen made to her evening with Tim, especially the Thai dinner they ate in a booth where they had to take off their shoes. The movie afterward had been the latest 3-D animation and Ellen described the plot to her no less than five times.

"Lydia said we should stop by A Good Yarn when you're finished working." Ellen hurried into the bookstore just before noon, Baxter bouncing beside her. "We can go there, can't we?"

"Yes, I was planning to." Anne Marie hoped to have another chat with her friend; Saturdays were often the busiest day of the week, however, and that might not work out. "I thought I'd pick up some yarn for my new project."

"Which project? The wedding one?" Knitting had become a bond, a subject of common interest between them, and Ellen almost always knit something right along with her.

"Yes, I was thinking I could knit Courtney something."

"What about a veil?" Ellen said.

That project was a lot more daunting than Anne Marie wanted to tackle. "She probably already has her veil. But Lydia gave me a pattern book and I found a bride's purse I liked. I'd use a cotton yarn with some metallic threads shot through it."

"A bride's purse?" Ellen repeated, her eyes glowing. "That sounds pretty."

"It would have a drawstring and hang from her arm. Courtney could use it on her wedding day."

As she'd expected, Lydia was busy with customers when Ellen and Anne Marie entered the shop. A large table was set up in the back, with pattern books stacked close by. The table was used for classes, too. Everyone who visited the shop seemed to gravitate to this natural meeting place.

Anne Marie chose another pattern book, one devoted to weddings, then pulled out a chair and sat down. She flipped through several pages until she located another bride's purse. She decided she preferred this one, but wanted Lydia's opinion—and Ellen's.

Ellen was at the front of the store petting Whiskers. Baxter and Whiskers tolerated each other and Anne Marie suspected cat and dog were better friends than they let on. Ellen held Baxter on her lap while she stroked the sleeping cat.

Lydia rang up a yarn sale, then joined Anne Marie. "I was just thinking I could use a break. Elise," she called out to the older woman who helped out on weekends, "could you take over for a few minutes?"

"Of course."

Lydia sat in the chair across from her, smiling tiredly. "How are you?"

Anne Marie shrugged. Usually people who asked that were simply being polite. All they wanted to hear was "Fine." That wasn't the case with Lydia.

"I'm coping," Anne Marie said. "Things are…confusing."

"I thought something was up. Tim parked in front of my store on Thursday. He went across the street, read Winter's specials on the board and then headed over to the bookstore."

"Did you see him when he left?" Anne Marie asked.

"I did," Lydia said. "And it was a different story entirely."

"He looked like a man ready to commit murder, right?"

"No," Lydia said softly. "But it didn't take much to see that he was upset. He stood outside his car for a few minutes, then banged his fist on the hood. After that he talked on his cell."

Anne Marie wondered whom he'd phoned. Then in a flash it came to her. He'd called his AA sponsor. Tim had mentioned the other man numerous times without ever revealing his identity. She was glad he had someone he could talk to whenever he felt the need. She envied him that, although she had friends of her own. Good friends, like Lydia, Barbie and Lillie.

"Mel and I went out last night."

"So I heard," Lydia said, glancing at Ellen, who still sat in the window, petting Whiskers with Baxter curled on her lap.

"We had a wonderful time."

"You always seem to when you're with Mel."

"He's so good to me and Ellen."

"But you aren't in love with him, are you?"

"No," Anne Marie had to admit. She understood what she found attractive about Mel. Her heart wasn't at risk with him. He couldn't hurt her the way Robert had when he'd had his affair—or when he'd died. The shock of both had left Anne Marie emotionally bruised, not quite as resilient as she'd once been. Not only that, she'd met Mel shortly after learning about Tim and Vanessa.

Lydia continued to study her.

"Earlier this week Mel asked me where he stood. I'm afraid I haven't been completely honest with him."

"Don't be so hard on yourself," Lydia said. "The one you haven't been honest with is you."

"I think I might learn to love Mel, given time," she said. He cared about her and Ellen. While he'd never spoken the words aloud, he showed his feelings in a dozen different ways. Not for an instant did she doubt him. Yes, he was almost twenty years her senior, but that had never bothered her. He'd do anything for her; all she had to do was ask.

"I agree," Lydia said thoughtfully. "Love is a choice. It certainly becomes a choice once the intensity of first love passes and you settle into everyday life. I choose to love Brad every single morning and I'm grateful that he chooses to love me back."

Anne Marie was impressed by her friend's marriage. Lydia and Brad's relationship was strong enough, solid enough, to include Casey, who'd been a difficult and troubled girl. Lydia had told her that Ellen's adoption had influenced their own decision to bring Casey into their family.

"Whatever your decision about Mel," Lydia said, "it'll be the right one."

Anne Marie stayed for tea and then picked out yarn and the new pattern for the bride's purse.

"I want to knit the same bride's purse as you. That's okay, isn't it?" Ellen asked before they left the store.

"Of course."

"Can I knit it without the beads?"

"If you want, but adding the beads isn't hard. Lydia and I can show you how."

"Okay."

"Who will you give the purse to?" Anne Marie asked. She didn't think Courtney would need *two* purses. Maybe Ellen wanted it for herself, for the fantasies she and April played at.

Instead of answering, Ellen asked another question, this one directed toward Lydia. "Can I knit it in pink?"

"Sure thing," Lydia answered, and led her to the shelf that housed the fingering-weight cashmere yarns. Ellen chose a light rose color.

"Mom likes pink. Right, Mom?"

"I do indeed," Anne Marie said absently, still focused on her conversation with Lydia.

Stepping over to the cash register, Lydia rang up the purchase. "That was a good choice," she assured Ellen. "If you have any problems, your mom can help."

"More than likely I'll be the one going to her," Anne Marie said with a laugh.

Ellen was quiet on the ride home. "Can I go to April's house with Baxter?" she asked.

"That's okay as long as it's all right with her mother." When they reached the house, Anne Marie phoned Natalie, April's mom, and learned that April had been at odds all morning, waiting for Ellen's return. Ellen had taught her to knit, and April was stuck and needed guidance. After a quick lunch, Ellen was out the door.

Anne Marie stood on the porch, watching her daughter race down the street, knitting bag in one hand, Baxter's leash in the other.

It seemed impossible that they'd moved only a week ago. Anne Marie had plenty to do and intended to stay busy. If she spent the afternoon sorting and unpacking, maybe she'd stop thinking about Tim and Mel.

Mel phoned midafternoon, inviting her and Ellen on an outing to the zoo Sunday afternoon. Anne Marie had taken Ellen to Woodland Park Zoo three or four times already, and since Monday was a school day, she decided a quiet afternoon might be best.

Mel accepted her decision graciously and didn't press the point, which struck her as a little unusual.

Not until she ended the conversation did she wonder what her reaction would have been had Tim suggested the outing. Mel might've hoped she'd recommend something else. She hadn't. Neither had he.

The fact was, she didn't feel any excitement, any compulsion about being with Mel. Not the way she felt about being with Tim...

Only he didn't phone.

For the rest of the afternoon, she waited to hear from him. When the phone did ring, around five, Ellen answered; it was obviously one of her friends.

"What's for dinner?" her daughter asked an hour later.

"What would you like?" Before Ellen could respond she added, "*Not* pad thai, and nothing with peanut sauce."

Ellen laughed. "I had that yesterday. I wasn't going to ask for it now. Can we have spaghetti?"

"Sure." Thankfully, that was quick and easy. Anne Marie wasn't in the mood to cook, or, for that matter, eat.

They were seated at the table for dinner when Ellen said, "Dad's eating at Grandma and Grandpa Carlsen's tonight."

"You spoke to Tim?"

Ellen nodded as she reached for the Parmesan cheese and sprinkled it liberally over her noodles. "That was him on the phone a while ago."

Anne Marie immediately lost what little appetite she had. Tim hadn't asked to speak to *her*. She toyed with the noodles, swirling them around her fork, but had no interest in her own cooking.

"Can we start knitting the bride's purse tonight?" Ellen asked.

"Sure," she said, hoping her voice betrayed none of her disappointment.

"Good." Ellen ate with relish, seeming to enjoy every bite. "I told Dad I saw you."

"Saw me?"

"Kissing," she said, and giggled. "You and Dad. You thought I was asleep but I woke up. We were in the car, remember?"

"Ah…"

"That day at the lake."

Anne Marie knew precisely when it had happened. "What did your father say?"

"Nothing at first, then he sort of laughed and said you were a good kisser."

"Did he, now?"

"Is Dad a good kisser, too?"

Anne Marie smiled. "He is."

"I saw Mel kiss you once."

That wasn't nearly as big a surprise.

"You kiss him different than you do Dad."

"Oh?"

"You like it more with Dad. I can tell."

For that matter, so could Anne Marie. "Mel's a good kisser," she said loyally.

"But not as good as Dad."

This wasn't a conversation Anne Marie felt they should be having. "How about dessert?" she asked, desperately trying to change the subject. Ellen shook her head, but the expression on her face said she knew exactly what Anne Marie was doing.

After dinner Ellen cleared the table and together they placed the dirty dishes in the dishwasher, washed the two pots and put them away.

"Church in the morning," Anne Marie reminded her.

"I know," Ellen said. "Can we start knitting now?"

"Okay."

Ellen ran into her bedroom with Baxter at her heels. She returned with the package from A Good Yarn, and they sat on the sofa, side by side. Anne Marie read the pattern all the way through and so did Ellen. It seemed relatively uncomplicated and wouldn't take more than a couple of weeks. Anne Marie cherished her knitting time. She used those quiet moments to think, weighing decisions and mulling over whatever troubled her, letting solutions come of their own accord. The rhythmic action of knitting calmed her mind, making her relaxed and receptive.

"I like the pink yarn," she told her daughter. "You never did say who you're knitting the purse for," Anne Marie said, completing the first row of her own project.

Ellen frowned as she worked the yarn onto the needles. Casting on was the most difficult part of knitting for her, because she insisted on using the long-tail method. At one time Lydia had said she felt it was the best way of starting a project. From that moment on, Ellen had refused to consider any other method.

They'd just finished their first rows when Ellen said, "For you."

Anne Marie didn't immediately grasp what she meant. "Oh, you're knitting the bride's purse for me?" She smiled. "That's very thoughtful."

"For your wedding."

"My wedding," Anne Marie laughed. "Did I become engaged and forget all about it?" she joked.

"Not yet."

"And just who am I marrying? Mel?"

Ellen stopped knitting, set her needles aside and hurried into her bedroom. When she returned, she was carrying the spiral notebook in which she'd listed her twenty wishes. She sat down next to Anne Marie and reverently opened the book.

In neat and even cursive writing, Ellen had carefully written each of her twenty wishes. Several had been crossed out, including the trip to Paris they'd taken almost a year earlier.

"I have a twenty-first wish."

"And what would that be?" Anne Marie asked, bending forward to read what her daughter had written.

Ellen rested the book on Anne Marie's lap. Sure enough, at the bottom of the third page was her twenty-first wish. *I wish my mom and dad would get married.*

"Your…dad," Anne Marie said. A tingling sensation went down her spine.

"You already said you like the way he kisses," Ellen pointed out.

"That's true." Anne Marie couldn't very well deny it now.

"And he likes your kisses, too." Ellen paused. "Sometimes wishes *do* come true. Look how many of mine already have," she said, smoothing the page.

The trip to Paris.

Finding her father.

Learning to knit.

Anne Marie couldn't read any further because the words began to blur as tears gathered in her eyes. "That's a very nice wish," she murmured. "But you have to remember that sometimes wishes *don't* come true. And sometimes, even if they do, it takes a long time."

Ten

May 5

April knows how to knit really well now. She doesn't
even need my help anymore. I told her about the
bride's purse I'm making and now she wants to knit
one, too, only she doesn't know anyone who's getting
married. Her mom is taking her down to A Good Yarn
on Saturday and she said I could come. Mom and I
have been knitting every night after dinner. I'm glad
I showed her my twenty-first wish. I wasn't going to,
but I did, anyway.

Anne Marie heard from Mel every day for the next week.
He phoned at least once and sometimes twice. Invariably
he'd invite her somewhere—dinner, a movie, even just coffee—but Anne Marie always found an excuse. Still, Mel
persisted. Finally, unable to put him off any longer, she
agreed to meet him for a drink on Friday night, after work.
Conveniently, Ellen had a playdate with another girl from
school.

Tim phoned, too, but he spoke only to Ellen and, other

than a polite exchange of greetings, he didn't have anything to say to Anne Marie. His lack of communication made her realize how much she'd come to rely on him and how much she'd looked forward to their conversations.

Lillie Higgins stopped by the bookstore early Friday afternoon. Lillie was not only a good friend, but one of Anne Marie's best customers. A voracious reader, she'd built up an extensive library and often purchased several hardcovers at a time.

"Oh, the book you ordered came in," Anne Marie said. She'd meant to phone and leave a message earlier, but had gotten sidetracked, which seemed to be the norm lately. She really did need to focus on business, she told herself, instead of the sad state of her personal life.

"I thought it must have," Lillie said as she walked up to the service counter. "It usually takes you about three days to get a special order in."

While Anne Marie retrieved the Mexican cookbook for her, Lillie wandered over to the new display Teresa had arranged. "I haven't heard from you since the move." She picked up the latest bestseller by a popular suspense author and flipped through the pages. "I got your thank-you note. Hector and I enjoyed ourselves."

"I really appreciate everyone's help," Anne Marie said.

"That Tim is quite the character, isn't he?" Lillie commented with a laugh. "While we were loading up the truck, he and Ellen were singing ABBA songs at the top of their lungs. He actually has quite a nice voice. Ellen, too."

At the mention of Tim's name, Anne Marie lowered her eyes. She didn't want to think about him, yet he was constantly on her mind. Not an hour passed without her being reminded of him in some way.

"My dear," Lillie said, placing one beautifully manicured hand on Anne Marie's arm. "What is it? Did I say something to upset you?"

"No…"

"Is it Tim?"

Anne Marie nodded. "We had a…falling out."

"Over Ellen?"

"Not exactly." Based on what he'd said to her daughter, he seemed to regret their argument. So did she. Perhaps he felt it best to keep his distance, step aside and give her a chance to work things out with Mel. She wasn't sure how to interpret this painful silence, this…discord between them. All she knew was that she had to find some way of resolving it.

"I remember how awkward it was when Hector and I first started seeing each other," Lillie said. "His family objected, and Barbie had her doubts, too. Neither of us wanted to cause problems, so we ended our relationship. I have to tell you, I've never been more miserable in my life."

"That's where I am right now," Anne Marie told her.

"Then *do* something about it," Lillie said. "If you have feelings for Tim, you need to tell him."

Lillie made everything sound so straightforward. Unfortunately, Anne Marie's situation was anything but. She liked Mel and enjoyed his company, but he didn't stir her senses, didn't make her feel the passion or excitement she felt with Tim. Mel was attentive and smart and she knew he loved her. But she didn't return his feelings. And there was nothing she could do about that. She couldn't force emotions that simply weren't there.

"You'll tell him, won't you?" Lillie urged.

"I… I don't know yet." One thing was certain: she couldn't move forward with Tim—if he even wanted to—

until she'd broken off with Mel. And that wasn't going to be easy.

Mel had suggested they meet at the Italian restaurant where they'd gone on their first date. So their relationship would begin and end at the same place. That wasn't a comforting thought. But there was no option other than honesty. Anne Marie would drink her glass of wine, then as gently as possible confess she was in love with Tim. After that, she'd be on her way.

She hoped.

By the time she arrived at Ti Amo Sempre, Mel had secured a table by the window. He stood as she approached and kissed her cheek. He'd already ordered her favorite wine, a Malbec from the Mendoza region of Argentina. His thoughtfulness made this final meeting even more awkward.

As she picked up her wine, Mel also raised his glass. "To Fridays," he said.

Anne Marie touched the rim of her glass to his. "To Fridays."

"You had a busy week," he said, leaning back in his chair.

Nervous, Anne Marie reached for a handful of the nuts their waiter had delivered with the wine. Her week had actually been slow, but she'd invented excuse after excuse not to see Mel, most of them related to the business, which led him to believe she'd been overwhelmed by a huge influx of new inventory and custom orders.

"You, too," she murmured, evading the truth for another few minutes—or seconds.

"Very busy," he said solemnly.

She responded with a weak smile, then drew in a deep breath and plunged forward, forgoing any further exchange of pleasantries. "I think you already know why I wanted to meet you this evening," she said quickly. Her stomach was in knots, and all she could concentrate on was saying what needed to be said.

"I asked *you* out, remember?" he said. "Now, relax and enjoy your wine. It's your favorite."

"I know...but I can't relax."

"Try." He gestured for her to take another sip. "The wine will help."

Anne Marie did, and Mel was right; the wine did make her feel calmer. "You came into my life at a turning point," she began.

"And you came into mine when I needed you."

Anne Marie nodded, trying not to wince, wondering how he'd react to her announcement. "I've really enjoyed our times together," she said.

"I have, too, which makes this all the more difficult for me."

Difficult for *him?* Anne Marie glanced up, unsure of his meaning.

"I've met someone else, Anne Marie," he said. "I've been trying to tell you all week, but whenever I called, you had some work problem that demanded your attention and we couldn't chat."

She blinked, certain she'd misunderstood him. "You've... met someone else?"

"Yes, a woman from my office, who's closer to my own age. We have a lot in common."

"When?"

"A couple of weeks ago. Remember the Saturday you moved? Renee was at the office, too. After my appointment, she suggested we grab a bite to eat. We had a great time. I had no idea what a wonderful sense of humor she has."

Anne Marie was having trouble assimilating all this.

"Mel, are you being honest with me?" She wanted to make sure he wasn't fabricating this story in order to ease her conscience.

"The truth is, I probably wouldn't have given Renee a second glance if it wasn't for the fact that I already knew I was losing you."

"Oh, Mel."

He gave her a wry smile. "I found out she's had her eye on me for quite a while."

Anne Marie laughed out loud. "You have no idea how much better this makes me feel."

Mel laughed, too, his expression almost boyish. "Tim's a good man."

"I think so, too."

"I regret the way I behaved earlier. I wish you both the best."

Rather than explain that she hadn't exactly worked out the situation with Tim, she let Mel assume all was well between them.

"I hope you and Renee find happiness together," she said. Mel had graciously wished her the best and it seemed only fitting that she do the same. Besides, she meant it. He deserved to be with a woman who cared about him with the same intensity she felt toward Tim.

"Let's keep in touch," he said.

"Let's," she agreed.

"I'll update you on what's happening with me and Renee."

"I'd like that."

They finished their wine, and after Mel had paid the bill they walked outside into the still-bright evening. On the sidewalk in front of the restaurant, they hugged, then went their separate ways. For the first time in weeks, Anne Marie felt she could smile.

Then she thought of the coming conversation with Tim, and all her anxieties returned.

Eleven

May 7

I doubt that I could be more surprised than I was
when Mel announced he'd met someone else. When
I got home my head was spinning. But I didn't really
have a chance to think about it because Ellen came
home soon after I did, talking up a storm about her
visit with her new friend Bailey. She's teaching Bailey to knit, too, and wants to start a knitting camp for
her friends during summer vacation. The backyard
will be perfect, since I plan to get a picnic table and
a large umbrella. She's going to invite Lydia to come
and teach. Ellen seems to have everything figured
out. If she teaches five friends to knit and each of
them teaches five friends, by the end of the summer
the whole school will know how to knit. Oh, if only
life was this simple...

Saturday morning the doorbell rang while Anne Marie
sorted laundry. She'd started taking every other Saturday off in order to spend more time with Ellen. When her

daughter didn't immediately rush to answer, Anne Marie
left the stack of soiled laundry in front of the washer and
hurried toward the hall. Baxter was barking wildly. She
calmed him and told him to sit—to her great satisfaction
he obeyed instantly—then opened the door.

When she saw Tim standing there, she nearly gasped
with shock. He was the last person she'd expected—and
the most welcome. While she yearned to yank open the
screen door and throw herself into his arms, she resisted.

"Hi," she managed, her voice, even to her own ears,
sounding breathless and strange.

"Is Ellen here?" he asked stiffly.

"Would you like to come in?"

"Not really. I came by to make sure her bike's working
properly after I fixed it."

"It's fine." His excuse was so flimsy, she had to suspect
there was another reason—one that had to do with *her*. Now
that he was here, Anne Marie had no intention of letting
him go. "Come inside, Tim," she said again, opening the
screen door to usher him in. "I'm glad to see you."

He met her eyes as if to gauge the sincerity of her words.

"I've missed you," she added.

"Good," he said mildly, although his expression gave
nothing away.

"Good?" she repeated. "You *wanted* me to miss you?"

He didn't respond, except with a smile. A very slight
smile.

"Did you miss me?" she asked.

"That's not the point."

"As a matter of fact, it is. I want to know if you thought
about me in the past week."

He shrugged.

"That's no answer."

"If I admitted you were on my mind every minute of every day, would you lord it over me?"

Her smile was so wide it hurt her mouth. "I might."

"That's what I figured. Women are like that. They demand their pound of flesh—and this time my Shakespearean quote *is* correct."

"Yes, it is, but the context is wrong." Anne Marie frowned. "You were doing very well until you said that. You should know I'm not going to let you make derogatory comments about half of humanity."

"You're the one who was going to lord it over me if I admitted I missed you—which I did."

"I already admitted I missed you, but I'll say it again." There, she'd extended an olive branch.

He grinned and looked so appealing that it was all she could do not to kiss him right then and there.

"Mom!" Ellen skipped out of the kitchen, clutching the phone in one hand. She stopped when she saw Tim. "Oh, hi, Dad."

"Hello, sweetheart."

"Mom, can April come over and play?"

"That's fine."

"Can she bring Iris, too?"

"Yes."

"Can she stay for lunch?"

Anne Marie nodded.

"Thanks, Mom." Ellen brought the phone back to her ear and returned to the kitchen, chattering as she walked.

"Okay, where were we?" Anne Marie asked, her hand on her hip.

Tim smiled again. "I believe you just said you missed me so much that your whole world's sad and gray."

Anne Marie felt her mouth twitch. "Ah...that's not quite the way I remember it."

"I was close, though, wasn't I?"

Anne Marie had a question of her own. "Why didn't you call?"

"I called."

"To talk to Ellen, but not me."

He sobered, and his smile faded. "How's Mel?"

"Very well. We had drinks last night."

A muscle tightened in Tim's jaw. "I see."

"I don't think you do."

"I'm here to check on Ellen's bike. I wouldn't want to take up any more of your time."

"Your being here has nothing to do with Ellen's bicycle." She wasn't going to play that silly game with him.

"If you're still involved with Mel, then I don't think we have much to say to each other."

"Are you always this obtuse?"

"I'm not the least bit obtuse."

That was when Ellen came back into the living room. "April's on her way over."

Anne Marie turned her attention to her daughter. "I'll start lunch in a few minutes. Right now your father and I are having a discussion."

Ellen remained where she was. "Are you fighting?"

"No," Anne Marie said.

"Yes," Tim said.

"We're having a difference of opinion," Anne Marie clarified, glaring at Tim.

"Did you tell him about my twenty-first wish?" the girl asked.

"No." Furthermore, she had no intention of doing so.

Ellen's face fell.

"What's your twenty-first wish?" Tim asked.

"I'll make lunch." Without waiting for anyone to agree or disagree, Anne Marie left the room. She searched the refrigerator, and not finding anything that suited her, took out a loaf of bread and a jar of peanut butter. Ellen would be happy with that, and she hoped April would, too.

The sandwiches were ready when Tim entered the kitchen. He pulled out a bar stool and perched on it. "Did you make me one of those?"

"No. Should I have?"

"It would've been the polite thing to do."

She extracted two slices from the loaf of bread. "At the moment I don't feel like being polite."

"So I noticed." He didn't say anything as she prepared his peanut butter sandwich, cut it in quarters, and set the plate in front of him. "Do you want a glass of milk, too?"

"I might shock you if I told you what I want."

She raised her eyebrows. "And what would that be?"

He leaned forward and braced his hands on the edge of the counter. "I have wishes of my own. I've never written them down the way Ellen has, but I've given those wishes a great deal of thought, especially in the last few weeks."

Anne Marie leaned against the counter, too, and waited for him to continue. "What kind of wishes?"

"Well, one wish was to find my daughter."

"That was granted."

"Thanks to you."

"Go on." She refused to let him sidetrack her.

"Another was to fall in love."

"Vanessa, right?"

"Fall in love *again*," he amended.

Still standing on the other side of the counter, she

pressed her palms against it. Their faces were only inches apart. "And?"

"I fell so hard, it was like nothing I'd ever felt before."

"Then…"

"Then I discovered that the woman I loved was involved with someone else."

"If we're talking about the same woman—"

"I think we must be."

"Then that…woman's been doing her utmost to explain that she's no longer 'involved' with this other man."

"No longer involved?" Tim repeated. "Since when?"

"Since last night when they met for a drink. However, the person she's been wanting to tell has been obtuse—yes, obtuse—and is severely trying her patience."

"Is that a fact?"

"It is."

"What I'd like to know is if this woman you mentioned is in love with me."

Anne Marie reached for a quarter of his sandwich and took a bite. "I think she must be."

"You *think?* You mean to say you aren't sure?"

"Well…it's a big decision to love another person." Recalling her conversation with Lydia, about how love was ultimately a choice, she used the word *decision* deliberately. Yes, the emotions, the sensations, might be involuntary, but real love was also something chosen. Something that had to be cherished and protected.

"I agree. Very big."

"There's commitment, to each other and to any children…"

Tim nodded. "One might suggest marriage as a way of keeping that commitment."

"One might."

"That's another of my wishes," he said.

Anne Marie set her piece of the sandwich aside. "Marriage requires a lot of trust."

"Yes, it does. It's—"

He stopped when Ellen and April walked in. Ellen immediately looked at Anne Marie, then at Tim and back again. "Are you two still fighting?" she asked.

"We aren't fighting," Tim assured her.

"We're discussing our wishes," Anne Marie said.

"Wishes?" April asked curiously.

"Mom and I made a list of twenty wishes," Ellen explained to her friend. "I have twenty-one now. I added one."

"I added one to my list, as well," Anne Marie said.

"You did?" Ellen stared at her. "Are you going to tell us what it is?"

Anne Marie nodded. "My wish is that you and Tim and I can one day be a family."

"I like that wish," Tim said in a low voice, a voice full of meaning.

"I do, too." Ellen pointed to the counter. "Is that our lunch?"

Anne Marie handed her daughter and April their plates.

"Can we eat in my bedroom?" Ellen asked.

"Yes, just this once. And don't feed the dogs."

"Okay."

The girls disappeared down the hallway.

"Now where were we?" Anne Marie murmured.

"I believe we were talking about wishes coming true. Even twenty-first wishes."

"I do believe you're right," she whispered.

Tim reached for her with the kitchen counter between them. It didn't take her long to skirt around it and find her way completely into his arms. Then they were laughing and talking between kisses, unable to stop touching and holding each other.

"I wasn't kidding," Tim said. "I want us to get married soon."

"I wasn't kidding, either—" But she didn't finish her sentence because Tim was kissing her again.

They were startled by Ellen's voice. "Mom," she said, standing in the doorway to the kitchen.

Tim and Anne Marie broke apart as Anne Marie straightened her blouse and tried to look as normal as possible.

Ellen wore a huge grin as she put the empty plates in the sink. "You're going to need the bride's purse I'm making, aren't you?"

Tim slipped his arm around Anne Marie's waist. "She is. How fast can you knit?"

"Real fast," Ellen told him, and then with her arms wide open she hugged them both.

September 10

This afternoon Tim Carlsen and I will be married in a private ceremony at the lake house with his family and mine in attendance. I'm so happy I can barely contain myself. Once I allowed my feelings for Tim to emerge, I was astonished at how deeply I cared for him. I had all along, but my pride had refused to let me acknowledge that. Tim is everything I want in a husband.

Ellen told us she's bringing her list of wishes to the ceremony so she can mark off her twenty-first wish as soon as we're officially husband and wife. I have a lovely pink summer dress that goes beautifully with the pink bride's purse she knit me.

This is the second happiest day of my life, the first being the day of Ellen's adoption. Who would ever have guessed when I made my very first wish—to find love again—that God would send me a daughter and then, as a bonus, her father. My husband. Tim.

September 10

Mom and Dad are getting married today. I always knew they would but sometimes adults need help. I can cross off my twenty-first wish now.

* * * * *